Praise for Vanessa Barneveld's *Under the Milky Way*

"Ms. Barneveld has done it again! This story is gorgeous. It has everything: romance, mystery, suspense. The speculative backdrop adds a delicious ambiance to this atmospheric tale. This is everything I want in a book!"
—Darynda Jones, *New York Times* bestselling author of the Charley Davidson series

"*Under the Milky Way* is out of this world. This novel has it all: Swoony romance! Alien abduction! Mystery!"
—Marlene Perez, bestselling author of the Dead Is and Afterlife series

"*Under the Milky Way* is the perfect read, tugging at your heartstrings while sending chills down your spine. Deftly paced and plotted, Barneveld keeps readers guessing through its exciting conclusion."
—Tina Ferraro, author of *Top Ten Uses for an Unworn Prom Dress*

"With prose that pops with supernatural charm, Vanessa Barneveld delivers a captivating story filled with earthly intrigue, extraterrestrial twists, and a romance that'll levitate even the heaviest of hearts!"
—Darcy Woods, award-winning author of *Smoke* and *Summer of Supernovas*

"*Under the Milky Way* is a thrilling paranormal romance sure to skyjack you from start to finish. Barneveld's writing is perfection, the story high-octane and the characters so tender and fierce, they will haunt you long after they're gone. Read this book. Read it now! You'll never see homecoming the same again…"
—A. K. Wilder, bestselling author of *Crown of Bones*

"Fun, riveting, and addicting. Vanessa Barneveld has crafted an out-of-this-world story suggesting that we're not alone in the universe, while exploring the heartfelt relationships—romantic or familial, human or alien—that keep us grounded on this earth. Prepare to giggle, gasp, and swoon!"
—Pintip Dunn, *New York Times* bestselling author of *Forget Tomorrow* and *Dating Makes Perfect*

Under the milky way

ALSO BY VANESSA BARNEVELD

This Is Your Afterlife

Live Fast, Die Young

VANESSA BARNEVELD

This book is a work of fiction. Names, characters, places, and incidents are the product of the author's imagination or are used fictitiously. Any resemblance to actual events, locales, or persons, living or dead, is coincidental.

Entangled Publishing, LLC
10940 S Parker Road
Suite 327
Parker, CO 80134
rights@entangledpublishing.com

Entangled Teen is an imprint of Entangled Publishing, LLC.

Visit our website at www.entangledpublishing.com.

Edited by Lydia Sharp, Stacy Abrams, and Liz Pelletier
Cover design by Elizabeth Turner Stokes
Cover images by
Couple © Shutterstock/Iaroslava Daragan
UFO © Shutterstock/rodnikovay
Interior design by Toni Kerr

ISBN 978-1-68281-573-1
Ebook ISBN 978-1-68281-582-3

Manufactured in the United States of America

First Edition August 2021

10 9 8 7 6 5 4 3 2 1

For Mum, who wanted to believe.

Under the Milky Way is a thrilling and romantic out-of-this-world mystery that will keep you on the edge of your seat. However, the story includes discussion of divorced parents and kidnappings, and there are scenes depicting use of needles and extreme physical pain. Readers who may be sensitive to these elements, please take note.

AUTHOR'S NOTE: This book features Deaf and also Dutch-Indonesian characters. Every effort was made to verify the use of American Sign Language and foreign-language phrases. Any errors in translation are that of the author.

TRACK 1

"You Shook Me All Night Long"

August 1977
The Nullarbor Plain, Australia

The feeble lights of Mitch Klaxon's Toyota van illuminated a stretch of Nullarbor highway that was more red dust than asphalt. They'd not passed a single dwelling since sunset, and the next township was at least sixty kilometers away.

Mitch didn't scare easily. At the Perth gig, even as he dodged beer cans—some empty, some half full—he'd kept on singing. Didn't miss a single note. That was one reason why he was a great front man for the band he and his brother Les had started in their mum's garage six months ago.

But one thing that *did* scare the leather trousers off of him was flying. Too many musicians had fallen out of the sky already. Patsy Cline. Buddy Holly. Otis Redding. He didn't want to be another statistic. Which was why he was taking the band on a thirty-six-hour road trip from the sleepy western end of Australia to the glittering lights of Melbourne.

If they weren't so broke, the rest of the band would have hated him for it. Didn't stop them from grumbling about the lack of air-conditioning or suspension. Despite the bumps from potholes and cracks, the guys snoozed in the back, their heads resting on guitar cases and amps.

Jangly strains of The Rolling Stones leaked quietly from the radio. Mitch frowned as static began to buzz.

"Bugger," he said, twiddling the knob in search of a station. Finding none, he flipped the radio off and squinted at the horizon.

Bright headlights glimmered far ahead.

Without warning, the van shook to a halt. The dash lights and headlights blinked once, twice, then extinguished.

"Shit," Mitch muttered, and turned the ignition key. Nothing. Decrepit as the van was on the outside, he knew there was enough petrol in the tank. And the engine was a die-hard block of Japanese iron. It'd take a meteor to demolish it. "Guys, we have a problem."

When none of his band mates replied, he faced them. All were fast asleep.

"Hey," he said, shaking his brother. "Les, wake up. Help me push-start this thing."

But Les remained dead to the world.

Mitch peered out of the windscreen, shielding his eyes as the approaching car's headlights grew brighter.

"Jeez, turn off your high beams, mate," he said, opening the driver's door so he could get out and flag the motorist down for help.

As Mitch's booted right foot touched the dusty tarmac, a vibration rumbled all the way up his body. His gaze was stuck on the oncoming car, which seemed to be rushing toward him at breakneck speed.

Immediately, the silence struck him. It was like he'd stepped into a vacuum. No crickets chirping. Nothing from his band mates in the van.

Most troubling of all, the approaching car was completely silent, too. Not even the rattle of a fender on the bumpy highway. And it was heading straight for Mitch's van. Growing bigger and bigger.

It was wider than the roadway, Mitch realized. As it came closer, more lights fanned out horizontally, and he glimpsed the shape of something smooth and elongated. This was no car. Not even semitrailers hooked together in the road trains that were common in these parts.

Mitch stood frozen in place. He couldn't turn away from those blinding halogen-blue lights. They burned his skin, pierced his eyeballs. Helpless, he tried to yell, but his throat felt like it was being squeezed by a giant invisible hand.

Now less than a hundred meters away, the lights pitched upward, lifting higher and higher.

It's a plane, Mitch reasoned with himself. Yes, a completely silent, propeller-free, massive plane flying just off the ground.

The craft slowed. The atmosphere around Mitch seemed to throb. He felt encapsulated by it, separate from the cool desert air. His eyes followed the craft as it hovered in place above him. Silver-white, blue, purple, and red lights pulsated in a peculiar rhythm, mesmerizing him. Soon he felt weightless. Like a feather being lifted to the clouds.

He saw figures moving toward him. Surrounding him. Judging by their small statures, he thought they were children. But then one poked him with something that seared his arm, bringing pain so intense he blacked out.

The next minute, Mitch was back in the van, radio blaring, engine idling. His limbs ached. Mitch touched his throbbing temples and felt warm blood oozing from a small wound. He checked on his band mates. All were present and accounted for. And breathing, thank Christ. They were in the same positions as before—legs, arms, and torsos twisted, trying to conform to the cramped interior.

"H-hey, are you guys okay?" Mitch called out, his voice

unnaturally high.

Eyes closed, Rocky, the drummer, mumbled an unintelligible reply. Jimbo made a grunting sound and flipped him the bird.

"What did you stop for, mate?" Les mumbled sleepily, his head still leaning against an amp.

White-knuckling the hard steering wheel, Mitch peered at the sky. Finding nothing but stars and scattered clouds, he shook his head. "A UFO. I think I saw a UFO."

He paused, waited for Les to fully wake up and tell him to stop being such a dickhead. But his brother had already fallen back into a deep sleep.

"I *know* I saw a UFO," Mitch whispered.

He put the car in gear and stamped his foot to the floor.

Mitch Klaxon would never mention the incident again. Not even to Oprah, when she would interview him many years later after he won ten Grammys. Nor would he ever again drive across any desert at night.

But that didn't mean he'd stop having nightmares about being probed by aliens until the day he died.

TRACK 2

"Beautiful Stranger"

Present Day
Dawson, Colorado

"Cassidy Roekiem! Earth to Cassidy Roekiem!"

I jolt awake at the mangled sound of my last name…and laughter. For the record, it's *ROO-keem,* not *Ro-ECKY-em.* The weight of twenty pairs of eyes burns into the back of my head. Damn. I'd fallen asleep in class. *Again.* A puddle of saliva marks the spot where my head had rested. I wipe it with my sleeve, and snatches of the dream I was in the middle of fade into oblivion.

It's not so much the public drooling that's freaking me out. For the past few months, my habit of falling asleep whenever, wherever, has gotten worse. A spontaneous snooze during class is bad enough. But what if it happens while I'm driving on the freeway? My parents took me to a sleep clinic a few years back, but the doctors there couldn't find anything physically wrong with me. According to them, the best cure is to get more *zzz*'s. Maybe just not in class.

My sharp-nosed biology teacher, Ms. Walters, continues. "Since you were here in body but not in spirit for the past ten minutes, you are cordially required to join me today at 3:15 for detention."

What kind of sadist gives out that kind of punishment

on a Friday? Doesn't she have something better to do? I open my mouth to protest, to tell her I have urgent business to take care of after school. But an audible yawn comes out instead.

Ms. Walters rolls her eyes. I sit up straighter and try to pay attention to her lecture on panspermia.

"Now," she drones on, "the theory of bacteria being distributed across the universe on dust particles and evolving into complex alien life-forms is an exciting one."

Somebody behind me pipes up enthusiastically. "Are you saying there are real E.T.'s out there?"

"Tony, when I say, 'complex alien life-forms,' I'm not talking about little beings with big eyes and glowing fingers. No, I mean bacteria and…"

Tony clicks his tongue in disappointment.

My mind drifts once more to anything but free-floating bacteria. The new kid in the seat beside me, Hayden McSomething, is playing with his phone, making the screen flash on and off. Out of the corner of my eye, I spy Hayden's jean-clad right leg sliding toward my chair, inch by inch. His seat squeaks as he quickly folds his leg back to its original position. I can't blame him for feeling restless.

I'm not sure what *his* issue is with this period, but I am more than ready to ditch my classes. I have Important Things to do for Mom. Even exploring the mysteries of the universe seems trivial in comparison.

White light persistently blips from Hayden's phone. It's annoying as hell. My head thumps to the beat—blip, blip, blip. Rubbing my temples, I sneak a sideways look at him, but he's not watching the teacher or his phone. He's staring at me.

Is he signaling me? Trying to tell me my clothes are inside out or that I'm still drooling? He catches my gaze and pockets his phone fast. Furtively, I do a quick grooming check.

Yep, my clothes are respectable and there's no more drool.

Hayden sends me the faintest of smiles. I blink in surprise.

He arrived in Dawson at the start of the school year and is rumored to be a track team superstar. His speed is unreal. This sport factoid alone earned him instant respect. And, really, anyone with a pulse seems to have registered his magnetic presence. Who wouldn't notice those serious but velvety-brown eyes? Dark floppy hair? That muscular chest and lean body? And he has to be smart if he's enrolled in AP.

Yet despite meeting all the criteria for instant popularity, he keeps to himself. That aloofness only serves to ramp up the curiosity factor about him.

I whisper, *"Hayden, is this class killing you as much as it's killing me? How about we skip to lunch?"*

Okay, I don't actually say any of that out loud. Maybe in another lifetime I would, when we're not surrounded by other students *and* a teacher who hands out detention slips like they're Halloween candy.

Slowly, Hayden's jaw drops as he turns toward me. His dark eyes are wide and deer-like. My heart strains hard against my ribs. Did I actually speak out loud? I clap a hand to my closed lips and cast a quick glance around the room.

In the back corner, Angie's studying her nails instead of a textbook. Others are cradling their chins with their hands and staring into space. Tony's lip is curled, unimpressed by the idea of bacteria being classified as aliens. But most are madly taking notes. There's no evidence I disrupted the class with an unsolicited pick-up line.

So that's good news. I blow out a relieved sigh. This one's loud enough to capture everybody's attention. Everybody except Hayden. He keeps his eyes on the chalkboard, lips flattened. That tiny smile is now a memory. Ms. Walters resumes scratching out a diagram of a bacterium hitching a ride on an asteroid.

When the bell rings later, Hayden practically jumps out of his chair. He jostles my shoulder.

"S-sorry," he says, his stammering almost drowned out by everyone's chatter. He focuses on shoving his notepad into a plain black satchel.

"No problem," I reply brightly. "Interesting about the pansperm—"

"I have to go," he breaks into my attempt at casual conversation. His tight smile is brief but apologetic. Then he's out the door before I can respond, a blur of dark denim and white tee.

Angie catches up as we funnel into the hallway. "Your spontaneous sleep sessions are getting ridiculous," she says, swinging her orange purse over her shoulder. Orange because it's fall.

Ever since I've known her, she's been prone to wearing colors to reflect the seasons. When December rolls around, she'll trade the pumpkin-hued flats for white knee-high boots. She's considering bleaching her hair platinum this year. I don't remember what her original hair color was. Today, it's maple-syrup brown.

Yawning, I say, "You don't understand. I need as much sleep as I can get."

"Liar. Something's keeping you awake all night. Or someone." Angie arches a single brow. It's a maneuver she mastered over countless practice sessions in front of the mirror. She wants to be an actress, so it was important to get that down pat. Angie can also cry real tears on demand, but only from her right eye.

"Someone? Like whom?"

She waves a hand toward a dark-haired figure in the hall up ahead. His tall form sticks to the center of the corridor, skillfully weaving around dawdling students. "Hayden McGraw. I saw him staring at you during class. He's obsessed."

"Don't make it sound creepy." Paradoxically, I keep my gaze locked on Hayden till he disappears around a corner. "I think he's just lonely."

Angie does the single-brow thing again. Practice makes perfect. "Well, jump right in there and ask him out!"

I groan. "Angie, I am truly thrilled you're now happily coupled with this mysterious Jacob from Whatever High, but that doesn't mean I want to be coupled with someone, too. Why do I need to 'jump' straight into dating? This guy needs a *friend*, for starters."

Angie isn't listening. She started swooning at the mention of her new boyfriend's name. He's from a rival school in Bartlett, and she first saw him at a football game. According to her, it was love at first on-field fight. "That's a pity. I wish you could have what Jacob and I share."

I smile wryly. She sounds like a character in a soap opera. "Yeah, someday my prince will come, but he'll probably turn into a toad."

"Such a cynic!"

"I'm a realist." I haven't had the best of luck in the romance department. Admittedly, it's through lack of trying. At my locker, a pile of books and notes fall out the second I open it. "I have zero time for dating right now. I've got a new project."

Here's when I would normally spill my guts to Angie

and tell her what I'm doing. And she'd fire question after question at me. Maybe even tell me I'm chasing phantoms. But right now I'm not ready for a verbal assault.

Angie *tuts*. She crouches on the floor with me and picks up paperclips with her tangerine-painted nails. "I told you not to do that advanced sign language course. You don't need the extra credit."

"Since when is extra credit a bad thing? Especially when I'm learning a useful skill?" Turns out I'm pretty good at it, too. It often surprises people to know that the language Deaf people use is totally different to spoken English. Learning the grammar rules of American Sign Language is challenging. I just wish I had more time to put it into real-world practice. Still, I tend to talk with my hands a lot when I'm talking to people who can hear.

Ultimately, I want to study languages in college and work at the United Nations. At the very least, I'd like to be able to have real conversations with the Indonesian relatives on my dad's side and my Dutch family on Mom's side. Of course, I've known the essential profanities in both languages since middle school.

But the UN is years from now. My current project is far more urgent.

Angie hands me one last paperclip. "True. But, excuse me for sounding like your mom—you're spreading yourself too thin. Look at you. You're falling asleep in class. You're working your ass off at your dad's office. When do you get to flake out and doom-scroll through your social media until five o'clock in the morning like us normal people?"

Suddenly, my throat jams up. Great. Just when I thought I had everything together, I'm on the verge of falling apart. In front of the whole school. Using my long hair as a curtain, I hide my face from Angie.

She isn't fooled. Angie pulls back my hair. The sympathetic tears forming in Angie's right eye unravel something inside me.

"Ohhh, Cassidy. I'm sorry. I didn't mean to mention your mom."

"It's all right," I say with a too-bright smile. "No need to pretend she doesn't exist anymore, okay?"

But that's the painful thing. Mom *does* exist. She just flat-out refuses to see me or Dad for reasons I'm sure make sense to her. Not to the rest of us, though.

"Got it. No more pretending," Angie says.

My mom is Nina Groen-Roekiem.

Yes, *that* Nina Groen-Roekiem. Every politician's nightmare. Her nickname at the *Times* may have been Rookie, but she was anything but. She got her start at *Rolling Stone* magazine and worked like a demon. Covering rock gigs is just as tricky as covering politics, according to Mom.

When I was in middle school, she missed out on a Pulitzer Prize for her series of articles about government inaction on climate change. My ten-year-old self was as crushed as she was. I'd spent hours with her on the road, watching her interview academics. We cried oceans of tears together.

She brushed herself off from the loss and got eyeballs-deep into researching a book on the disappearance of Jane Flanagan, President Flanagan's five-year-old daughter, in the mid-eighties. There are conspiracy theories galore, yet nobody knows for sure—is she dead or alive? Helena Flanagan is on record saying, "Call it a mother's instinct, but I *feel* Jane is out there somewhere. I won't rest until she's home."

And my mother, who acted on gut feelings her whole

life, understood. Moms have a spooky intuition when it comes to their kids. At least, that's what mine believes. Until—God forbid—a body turned up, Mom wouldn't give up hope. One way or another, she wanted to find out what happened. Bring some peace to the Flanagans.

Mom traveled back and forth to DC for months, trying to get answers, but hitting roadblocks at every turn. Mom's obsession, as Dad called it, strained their marriage. It wasn't a secret—their arguments were impossible to avoid. How I wish I could have slept through them. It got to the point where I'd jolt every time anybody raised their voice. When they split, it was almost a relief.

Almost.

That's when Mom *really* threw herself into research. Because she didn't have time to find a new place, Dad said she could stay in the tiny guest house on our property. But since she was always on the road anyway, that arrangement turned out better than Dad expected. We never saw her.

Then finally, the inevitable happened earlier this year. The Breakdown. Years of running at full speed but getting nowhere got the best of her. In June, she checked herself into a high-priced mental health facility, without consulting us. We since learned she was moved to a super-exclusive "wellness" resort called Eden Estate. I've looked into it. No Google reviews. No Yelp. Definitely no Facebook fan page.

That's three million kinds of messed up.

Inexplicably, she won't see me or Dad, not even on FaceTime. Sure, my parents have been divorced for a couple years, but they don't hate each other *that* much. My mother is a woman of her word. She doesn't say anything she doesn't mean.

Eden's front line is just as hard to get through. I've begged, pleaded. I'm about ready to start a petition. Every time I'm told by the same snooty-voiced receptionist, "We're sorry. Visitations are not possible today," a piece of my heart gets cleaved off.

What kind of a health facility doesn't support visitors from friends and family?

Last week, I added a bunch of new songs to the playlist Mom made for me not long before she started treatment. Songs that influenced her when she was in college. Songs with lyrics that stirred her emotionally, politically. Songs that were the soundtrack to her life. I thought sharing music with her would melt whatever defenses she'd put up.

She didn't respond.

Twisting the strap of her bag, Angie says, "I meant what I said. I see you constantly running in circles at a hundred miles an hour. It's almost like…"

"Like what?"

She stares hard at me. "Like if you stop for a minute, you'll see there's something missing in your life."

I slam my locker door. "There is. My mother."

"No, it's more than that."

"I really don't know what you're talking about."

Angie, good friend that she is, sees through my bravado and makes soothing noises. Despite her intentions, I wish she'd stop, because I'm about to slide off that verge.

Squaring my shoulders, I pull myself together both physically and metaphorically. Mom's in a very dark place right now. And it's up to me to get her out of there.

In the end, Ms. Walters held me in detention for a grand total of five minutes. She had somewhere to be. That made two of us.

But I doubt Ms. Walters's "somewhere to be" is as shiver inducing as mine.

Eden Estate.

Long shadows of the impossibly tall, locked gates on a secluded road off I-15 loom over the little Fiat I inherited from my mother. The guard booth stands empty. With cobwebs clinging to the windows, I'm thinking it's been empty for some time.

"This can't be it," I whisper to myself, then check my phone for the address that was buried deep in the bowels of an intensive Google search. It finally came up in the results when I punched in Eden's phone number.

Super-exclusive? Resort?

Now I'm worried. I've had nightmares about places like this.

The boxy, two-story building's paint might have been bright white fifty or sixty years ago, but today it's gray and flaky. Weeds are growing out of what little I can see of the flat roof. Chunks of stucco have fallen off the front portico. Hard to believe anyone can see through those chalky windows and look out over Saddleback Ridge.

There are no patients wandering the grounds. Why would they? The grass is overgrown in some places, dry and yellowed in others, and there are more nettles than roses in the flowerbeds.

Ivy clings to a rusty comms box outside the guard booth. I open my window, press a faded red button, and call out loudly, "Hello?"

A few seconds pass, then static crackles through the speakers. No voice. Just static.

When it stops, I press the button again. "Um, hi? This is Cassidy Roekiem. I'm here to see my mother, Nina Groen-Roekiem."

More static and electronic squealing vomits from the speaker.

Frowning, I check around the gates for surveillance cameras. But unless they're cleverly hidden behind the weeds, there aren't any.

"Is anyone there?" More static. I unlock my phone and find the contacts app. "Okay, I'll just *call* your office, then. I really need to see my mother."

But as soon as the phone line starts buzzing, the gates swing inward with an ominous, creaking groan that seems to intone, *"Enter if you dare."*

I rev the engine in response. "I dare, all right."

TRACK 3

"Under Pressure"

Two Weeks Ago

Hayden paced the basement like a caged animal. The ceiling was mere centimeters above his head, and the beige carpet and walls felt suffocating. But this was the McGraws' safe place in the new house. Soundproof, earthquake-proof, flood-proof. Whether it was sinkhole-proof was not among his concerns.

He rarely called family unit meetings. It was most often his mother who scheduled them. He sensed his parents' surprise when he made the urgent request within an hour of starting his first day, but they humored him. Lindsay, Sam, and Trudy watched him apprehensively now, each with identical frowns on their faces.

"Life's short, Hayden. Why don't you just blurt it out?" his little sister said as she played tug-of-war with her new pet dog.

"Fine." Hayden stopped pacing. He gazed at Trudy, then their parents. "I've detected a former captive."

"You're certain this time?" Lindsay's hands clenched the sofa. "It's not like you can do a retinal scan to be sure."

He bristled at the "this time." He was absolutely certain this time. There would be no repeat of what happened in

Maine, when he almost revealed his true self to the wrong person.

"And it's not like you know I *need* Aguan equipment to do that," Hayden replied.

"Yes!" Trudy exclaimed. "Try my light test. I've been experimenting with different spectrums—"

Sam cleared his throat. "We've talked about this ad nauseam. We're Observers. No experiments. No in-depth studies. No development of equipment. Leave those things to the Grays."

Hayden's stomach twisted. He'd been thinking how much he would like to study Cassidy. His fascination with her went beyond knowing she was one of the few marked captives on Earth, someone who'd previously given to the cause. The DNA of captives changed irrevocably. When he looked at Cassidy, that transmutation was like a siren call. It reverberated through every cell of his body.

"Does this captive seem…affected?" Lindsay asked.

Is she haunted-looking? Is she jumping at every little noise? Is she tweeting her experiences in all caps to the entire world? Hayden shook his head. "If she remembers, she's good at hiding it. She's amiable, if a little distracted. However, I suspect she remains clouded."

He sensed within Cassidy an innate sense of duty that aligned with his. It made him want to reach out to her. But he knew he had to be careful. Watch her from afar.

Sam turned to Lindsay. "So what protocol should we follow? We obviously can't move again. Not for at least six months."

"Yes, we need to stay put." Firming her jaw, Lindsay mulled over the options.

"What if she becomes unclouded?" he said.

"I doubt that will happen. There would have to be an

extraordinary chain of events."

"There's another thing." Hayden said. He drew a deep breath. "She reminds me of Kalexy. Not in looks so much, but the way she holds herself."

Sam cleared his throat. "That must be difficult for you, son."

"Kind of." His shoulders drooped.

News of Kalexy's untimely passing last Earth year had hit him hard. Intellectually, he understood that although Cassidy and Kalexy shared some physical similarities—shimmering dark hair, lean legs that went on for days—they were not the same beings. Comparing them against each other was unfair. He couldn't help but wonder if fate had put Cassidy in his path as a way of helping him adapt to Earth. Either that or it was a test courtesy of the superiors, to see if the McGraws really were suited to their mission.

"You have to put that out of your mind," Lindsay said firmly. To Trudy, she added, "Tune down your light experiments. We don't know what could trigger this girl or any other captives we might come across."

Sam nodded. "You don't answer to just your mother and me. The bottom line is *don't interfere*. No matter what. Our lives here depend on it."

TRACK 4

"Sorrow"

Present Day

No one greets me when I enter the facility.

Which is fine, because the moment I set foot inside and look around, I'm awestruck. I stand in one spot and turn around.

It's nothing like the austere exterior.

Yes, the structure fits in with the outside. All straight lines. No features like crown molding or warm, polished wood. The walls are white but tinged yellow, like the pages of an aging paperback.

The furnishings scream old-world luxury. Gilt-framed mirrors and faded landscape paintings. Elaborate chandeliers are dusty but still glittering. They catch every ray of light and throw rainbows onto the ceiling. Persian rugs are planted strategically over the utilitarian linoleum tiles. A lush carpet runner covers a wide terrazzo staircase with black metal banisters. It's like someone tried their hardest to soften the Spartan architecture, but the effect is incongruous.

There's nothing resembling a reception desk, nothing that indicates Eden is a place for the very sick. I don't see workers in lab coats or scrubs wandering around, or hear any movement.

The fact that it's like a decorated royal palace inside should bring me some comfort. But it doesn't. The atmosphere is odd and stale, like nobody hangs around here much.

"Is anyone here?" My voice echoes. Then comes the sound of a door opening.

"Ah, you must be Miss Roekiem."

I whirl around to face the person who pronounced my name perfectly. A tall man with silver hair and gaunt, wrinkled cheeks steps in from a room off the foyer. He peers at me with watery blue eyes framed by gold-rimmed glasses that don't seem to fit his head. They keep sliding down his narrow nose. Pure white teeth gleam as he smiles. There's something about that smile that puts me on edge right away. It's too wide, too friendly. He straightens his white lab coat and holds out a meaty hand that's covered with pigmentation spots.

"I'm Cassidy," I say, nodding. His grip is so cold it sends a shiver down my back. "Dr. Davis" is monogrammed in blue above his coat pocket. "Thank you for letting me in. I've tried for a long time to even speak to my mother, so being able to see her now is awesome."

"Yes," he says before pressing his lips into a taut line.

Great. I can already sense that getting any information out of this doctor will be like trying to squeeze champagne from a potato.

"Is there a reason why I couldn't see her before? Was she…" I force a lump of emotion down my throat. Images of old horror movies and patients languishing in straitjackets jump to mind. "Was she too sick to even pick up a phone? Shoot me a text?"

He's silent for a moment, and the walls feel like they're

closing in on me. When he speaks, his words are slow, measured. "There were some issues that needed addressing."

"Issues?" My chest squeezes. "What kind?"

Dr. Davis stares down at me with a faint air of disapproval. "We take patient confidentiality very seriously here, as I'm sure you can appreciate."

"Even from family? I'm her *daughter*."

"Even so." He gestures for me to enter another room off the foyer. Worn red velvet sofas and armchairs are arranged around a coffee table. "So, Cassidy, I have heard a lot about you."

"Oh, really?" A glimmer of hope sparks. If Mom has talked about me that means she's been thinking of me, at least. I sit on an armchair. Its springs dig into my butt. The air in here is stale, too, as if the windows haven't been opened in a while. "But why doesn't she want to talk to me?"

"I know the months she has been working on herself here must feel like a lifetime to a young person." That too-wide, too-white smile flashes for a split second. The man's got to be in his seventies, but he moves like a lion prowling on the savanna. He sits on a sofa opposite me, and light from the closed windows behind him turns him into a silhouette. "But Nina isn't ready for family therapy, so you and your father aren't scheduled to see her for some time. Your father is aware of this, of course."

My lips tighten. Yeah, Dad knows. He's content to go along with the doctor's "advice." It's a sticking point between us, but when it comes down to it, my parents are no longer married. He has no say in what happens with Mom anymore. Neither do I.

"I didn't come here for therapy. I'm here to visit. Just to talk to her." I can't keep the edge out of my voice. I wanted to sound grown-up and controlled, but months of frustration have taken a toll, and this man's attitude is stomping on my last nerve.

"Yes, but you must understand," he says smoothly, "isolation is quite necessary for recovery in this case. Nina explained the visitation policy to you, yes?"

"She did," I say, forcing the words out through clenched teeth. Mom had written a letter—a letter!—explaining that she needed time out from life, and that it was all in the name of recovering from her nervous breakdown. Her words didn't comfort me. They only told me that I couldn't be part of the solution to her problems. That hurt more than a karate-kick to the groin.

"I can see you're upset with your mother about the policy," Dr. Davis says.

Anyone in my situation would be angry. Doesn't take a genius to realize that.

"I'm here now. I'd just like to see her," I say, injecting steel into my tone, "if that's okay with you, Doctor?"

He checks his watch. "It's very short notice, and she has just received her medication."

"What kind of medication?" My pulse rises at the thought of my mother needing to be drugged. She never took anything stronger than ibuprofen in the past, as far as I know.

"A mild sedative," he says.

Wait. *What?* "Why does she need a sedative? Shouldn't she be feeling much calmer now that she's being treated properly?" The steel in my voice melts a little as an image of my anxiety-riddled mom haunts me.

"It's part of her ongoing therapy. Many patients with her condition benefit from this particular drug. It's perfectly safe." Dr. Davis stands, his face no longer in the shadows. Overgrown gray brows lifted, he regards me like I'm the one who needs a sedative.

"If she's…sedated, then it's okay to see her, right? It's not going to stress her out?" I lock my arms around my body as I stand.

He hesitates for a moment, the first time I've seen him appear unsure. That rattles what little confidence I have in this treatment facility. "She might be a little drowsy," he says, "but yes, you can see her. Briefly."

I breathe out six months' worth of tension. "Great. Thank you."

He crosses the room and I start to follow, but then he says over his shoulder, "Stay in the waiting room. I will bring her downstairs to you. It's protocol. And you'll both be more comfortable here."

I don't know about feeling comfortable in this stuffy room, but at this point, I can't be too fussy. I'm finally getting to see my mother after all this time apart.

This waiting room doesn't offer a single magazine or even a pamphlet to read. And with my phone getting zero bars, there's nothing to help pass the time.

After a while, the faint sound of something tapping skates on my nerves. I search around for a clock, but there isn't one. I head to a window and find it not only locked, but also free of nearby trees and branches that could be making the noise.

The door opens with a soft squeak. I'm so on edge that the sound makes me jump. I turn. A ghostly figure stands in the doorway.

My throat catches. "Mom?"

She looks scared, like a lost rabbit. Her blue eyes are wide and round. Instead of the colorful bohemian dresses she loves, she's wearing a gray robe. Its belt encloses a waif-like waist. Her cheeks are sunken. Skin dull. All the vibrancy has been knocked out of her.

This is not my mother. Not the one I know anyway.

Dr. Davis nudges her from behind. "It's okay, Nina."

I rush across the room toward her, but then stop short when she seems to shrink back. "Mom? It's me, Cassidy."

"Cassidy... Cassidy..." She repeats my name as if sounding it out for the first time.

"That's right. Your favorite daughter." I try to keep my voice even and light, but inside I'm shaking. My own mother doesn't recognize her only child. What kind of sedative are they giving her? I thought this place was supposed to help her get better. Instead, she looks worse than the day she checked herself in.

A few seconds pass, and then her expression clears. "Oh...baby."

She takes a couple of steps and folds me into her arms, every bone in her rib cage pressing against me. Still, her touch calms me. I let out a sigh, grateful she knows who I am. I want to hug her even tighter, as if that would somehow transfer healing vibes to her. But I'm half afraid she'll break.

"I'll give you some privacy." Dr. Davis offers a thin smile and reaches for the doorknob. "And I apologize for any construction noise you might hear. We're currently refurbishing the estate from the inside out."

Ah. One mystery solved.

As soon as he's gone, I pull Mom down onto a sofa with me. "How are you doing? I've missed you so much!"

"I'm wonderful, baby. Really." She sits back, eyes darting around like she's not sure she's allowed to get comfortable. I contemplate her response. She's either lying or she's forgotten what the word wonderful means. "I've missed you, too," she says. "Why haven't you come to see me before today?"

"Um, because you told us not to come," I say, puzzled. *And you said it like you meant it.*

Mom's smile drops. "Oh. Yes. Yes, of course."

"I'm so glad I made it past the front gate. Through the front door, even." I grab both of her hands. It's hard to believe I'm actually touching her. "I hate being cut off from you, especially now when you're in this weird…resort? What is this place, anyway?"

Mouth agape, she peers around the room as though she's never seen it before. "Isn't it beautiful?"

"Yeah…it's nice." I suppose beauty is in the eye of the beholder and all that. "You're comfortable? Eating enough? How are they treating you here?"

Her eyes shutter as if the barrage of questions is too much to handle. The purple shadows under her eyes look like bruises. "You should have listened when you were told not to visit."

Pasting on a hopeful grin, I say, "But you're thrilled to see me, right?"

Her silence exacerbates the emptiness of the place. Even the hammering has stopped. It's like we're in a vacuum.

"Yes," she whispers after a long, excruciating time.

Her hesitation beckons tears to my eyes. The old Mom wouldn't have left me hanging like that. Old Mom would've replied in a split second, *"I'm* beyond *thrilled."*

I try again to inject brightness and sunshine into my words. "So, when can you come home?"

Another pause, then, "When I'm better."

I bite my lip. "That seems kind of vague."

"Mental health issues are challenging," she says robotically, almost like she'd rehearsed it. There's a stoniness in her gaze now that's completely foreign to me.

I squeeze her bony hand. "I'm doing everything I can

to get you out of this place."

For a nanosecond, her rigid, masklike expression flickers. A light seems to shine from those blue eyes. She whispers, "Out?"

"That's what you want, isn't it? Your own bed, your own tiny house. Your own life? Even your career?" That brief light in her eyes extinguishes as soon as she hears my last word. I've blown it. "It's okay, Mom. No one could blame you for feeling down."

"There's more to it than 'feeling down.'" Her sharp tone cuts through the air like a blade. She twists away from me and walks to one of the windows.

"You're right. That was…that was brainless of me. I'm sorry." Damn, why do I keep saying the wrong thing? It used to be so easy to talk to my mother. Now I feel like we're strangers to each other. "I was thinking maybe there's a way I can help with your treatment."

"I'm getting all the help I need, sweetie," she says in a voice so soft I have to strain to hear it.

"I'm not talking medically. But…professionally?"

She faces me and squints. "What do you mean?"

I take a big breath. "I will solve the Jane Flanagan investigation you started, and that would bring you some closure, and you can start to heal. I have your laptop. I'm getting it fixed. I'll continue where you left off. And I've already got a lead. Okay, you probably uncovered it already. But it's a good idea to start from scratch, right? Get a new perspective?"

"Investigation." Mom's eyes glaze over. I'm talking way too fast. I know I am.

"Jane. Flanagan. You worked day and night on your book. Remember?"

How could she have forgotten the thing that put her in

treatment in the first place? Are the sedatives *that* good?

Or conversely, are the sedatives *that* bad that entire chunks of her life have been wiped from her memory?

A spark of recognition finally crosses her features. "The president," she whispers.

"Yes, the former president's daughter. You were so pumped about that investigation when you started it." I start pacing around her. "Then you said working that case was like going over an obstacle course, but I can start with a fresh angle—"

"No!" She jerks her head sharply, hands whipping through the air.

My jaw falls open. "Why not? It's a great story. An untold story. I'm going to finish it for you."

Giving her blond head a vigorous shake, Mom says, "It's a terrible idea. Trust me."

"But you used to say if the right people talked—"

"No! You won't find anything! No one will talk," she snaps in a totally non-Mom way. "It was a hopeless investigation from the start. Save yourself the heartache. Just… just go on with your life."

She stares hard at me, her gaze no longer vague. It occurs to me then that maybe she wanted to finish the job herself when she gets out of this place. I shouldn't have asked, knowing how protective she was of her work. However…

"Mom, please." My voice cracks. I fight to sound a little tougher. "Solving this case doesn't just help you or me."

"I'm sorry," she says, turning away. "I don't want you to take on the investigation. Look where it got me—"

A hard knock at the door startles me.

Dr. Davis stalks back into the room. He flashes that too-white, too-wide, too-friendly grin on me. "Apologies for the interruption, Cassidy."

I glare. He looks sorry-not-sorry. "Yes?"

"Nina, it's time to resume your treatment."

"Yes, Doctor." Mom starts to move. I put my hand out to stop her, but she slips away from me to stand beside him. Two against one.

"Mom, wait." I laugh awkwardly. "Let me visit you every week. Or every other weekend? It'd be great for both of us. Therapeutic, even."

Mom shakes her head. "No, Cassidy. Please understand. There are good reasons for me to recover in private."

"But… But I'm your daughter."

"It'll be okay, sweetie. Be patient." Mom squares her posture.

My gaze slides to the doctor, who nods solemnly as if to say, *"See? This is what she wants. No one's forcing her."*

Dr. Davis's hand moves to her shoulder, angling her toward the door. "Go on ahead to the treatment room, Nina. I'll be right with you."

"Wait!" I lunge for Mom, hugging her so hard she gasps. "I love you, Mom. Call me anytime. Or text, whatever."

"I love you, too, Cassidy." She pulls back and does that classic mom gesture of brushing hair out of my eyes. In that brief second, I see the old Nina Groen-Roekiem. "I'm getting help. Tell your dad everything's fine."

"One more thing—" I rush to my bag and pull out a package the size of a brick. "I almost forgot these. The food of our people."

For a dessert-lover like me, growing up with a mom of Dutch descent and a first-generation Indonesian dad has its culinary advantages. Winters weren't complete without spiced Dutch cookies and a glass of warm milk. Indonesian coconut and pandan jellies made with love by my great-aunt Carole often put me into food comas on the back porch during long, hot summers.

"*Speculaas*!" With trembling hands she brings the package to her nose. There's no way she can smell the sweet cinnamon and nutmeg shortbread through the red foil.

"I found them at the Dutch deli," I say, loving the light in her eyes. Sure, it might be a reflection of the cookie packet, but I choose to believe it's something more. It gives me hope that she can find her way back.

"Thank you, sweetie." Mom smiles tightly and blows me a kiss.

As she drifts down the hall without looking back, gray robe clinging to her bones, all I can think is that everything is *not* fine.

Dr. Davis clears his throat and steps toward me. I'm fairly tall, but he's even taller, even with a bit of a hump in his back. "I hope you can see now that your mother's wishes need to be respected. Remember, it was she who checked herself in."

"Then she can check herself *out*, right?"

"When the time is right and when she meets certain criteria," he says. "Emotionally, she's in a very delicate place. She has deep-seated issues. It may take years to resolve them all. I have to insist that you don't visit again until Nina says she's ready."

"You're saying I could be out of college before I can see my own mother again?"

"It's difficult to put a specific time frame on these things. The mind is rather complex. Often unpredictable. Like your mother said…be patient." His tone is meant to be soothing, but I'm not soothed by it. At all.

I meet the doctor's glacial blue eyes. There's harshness in that gaze where there should be sympathy, understanding.

He widens his stance, forming a sort of roadblock. A vein in my head throbs like a drum in response. In this moment I hate everything about this dusty, antiquated place, and he's at the top of the list.

I've got to get Mom out of Eden. Pleading with her or getting past Dr. Davis isn't going to work. The only way is to find Jane Flanagan, dead or alive.

Whatever it takes.

TRACK 5

"Working Class Man"

September 14, 1947

As the "D.W." in D.W. Prospecting, Derek Watkins was accustomed to working seven days a week. But his board members—Goldstein, Sharpe, and Canley—were more likely to spend their days on the golf course.

Particularly on a Sunday.

All of them looked at him, on this fine and glorious day, with bare contempt. Good-for-nothing sons of bitches. Watkins didn't care about them.

But he did care about his mining crew. Believed in them.

"Gentlemen, thank you for attending on short notice. I know I'm taking you away from your wives and families."

Goldstein snorted. "Get to the point, Watkins. What are we here for?"

Watkins hesitated. He'd been doing a lot of that lately. Glancing out at the thickly forested Saddleback Ridge, he said, "I'm concerned about this story in the *Gazette*. The one about ships from outer space kidnapping our workers and then dumping them hours later."

"You don't seriously believe those men?" asked Sharpe. And indeed his tone was sharp.

"Gary Bueller said it was true," Watkins bit out. Bueller

was a man you could count on in a scrape. A man who called a spade a spade. A spacecraft a spacecraft. "That's enough for me."

"It's unadulterated nonsense," Sharpe said. "Declining production is what we need to focus on right now. What are we gonna do about that?"

"Not a lot if a big chunk of our workforce is sick." Watkins tossed files onto the table and fanned them out. "Look at these absentee records."

"What do you mean by sick?" Canley asked, finally looking interested.

Watkins jabbed each of the files. "Robson, third-degree burns. Smith, nosebleeds—"

"Nosebleeds?" Sharpe scoffed. "What else? A broken fingernail? I survived two bullets on D-Day, for Chrissakes. Just fire 'em. We'll find a new crew."

Watkins glared at him. "Some of our men fought on the front lines, too. We need to look out for them."

"What do you suggest we do? Send them on vacation to recover? All expenses paid?" Goldstein laughed.

"Hilarious," replied Watkins, grim faced.

Canley spoke up. "I know a doctor. Works for the government."

Watkins turned to him. "What kind of doctor?"

"The kind who's interested in this UFO stuff. He's a shrink." Canley idly leafed through the files. "Leave it with me. I'll see what he says. I'm sure he can knock some sense into the crew."

When Watkins drew the meeting to a close, the other board members bolted from the room like it was on fire. Watkins stared out the window as Canley, Goldstein, and Sharpe drove away in their company Oldsmobiles. Warm fluid trickled from Watkins's nose.

"Dammit. Not again."

Turning from the window, he reached into his pocket for his handkerchief. He swiped at his nostrils, then inspected the monogrammed white linen.

Watkins wasn't faint of heart. He'd seen a lot in the war, too. But the sight of the deep red blood clots in that handkerchief shook something inside him.

A new battle was about to begin. This time, he wasn't sure who the enemy was.

TRACK 6

"Chances Are"

Present Day

Before I even dream about driving home from Eden, I rest my head on the steering wheel. The tears have dried up, but my heart's still galloping harder than a thoroughbred in the Kentucky Derby. A series of text message alerts start firing out in quick succession. I fumble for my phone. The first is from Angie, obviously sent while I was in the mobile reception black hole.

Angie: Good luck with your mom!

Angie: Have you talked to her yet?

PC Brigade: Hi, Cassidy. It's Javier. I tried to leave a voicemail, but it went wonky. Technical term. So, it's bad news for your laptop. It's dead. Sorry about that. Come pick it up anytime and I'll explain everything. Thanks.

I groan. It's not my laptop. It's Mom's. I "borrowed" it when I first got the idea to hunt for Jane Flanagan, but I couldn't get it fired up.

Angie: You have to come to the lake party. Bringing Jacob so you can finally meet him. Love of my lice.

Angie: *life

Angie: What's happening???

There are ten more messages from Angie, most of them

containing single words or emojis. Sucking in my cheeks, I scroll down. I love my best friend, but the one message I was really hoping to see isn't one of hers—and it's not among any of the texts.

But then, Anna Kingston doesn't strike me as a texting kind of woman. She did, after all, respond with an email when I first reached out to her.

Anna was a young White House intern when Jane Flanagan disappeared. She was named in an archived *Washington Times* article from 1985 that I found online. Wiki says she served in the Senate before retiring early when she became ill. I quickly check my inbox and find only newsletters from my favorite authors and sales alerts from Sephora. Nothing from Anna.

I tap out a text to Angie in case she's already commissioned a search party for me.

Me: Hey Ange. It was so awful. The worst. You should have seen her.

My thumb hovers over the send icon. Chewing my lip, I decide against telling Angie my mother was less animated than a department store mannequin. Except when she told me to stay away from the Jane Flanagan case. No, giving Angie the unvarnished truth would only invite more questions from her, and frankly I can't deal right now.

I jam my finger on the backspace key.

Me: Hi! I got to see Mom. She's doing fine. Driving now. Talk later!

Angie's reply is immediate: WTG Mom! So great. I'll see you at the lake. Tell me everything then.

Feeling sharp stings of guilt from all the lies, I toss my phone face down on the passenger seat. I'm pretty sure I hadn't committed to going to tonight's pre-homecoming party at the lake. In fact, all I'm committed to is crawling into bed as soon as I get home. By the sound of things, Mom's laptop isn't going to be of any use, so it can wait till tomorrow.

Starting the car, I crane my neck to check for other vehicles and visitors before rolling back. There's not much in the way of life here except for weeds poking up through a multitude of cracks in the asphalt and a couple of lizards. No other cars, either. The doc mentioned construction was going on. I guess the workers parked their trucks around back?

The surrounding forest casts long shadows. I frown at the dashboard clock. How could it be quarter to six already? Had I really been inside for two hours? It seemed like only a few minutes. Then again, it did take an excruciating amount of time for Mom to come down from her room.

By the unmanned guard's hut, the front gate judders open for me. A little ways down the road, the steel-gray paint of an old pick-up truck appears. I tap on the brake and wait for it to pass. Only it slows down and eventually comes to a stop, blocking my exit. It dwarfs my tiny, adorable-but-not-the-best-vehicle-for-the-mountains Fiat 500.

"What's your problem, buddy?" I mutter while gesturing for them to scooch a little farther so I can leave. But they don't move. Groaning, I step out, just as the truck bunny-hops and stalls. I stride over the crumbling asphalt to the driver's side.

A scratched window winds down manually.

And I'm face-to-face with Hayden McGraw. He stares at me with bulging brown eyes as he fumbles with the ignition. The engine starts, but he messes up with the clutch and the truck hops and stalls again.

"Hayden?" I step back as he opens his door. My fingers brush the windowsill, and a zap of static electricity makes the hairs on my arms stand up. "What are you doing out here? Are you lost?"

He climbs out of the car and rakes a hand through his hair, revealing a crumpled brow. His gaze darts from me to Eden, then back again.

"I…I was, uh, coming back from a job interview and thought I'd take a tour of Dawson…" Hayden's lips quirk into a sheepish smile. A deep burgundy flush spreads across his cheeks and spills down his neck. He scuffs the soles of his Timberlands on the asphalt. "And, yeah, I'm lost now. My GPS stopped working around the turn-off from the highway back there. Weird, huh?"

"Very."

"I feel like I've been driving in circles." He tosses another glance at Eden. "So how about it? Can you tell me where on earth we are?"

My gaze travels back to the decrepit building beyond the fence. Just looking at it puts ice in my veins. I'm ashamed to tell him that's where my mother's living.

No, not living. Existing.

I don't want him to think my family dumped her in a place like that on purpose. God, if I'd known how bad it was here, I would have tried to stop her somehow. Barricaded her in the house. Anything.

"We're outside a 'health resort,'" I say with air quotes, feeling my throat constrict. "It's for people with anxiety issues and things like that."

He squints at Eden, then at me. "Looks more like a last resort."

"That's what I thought, too. Apparently, they're in the middle of renovations."

"But they're still treating people while that's going on? As in-patients?"

Good point. Flying sawdust, construction workers yelling over the buzz of power tools, demolition shaking the foundations—all of those things would only add to the patients' stress levels. *Mom's* stress level.

"Yeah," I say. "That's not how I'd run things if I were in charge. I didn't actually *see* any construction or contractors." On the first floor, a dim light turns on behind filmy curtains. Could that be Mom's room? Tentatively, I wave, despite not seeing anyone moving.

Hayden catches me waving. There's a mix of curiosity and warmth in his eyes that makes my insides wobble. The atmosphere around us seems to throb, like it does when summer storms approach. Except it's fall.

"Do you know someone in there?" he asks, face softening.

A lump of emotion in my throat stops me from answering. I can only nod.

"I'm sorry." He starts to reach for me, but then thinks better of it, folding his arms tightly across his broad chest. I'm glad he didn't hug me or anything. I would've totally lost it.

"It's fine." A blatant lie. He tilts his head like he knows it, too. Brightening my voice, I say, "The inside is nothing like the outside. It's kind of old-school opulent. If you like antiques and oil paintings of unhappy-looking subjects. Not the mid-century aesthetic she likes, but it could be worse."

His smile is a reassuring one. "I bet your mom will be out of there in no time."

"I hope so—" My eyebrows knit together. "Wait, how did you know I was talking about my mother?"

Hayden's leg collapses for a second. His entire face turns an even deeper shade of burgundy this time. Plum, even. "Sorry. When you said 'she,' I…I just assumed."

I peer at him closely. Does he have a sixth sense? I cast

my mind back to our morning biology class, a lifetime ago, where he seemed to react to what I was thinking. Then there was the "last resort" comment, which echoed my thoughts about Eden *exactly*. Maybe we're in tune somehow.

It also could be my imagination running away with me. Wouldn't be the first time.

But am I also imagining the electric current pulsing in the air?

I shake my head. *Of course* I'm imagining it. I'm letting Angie's melodramatic influence get to me. She believes in romanticisms like sparks flying and chemistry bubbling between two people. The only electricity here is coming from the power lines running parallel to the road.

"It's fine. Don't worry about it," I say, keeping my fingers crossed that Hayden really isn't a mind reader. "But don't spread it around. Most of my friends know my mom's getting help, but they don't know every detail."

He nods solemnly. "I won't tell anyone. You can trust me."

My stomach churns as I look at Eden. Once again, I can't shake the feeling that it's the wrong place for Mom. I swing around to my car and send a glare in the general direction of Dr. Davis.

"I take it visiting hours are over?"

Tossing my head, I say, "They don't have visiting hours, period. I'm surprised I got in today at all."

"That's weird." He stares at me for a long while. "You'll get back in there."

"Oh, I intend to." Sighing, I say, "I'd better head home, though. There's not a lot I can do about it now."

Short of a court order. Or maybe a SWAT operation.

"Right." He snaps his fingers. "I'll get out of your way."

"Thanks. And, uh, you'd better follow me." I hide a grin.

"Can't have you driving aimlessly. You might end up in Canada."

He laughs, sheepish. "It's okay. I'll figure it out. Besides, I need to stop for gas. I don't want to hold you up."

We lean on our respective car doors and stare at each other, just ten feet apart. It doesn't look like he's going anywhere.

Then I remember how it doesn't seem like he's gelled with anyone at school yet. He must be dying for company.

"Hey, uh, you should come to the lake party tonight," I say. "Hang out for a bit."

"T-together?"

His doubtful expression drills a tiny hole in my heart, but I push that aside. "We don't have to go *together* together. I mean, it's a traditional senior class thing and you're new in town and people are curious about you."

Hayden recoils. I'm not sure if that's because he finds my rambling distasteful or if he's uncomfortable about being thought of as a curiosity. "Uh…"

"Look, it's no pressure. I understand if you want to skip it. It'll just be kids standing around a bonfire and seeing who can burp the loudest and longest. And that's just the cheerleaders."

A deep, genuine laugh erupts from Hayden, making me feel like a comedienne.

"Fine. I'll think about it, but just to let you know, I'm physically incapable of burping, so I'd sit that contest out."

Rolling my eyes, I say, "Sure, Hayden. But one day you're gonna have to prove you're human like the rest of us."

TRACK 7

"Skin Deep"

MEMORANDUM FOR THE DIRECTOR OF THE CENTRAL INTELLIGENCE AGENCY

CLASSIFICATION: TOP SECRET

SUBJECT: PARALLAX

November 3, 1947

The Parallax Human Intervention Unit has been initialized. We project a $2 million Black Budget running cost for the 1948 fiscal year, rising to $2.7 million in 1949, and $3.2 million in 1950. This includes a one-time compensation package with D.W. Prospecting for the use of their employees, henceforth to be referred to as Subjects, and facilities.

Professor Jonathan Taylor, formerly of Harvard Medical School of Psychiatry, has completed an assessment of fifteen Subjects. All satisfy eligibility and suitability requirements. Each Subject will be adequately compensated at $40 per week. All food and emergency accommodation costs are included in the budget figures above. Binding confidentiality agreements signed by the Subjects are enclosed herewith.

Stage I experiments will commence November 11, 1947.
For the Parallax Human Intervention Unit,

Dr. Harold P. Elsworth

TRACK 8

"Say My Name"

Ten Years Ago

Though his eyes were closed firmly, the boy knew it was morning. The blackout curtains did their job keeping the sunlight out, but intense summer heat throbbed through the glass. He threw his covers off the bed and tossed over onto his stomach, then onto his back again.

He'd slept poorly since the arrival, so he was determined to snooze just that little bit longer. Last night he had a nightmare about Kalexy, his best friend. Dreamed he'd never see her again.

He rubbed his swollen eyes. Seemed he'd cried sometime during the night.

The boy listened to the quiet murmurs of his parents as they fussed around outside his new bedroom. He heard them utter words like "too soon" and "this isn't what we were told" and "they're not like us at all."

At least it sounded like they were in total agreement with each other. Still, those words contrasted sharply from the ones he'd overheard in the past year, such as "mission objectives" and "avoid detection."

His parents' work was important. Special. He'd known that from the day he was born. Or since he was old enough to understand, anyway. He also knew they were more than just a family. They were a unit. And they had to work together for the greater good.

Years of training had gone into the arrival. But now that they were here, the boy couldn't help feeling there were gaps that needed filling. Like, how was he meant to integrate if he wasn't allowed to make friends? What should he say if someone asked him where he came from? Was it going to be possible to hide all of his abilities?

A soft knock preceded the turn of the doorknob. The boy rolled over again, finally opening his eyes. Through the small gap in the door, he could see his mother's flushed cheeks.

"Rise and shine, sweetheart!" Yes, she was smiling, but even at seven years old the boy could see tension in her eyes. Her neck muscles looked taut and strained.

"Lindsay," he said, yawning.

She lightly bounced a pillow on his chest. "We've discussed this. You must call me Mom. Remember, we don't want to draw any attention to ourselves while we're getting settled, all right?"

He allowed her to pull him onto his feet. Digging his toes into the shaggy carpet, which he had to admit felt a hundred times more comforting than his new bed, he stretched and yawned. "All right, *Mom.*"

"Thank you. It has a nice ring to it, right?" Lindsay, aka his mother, jerked his cotton pajama shirt over his head and replaced it with a blue cotton T-shirt. "Now, what's your name again?"

The little boy stared at his image in the mirror over a dresser for what seemed like an eternity. Dark, burdened eyes stared back. He'd been coached within an inch of his short life. He'd studied the data from previous arrivals and aced all the tests. Could he now ace real life? His *new* real life?

"Sweetie, I know this arrival has been hard for you, but—"

"Hayden," he blurted before she could give another speech about the importance of their work. "My name is Hayden McGraw."

TRACK 9

"If I Could Turn Back Time"

Present Day

As soon as I arrive home from Eden, I get a message that makes my heart jump. A witness whose name I dug up from a decades-old *Washington Times* article wants to talk. I grab a quick bite, then FaceTime her on my iPad.

A low-angle shot of an elderly woman appears. She pushes her frameless glasses up her nose. A collection of at least six cuckoo clocks on the wall behind her peal at the same time.

"Hello, Mrs. Parkes." I wave. "Thank you so much for meeting me. I really appreciate your time."

She leans forward, I'm guessing to get closer to the speaker. "It's my pleasure, dear. So clever of you to find me."

I chuckle. It wasn't really, but I don't want to diminish her opinion of me so early in the conversation. The article said she was a dental assistant and the mother of twins. All I had to do was check out some ancestry websites and cross-check them with Facebook. Mrs. Parkes's profile was wide open for all to see.

"Mrs. Parkes, I know it was such a long time ago," I begin. The clocks behind her stop cuckooing. "But can you cast your mind back to the day Jane Flanagan went missing?"

"To be honest with you, dear, I'm not sure if I can help." Her glasses slide down again, revealing cloudy blue eyes and a deep furrow of uncertainty between her sparse brows.

"You never know. Sometimes details that don't seem important at the time can actually turn a case around." I check notes I'd taken from Wikipedia. "Okay, so you and your kids were at the Children's Playground in Georgetown?"

"That's right. We lived on 31st Street, and I worked close by. I used to take my twins to that playground every day. Of course, after the kidnapping, never again." She grimaces.

"Very wise." I nod. "On the day of the kidnapping, did you see Jane at the playground?"

"Oh yes," she says. "My Ruby was about to go down the slippery slide, but she was stopped by the Secret Service so Jane could have a turn first."

"I'm guessing that didn't go over well with Ruby."

"Believe me, normally she'd stomp and pout. That day? Those agents terrified her into submission. There were six of them, I remember that. And a nanny." She gives a wry smile. "But *I* was the one who stomped and pouted. I marched over and gave them all a piece of my mind. Out of earshot of the children, of course."

"What did you say to them?"

Chin raised, her face takes on a look of defiance. "That everyone, no matter how rich or powerful, needs to wait their turn. Or something like that. I might have used a cuss word or two."

She takes off her errant glasses and pinches the bridge of her nose.

"Mrs. Parkes?"

Not looking at the camera, she shakes her head. When she lifts her face again, it's marked with what I can only describe as shame. "It just dawned on me that if I hadn't gotten a bee in my bonnet about the pushy agents, they wouldn't have been distracted, and that little girl might be here today."

"It's *not* your fault, Mrs. Parkes," I say softly, crossing over into the role of amateur counselor instead of amateur investigative journalist. "The person or people who stole Jane away from her family already planned it. This is on them, not you. You can't beat yourself up over it. As far as the agents are concerned, they thought letting Jane go down the slide first was part of their job, too. No disrespect to you, they would have been focused on her, not your kids. They're pros."

She puts her glasses on again. "You're kind to say that, dear. I suppose you're right."

I peek at my notes to get back on track. "Mrs. Parkes, did anyone ever question you? The police? Secret Service?"

"Apart from the reporter who accosted me on the way to work the next morning... Nobody." She shakes her curly gray head. "I neglected to tell you one detail. My girls and I left the park right after I argued with the agents. Little Jane and the entourage were getting ready to leave."

I sit up. "Did you see anything unusual? Maybe a car or delivery van that looked out of place? Or a person you'd never come across in the neighborhood before?"

"No..." She scratches her head. "I remember trying to calm my girls down because we were leaving earlier than planned. There was a lot of stomping and pouting and screaming *then*."

In the background, I hear two women yell in unison, "Mother!"

"Some things never change." Mrs. Parkes laughs, then turns thoughtful. She drums her fingers on her cheek.

"Mrs. Parkes?"

"Excuse me, dear. I'm just thinking about something now that you've mentioned a van." She closes her eyes as if casting her mind back to the day. "There was a van driver waiting to parallel-park a block away from the playground. The writing on the van kinda jumped out at me."

"What did it say?"

"DC Medical Supplies...or Suppliers."

"What was so special about that?"

"I worked as a dental assistant. The office manager had been complaining nonstop about inferior masks from our regular supplier. She was threatening to break a contract with them." She frowns in concentration. "There was a logo of sorts. Come to think of it, almost like four moon phases all in a row underneath the writing on the side panels."

"Very, very good." I lean forward, my Spidey senses piqued. What do moon phases have to do with medical supplies? Was it bad graphic design, or something more? "Was there a phone number or address painted on the van?"

"Yes, just a phone number. I even wrote it down and gave it to the office manager much later." Mrs. Parkes purses her lips. "Donna never liked me. And she disliked me even more when it turned out the number wasn't connected."

"That's...interesting," I say slowly. In my notes, I write *fake phone number on getaway van?*

"Of course, I might have written it down incorrectly in the first place."

Deep in thought, I tap the pen to my lips. I take a breath and try to channel Mom. What else would she ask an interview subject at this point? I snap my fingers as an obvious question pops into my mind. "Did you get a look at the license plate?"

She shakes her head. "I didn't think of it at the time.

Too busy writing down the phone number and wrangling the twins."

"No problem," I say. "What about the make and model of the van?"

"Oh, that's easy. I grew up in a family of car fanatics. It was a gray 1980 Ford Econoline. My brother could tell you the paint code without looking it up if he were with us today." She kisses her hand and touches the air.

"That's excellent, Mrs. Parkes."

She nods while covering a yawn. "Do you have all the information you need, dear?"

"Yes, thank you very much."

While I'm bummed Mrs. Parkes wasn't able to pinpoint a kidnapper or a person of interest, her account did give me more info to work with. There had to be a confluence of events that resulted in Jane's disappearance, and to find that connecting thread, I have to unpick them one stitch at a time.

TRACK 10

"I Second That Emotion"

Present Day

"Know what you're ordering?" Dad asks while reading a laminated breakfast menu at Goldie's Diner. Given the menu hasn't changed since God was in kindergarten, I don't know why he's reading it. But the lack of progress here is part of the charm. It's comforting.

We're sitting in our usual booth in the corner. The window curves right around, giving us a panoramic view of comings and goings. Newspaper-print wallpaper spans the length of the long, narrow diner.

"Chicken-fried lamb's brains," I say. "What else?"

He grins. I'm pretty sure we're both thinking about our family vacation to Sumatra, when I was eleven. He'd proudly taken us there so we could see where he lived as a boy, in a village of fifty people and twice that many cows.

My late great-grandmother Gigi, who was all of four-foot-ten, cooked for days before our arrival. She prepared an Indonesian banquet fit for royalty on a two-burner stove in her modest cottage. Spring rolls, sticky rice sprinkled with toasted coconut, tender beef *rendang*. For her, cooking was an expression of love. One dish I couldn't get enough of was her specialty "popcorn"—soft and silky morsels coated in a spicy batter that danced with my taste buds.

"I love this popcorn tofu," I said at the time, licking the juices off my fingers. Mom's lips quivered uncertainly as she watched me eat.

"Um, it's not tofu, Cass," Dad replied as he reached for another helping. My great-grandmother chortled and gave a detailed, animated explanation in Indonesian. Which Dad translated as, "It's, um, lamb's brains. Everything tastes better when it's deep fried."

My brain, once it had an official name to the morsels, decided it couldn't deal, much to my family's amusement.

I miss my sweet great-grandmother. I'm grateful for that one trip to meet her and explore our heritage. The brain-corn? Not so much, but the thought of it and Gigi's giggling still makes me smile. There aren't any Asian restaurants in this town—Panda Express excluded—let alone an Indonesian one. I'm not likely to taste lamb's brains again, even if I wanted to.

A waitress fills our coffees and takes our orders—innocuous peach crepes drowning in maple syrup for me, not chicken-fried offal.

Dad stirs fake sugar into his mug and neatly folds the empty paper packet into quarters. I peek at his upright posture through the steam wafting over my coffee. My father doesn't do casual. His wardrobe consists of long-sleeved business shirts—never short-sleeved, even in summer—sharply tailored suits and ties. On Saturdays, like today, he'll skip the ties and maybe wear leather loafers to replace lace-up brogues.

When he's outside of a courtroom, he's a man of few words. Sometimes it's hard to know what's going on behind those dark eyes. I do know from experience that he likes to get to the point, so I take a breath and plunge right into the touchiest of subjects.

"I went to see Mom yesterday."

As soon as I said *Mom*, a range of conflicting yet indefinable emotions crossed Dad's face. But now, he holds them back. "Oh?"

"We need to get her out of there. It looks like a place where linoleum goes to die."

Now confusion is clear in his eyes. "Eden Estate? Charlie said it was the finest..." He trails off, unable to call it what it is—an institution.

"Has Charlie ever actually been there? Have *you*?"

With his finger, he traces the patterns on the ancient Formica table. I guess, since the divorce was final before she checked herself in for treatment, he feels like it's no longer his place to look after her affairs. Then again, aside from me, my mother has no one else. Her ancestors moved here from the Netherlands during the gold rush. My maternal grandparents passed before I was born, but I'm told I inherited Oma Josephine's *sterke* nose and jaw, and sturdy long legs. Poor Opa Henk apparently had a permanent hunch in his back thanks to laboring in the mines. Knowing that, I'm always conscious of my posture.

"No, I haven't been there." He shifts in his seat and brushes grains of fake sugar into a pile with his fingers. "How was she?"

"She looked...awful." Picturing the dark circles under her eyes now, stark against her pale skin, and the blankness in her eyes makes me shudder. "Her clothes were hanging off her like she was nothing more than a coat hanger."

"And emotionally? Does she seem better?"

"The doctor said he sedated her. She was really out of it." I try to shake the image of depressed Mom from my head. "Isn't there a better place for her to get treatment?

Somewhere not so isolated, where they let people visit? She doesn't deserve this."

"It's where she needs to be. More importantly, where she *wants* to be," he insists. But his words don't match his miserable expression. He still cares about Mom. Enough to do anything for her, though?

I reach for his hand across the table, squeezing so hard my knuckles whiten. "Promise me you'll call."

Releasing himself from my grip, he says, "She's not going to be happy if I interfere."

"She's not happy *now*."

Dad winces like I stabbed him with my fork and poured the contents of the saltshaker into the wound. "It's just that… I can't go into every detail about why your mom and I split up. Especially in the middle of a crowded diner. It's between the two of us. But I have to say she was clear on one thing—I had to butt out of her life."

The look of bewilderment and torment on his face makes me want to sob all over the table. Discreetly, I turn to the side and stop a tear with my napkin. Once I get a grip on myself, I ask, "But you still have power of attorney over her, don't you? You *can* have her removed if you think there's a better option."

"No, she revoked it." He leans back as our server returns with the food. When she leaves, he continues in a low voice. "I'll call her before I leave for Copenhagen. See if she'll allow me to help. How does that sound?"

My dad's due to give a keynote speech on environmental law at a conference soon. He'd never tell me as much, but I know he's nervous as hell about it. And now I've heaped more pressure on him. I'm passionate about conservation, too, and proud of what he does in his work, but Mom's happiness and future are just as important.

"Sounds good, Dad." Well, under the circumstances, anyway. What else could be done apart from snatching her from Eden in the middle of the night? I reach for my phone. "I'll email you a list of clinics I Googled last night. Some of them are out of state, but could be worth checking out."

He squeezes my hand gently. "Okay. I'll get on it."

The glass entrance door swings open, and a bunch of jocks surge into the diner. At the tail end is a flush-faced Hayden wearing a tight white polo shirt. As if by instinct, he turns his head and immediately manages to lock onto my gaze.

Then just as fast, he disengages. His face turns an even deeper red, the flush extending down his neck and—I'm sure—right down to his toes. Hayden sends me a half wave before pointing and shrugging as his jock friends take a booth at the opposite end of the diner.

It's not surprising that he seems less than eager to talk to me. Despite my witty invitation, he didn't turn up to last night's party.

I admit I spent *some* of the time looking out for him at the lake, perking up every time I spied a new group of kids spilling onto the pebbled shore. And I also can't lie about the odd pang that hit my chest every time I realized Hayden wasn't among them. But I promised myself I wouldn't send him desperate "Where are you?" texts. For most of the night, Lisa Cannon and I were busy consoling Angie because Jacob bailed on her. And apparently it wasn't the first time.

I stare at the brunch sitting before me. The peaches are bright orange islands in a lake of melted ice cream. I'm no longer hungry. Not sure I ever was. My gaze drifts to the newsprint wallpaper. I never paid it much attention before because, well, it's wallpaper. It's meant to fade into the background. The articles are from different eras of the

Dawson Gazette. I study one piece about a fundraising picnic for miners' children, dated February 1948. Scintillating stuff.

A burst of laughter echoes across the diner. I swivel my head and find Kevin Williams "entertaining" the track team girls and guys by sticking napkins up both nostrils. Such a charmer. He's a junior, but his maturity level is stuck in middle school.

Hayden's perched on the outer edge of a banquette. He's smiling, but the amusement doesn't reach his deep brown eyes. He doesn't seem impressed by Kevin's antics. I mentally put a checkmark of approval by his name for good judgment.

He catches my eye again. I know it sounds silly, but that connection makes my heart do a little jump. No, a somersault. Thinking rationally, though, it's probably the effect of a second cup of black coffee.

"Aunt Carole says you've been doing a great job in the office." Dad jabs at his poached egg. Gooey yolk slides onto the sourdough toast like lava. But he can't bring himself to actually eat his food, either. He pushes the meal around his plate, creating a bright yellow mess that reminds me of a Jackson Pollock painting.

"Thanks, I'm trying." I dig into my crepes, unappealing as they look now. It's sinful to let food go to waste, as Gigi would've said. "There's a *lot* of old files to digitize."

This past summer, not long after Mom went into treatment, Dad bought out his elderly partner, Charlie Hobart. His first order of business in this new era? To bring the office into the twenty-first century—decades after it started. Part of that means sorting and scanning reams of crusty old papers, and releasing them like doves to the sky. Sounds cushy, but it's labor-intensive as hell. Plus, I have so many paper-cut scars crisscrossing my palms that they'd confuse even the most skilled fortune-teller.

"I know. Which is why I hired you to take care of it." Dad winks.

"Well, I've done the math. Four-hour after-school shifts, two times a week? I figure I'll be out of college—no, grad school—by the time every scrap of paper has been scanned and archived."

Out of the corner of my eye, I pick Hayden out of the brunch crowd again. It's almost as if I have internal radar tracking his every move. He's frowning into his open wallet.

"Are you saying you want more shifts?" Dad asks. He jerks his head. Slick black hair, streaked with fine strands of silver, barely moves. "As much as I love having you in the office, I don't want to distract you from schoolwork. Especially since this is an important year for you. So the answer to that is no."

"I wasn't asking for extra hours."

His issue with my extracurricular activities is something we've gone over again and again. Which is why I haven't told him yet about my decision to single-handedly solve the Jane Flanagan case on Mom's behalf. A) He'd berate me for my ceaseless multitasking. And B) part of me feels like he'd say I don't have the skills to investigate a missing person case. Particularly when that case landed my mother where she is now.

Hayden's making his way to the entry foyer. His eyes are glazed. Upset, even. In an instant, I remember he mentioned he was job-hunting when we crossed paths outside Eden yesterday. If this isn't kismet, I don't know what is.

"Dad, Dad," I say, interrupting him mid-chew. "What about hiring someone to help me? For just a few hours a week?"

"*You* want an assistant?" He puts his fork down and smiles wryly.

"Not an assistant, a partner. Based on what you just said, I need one. And you want everything digitized *yesterday* so you never have to trawl through papers ever again, right?"

Dad sighs. "Guess I can't argue with that. Okay, we can look at hiring."

"Great!" I slide out of the booth. "I know just the right person for the job. Wait here."

"Who?" Dad asks on an exasperated sigh.

I duck and weave around busboys. Waving, I call out, "Hayden!"

Eyes to the checkerboard linoleum, he walks faster. But not toward me. *Away* from me. I almost crash with a server as I bound between tables. She glares at my swift apology and continues to the kitchen.

I get to the front door just as Hayden presses down on its handle.

"Hayden!"

"Hi, Cassidy," he says, gaze darting. "Hey, I'm really sorry I couldn't make it to the lake."

I wave his words away and accidentally touch his wrist. He eyes my hand like it's a serpent. "I'm sorry, too. For touching you. With sticky fingers. Gross."

Hayden chuckles. "Apology accepted."

A young family on the other side of the glass door gestures for us to get out of the way. I open it for them and beckon Hayden to the side.

"I see you're in a hurry, so I'll be quick." I squirt hand sanitizer into my palm from a pump in the foyer. "You need a job, right?"

"Um, yeah." He checks his phone. "I'm heading out to see—"

"Great! Come with me. I've lined up a job interview for you."

"Now?" Hayden smooths his shirt down. It's hard not to notice the shape of his ab muscles against the cotton fabric. "What's the job?"

"You'll be an assistant at my dad's law firm downtown," I say, like he's already accepted the role. Because why on earth would he say no? "Great conditions. Decent pay. And you'll be working with the other assistant—me." I flash a grin. "Sound good?"

Hayden just gapes at me.

"I'll take that as a yes."

TRACK 11

"Gimme Shelter"

MEMORANDUM FOR THE DIRECTOR OF THE CENTRAL INTELLIGENCE AGENCY

CLASSIFICATION: TOP SECRET

SUBJECT: PARALLAX BUILDING EXPANSION

April 16, 1950

Building works to extend the current Colorado facility will commence May 1, 1950. The expected completion date is June 15, 1951. Contractors have undergone the orientation and confidentiality training.

The five-story subterranean complex will contain power and cooling plants, two surgical theaters, an upgraded pathology unit, and ten additional clinical rooms with adjacent observation rooms. We are liaising with Headquarters on audio and visual surveillance equipment procurement; these will be integrated into the Control Room. Protective custody accommodations will house up to fifty Subjects. Location scouting for a radio telescope array is underway.

Thirteen of the original fifteen Subjects have been deemed suitable to continue with experiments indefinitely. Subjects No. 006 and No. 009 are halfway through a six-month debriefing program. Given their current psychological states, we recommend they be transferred to Project XU-891B.

For the Parallax Human Intervention Unit,

Dr. Harold P. Elsworth

TRACK 12

"The Whole of the Moon"

Present Day

"Where is he?" I mutter, keeping my gaze glued to the glass entrance doors while stuffing files into an archive box.

I'd just finished scanning one of a hundred million files dating back to the 1950s when Charlie Hobart's father started the firm. The task of scanning is monotonous but oddly soothing. It gives me time to think about my next move in the Flanagan case. To be honest, I'd rather be out there scouting for leads, interrogating witnesses. Anything to get Mom one step closer to home. Every now and then, a paper cut jolts me out of relative serenity. I can't wait for Hayden to join me in solidarity.

My great-aunt Carole—and Dad's receptionist—squints at her iMac's clock. On her screen, a live stream from the International Space Station shows a spectacular view of Earth. "It's 3:54," she says. "He starts at four, doesn't he?"

"I just don't want him to get on Dad's bad side." It's crystal clear that Hayden needs the money. That desolate frown on his face when he peered into his wallet the other day really got to me. Dad's giving him two after-school shifts to start with for a trial run.

"Ethan doesn't have a bad side!" Aunt Carole says. She

smiles at an email newsletter she's putting together. It's got Dad's picture in one corner. He looks serious, but not intimidating, which is the look he was going for when I snapped the shot. In Carole's eyes, my dad can do no wrong. She immigrated to the U.S. from Indonesia back in the quote/unquote "swingin' sixties." The photos of her in teeny-tiny miniskirts with sky-high beehive hairdos are hysterical. When Dad came here to study, she promised her older sister—my Gigi—that she'd take him under her wing. And feed him tons of buffalo wings.

Aunt Carole sits back and adjusts her black-as-black hair. She's toned the beehive down over the years, but it's still a thing. "Didn't you say he's new in town? I bet he's lost."

A figure appears at the door. I dust off my hands. "Oh, look! Now he's found."

Eyes to the cream carpet, Hayden steps in. He skates a hand through his wavy dark hair. If I'm not mistaken, there's a slight tremble in his fingers. His crisp blue business shirt, skinny black tie, and stovepipe black trousers make a sharp contrast to my faded jeans and V-neck green T-shirt. My red Converse shoes are fit for a boat deck, not a downtown law firm.

"Hayden!" I rush toward him. He pauses for a split second, and I realize I sounded super excited to see him. Which I am, of course, because many hands make the load light and all that. Plus, I'm happy he's now able to earn some cash for himself. Spring for a new GPS in his truck. Maybe even a newer truck. Eventually.

"Well, hi there. I'm Carole," my great-aunt says brightly, holding out a hand. Her long fingernails are alternately painted gold and purple. They're occupational hazards when it comes to typing, but they look awesome on her.

He glances at our casual clothes, then eyes his polished shoes. They're a far cry from his usual bulky Timberland boots. It strikes me then that he'd modeled his get-up on the one Dad was wearing during their impromptu job interview at the diner. For a moment, my mind goes down a rabbit hole, trying to decide whether he's hotter in street wear or in Wall Street wear.

Either way, I can't tear my gaze off him. My whole body pulses in time with my heart.

"Hello. Hayden McGraw." He gives Aunt Carole a nervous grin. He's like a deer in halogen headlights. And that's kind of endearing. I'd be less impressed if he swaggered in here like some slimy entrepreneur. "Hi, Cassidy," he says. "I hope I'm not late? I spent way too much time ironing this shirt."

"It was worth it. Not a wrinkle in sight." Aunt Carole smiles her approval. "But just so you know, jeans and tees are acceptable in this office, too."

"Oh…okay." Blushing, Hayden shifts from foot to foot.

"You and I will be in the back offices most of the time, out of the clients' sight," I explain. "But if you did have to be on the front line, that outfit would totally work."

"Good to know," he says, eyeing the plastic lunchbox Aunt Carole is thrusting under his chin. It's got the remains of the sesame seed cakes she made over the weekend. He glances uncertainly at me before shyly popping a tiny cube in his mouth. "Wow. This is *delicious*."

Aunt Carole beams as he takes a second, slightly larger cake. He's passed the first new-employee test as far as she's concerned. She pushes a bottle of hand sanitizer his way and settles back in her chair. "Cassidy will show you the ropes and take you on a tour from here. I've got to get back to work now. These riveting newsletters aren't going to write themselves."

Hayden trails me down the hall, his shoes making soft squeaking noises. He keeps slowing down, like that'll stop the squeaks, but it only makes them more obvious. I show him the kitchen, staff room, storage, and boardroom. We tiptoe past Dad's office, which is shut tight because he's with a client.

In a wide corridor, I stop at a plate-glass window overlooking the wide avenue outside and point out some of Dawson's landmarks. "Over in that strip mall is Hot Tamales. You'll need a fire extinguisher for your mouth if you're not used to spicy food. To cool down, there's an ice-cream shop. Not thirty-one flavors, but thirty-*two*. That extra flavor makes all the difference."

"You're making it really tempting to blow my first paycheck instead of banking it."

I laugh. "Yeah, well, the pay isn't exactly going to make you an instant millionaire, so you're smart to save it."

A couple of feet away from me, he stands by the window and eases his tie a fraction. His expression grows serious. Intense, even. Made even more so by the pulse of energy his presence seems to give off. "Hey, um, thanks a lot for this."

"The tour? I hate the thought of you getting lost in this maze. But rest assured I'll be in charge of the search party if that ever happens." Grinning, I turn around and lean back against the window.

"No, I mean the job." For a fleeting second, I swear a look of shame darkens his face. But it's soon replaced with pride. He toughens his jaw. "You—and your dad—swooped in at just the right time. Although...I didn't picture myself working in a law firm. I would've been just fine working nights as a janitor."

"You're kind of a loner, aren't you?" I ask softly.

"I'm...I'm an observer. You learn a lot about people that way." Again, he fiddles with the knot of his tie. Loosening. Tightening. Loosening again. I catch a glimpse of another blush creeping up his neck. Exhaling heavily, he says, "Anyway, yeah, I wanted you to know I'm grateful. My parents...are in a bind. I'm trying to do my bit to help out."

My stomach churns, thinking about my mom. I blink rapidly to ward off tears and focus on what's right in front of me. "Do you want to talk about it?"

Hayden's mouth flaps open and shut a couple of times, then words finally tumble out. "They made a bad real estate deal. So, yeah, having a job means a lot."

"Times have been tough for everyone. I'm happy I could give someone a break." I purse my lips. To lighten the mood a little, I add, "Even if your paycheck can only buy you thirty-one of those thirty-two flavors. Plus, I had an ulterior motive. I needed someone to share my pain. And I warn you, there is a lotta pain involved in this job."

I show him the thousand paper cuts on my palms. He stares at them, brow furrowed. Slowly, he starts to reach for my right hand. My breath quickens as I realize I'm leaning closer and closer to him. It's like he's got the gravitational pull of Jupiter, pulling me into his orbit. The air in the corridor seems to get sucked out somehow, somewhere. The atmosphere feels charged. Alive with electricity.

My palms? They're bursting into a spontaneous sweat. When he jams his hands deep into his pockets, I'm almost relieved.

Almost.

No guy has ever made my palms sweat with anticipation. Revulsion, yes. There have been plenty of those kinds of sweats in my dating past.

There's an unmistakable attraction. Me to him. But him

to me? The jury's still out on that, especially as he seems intent on putting space between us now.

Down the corridor, a door opens, then Dad strides toward us, iPad in hand. He's so deep in thought he almost walks right by us.

"Dad, hey." I hook him by the elbow.

His serious face cracks into a distracted smile. "Hi, honey. And, Hayden, good to have you aboard."

"I really appreciate you hiring me, sir." Hayden practically bows to him. There's real sincerity in his eyes and slightly parted lips.

"You know," Dad says, crossing his arms, "it occurred to me as I was signing your paperwork, you're a McGraw."

Hayden swallows audibly. "Yeah…"

Confused, I look from Hayden to Dad. Why is that so significant?

"You're the same McGraws who bought that entire subdivision near Saddleback Ridge?" Dad asks.

My stomach drops. Everyone knows about the subdivision. I just hadn't connected it to Hayden's family.

Wow, he was right about being in a bind.

A developer built fifty McMansions, with plans to build two hundred more. Then rumors about old mines destabilizing the houses surfaced. No one wanted to live in a less populated part of Dawson, where jobs are scarce. And where your house could fall into a sinkhole without warning.

But for just ten grand, you could buy the entire development, sinkholes and all.

When that deal went through, my dad had lots of feelings about it. Most of them negative. He ranted for days about greedy, irresponsible developers donating to governments and wack-job bargain hunters.

"That's us, sir," he replies. "My parents had engineers

inspect the whole area, but they say our block is the safest."

Dad doesn't look convinced. His eyebrows rise. "Has anyone else moved in?"

"No, not yet," Hayden replies evenly. His expression gives little away.

"That sounds lonely for you guys," I say. And no doubt they'll be alone in that neighborhood for years to come. Who else would risk moving their precious family into a precarious neighborhood, even if the rumors turn out to be false?

Dad turns a penetrating stare on him, the kind that makes people squirm on the witness stand and wish they were in the middle of a viper pit instead. The only reaction from Hayden is the visible clenching of his jaw. Suddenly, I understand the urgent need for Hayden to find work. He's trying to scrape money together in case of an emergency. Such as his house falling into a mile-deep hole—hopefully after his family jumps clear of it.

"Okay, well, if your mom and dad need legal help, you know where to find me. I've got plenty of contacts who can help with surveys, too." Dad gives him a tight smile and continues down the corridor. "In the meantime, welcome to the firm."

When he's out of sight, Hayden exhales. "Your dad thinks my parents are jerks."

"I'm sure he understands they had their reasons for buying the estate. And everyone deserves a roof over their head." I try to arrange my lips in a supportive smile, but I'm sure it looks more like a grimace. "I can't help but feel kinda…concerned? Aren't *you* worried about your house plummeting into the bowels of the Earth without warning? With your entire family inside?"

Hayden gulps again, and in that moment I know the

very same thoughts have rushed through his mind, too. In a defensive tone, he says, “My mom and dad don’t have a death wish. Our house is stable. Really.”

“If you say so.” I throw him a doubtful look. That strong jaw clenches again in response. “This does explain a few things about you, though.”

Now Hayden’s eyes take on a piercing stare. “What things?”

Ugh, why did I say that? I wish *this building* were on a sinkhole so the floor would open up and send me into an abyss. “Nothing. I shouldn’t have— ”

He puts a hand on my forearm. It’s a light touch, but it’s enough to arrest me. “It’s okay. You can say it.”

“Well…” I draw out the word, looking up at him from under my lashes. “You’re always staring at me. I know it can’t be my staggering beauty.” He makes a noise, a kind of protest, which is sweet, but I push on. “Are you silently imploring me for help?”

Hayden looks away in what could only be a conscious effort *not* to stare at me. “Oh. I didn’t realize I was doing that.”

“You’ve, uh, been doing *that* all week, like I’m a new, unidentified species.” I pause, as a thought crosses my mind. “And your truck stalled right by Eden the other day, just as I was leaving. Which, I understand could be completely coincidental, but… Was it?”

He splutters loudly and doubles over. Tears squeeze from the corners of his eyes.

“Are you okay?” I pound a palm on his back. “Is this helping?”

“Thanks,” he croaks, sliding out of reach. “Sorry, I had some dust in my throat.”

My head tilts. Why would he lie? Dad’s office is pretty

much hermetically sealed thanks to a recent renovation. He has it cleaned each morning *and* deep cleaned every week. If there's a speck of dust anywhere, it'd stand out a mile.

"The last thing I want is for you to think I'm some stalker creep." Hayden's brown eyes are wide with horror. He takes two steps back to prove his point.

"I don't feel creeped out," I say slowly. If I were to describe the way he looks at me, I'd compare it to someone who's watching, say, penguins at a zoo. He's curious, but he doesn't want to get too close because, despite being adorable, penguins reek. "You don't give off serial killer vibes, anyway."

He exhales. "That's a relief."

"But was it a coincidence? When you ended up outside Eden just as I was leaving?"

"I really was lost." His cheeks glow red as I give him a penetrating stare of my own.

"Aside from getting you acquainted with the concept of a navigation app, I could help you with that," I suggest. "Take the tour outside of the office and into greater Dawson. You'll never be lost again."

"Maybe," he says softly. I'm skeptical. He's already blown off one social invitation from me. "As for the staring… I'm sorry. It won't happen again."

I wave an arm. The jade and pink quartz bangles I bought in Indonesia clank gently together. "Oh, you stare at me all you want. As long as you don't do it in front of Angie, because she thinks you have a thing for me."

The moment the words leave my mouth, I want to reach out and pull them back into me. Now he knows I've been talking about him to my friends. Great. Any hint of coolness I had about me has been shot to pieces. Although, if he *has* been studying me that closely, he already knows I'm not up there with the coolest of the cool.

Hayden lifts an eyebrow in a very Angie way. But he chooses to, thankfully, get back to the topic at hand. "It's just that you're…"

I wait for him to finish his sentence, then jokingly suggest, "Drop-dead gorgeous?"

He reddens and averts his gaze. "You remind me of an old…friend. Just your mannerisms, the way you carry yourself."

There's a raw spike in his voice that tugs at my heart. A little part of me is disappointed that he didn't say he's been drinking in my breathtaking beauty all this time. But it's all been a case of mistaken identity, not speechless infatuation. Can't wait to tell my friends. Yay. "Oh, you mean I talk with my hands?" I say, brushing aside the dent to my ego. "I'm actually practicing sign language. Trying to keep my skills up."

"It's more than that. You move fast, like there's no time to waste."

I chuckle. "Nailed it."

Hayden nods, but the faraway look on his face tells me his thoughts are somewhere else. Or on *someone* else.

"So…it sounds like she meant a lot to you." Suddenly I find it hard to swallow. Like, if he were to tell me he's talking about his ex, it'd make me feel jealous. Which is totally silly. I have no claim whatsoever on him. "When did you last see her?"

The few seconds it takes for him to answer feels like an eternity. Misery mists his dark eyes. "In my nightmares."

TRACK 13

"Don't Ask"

Present Day

"There you are!" With impeccable timing, Aunt Carole bursts into the corridor. The musky fragrance she liberally douses herself with every hour on the hour wafts in around me.

Involuntarily, I cough.

"Are you coming down with something?" Aunt Carole presses the back of her hand to my forehead. She's very aware that coughs aren't caused by dust mites here, so naturally she assumes I'm sick.

"Oh, just a mild inferiority complex," I mutter. I'm Hayden's worst nightmare? Granted, he merely said my *lookalike* was in his nightmare. But his opportunity to elaborate just vanished in a cloud of perfume. In a louder voice, I say, "It's nothing. Do you need me?"

"Can I borrow our newest employee for a few minutes?" she asks. "I just found a key I've been looking for. I need help moving archive boxes from one of Charlie's old storage rooms. It's being detail cleaned tonight."

"On it." Hayden practically clicks his heels. I'm surprised he doesn't salute.

"Hey, I can do that for you," I protest. "I've been

carting boxes from place to place for weeks. My biceps are phenomenal." I note that Hayden makes a concerted attempt to *not* check out my arms. He focuses on tying a shoelace that was already knotted into a perfect bow.

"Yes, they are, dear." Aunt Carole grins. "But I figure I'll give you some time to let those paper cuts you've been moaning about heal. Could you look after the front desk while we're gone?"

"Sure," I say, feeling a breeze as Hayden bolts to Aunt Carole's side like he can't get away from my riveting office tour fast enough. "Oh, and if you see any archive boxes from 1984 to 1986, can you please bring them out for me?"

"Will do," Hayden says. This time he *does* salute. A small, respectful gesture, not a defiant two-fingered one.

As I man the front desk, thumping sounds as well as exclamations of "Oof" and "Arrhhh" from Aunt Carole float out from the back offices. Seems the task is going to take eons or longer.

Which gives me time to do a little more trawling of the net in search of anything to do with Jane Flanagan. I bookmarked a trove of 1980s newspaper archives and was hoping to find a few more witnesses' names or connections. No doubt some, maybe all, of those people might be dead by now. But who knows? They might have talked to friends or family members who are still around.

I wake up the reception desk's computer. Numerous tabs are open on the internet browser—hilarious cat vids, recipe sites, celebrity gossip news. One shows a tabloid site's screaming headline: *Aliens Among Arizonians.*

"Oh, Aunt Carole. Can't resist click bait, can you?" I lean my elbows on the desk and continue reading. Because I also can't resist click bait.

Residents of Phoenix are no strangers to unidentified

flying objects. In 1997, and in the years since, thousands of witnesses from all walks of life have reported seeing lights on a large "ship" unlike any other in the skies above the city. Now one woman says the ship has not only landed, but also its occupants have walked among us.

"They can take on any form they want," claimed the forty-three-year-old former RN, who now runs a UFO research—

"And…we're back," Aunt Carole says, rounding the desk. "Thank you for filling in for me."

"No problem," I say absently, still reading the article.

Aunt Carole reaches into her bag and applies two more squirts of Tabu. It's all I can do not to pinch my nostrils shut.

Hayden rolls in a chrome cart that's filled with a grand total of two archive boxes and stops by the water cooler. He fills two cups and hands them to us before pouring a third for himself.

"Good workout lifting all those boxes?" I ask him. My eyes want to stray to his biceps, see how they're faring, but I rein myself in.

"These are heavier than they look," he says before draining his cup. "And in my defense, I had to move twenty-one boxes in order to get to those two babies."

"Huh. What a nightmare," I say without thinking. Then I catch Hayden's barely perceptible frown and remember what he was trying to tell me earlier. His nightmares about me. Or rather, about someone who looks kind of like me. It makes me super curious. Who's the girl? Why did he look so haunted? She must've meant a lot to him if she's still on his subconscious brain.

He gestures at the monitor. "What were you grinning at earlier? Cat GIFs?"

"Yup, and UFOs."

Hayden shifts his weight from foot to foot. "Oh."

Aunt Carole taps me on the arm with a golden nail. "Wasn't that article amazing?"

"Amazing isn't the word that came to mind," I scoff.

"You sound like a nonbeliever," Hayden says.

"I'll believe it when I see it."

Aunt Carole scrolls through the story. "It says they're seven feet tall, but they disguise themselves as basketball players."

I look over her shoulder. If my ex-boyfriend Sean turns out to be an alien, that would explain so much about him. "Riiiight. I didn't read that far. Do they speak our language?"

"Yes, English, but a witness said they had a European accent."

Turning to Hayden, I watch him carefully. "Do *you* believe in this stuff?"

Hayden takes one slow step at a time, his face a jumble of fascination and…fear? The fear makes sense if he feels like his brain will melt from being forced to read this garbage. His lips purse as he looks at the screen.

Actually, no. He's staring into deep space.

I wave my hand in front of his face. "Hayden?"

He snaps out of his trance. "It's kind of arrogant to think we're alone in the universe. Or that our universe is the only universe. There's got to be other life-forms out there. Like our teacher said in class the other day."

"Yeah, but she was talking about bacteria."

Aunt Carole elbows me. "I pulled up a sighting on YouTube. Hayden, come on back here."

She plays a blurry clip of a shiny silver object hovering behind a brick house in Maryland. People in the background chant "Oh my God!" over and over.

"Look at how out of proportion that thing is." I smirk. "That's a lampshade, not a freakin' UFO."

Rolling her eyes, Aunt Carole finds another video. "These are the Phoenix Lights, the ones from the article."

Hayden enlarges the video window and leans in for a closer look. It's not going to do him any good; the image is fuzzy.

The "footage" shows a series of steady amber lights aligned in a V-shape. They hover over the mountain range bordering the city.

"How do you explain that?" Aunt Carole asks. "Even the mayor and military people swear they saw this ship."

Hayden squints at the clip. "It's pretty compelling."

"But is it real or fake footage? Anyone could doctor it." I wave my hand dismissively at the screen. "Besides, why can't anyone get clear video or pics of a UFO? Every woman and her dog have a camera in their pockets these days."

Hayden's jaw clenches. He's taking this way too seriously—they both are. "Maybe because people report their equipment failing when UFOs are close," he says.

"Yes!" Aunt Carole clicks her fingers emphatically. "That happened in a movie I saw."

"Uh, you're citing proof of UFOs from a movie?" Aunt Carole is at the front line of a firm that deals in facts and evidence. What the hell? "Until I see one for myself, UFOs and aliens don't exist. Now, let's start scanning these files"—my lips twitch—"before Darth Vader comes down and slices us in half with a lightsaber."

After work, I toss my bag in the back seat of my car. "Do you really believe in UFOs?"

"I'm open to it," Hayden replies. But his tone sounds defensive.

I offered to drive him home because his dad needed his truck and had dropped him off earlier. I punch his address into my navigation app, then give him a reassuring smile and say, "I don't think any less of you for it. But I'd be careful about broadcasting that to the world."

Hayden swivels in his seat to face me. "See, this is what bugs me. There's no definitive proof that a god exists, and no one cares if you worship one. But are you automatically labeled cuckoo because of your belief in a god? No, because it's all about faith. I don't see belief in aliens as any different."

He makes an interesting point. But that doesn't mean I'm convinced.

I stop at an intersection. The bright neon lights of the thirty-two-flavor ice-cream parlor wash pink and yellow hues all over Hayden's face, making his cheekbones stand out in a way that'd make a catwalk model jealous. "Is that why there's a religion based on the Jedi knights from *Star Wars*?"

"What? There is?"

"Yeah. Twenty thousand members in New Zealand alone."

"Wow." He sits back in his seat, looking thoughtfully at the dash.

I keep one eye on the traffic signals. "Tell me you're not actually thinking of joining."

His head lolls toward me, and a swath of hair falls over one eye. He pushes it back, but not before a thought flits across my mind. *Hayden is Hot. Capital H.*

I shelve the thought immediately. If we're going to work together, I need to keep it professional. He blasted through digitizing five boxes of files in less than two hours, though. All with zero paper cuts and minimal wrinkles to that starched shirt. So at this rate, the project would be done within a couple of weeks. Unless, of course, Aunt Carole discovers a warehouse full of old files.

"Worship fictional characters? What's wrong with that?" He winks.

Exhaling loudly, I say, "Thank Jedi. You were joking."

It's great to see Hayden has a sense of humor underneath that too-serious exterior. The traffic signals change, and I step lightly on the gas.

"People should be open to unknown things, like UFOs and stuff," Hayden continues. "Do you know some governments are declassifying documents about UFOs?"

"For real?"

"Yes, for real!" He turns in his seat, growing animated and gesturing as he speaks. "Sooner or later, this world will acknowledge that we're not the only intelligent life in the universe. We already know there are other universes, other Earth-like planets. We need to be careful—" He claps his mouth shut like he's said too much. Or he's embarrassed he said anything at all.

At first I thought Hayden was just humoring Aunt Carole, but now it seems he literally got brainwashed by the likes of *Inquiring Minds* magazine. "Careful about what? Being abducted by aliens? According to those UFO stories, you don't get much choice."

Hayden turns his face to the window. Finally, he laughs. But it sounds forced. Hollow. He checks his phone and fires off a quick text.

My own urge to laugh dies in my throat. I've definitely hit a nerve. Feeling awkwardness stretch between us, I switch from the GPS navigation to a playlist.

"The Whole of the Moon" by The Waterboys starts, filling the silence.

"Great song," Hayden says after the first chorus.

"Yeah, my mom said it was a big hit when she was a kid." I drum my fingers on the steering wheel in time to the staccato beat. "She put together this playlist of her favorite songs, and told me I need to listen not just to the melodies but to the lyrics. Find meaning in them."

He tilts his head toward the speaker. "And what does this song mean to you?"

"My interpretation? Seeing the whole picture and not taking things on face value. There's always more to every story. Like, with the moon, some people see a crescent. And others see—"

"The whole moon," he finishes.

"Right. How about you? Big music fan?" As I accelerate around a corner, I suddenly remember what Mabel Parkes said about the logo on the van. The moon phases. Is *that* why Mom put this song on the playlist? Because she'd found the clue? Maybe she pursued that line and it turned out to be yet another dead end. After all, if it was *the* van involved in Jane's disappearance, that could have broken the case. And she wouldn't be stuck in Eden Estate right now.

I wish I could access Mom's notes. Better yet, talk to her about Jane again. But if I ask her, I'm afraid she'll snap. I can't take that risk. She's still fragile.

"I'm sure I could play if I put my mind to it." Hayden mimes playing keyboard chords. "What I'm really into is flying."

"Oh yeah?"

"I got my pilot's license as soon as I turned sixteen. But I have to give it up." He shakes his head. "Flying is an expensive hobby. And to be completely honest? I'm waiting for teleporting to be a thing again."

"Again?" I throw him a puzzled look. "I wasn't aware there was *ever* a teleporting thing outside of movies."

Hayden coughs and clears his throat repeatedly. "Yeah, uh, I got my tech screwed up. I meant to say supersonic jets. Like the Concorde. Those things flew at twice the speed of sound."

"Sounds awesome. Promise you'll take me for a ride if you ever get your hands on one."

"Deal," he says, grinning.

I approach the final kinks in the road to his cul-de-sac. It's not hard to figure out which of the almost identical craftsman-style houses is casa McGraw. There's only one house on the block with lights blazing. The other two-story homes are dark. Silent.

Eerie.

Like all the others, Hayden's is made of engineered timber, with a faux stone chimney facade. The portico is topped by "wood" shingles. A curtain in a front window swishes, and a short, silhouetted figure presses against the glass.

He peers at the house, lips twisting as if he's trying to make a decision. At last he says, "Are you hungry? I'm pretty sure my family would love you to stay for dinner."

"Pretty sure, huh?" I grin. My stomach rumbles at the thought of food. Dad's gone out with a client to dinner. I had firm plans to devour a pint of ice cream and study old newspapers. On the one hand, I didn't want to lose any more research time. But on the other hand, Hot-with-a-capital-H Hayden McGraw is inviting me into his house. I could spare an hour. "Yeah, I'd like that."

"Good," he says. "I've told them all about you."

A huge, unappetizing lump lodges in the pit of my stomach. A meet-the-parents moment already? I mean, it's not like we're dating, but still… I squirm. "Um, what have you told them?"

And…*why* has he told them all about me?

"That you're the first real person I've met in Dawson." He gives me a tight grin and opens the passenger-side door.

"Ah, so you figured it out. All the kids at school are cyborgs."

"Not all. Just the ones in the Calculus Club." He moves his head and arms jerkily like a robot, making me snort-laugh. He opens the door and steps aside. "Come on in."

Right away, the intoxicating smell of stewed tomatoes and roasted garlic hits me, making me forget the anxiety of meeting my new not-boyfriend's parents. Two minimally furnished rooms open up on either side of a double-height foyer, but there's no one in either of them. The sound of crockery rattling comes from the rear of the house; the kitchen, I assume. A golden retriever puppy scrambles down a polished timber hallway and barrels into Hayden's shins.

"Yoda!" He kneels, and the dog jumps into his arms. Standing up, he holds Yoda at my eye level. The puppy's pink tongue unfurls and almost hits my nose. Its yips echo around the room.

I scratch Yoda behind the ears, and he bats my arm with the pads of his fluffy feet. Laughing, I say to Hayden, "You really are a *Star Wars* fan."

He shrugs. "It's the greatest story ever told. That and *Close Encounters of the Third Kind.*"

"What's that?"

"You've never heard of *Close Encounters*?" Wide-eyed, he puts Yoda on the floor, and the puppy sits with his back legs splayed under his chubby body. "We'll have to fix this. Soon."

Elsewhere in the house, something heavy crashes to the floor and an obscenity rings out. Hayden reddens and shrugs it off. He leads me forward, until we reach a swinging door at the end of the hall, then he pauses.

"I need to warn you about something." Hayden draws in a deep breath.

My heart stutters. "Yes?"

"My folks are normal humanoids," he says. "But my little sister—"

A bright white light hits me right in the eyeballs. I shield my face and squeeze my eyelids shut. "Hey!"

"Trudy-Rudy!" Hayden exclaims in an exasperated tone. "Put that flashlight away."

"But I was conducting an experiment," a little girl's voice whines. "You can open your eyes now. It's safe."

"Phew." I sigh in mock relief and blink to adjust my vision. All I can see at first are giant transparent yellowish orbs. Then I look down to find the girl's impish face staring up at me. She's maybe five years old, and her dimpled cheeks put her on a level of cuteness with Yoda the dog. I try to recall whether I could perfectly pronounce words like *conducting* and *experiment* at her age, let alone know how to use them in a sentence. She clutches a small Kermit-green Maglite to her puffed-up chest. "You must be Trudy," I say. "What's the experiment?"

Hayden gently reefs the flashlight from Trudy's hands. He throws an *"I* tried *to warn you about my sister"* eye-roll.

Trudy scowls at him, then cranes her neck to gaze up at me. In a sweet voice to match her sweet face, she says, "To see if you're an alien, too."

TRACK 14

"Reasons to Lie"

Present Day

"Trudy!" Hayden pulls her to his side and ruffles her pigtailed brown hair.

"Wow, you McGraws really can't get enough of sci-fi, huh?" Smiling uncertainly, I look from Trudy to Hayden and back again. Sure, I'm wearing a green shirt and my high ponytail is pulling my face taut, but in no way do I resemble an alien.

Hayden chuckles awkwardly. "As I was saying, my sister's a little monster. She's just being silly. It's a game we play sometimes, called, um, Find the Alien."

"Oh. That's cute." I fold my arms across my chest, feeling self-conscious.

"It's not a game, it's an experiment," Trudy says, pink bottom lip protruding.

"No more alien experiments tonight, okay?" he tells her. "Cassidy's…sensitive."

She glances at me, then nods reluctantly. "Okay."

"Sorry about that," he says to me in a low voice, his hands covering Trudy's ears. "Don't take any notice of her."

"I can hear you," she retorts loudly.

"Have you set the dinner table?" Hayden says.

"Nope." Trudy grins. "It's your turn."

"Bummer, I was hoping you wouldn't remember." Hayden growls playfully and spins her around to face the door.

"I've got a perfect memory," she says, looking over her shoulder at me before pushing into an expansive kitchen and dining area. Sliding glass doors form the entire back wall. Outdoor lighting shines on a stone terrace and pool, but there isn't a single plant out there. I guess they haven't gotten around to landscaping yet. Inside, though, the house is sparsely decorated despite its enormous scale. Just basic furniture for a family of four and maybe a guest or two.

Hayden holds the door open for me, but I hang back. "What did you mean I'm sensitive?"

"Nothing," he says. "It's just part of the game. The only way to get her to stop is if she thinks you can't handle her experiments."

"Told you I'm not a monster!" she singsongs from a distance.

I flash a grin and brush past Hayden, still trying very hard not to think about meeting a guy's parents for the first time. Cute but precocious siblings, I can deal with. I tell myself to get over it. If Hayden and I were dating, it would be a whole different situation. Since we aren't, there's no need to be nervous.

And yet, I feel like I have to try my hardest not to screw anything up. What the hell am I doing in Hayden's house? I'm supposed to be in my pajamas right now, eating butter pecan ice cream straight out of the cardboard tub.

At the stove, a slender woman stands with her back to us, staring intently into a stockpot. Classical music plays from a speaker on a bench. Trudy clambers onto a barstool at a huge stone island and starts work on a coloring book.

"Hey, Mom," Hayden says. She jumps at the sound of his voice. A wooden spoon clatters onto the stovetop. "Sorry. I didn't mean to scare you."

"Well, you did—" She turns, and freezes when she catches sight of me. Right away I see how much Hayden resembles her. Tall, with glossy dark hair. Except her eyes are greenish, not almost-fathomless brown. They're also wary. Guarded, even. Her brief, questioning look at Hayden compounds my uneasiness. "Oh, you must be Cassidy. Hello."

There's a weird, charged atmosphere in here, like we've just walked into the middle of an argument.

"Yes. Hi." I step forward and give Mrs. McGraw my warmest, glacier-melting smile. And it seems to work its magic. The tense lines around her eyes and mouth relax a smidgen. Hayden motions me toward the stools. My instinct is to cling to one like it's a buoy; I can't help feeling like an intruder. Instead, I take a seat and perch on the very edge.

"You got my text about my plus-one for dinner, right?" Hayden asks his mom. She gives him a nod and a taut smile. "Where's Dad? I can't believe he's letting you anywhere near his Bolognese."

I peer at mother and son. The change in him is very interesting. At school, he's the one who's tense and guarded, much like his mom is now. Here, though, he seems like the master of his domain. Which is understandable, I guess. More and more I realize he's an introvert. He doesn't need or want to be the center of attention.

Mrs. McGraw turns to me, her hands up. "I promised I would stir, and stir only. I'm the worst cook. I *really* have to concentrate. My family would starve if they had to rely on me for dinner."

"I can cook," Trudy says, not looking up from her artwork. "I learned from the best—Nigella Lawson."

"You said Curtis Stone was the best yesterday," Hayden teases. He sees my puzzled frown and explains, "We're talking about celebrity chefs. Trudy's obsessed with the Food Network."

Trudy shrugs. "Curtis's accent is funny."

"Darling, we don't judge people's cooking, or people in general, by their accents," Mrs. McGraw says, swiping up red splotches on the floor.

"Is Dad around?" Hayden asks her.

"He's on the lower terrace setting up his equipment." She frowns at a red smudge halfway up the subway-tiled wall. "How the hell did I get sauce up there?"

I lean back and peer toward the terrace. "What kind of equipment?"

"He's got some shiny new toys. Telescope and camera gear—"

"Trudy." There's a warning note in Hayden's voice. She pokes her tongue out at him. Classic little-sister move. He catches my inquisitive look and explains, "Dad's into astronomy."

"Oh, is he looking out for the Death Star?" I wink at Hayden, but he looks queasy. I guess he's had enough of the *Star Wars* references for one night. Never mind the fact he has a permanent reference in the form of a pup named Yoda.

"Hey, we've got a visitor!" Mr. McGraw calls out from the sliding doors, where he wipes his feet on a mat before entering. He sounds surprised, but like he's trying to hide that surprise behind an overly cheery facade. He's a bit shorter than Hayden—and Mrs. McGraw—and stockier. But like Hayden, his body radiates tension. Like he's burdened by something. Maybe it's the stress of the real estate gamble he's taken on this neighborhood. That would also explain why his wife seems so jumpy.

"Hello," I say.

"I'm Sam," he says, shaking my hand. He nods at Hayden's mom. "I see you've met Lindsay."

"Oh, yes, I forgot to introduce myself." Mrs. McGraw steps back and brushes an imaginary piece of lint from Hayden's shoulder. It's a sweet gesture, but Hayden's exaggerated grimace is priceless.

Feeling weird about addressing them by their first names, I go with a simple, "Nice to meet you both. I'm sorry for dropping in on your dinner."

"Don't be sorry." Lindsay returns to the other side of the island. She checks on the oven before casting a super-bright smile on me.

Sam adds, "We love meeting Hayden's friends. We're looking forward to being active in the community."

I take in his ultra-wide grin and glance at Hayden. His parents seem to be working really hard at presenting a shiny, happy front. But there's that undercurrent of tension. His mom's posture looks stiff and hyper-alert, and his dad looks like he's barely keeping it together.

"Or just...*in* the community," Lindsay amends.

Sam's grin dims. He turns his back on us and inspects the simmering sauce.

"Consider me part of the unofficial welcoming committee," I say, deciding to go along with the game of pretending everything's okay. I can play very, very nicely. "I'm offering daily tours. Right, Hayden?"

"Yep, and jobs, too," he says. His dark gaze darts between his mother and father. Is he hoping against hope that they don't start arguing in front of me? Because I have been in that situation with my own parents and don't wish it on anyone.

Trudy has stopped coloring. Looking at her handiwork, she's clearly an outside-the-lines kind of girl. She stares at me in a thoughtful way, like she's trying to figure out what to say next. And that's so unlike any kid that age I've ever met.

I pull a face at Trudy. Thankfully, instead of wailing and running away at full speed, she crosses her eyes and sucks her cheeks in. We giggle.

"Cassidy, Cassidy. Come here." She pulls me close. Her whisper tickles my ear. "*Terlalu banyak bawang putih.*"

The whisper might as well have been a hundred-decibel scream. I almost fall off my stool. "What?!"

Trudy studies me, eyes narrowed in confusion. "You don't understand Indonesian?"

"I...I do. *Sedikit.* A little bit," I stammer. But how did she know, out of all the languages in the world, how to say "too much garlic" in my dad's first language?

"Hey, Trudy-Rudy, stop showing off." Hayden clears his throat and plays with his sister's hair. "She wants to join Mensa."

Isn't that a club for geniuses? Although, that explains a helluva lot. Perhaps she could tutor me.

"You know, Dawson really is a *lovely* area," Lindsay continues. Obviously she's accustomed to her very young daughter using Southeast Asian languages. "Beautiful lakes and hiking trails. I would love to take a tour."

"And it's quiet. Very quiet." Hayden smirks. He starts taking plates from a butler's pantry off the kitchen. "Are we eating on the terrace tonight? I can light the fire pit."

"Great idea," Sam says before taste testing the Bolognese. "We can look at the stars. You know, I still can't get over how bright they are out here."

"Sam." Lindsay says his name in a way that makes me

think of our school principal. Like he's in trouble and about to get suspended.

Face red, Sam sidles up to Lindsay and whispers something. Lindsay's hands fist in response and she shakes her head sharply. That confirms my fears. I've walked into a lull between battles. I wonder what on earth the war could be about.

Feeling awkward, I join Hayden in the pantry. "Is everything okay with your folks? They seem kind of tense."

His answer comes quickly and doesn't sound natural at all. "Everything's fine!"

Skeptical, I peer at his family in the next room. "Listen, I can skip dinner and give you guys some space. Believe me, I understand family dramas."

Hayden's hand whips out and snags mine. "I want you to stay. *We* want you to stay."

I glance at his grip and he lets go. "Are you sure?"

"Of course. I know I said my parents are normal human beings. But the reality of moving here is starting to freak them out a little."

"Are they worried about the sinkholes?"

He winces. "Something like that."

Bouncing on my toes, I say, "Don't sweat it. No houses have ever been swallowed up here. I bet it was just a rumor to bring down the prices."

"I'm sure you're right," he says, casting a look over his shoulder toward his family. His mom and dad are still in an intense conversation. The puzzle known as Trudy-Rudy is singing to herself, seemingly unaware of what's going on around her.

"What can I do to help?" I ask brightly, intending to keep his mind off his parents and sinkholes.

He points behind me. "All the silverware's in those two

drawers if you wanna take care of that."

"I didn't mean help as in provide manual labor," I say, chuckling.

"I know," he replies, not looking at me.

"Um, okay. So the silverware's in here?" I pull open a drawer. The recessed ceiling lights shine onto the cutlery and reflect back into my eyes. Someone in this household takes silverware polishing seriously.

Hayden nods. "And the one next to it has salad servers and stuff like that."

"Boys know about salad servers?"

"This boy does." He sets five dinner plates and five bread-and-butter plates on the bench. "It's the twenty-first century, Cassidy! Get with the times. I also know about cake servers and napkin rings. Ask me which of those spoons are used for dessert. I dare you."

"Okay, which ones?" I sweep my arm like a game show host.

He picks up a wide-bowled spoon and displays it inches from my face. "This is a dessert spoon."

"Huh. Looks like a soup spoon to me," I say haughtily. He covers the end of my nose with the spoon. Laughing, I push him away.

"Wrong! A soup spoon has a deeper bowl. Like this." He rummages in another section of the drawer. "See?"

"Amazing," I say in a flat tone. "I can use this information when I visit Buckingham Palace."

"You're welcome," he teases. Picking up the plates, he says, "Come on, I'll show you how to set the table for a state dinner."

"Ha! I'll be right there."

He walks out of the pantry, crockery rattling. I start gathering cutlery, and a silver flash in the back of the drawer catches my attention. Much more lustrous than the glint of a polished knife. Almost gem-like. Curious, I pull the drawer out farther.

My fingers close around the cool metal. As soon as I touch it, something shutters over my eyes. Just for a split second. Like someone turned out all the lights.

The utensil looks like a surgical instrument. About five inches long. One end is tapered, while the other end has two prongs on it. It couldn't be more than a couple of millimeters thick. I stare at it in fascination.

But the fascination doesn't last long. Somewhere deep inside, a voice tells me this thing could do a lot of damage. Cause a lot of pain.

A loud roar thunders in my ears, and it takes me a few seconds to realize I'm hearing the sound of my blood pumping.

"Get a grip, Cassidy. It's just a kitchen gadget," I whisper as if to override that inner voice.

My knees give way. I hold onto the counter for support. The shuttering effect on my eyes gets more frequent and intense.

The last thing I see before total blackness inches over me is Hayden, and a look in his eyes that screams of terror.

TRACK 15

"Clocks"

Present Day

As I slowly return to consciousness, I hear bits of sentences in hushed voices around me.

"…an experiment…"

"Didn't let up…"

"…the hospital…now…"

Frowning, I murmur, "Experiment?"

"Cassidy made a noise! She's awake!" a high-pitched voice chirps close to my ear. Trudy-Rudy.

I open my eyes. Three anxious-looking faces hover above me. I struggle to sit up, but the McGraws' fat-cushioned sofa is threatening to swallow me whole.

Heat and dizziness overcome me. Flopping deeper against the cushions, I mumble, "I fell asleep. I can't believe I fell asleep."

"No, you *passed out.* I was about to call your dad," Hayden says in a grim tone. He holds a palm to my forehead. For some reason, his touch makes me feel faint all over again. It's hot, scorching.

Trudy pokes my foot, staring at it like it's the most fascinating object in the universe. Then, biting her lip, she slides a furtive gaze at her mother as if to say, *"Am I in trouble?"* But her mom's pacing, watching me.

Experiment. Did Trudy perform one of her experiments on me? I rub my temple. No, that can't be right. She wasn't in the pantry. She was busy with her crayons.

And her experiments are just a game. They aren't real. *Snap out of it, Cass.*

"Please don't call my dad. The last thing I want to do is worry him. Besides, he knows I've got this habit of falling asleep in strange places!" I laugh awkwardly, but not one of them smiles with me. This time, when I try to sit up, I actually succeed. "How long was I out for?"

Worry lines crease Lindsay's forehead. "About ten minutes. Hayden caught you before you hit the floor."

"I can't believe how fast you went down," Hayden says. I can't get over the concern in his voice and eyes. I'd probably given him one hell of a shock.

"Maybe a rattlesnake came in and bit her," Trudy offers. She climbs onto the couch next to me and sits so she's almost on my lap. "There are rattlesnakes in Colorado, you know."

"Oh, I do know, Trudy. But I don't remember seeing a snake in your pantry." I'm positive I'd be writhing in agony right now if I was bitten. Squinting, I try to remember what I was doing when I blacked out. There was a rattle, though…

No, that was the sound of plates clattering.

Feeling stronger but still beyond embarrassed, I stand. "I'm sorry to ruin your family dinner. I should go home."

All of them protest at once. Hayden's voice is the loudest.

"No, really," I say. "I'm not hurt. No broken bones. I'll head home. Get some real sleep."

"I understand," Lindsay says, squeezing my arm.

"At least let me pack you a to-go bag." Sam heads for the kitchen in swift steps.

"I'll drive you." Hayden goes to a sideboard and fishes keys from a ceramic bowl.

"I was just about to suggest that, sweetie," Lindsay says.

It's bad enough that I'd collapsed in his pantry—I bet they found me drooling and spread-eagled on the floor. I don't want these nice people thinking I'm totally helpless. Holding up my hands, I say, "Seriously, I'm fine. It's a twenty-minute drive over Saddleback Ridge. Ten if I take a shortcut."

"Ten minutes? That's all? I've got a free ten minutes," insists Hayden. "How about you drive your car and I follow you?"

"Fine, fine," I grumble. In reality, I'm touched by his thoughtfulness.

His dad puts a Tupperware container in a bag and hands it to me. "Careful, it's piping hot. You won't even need to microwave it when you get home."

"Thank you," I say with a wobbly smile.

Outside, Hayden's parents and sister stand on the sidewalk and wave as I pull away. The dash clock glows 7:30. With deep darkness surrounding the car, it feels much later. Behind me, Hayden follows in his truck, close enough for me to see his face in my rearview mirror. He looks serious and pale. What I didn't want to admit to any of the McGraws was how freaked I was. And still am.

Falling asleep standing up? Blacking out for no reason? Or maybe there is a reason. Maybe it's a tumor…

I point my car toward the ridge. This is a shortcut I'd never attempt by myself at night, not with its steep hills and a border of thick forest. There are no streetlights, no road markings. The occasional sign warns of hairpin bends and deer crossings. Over the tree line, lightning jags, but it brings no thunder.

Hayden tails my Fiat like a cop in pursuit of a perp. Well, maybe not that aggressively. But he does stick to me like he's being towed. I concentrate on keeping the car on the asphalt road. The soft noise of the wind rushing by soothes me, helps ease my worries about a possible tumor. Before I know it, I'm pulling into my driveway.

I nose the car up to the garage door. Hayden parks right behind me and runs up to my window before I even turn off the ignition.

"Hey, Cassidy, are you okay?" He pants like he's just run a marathon. Leaning on the windowsill, he peers inside my car, eyes wild.

"Um, yeah."

Hayden searches my face. He can't seem to haul enough breath into his lungs to answer me. "What's the matter? Did you notice something wrong with my car? Do I have a flat?"

He frowns deeply and steps back from the car. "No, your car looks fine. Fine."

Turning off the engine, I say, "Good. You, on the other hand, are not fine."

"I...I just thought..." Jamming his hands in the back pockets of his jeans, Hayden looks up at the stars for a moment. He mumbles, "Your car weaved around a few miles back, that's all. Maybe, uh, get your wheel alignment checked out."

"Wheel alignment. Got it." I give him a thin smile. The car had been serviced just last week. Top to bottom. Bumper to bumper. What's going on with him?

Hayden straightens and turns toward the street. Unspoken emotions churn on his face.

He looks at the sky again, then back at me. Judging by his firm nod, he seems to make a decision. He lunges forward and opens my door. "You should get inside. Now."

"What's the hurry? Is that storm getting closer?" From our hilltop vantage point, there's no sign of the lightning I'd spotted earlier. The night's so clear I can practically see the entire Milky Way.

As he stares at his watch, he swallows. "It's late, that's all. Wouldn't want you to break your curfew."

"Hayden, please. The sun only went down an hour or so ago." But it's sweet of him to worry. Unless all he's concerned about is not getting on his new boss's bad side. Twisting my mouth in skepticism, I power the window up and grab my bag and the Tupperware container.

On the curved brick path to the door, my legs feel kind of numb. I stumble and hold out my arms for balance.

"Are you sure you're okay?" Hayden grabs my elbow. I wince as his thumb presses into me. He stares at me like he's trying to read my mind. His pink mouth is pursed tightly. Is he holding his breath?

"Yep, totally fine." I wish he'd stop asking me that. Although, come to think of it, I *don't* feel so hot. The spot where he grabbed my elbow is throbbing. I just want to crawl into bed and sleep for a week.

"Okay." Hayden escorts me to the hefty front doors. As I fumble for my key, I notice his skin feels kind of clammy. If anything, I should be worrying about him. Aside from being fundamentally hot, he looks like hell.

"Maybe we're both coming down with something," I admit, trying to put the key in the lock. Keep missing it. My coordination is out of whack. Maybe he was right about me swerving on the road. "You know, because I fainted for no apparent reason. And you seem kinda feverish."

"That's…a possibility." Pointing at the key in my hand, he asks, "Need help with that?"

"I've got it." The door swings open. Feet on the threshold,

he leans in and eyes the alarm keypad inside the front doors. "Aren't you going to disarm that?"

Lowering my voice, I say, "That's just for show these days. Mom insisted on installing it, but Dad and I can never remember the code."

I put my bag and the Bolognese on the hall stand. Soft light rains down from the chandelier when I flip a switch. Rolling up a sleeve, I check out a zit-sized red bump in the crook of my right elbow. It looks like a fresh insect bite, but I don't remember how or when it happened. Frowning, I wipe away a speck of…blood?

"What is that?" Hayden stares at my arm and absently scratches his leg.

"It's just a mosquito bite," I say, scratching the bump. "I'll live."

Hayden nods slowly. Peering around me and into the house, he doesn't seem to be in any hurry. He finishes scanning the foyer and sends me a fleeting smile.

"So…thanks for seeing me home," I say.

"You're welcome." He clears his throat. "Do you want me to stay?"

"Um…till Dad comes home?"

Hayden looks over his shoulder, then back at me. His face is deeply troubled. "I mean stay the night."

"You want to stay here? Overnight?" Collapsing into my warm, comfy bed is all I can think of right now. "Why?"

He sways ever so slightly and says, "For protection."

At least, I think that's what he says. His voice is so soft.

"You don't need to protect me. I can look after myself," I scoff. What century does he think we're living in? "But if it'll make you feel better, I'll try to remember the alarm code and switch it on."

Blinking hard, he steps back. "Sorry. I don't know why

I said that. Sorry, Cassidy. Just…erase everything from… Just erase it all."

Before I can even draw a breath, he slams the door shut and jumps into his truck. He literally burns rubber on the driveway. The acrid smell lingers. By the time I wrench open the door, Hayden's taillights are already disappearing over a crest.

Zombie-like, I close the door and grab the Tupperware. It's only when I put the food down on the kitchen island bench that I realize the container that was superhot when I left Hayden's house is now cold.

Puzzled, I tilt my head and catch sight of the oven clock. As the colon between the bright green numbers blinks intermittently, my heart pounds in time. Hard.

9:53.

"That can't be." But the phone I fish out of my jeans pocket confirms it.

I've lost over two hours of my life.

TRACK 16

"Up Around the Bend"

Two and a Half Hours Ago

Distant lightning flashed beyond the treetops. There wouldn't be a storm tonight. Not over Dawson anyway.

Accelerating out of a hairpin corner, Hayden shifted into third, wincing as the gears crunched. He'd practiced driving as much as he could since obtaining his license six months ago. Operating a manual transmission vehicle had not come as intuitively as flying. Of course, where he came from, flying was as easy as pressing a button on a glass control panel and letting the machine do the rest.

That kind of automation was not an option in this time, in this place, in this primitive vehicle. He had to make do.

Fragrant Douglas firs towered on either side of the narrow road, their canopies stretching overhead and forming a living tunnel. The headlights of his truck were feeble and the few-and-far-between streetlights even weaker, but he could see better than most apex predators without any aids. He'd learned the hard way that driving without lights would only draw more attention to himself.

Cassidy's car was little more powerful than a lawnmower. Yet the car was nimble thanks to its light weight. She zipped up Saddleback Ridge's inclines while he lumbered, and then slowed down on the flatter stretches of road so he could catch up.

But up around the third or fourth hair-raising bend, he lost her. A dying flare planted on the road's yellow centerline burned white-hot, lighting up the tree trunks. A thin plume of smoke angled with the wind.

He slowed down. Stopped. Shielding his eyes against the flare, he searched for taillights on the straight road ahead and found none. His heart thundered hard against his ribs. Something felt very, very wrong.

He checked his phone, but somehow he already knew there would be no mobile reception. As he swung out of the car to listen, twin red lights to his left caught his attention.

Heart pumping even harder, he steered the car left onto a lane hidden by brush. The asphalt was so thin and cracked it might as well not be there. Overgrown branches batted at the fenders. He knew the truck was going to look like it'd been sandblasted in a desert storm once this was over.

The winding, twisty lane gradually widened, the woods on either side becoming less dense. Hayden veered to the right, into a clearing, and his overworked heart came to a crashing stop.

He lost control of the clutch's friction point and stalled the truck. He would've stopped in any case, because blocking his way were three bulky beings in black hazmat suits. Giant helmets made of a stiff plastic material covered their heads and faces. They surrounded the truck's cabin. Hands gloved in padded fabric grabbed at his door handle and dragged him out.

"Where's Cassidy? Who are you?" he demanded, but they didn't answer. His eyes wild, he frantically looked for Cassidy. He slipped out of two pairs of strong hands. Again they grabbed him, and again he evaded them. On the third attempt, Hayden's training finally took over. *Don't interfere. Observe only.* He might not have conquered stick shifts, but he was a master pretender. Hayden pretended to struggle, pretended he wasn't fifty percent stronger than most humans on Earth.

The beings blindfolded him and bound his hands and feet, then hauled him to a vehicle. Not one of them said a word. They roughly threw him inside. He came to a skidding halt against a metallic wall, on a floor made of something smooth yet unrelenting. Doors slammed, making his head throb.

The sound of steady breathing inside the vehicle was like a beacon in the darkness.

"Cassidy," he panted. "Are you all right?"

No response. Not even a murmur.

He sensed footsteps treading heavily toward him. He knew the cadence of Cassidy's light gait, knew the being coming his way was not her.

And certainly knew it wasn't Cassidy who stabbed a needle full of something stupefying into his thigh.

TRACK 17

"Rumour Has It"

Present Day

The next day, my head pounds with every step I take along the linoleum halls. I'd gone through my morning classes like a ghost. Not interacting. Not reacting.

I didn't see Hayden till after second period. He totally blew me off, sidestepping into the chem lab without so much as a hello. Just a hasty wave, and he was gone. My texts to him went unanswered, too.

Is it possible he's avoiding me because he also realized we missed a few hours of our lives? If that's the case, wouldn't he *want* to talk to me about it and figure out what the hell happened?

I follow Lisa and her girlfriend Billie into the cafeteria, and dump a salad and water onto my tray. After I shake off this nausea, I plan to do some Jane research in the library, make a few calls. Corner Hayden.

My brain throbs just thinking about my to-do list. Could Angie be right? Am I trying to fill some void?

I dismiss that idea right away, along with a feeling of fear that pops up occasionally. Fear of not being able to finish what I start.

"Weather balloons, my ass. They've been using that

excuse since Roswell. Can't they think of a more creative explanation?" Shaking her head, Billie scrolls through something on her phone. She rolls up the sleeves of her oversized charcoal-gray sweater and sighs in exasperation as they slide back down again. Her black jeans, in contrast, cling to every curve. A skull-print headband holds a riot of curly brown hair away from her face.

The cloying smell of congealed mac and cheese on her plate permeates the air and mingles with Lisa's vegan "not" dogs. I crack open my water bottle and chug to wash my nausea away.

Looking over Billie's shoulder, Lisa says, "I heard it was just kids playing with lasers."

"What do you think, Cassidy?" Billie thrusts her phone under my nose.

I squint at shaky footage. Pinpricks of white light dance in a video. "What exactly am I looking at?"

"Ah, wouldn't we all like to know?" Lisa says.

"It's a UFO. Or UFOs, plural. Clearly." Billie takes her phone back. She pushes aside her tray, bringing that oozing cheese mess closer to me. I fend off another wave of sickness. "They were seen over Bartlett last night. Didn't you hear?"

I shake my head and drain the water bottle. My stomach is doing cartwheels and somersaults. All I can think about is the location of the nearest exit.

Billie goes on, her brown eyes lighting up. "You know, with the CIA and FBI and God knows what other black-ops government agency, they all know UFOs are real. Even air force pilots have made reports about sightings. Jimmy Carter's on record about seeing a UFO, too. The authorities just deny, deny, deny." She takes a bite out of her sandwich. "But…I heard the CIA is actually in on alien abductions."

Eyes bulging, I say, "That's ridiculous."

"Not really." She looks around to see if anyone's listening in. "They're covering up the abductions in exchange for alien technology."

Angie scoffs. Today she's dressed in maple-leaf crimson. She flicks crumbs off her pleated wool skirt. "Okay, that's what I call a conspiracy theory. The government wouldn't do that."

"How do you know?" Billie asks. "I hate to sound like some paranoid crackpot, but there's a lot of stuff governments around the world don't tell their citizens. Can you imagine what would happen if people knew the CIA was selling them out to aliens?"

"That can't be true." Angie frowns and starts picking at her food. "Remember what Lincoln said. A government for the people, by the people, et cetera, et cetera."

Billie shrugs. "Sorry to burst your bubble, but the government's made up of real people who aren't necessarily in it for the greater good. Have you heard of Lewis Blake?"

We shake our heads.

"Totally nefarious guy. A senator. He's actually from Colorado." She leans forward, eyes bright. "One of my dad's college buddies stayed with us for a few days. I kinda sorta eavesdropped on him telling a bunch of stories from his CIA intern days back in the eighties. This Blake guy was in charge of a project about mind control. Helping soldiers mentally block out torture in case they were captured or to prevent them from giving away army tactics. That kind of stuff," Billie says. She reaches for my phone. "Let me look him up."

"Um, what's wrong with your own phone?" Lisa teases her as she winds her copper-colored hair into a lopsided bun.

"The battery's dying," she says, tapping my screen. "Turns out he messed up a lot of people by using the wrong techniques and not bringing people out of their trances the right way. There was an accident where an ex-soldier went on a rampage in the Bronx because he fully believed he was still fighting in the Vietnam War."

Angie sighs. "God, that poor soldier."

Billie gives my phone back to me and pokes at her lunch. "Ugh, can you imagine what aliens would think of the food standards here? This looks like smashed-up cerebral matter."

"They probably eat dehydrated steak like NASA astronauts," Lisa says. Her grin slips when she glances at me clutching my stomach. "Hey, are you okay?"

"Mm-hmm." I shove my salad at Billie. "Here, all yours."

I throw my bag over my shoulder and run to the restroom, ignoring my friends' shouts of concern.

Later, I splash cool water on my hot cheeks. The reflection in the mirror shows purple shadows under my eyes, reminding me of Mom.

Is this how she felt in those last few days before she got help? Confused? Sick to her stomach? Aching all over?

Obviously, our situations are different. She was under enormous pressure from her work. And me? I don't even know what happened for me to feel so muddled.

I scratch the insect bite from last night. It's raised and red. There's a tiny hole where the fucker sank its beak into my arm.

I tilt my head thoughtfully. Maybe I've caught a virus. West Nile or Lyme. I'm not even sure if those things are common in this part of Colorado.

My legs feel like columns of lead as I shuffle to a bench. The unforgiving steel gives me a chill. I tap out a message to

Mom, knowing I shouldn't hold my breath for a reply. She hasn't responded to a hundred or so messages in months.

Minutes pass and I'm indeed glad I didn't hold my breath. Although, if I stay in this restroom any longer, I might have to.

The bell rings right after I step out. Soon I'm engulfed in a crowd. Up ahead, I spy Lisa and Billie, strolling hand in hand out of the cafeteria to their next classes. The pounding in my head returns as a cacophony of different voices overwhelm me. A deep droning noise underlies them all.

At the other end of the hall are the main entrance doors. I'm there in seconds, looking out the glass at my car in the parking lot and the hazy mauve outline of Saddleback Ridge beyond.

Air. I need some fresh goddamn air.

And I need Mom.

With only the tiniest bit of guilt, I push through the doors and run before someone catches me.

TRACK 18

"Life On Mars?"

Present Day

"You're sure it's dead?" I say. "You tried everything?"

After leaving school, I drove to Bartlett, staving off more stabs of guilt by focusing on Mom and helping her get the hell out of Eden. This mission is worth another detention. Maybe even expulsion.

Javier, the tech at PC Brigade, gives me a look that could burn down the Amazon in five seconds or less. He slides Mom's old MacBook Air across the counter with one stubby index finger. "I don't know what else to tell you. The hard drive is toast, and it wasn't backed up to anything. This model's older than my first-grader. They're workhorses, sure, but they don't last forever. Promise me you'll give it a decent burial or at least recycle it, all right? I spent three whole days on it."

I clutch the laptop to my chest. In some ways, it's symbolic of my mother. Her heart and her soul are etched on it. "I'll never get rid of this."

"Oh!" Javier touches a hand to his chest. "That'll be $180."

I wince. There goes a big chunk of my savings. But I have to do whatever it takes to access Mom's files. I'm not letting a dead laptop get in my way. I still have options. While the transaction is going through, another customer walks in behind me.

"Hello, Javier," a woman says.

"Oh, hey, Moira," Javier says with a nod. "Another drop-off?"

"Yes," Moira intones. "May I?"

Javier gestures at the one place on the counter that isn't covered in trays of circuit boards and USB sticks and other PC pieces for sale.

Moira eases past me. I take in her floor-length black dress; its long sleeves are tight from shoulders to elbows, then flare out past her wrists. Very Countess Dracula. Her skin looks like burnished copper. Fine gold liner emphasizes and elongates her eyes. With careful and deliberate moves, she places the flyers in a neat stack.

I can't help but read the one on top. "Alien Abductees Anonymous?"

Has the whole state gone alien crazy? And flyers, for F's sake? Hasn't this woman heard about Facebook invites? She doesn't look *that* old.

"Yes," she says. "There's high demand for spots in our support group."

My jaw drops. "How can there be so many people who claim to have been taken by aliens in one town?"

"These people are traumatized in a way you could never understand." She stares at me like I'm a piece of gum on an alien's shoe. Or webbed foot? "And they don't just come from Bartlett."

"I'm sorry," I stammer. If anyone can understand the ripple effects of trauma, I can.

"There was an event last night," Moira says, addressing Javier, not me. Something about the way she says "event" makes it seem like an unholy word.

"So I heard." Javier's eyes darken. "You might have a few more people turning up."

Moira gives a single solemn nod. "I'm afraid you're right. This is why I felt it was necessary to schedule an emergency meeting for tonight. I'm doing everything I can to put the word out."

"Do you have to be an abductee to join?" I ask, trying to inject as much respect as I can muster into my voice.

Moira arranges her long dark curls over one shoulder. "No. There are loved ones of people who have been taken and never returned. We are there to support them, too."

I wrinkle my nose. "How do they know that their loved ones were abducted if they never came back?"

"Because they witnessed the event." She stares me down, like she's challenging me to say something stupid again. Now I get what she means by "event." It's definitely not an occasion I'd want to RSVP to.

Javier hands over my receipt. I step forward, eyeing that stack of flyers, my hand hovering above the counter.

I won't say something stupid. But I might *do* something stupid.

"Thanks for…not fixing this," I tell Javier, then take my receipt, grab a flyer, and get the hell out of there before this gets any weirder.

I'm not even a mile out of Bartlett before fatigue hits me. At least the headache and nausea are gone, but my heart is still sick about Mom's laptop. Despite it being dead, I put it in my satchel and take it into the restaurant. Seems Moira had made her presence felt here, too. No less than four of her support group flyers are pinned to a community notice board in the foyer.

Again, I have to wonder how effective this form of advertising is for an "event" that's happening imminently. However, the restaurant *is* almost full, so plenty of people would have passed it.

Two very small fish tacos and a large empanada later, I open up the old MacBook. My fingers glide across the keys as I picture Mom tapping hard and fast. If only I could mentally extract her research from the hard drive.

I swirl the ice in my pink lemonade, thinking back to how she reacted when I told her I wanted to take the Jane Flanagan case. The way she snapped at me, warning me off. I've never seen her look so cold before. It occurs to me now that she was saying I'd be putting myself in danger.

Yes, working on the investigation endangered her on a psychological level. That was bad enough, because look where she ended up.

But there had to be something else to it. Had she been threatened by someone in the government? Why, though? I'd think the feds would be just as invested—even more so than Mom—in solving Jane's disappearance. She's a former president's daughter.

Yawning, I check my emails again, noting my phone battery is marching toward death. There's still nothing further from Anna Kingston, the Flanagan-era White House intern. I'm trying not to take it personally. After all, she's probably a busy person. Though she was on the bottom rung of the political ladder when Jane vanished, maybe she heard something, saw something that would help me. I leave a brief, non-whiny message on her voicemail, asking her to call me back at her earliest convenience.

A group of people in fluorescent construction vests

amble into a booth across the aisle from mine. They chortle over the video of last night's light show.

"It's so stupid," one guy says, slurping hard on a bucket-sized soda. "Why would aliens want to come here?"

A bearded man flaps a napkin before tucking it under his chin. "To scope the place out before they annihilate us all and take over."

"Because they're running out of water on their own planet?" suggests another, more thoughtful-sounding worker with a Scottish accent.

"They've landed in the wrong place, if that's all they're after. Freshwater is scarce on every continent," I blurt.

I could have reeled off depressing stats embedded in my brain thanks to school assignments and working for an environmental law specialist who happens to be my dad. But the men throw me a collective *Who the hell asked you?* look, then continue disseminating the supposed UFO footage amongst themselves.

Moira's flyer pokes out from my bag, and I give it a sidelong glance. I'm not sure what possessed me to take it. I've never been abducted by aliens. I sure don't know anyone else who has. If something like that had happened to Angie, she would've texted me while on board the spaceship.

I turn the flyer over and start jotting down ideas about the Jane Flanagan case. I'm basically starting from scratch. I've almost covered the page with my semi-legible handwriting when a voice intrudes upon my thoughts.

"...and then the guy said he couldn't account for missing time. One minute he was walking his dog at six o'clock like he always does. He blacks out. Next minute, he's in the middle of a field, an entire hour later. The dog's *frantic,* barking its head off—"

Missing time? What?

As he speaks, a kernel of fear starts to roil inside me.

I turn to the group of construction workers. "I'm sorry to butt in again, but wh-who said that? Who couldn't account for time?"

The bearded one looks annoyed at being interrupted, but answers me anyway. "Some old Chilean farmer back in the seventies." He turns his attention back to his coworkers. "So he's standing there and he realizes half his hair has been shaved off— "

"I...I'm sorry. Me again." I give the man an embarrassed grin and take a tentative step toward their booth. Now all of the men are frowning at me. "Is it possible that this farmer just...blacked out? You said he was old. Maybe he had a stroke."

"No, kid. None of the above," he retorts. "To make a long story short, he got hypnotherapy years later and it turned out he was abducted by a UFO."

My knees turn to jelly. That kernel of fear pops like a full-on explosion in my chest. I double over.

"Whoa, now. Are you okay?" the Scottish man asks, holding me up.

I work hard to haul air into my lungs. A vision of Hayden's concerned dark eyes last night swims before me. He looked spooked when he pulled up behind me on my driveway last night. Okay, he and his family were already acting weird *before* I fainted last night. But the fear etched on his face was inexplicable. He saw something disturbing.

And now I have a good idea of what that something was.

"I'm okay," I gasp, pulling away from the man. But I'm not okay. Not by a long shot. Is Hayden?

I race to my car as fast as I can with one thought screaming through my rattled head: *Aliens abducted me.*

How else to explain the missing time?

A week ago, my rational side would have said this was a ridiculous conclusion. If I hadn't been drawn into Aunt Carole's UFO "research," alien abduction would so not be on my radar. But right now, I can think of nothing else because my rational side has gone AWOL. I can't even begin to imagine the hows and whys of when they got me.

I spear a charging cable into my iPhone. My fingers, shaking and slick with sweat, trip over themselves as I try to find Hayden's number. I'm about to give up and say, "Hey, Siri, call Hayden," when a call from the boy himself flashes on the screen.

I pause before answering. I'm not a believer in the paranormal, but is it possible Hayden is psychic? How many times has he preempted me in the past few days? It's beyond weird that he's contacting me right now when I'm trying and failing to do the same.

Shaking my head rapidly, I accept the call. I'm not worried about Hayden having psychic abilities. I'm worried about freaking UFOs and aliens messing with me. With us.

"Hayden! Where are you?!"

A pause, then, "On my way home. The more pressing question is where are *you*? You weren't in Latin class. I was worried about you."

"You were?"

"Yeah, I would have texted you earlier, but I heard a rumor about a pop quiz for chem and had to scramble."

"Oh," I say, swallowing thickly. So that's why he blew me off at school. "I'm worried about you, too."

"Me?" He scoffs, sounding surprised. "*You're* the one who fainted in my pantry last night."

"I'm not talking about that," I say. And to think I was embarrassed then about being found drooling on the floor in front of my not-boyfriend's parents. That's nothing compared to alien abduction. "I mean what happened afterward. Do you remember driving to my place? How it took way, way longer than it was supposed to?"

"Cassidy, you're kinda not making sense," he says, sounding genuinely puzzled, if a bit impatient.

"Yeah, my brain is like scrambled eggs." My heart thuds hard. Did *aliens* rewire my brain? Isn't that what they do to people, fuck them up forever?

My gaze falls on Moira's flyer. The conversation I need to have with Hayden can't happen over the phone. I want to see him face-to-face when I tell him my suspicions. Who knows how he'll react? At least I can be there for him. Even loners need support when they're told they're a possible—probable—alien abductee.

"Cassidy?" Hayden prompts.

"I'm at Taco Heaven in Bartlett," I say. "There's something I need to show you. How soon can you get here?"

TRACK 19

"Fade to Grey"

Five Years Ago

Though it was mid-June, the twelve-year-old girl slept under a feather duvet made for snow days. Dead to the world. A slice of brilliant white light speared through a windowpane. It illuminated the foot of the bed, then slowly traced the rest of the girl's huddled form.

The light concentrated on her face, intensifying in heat, turning her brown hair silver. Her eyelids fluttered like butterfly wings, then snapped open.

Startled, she shielded herself from the light. A single word choked from her throat. "Mommy?"

There was no reply. Just a low-frequency pulse that seemed to be coming from a long way away.

She slid out of bed. But not by choice. *Something* compelled her to put one bare foot in front of the other. Entranced, she followed the light as it guided her down the hall, passing her parents' closed bedroom door. It was impossible for her to look left or right, up or down.

She neared the top of the stairs, where a silhouetted figure waited. The temperature had dropped. Her cotton Donald Duck pajamas were a weak barrier against the frigid air. The pulsating sound grew more intense. Terror shook every cell in her body. She wanted to run, to scream, but she couldn't physically attempt either of those things.

The figure reached out. Long, strong, and spindly fingers clamped her wrist. It led her outside to a sparkling light that resembled a tornado funneling down from the sky. But this was no weather phenomenon.

Right above the fir trees, a dark triangular ship hovered. She stared at it. Transfixed. Fascinated. Dizziness overwhelmed her, and she realized she was floating, getting vacuumed up by the light.

She landed gently on her feet in a room with features that were bleached out by blinding lights. There were no shapes, no shadows. The air was so thick it seemed to cradle her. It was comforting. Almost.

A distant whimpering sound nearby distracted her. She couldn't tell where it was coming from, but it sounded like someone young. A girl. Someone like herself maybe.

The whimpering suddenly intensified into screams. Ignoring the girl's pain wasn't an option. She *had* to help.

TRACK 20

"Need You Tonight"

Present Day

"Is this part of my tour? Are you here to show me heaven?" Hayden smiles through my open car window. He jacks his thumb toward Taco Heaven behind him. "Because I've already tasted the hot 'n' spicy enchiladas here. I died and saw the angels."

"Get in the car," I say. No preamble, no niceties. His eyes bulge, then he gives the same respectful salute he gave at the office yesterday.

God, yesterday seems like a lifetime ago. Time flies.

Or disappears.

As Hayden walks around the back of the car to the passenger side, I catch his worried expression in the rearview, bottom lip clamped under his perfect teeth. I shouldn't have snapped at him like that. He drove all the way out here to see me and didn't even question it. Obviously my rational side has yet to make its triumphant comeback.

But I do have the presence of mind to quickly pop a Tic Tac into my mouth. Fresh breath after tacos should always be a priority, no matter what. I slap the thick folder containing my Jane paperwork on the rear seat.

By the time he gets in, Hayden's frown lines have

disappeared and the easy grin is back. In my tiny car, he has to fold his tall frame like origami paper. He's so close I can smell heady, outdoorsy sandalwood on his skin.

Now I want to order Hayden *out* of my car, because I've started thinking about snuggling his neck and that's so inappropriate for a thousand different reasons. I force myself to keep on track.

"I'm sorry for sounding like a drill sergeant," I say, wincing at the way I spoke to him. "Just because I'm your boss's daughter doesn't mean I get to order you around. Especially when we're not at work."

"Apology not needed but accepted." That perfect smile flashes white. He shifts in the seat, putting more space between us, then he grows serious. "So what are you doing here, other than breathing in Tabasco fumes?"

"Oh…" I fiddle with the key chain swinging from the ignition. "I'm quietly freaking out."

"About…?" He peers at me closely. Nothing in his gaze shows me that he's freaking out about *anything.* Not even about being summoned ten miles out of his way to a Mexican restaurant. Then a look of clarity—and concern—crosses his features. "Has something happened to your mom?"

My breath catches. I'm touched that he remembered her. "No, there's no news. Dad's working through the list of new treatment centers I gave him. I'm doing all I can to get her out of Eden in my own way." There's no time to give him the whole spiel about me taking on the Jane Flanagan case. I circle back to the problem at hand. "But that's a different kind of freak-out. *This one* affects us both."

He sits up, eyebrows knitting together. "Okay, I'm listening."

"Something weird happened to me on the drive home

last night." I watch him carefully, checking his reactions.

"Ohhh?" Hayden draws out the word, turning one syllable into four. He sounds wary. His wide shoulders square up.

"Maybe you can help me figure it out. You were right behind me. The entire time."

He nods. "And I was extremely impressed by your defensive driving on those dodgy roads."

I squeeze my eyes shut for a moment. Is he being evasive or are we just not on the same page? "Did I stop for any reason?"

He shakes his head. "I noticed you did a perfect rolling stop at that last intersection before we got to your house."

I sigh. Not only are we not on the same page, but we're not even on the same book. "But did I pull off the road and stop for a while?"

"No," he says finally.

"You're sure?" I lean closer. He leans back. It's just a small move, but it's significant. He folds his arms across his chest.

"Yes," he says. "And I'm glad you didn't, 'cause those woods are hellishly freaky in the dead of night."

Dead of night. Interesting choice of words. "Do you know what time it was when we reached my house?"

He sucks in his cheeks. "No idea."

"I do." I give a dramatic pause. "It was 9:53."

"Um, did you miss your curfew?" he asks, seemingly unmoved by my amateur theatrics. "I'd be happy to explain to your dad..."

Narrowing my eyes, I say, "Hayden, don't you see? That ten-minute shortcut? It actually took over two whole hours."

"That's...impossible."

"Two hours and thirty-three minutes, to be exact. And

that means your return trip would have taken another two hours and thirty-three minutes, and you would have arrived home after midnight."

"Ah, but I didn't," he says, holding up a finger. "I went home another way because I didn't want to drive that mountain road by myself. I'm not as brave as you are."

"Flattery will get you nowhere."

"Obviously not with you," he says.

"So tell me, what time did *you* get home?"

He shrugs. "Don't know. Dinner was waiting. I did my homework. And that was it. My exciting night." He lowers his voice. "It was more exciting when you were with me."

"Hayden…"

"Right, I forgot. No flattery necessary."

My mouth twists. He's being obtuse. Annoyingly so, but he can still make me smile.

"Look," he says, "I'm not sure what you mean. The trip didn't seem that long to me."

"That's the problem! Don't you see? I know that shortcut. It's called a shortcut for a reason."

He inhales sharply, his chest expanding far enough to strain the seams of his slim-cut sweater. "Okay…what are you saying?"

"I'm saying we're missing almost three hours out of our lives. Didn't you notice?"

Hayden swallows hard again. He looks away guiltily.

"Why aren't you answering me?"

"Yeah, I…I noticed." He slips his hand down to mine. It's like he's trying to stop himself from drowning by hanging on to me. He's shuddering. Seeing that vulnerability in him makes me melt.

He's scared.

And that makes me scared, too. But we don't have to

be scared. Knowledge is power, so the cliché goes. There's also safety in numbers. Another cliché. I hardly care what my English teacher would say about it at this point.

"I know where we can find answers. Or find help, anyway." I pluck the Alien Abductees Anonymous flyer from my bag and hold it inches from Hayden's nose. "At this meeting. Tonight."

TRACK 21

"I Forgot to Remember to Forget"

Present Day

As soon as I step into the shoddy, windowless room with its semicircle of mismatched plastic chairs and faux wood paneling, I immediately want to step back out. The decor isn't the repellent. No, it's the lean man—or being?—in the gray alien mask, standing with his back against a chalkboard. A plain black tee and dark blue jeans complete his look. I hope to God he really is human.

I whisper to Hayden. "Why would anyone go to an alien abductee support group dressed like that?"

Hayden glances at me. Color drains from his face. "Desensitization technique? To try to normalize aliens?"

At a makeshift table, we write our names on tags and stick them onto our shirts. I notice Hayden has dubbed himself *Anonymous.* After a few seconds of thought, I discard my tag with my real name on it and scrawl *867-5309* on a fresh sticker.

"Aliens are not normal. Not on planet Earth, anyway," I reply in a dark tone. I steer Hayden to a pair of empty seats as far from the "alien" as possible. The chairs are spaced a few feet apart from one another.

"Oh, you're an expert now?" Hayden teases. "Maybe he's

taking the 'anonymous' in Alien Abductees Anonymous seriously."

"Could you please stop saying that word?" asks an older man in the chair next to Hayden. His name tag reads "Richard." He's wearing a light-yellow short-sleeved business shirt and black polyester trousers. The end of his tie looks like it has been dipped in coffee by accident. It couldn't be by design. He clicks a ballpoint pen repeatedly.

"I'm sorry. Uh, which word?" Hayden asks warily.

"The 'A' word," is Richard's tense reply. *Click, click, click.*

Hayden and I exchange confused glances before he says, "I'll do my best."

"Appreciate it." *Click, click, click.*

The room fills up slowly. I try to keep my eyes off Alien Man, as does everyone else. By eight o'clock, I'm surprised to see only a couple of chairs remain unoccupied. I count ten of us here.

Discreetly, I check everybody out. Our fellow abductees are a snapshot of North American life. There's no common demographic thread here. We're all different ages, all shapes, all sizes.

A man named Bill, identified by his name tag and by the embroidered patch on his coveralls, stares wearily at the floor. Bill's bulky form dwarfs the chair, making it look more suited to a kindergartener. The fabric on his chest and thighs are smeared with black, oily handprints. Obviously soap and hand towels are in short supply where he works.

In contrast, a reed-thin woman in her forties with fresh makeup and an immaculate suit sits upright. The letters on her name tag, spelling out "Julia," are also sharp and upright. Her dark eyes are wide and alert. Despite her patent-leather stilettos, she looks like she's ready to sprint downtown.

An elderly woman contemplates a seat beside me, groaning and sighing as if every move she makes causes immense pain. She grips the back of a chair with knobby fingers. Purple veins pop up under the surface of her crepe-thin skin.

"Are you okay, ma'am? Can I help?" I ask. "Katherine" is written on her name tag in shaky letters that gradually slope downward.

Leaning heavily on a cane, Katherine plants her hunched body with a heavy thump. Her watery eyes are magnified behind thick gold-rimmed glasses. Patting my arm and smiling kindly, she says in a croaky voice, "I'm dying, but I'll be all right."

"Oh my gosh. I'm so sorry!" No wonder she looks so frail. Now *my* eyes are watering.

She chuckles. "Don't worry, child. I'm not the only one. We're *all* dying."

"What…?"

"Radiation," Katherine says. "From the abductions."

Click, click, click.

I stare at her in shock. My heart stammers in time with the clicking pen.

"No one's ever told you about galactic cosmic radiation? GCR?" Katherine asks. "Don't they teach you kids anything in school these days?"

"I…I take AP classes," I stammer. "Of course I know about GCR."

Katherine grunts and folds her arms.

The door opens with a *whoosh*, sucking warm air out and pushing cool October winds in.

"I'm sorry I'm late, fellow travelers." A figure in green, purple, and red glides past us and takes a chair at the right-hand end of the semicircle. Moira, our fearless leader. She drops a satchel on the floor and unwraps a red silk scarf from her neck. Even seated, her larger-than-life presence fills the whole room. "I was held up."

A woman with pin-straight black hair frowns with concern. "Were you abducted, Moira?"

I cast a look at the man beside Hayden to see how he reacts to an "A" word. The pen now in his shirt pocket, he sits on his hands and leans forward. Alien Man lingers by the chalkboard.

"No, Minh. I got caught up at work," Moira says, stripping off more of her outerwear, finally revealing the black dress she had on earlier. I note her gold eyeliner has been replaced by tons of purple glitter. She looks spectacular. And really out of place in this drab room.

"Are you sure?" Minh persists. "Did you lose time? What's that mark on your neck? You didn't have that last time I saw you."

"I'm fine, I assure you. It's only the same mole I've had all my life," Moira says. She glances at Alien Man standing awkwardly by himself. "Hi there, fellow traveler. Come on and sit down."

We all watch as Alien Man waits ten seconds, then slinks toward an empty chair. I notice he's wearing a name tag, but it's blank. If his plan was to be invisible or unobtrusive, it wasn't working. His rubber soles make a squeaky noise on the linoleum.

"It's nice to see some old friends again. And new faces," Moira says. There's a flare of recognition in her eyes as she looks my way. "Thank you for coming at such short notice."

Everyone murmurs.

I shudder—not just at Moira's "fellow travelers" catchphrase.

"We should go over some ground rules. No ridicule, no

judgment." Moira glances sideways at Alien Man, who's clutching his phone. "And definitely no recording on any device. What goes on inside an AAA meeting stays inside an AAA meeting."

"Hey, guy, are you filming us?" Richard asks in a shrill voice.

Alien Man rapidly shakes his head while pocketing his phone.

"Now that we've got those rules out of the way, let's talk about last night's reports." Moira's gaze skips over me and lands straight on Hayden. "You look particularly…haunted to me. Tell us what brought you here."

Hayden coughs into his elbow. He crosses and uncrosses his arms over his sweater. I can almost feel the "I hate being called on" vibes shimmering off of him. His eyes meet mine and I send him a silent apology. Even though it's Moira who should be sorry for putting him on the spot like this.

"Well, my name's…Anonymous. I'm only here to observe, really," he says, coughing again. "I don't know what people think they saw last night. I'm pretty certain I haven't been abducted by aliens, so I wouldn't say I'm haunted by anything."

"What makes *you* so sure?" Moira asks Hayden. She leans forward, her gaze so intense it could burn holes into a brick wall.

"I would remember something like that," he replies simply.

Laughter erupts around the semicircle of "fellow travelers."

Hayden and I glance uncomfortably at each other. What is so funny?

"Most of the time, they melt the part of our brains that deals with recall," Bill says, his voice sounding like his throat has gone through a shredder.

Richard's nose makes a high-pitched noise, while Katherine murmurs knowingly.

"That's not *quite* true," Moira says in an authoritative tone. "They just disable memories, if you will. But they can be enabled again."

"How?" I ask.

Moira squints at my name tag. "I take it you're Anonymous's girlfriend, uh, 867-5309?"

"Is that the number the aliens assigned to you?" Julia asks.

Jon, a man with long brown hair streaked with silver, laughs. "It's a song, right? By Tommy Tutone, right?"

"Yeah, my mom loves that song." My lips tug into a smile. "It's on a playlist she made for me."

Moira clears her throat. "Well, 867-5309, hypnosis is one method. I myself am a trained hypnotherapist—"

"Jenny," Jon interrupts. The fluorescent tube right above his head flickers. "That's the name of the girl in the song. That's *your* name, too, right?"

"Um… Sure, yeah. Right," I say. Jon pumps a fist like it's the first win he's had in his life.

"Good. Jenny." Sounding eager to move on, Moira clearly doesn't care what my name is. "Tell us about your experiences."

"Okay, other than telling you Hay— Anonymous is not my boyfriend, I can't tell you a whole lot." I glance around the group. "But this is what I know. We drove over Saddleback Ridge to my house last night, around 7:30. Separate cars. I had a boiling-hot Bolognese in a bag beside me."

"What's that got to do with it?" asks a frizzy blonde on the far side. I can't read her name tag, but I can read her face—there's boredom written all over every wrinkle.

"I'm getting to that," I reply, smiling tightly. "I've lived in Dawson all my life. Made this trip dozens of times. I get past a curve in the road that I always take at twenty miles per hour, rain, hail, or shine. One minute, I'm looking at distant lightning, wondering when the storm is going to hit."

As I speak, the fluorescent light blinks intermittently. Two seconds on, two seconds off. Everybody is focused on me. How is it possible they're not bothered by the light situation?

"And the next minute?" Moira prompts me.

"Sorry. Th-that light tube is distracting," I stammer, pointing at the ceiling. Two seconds off… "The next minute, I'm pulling up in my driveway. The pasta is stone-cold. And it's 9:53."

"Same exact thing happened to me! Missing time!" Minh exclaims, sympathy oozing from her dark gaze as she nods. The bored frizzy blonde seems unimpressed by my story.

"Apparently." I sink down in my seat, using a hand to shield my eyes from the stupid light.

"And, Anonymous, where were you?" Moira asks. "Jenny said you were in separate cars?"

"Yes, I was following in my truck. It's heavier and can't take the curves as fast, so I kept losing sight of her." Hayden shoots me a glance, his brow furrowed. "But I didn't see any aliens."

"Ah, but did you see a UFO?" Jon asks.

"No, like I said, I would have remembered something like that…" Hayden's voice fades. The light is still proving to be a major distraction for me and only me.

Parting my fingers, I glance up at it. Two seconds on, two seconds off. Two seconds on, two seconds off. It's unrelenting. Unnerving. Even Richard's pen-clicking wasn't this level of annoying.

Two seconds on, two seconds off…

A sharp jab into my abdomen makes me scream. The heat that follows has volcanic intensity. My whole belly feels like it's being ripped to pieces. Panicked, I try to lift my head to see what the hell they've done to me. Two beings pierce my skin with the longest, fattest needles I've ever seen. Roughly, they wriggle the needles, making me scream and scream again.

"Jenny?" says a far-off voice. "Jenny, do you need a moment?"

A croaky voice calls, "Jenny?"

I feel something jabbing into my side. It's not sharp like a needle. But it is invasive enough to make me cry out.

"Jenny? Oh, for heaven's sake, Anonymous, wake poor Jenny up," orders the croaky voice.

Who's Jenny?

"Cassidy." Hayden's breath is warm against my ear. I snap out of my trance. Blinking, I stare into his deep brown eyes. "It's okay. You're safe."

"Hayden," I whisper. The room falls away as I focus on his face.

"I'm here. Everything's fine." He smiles and brushes my cheek. A spark zaps up and down my body in response.

"Somebody get her a coffee. And do something about that light, for heaven's sake. It's driving me batshit crazy," Katherine says. She's leaning on her cane beside me and that's when I realize *she* was the one who jabbed me. And thank God she was there to help me out of the bad memories.

Hold up. Memories?

Is it possible? Have I somehow *enabled* the part of my brain that stored memories of my abduction?

Hayden steps out of the way. Seconds later, a steady hand presses a lukewarm cup of coffee into my grip. I look up. Looming over me is Alien Man. He bows his head. I send him a wobbly thank-you smile and he returns to his chair.

Jon gets busy taking the faulty fluorescent tube out of its socket. It's not a huge loss to the decor. The place is that little bit dimmer.

Moira cranes her neck at me. "Are you okay to continue, Jenny?"

I open my mouth to speak, then catch sight of Hayden. His expression is full of concern. He assured me we're safe.

But are we really?

We're in a room full of alleged UFO abduction veterans. Surely the aliens could grab the whole lot of us in one hit if they decided they wanted to take another stab at kidnapping?

My chest starts heaving again. I sip the coffee, even though I know it'll make me even more jittery.

Without looking at Hayden, I speak up. "That's…that's all for now, if that's okay."

"Sure." Moira looks around. "Anyone else?"

"Moira, can't you command that traveler to take off his offensive mask?" Richard says, clicking the pen madly.

"I can't *command* him," Moira replies, then swivels to Alien Man. "But I can politely ask and he can politely refuse. So, you're among friends here, fellow trav—"

"Just take the goddamn mask off, son. You're giving us all the heebie-jeebies," snaps Katherine, saving us all from hearing "fellow traveler" for a fourth time.

Everyone stares at Alien Man. The mask's enormous black eyes, though plastic, somehow make him look scared. Cornered. His shoulders go from rounded to straight as he seems to make a decision.

Millimeter by millimeter, his slender brown fingers pull the mask upward, first revealing a muscled neck, then a strong, stubbled jaw. Short, curly black hair frames ears pierced with intricate ivory studs. Then cheekbones that look like they were carved by an artist…

"He's *human*," Minh says, as if that was ever in doubt.

Alien Man's lips form a tight smile in response. He looks my age. Maybe seventeen, eighteen. I tilt my head. That smile looks so familiar. Finally, he whips off the mask and it drops to the floor by his sneakered feet. I look up and stare into deep hazel eyes framed by long black eyelashes. He's human and he's beautiful.

And Hayden's gaping at him like he's just landed from outer space.

TRACK 22

"Boys Don't Cry"

Abduction #4 - XU-891B
Two Years Ago

"Jake," Cassidy whispered, turning her head. He lay on the bed beside her, close but just out of arm's reach. A thin sheet covered him from below his chin right down to his toes. "Are you awake?"

He moaned softly but didn't open his eyes.

The aliens had been tough on him. Taken pints of dark crimson blood. Scraped cells from his nostrils, their instruments making stomach-turning squelching noises as they dug deep. Drew fluid from his gums. Ignored the cries of their "patients." They went about their sadistic work without a word.

Cassidy had done enough experiments in biology class to imagine what the aliens would attempt next.

Dissection.

But for that, they'd have to kill them first. She wouldn't let that happen. She didn't think the aliens would have any qualms in taking slices out of their brains with laser-like scalpels while they were still alive, anyway. She was sure of it.

"Yeah, I'm awake. Just…resting." He swallowed thickly. "They've left you alone so far."

"They didn't abduct me for nothing. My turn will come." She shivered uncontrollably and studied him. "Are you in pain?"

"Of course not."

She wasn't buying his brave hero act. In her eyes, there was no shame in admitting the truth.

The door opened.

They were back.

Cassidy's hands clenched into tight fists. Her back stiffened. She squeezed her eyes shut. That's about all she could do to defend herself. Bindings kept her rooted to the table. Virtually paralyzed.

A presence swept between Cassidy's bed and Jake's. It wasn't a presence she'd come to recognize as the aliens'. For one thing, it had a delicate smell. Like freshly rained-upon jasmine flowers.

Beside her, metallic surgical instruments clattered, followed by the sound of Jake struggling against his restraints. Cassidy's heart panged in sympathy as he groaned.

"Jake, fight it!" she said, but her words were wasted on him. In mere seconds, he stopped moving.

And she started shaking, knowing the stage was set for more torture.

Featherlight fingers touched Cassidy's shoulder. Not the usual rough push or prod or poke. For a fleeting moment they calmed her down. Mint-fresh breath grazed her ear, whispering her name.

Involuntarily, her eyelids jerked open and her gaze landed on the face of another being.

A *human* being.

TRACK 23

"Mr. Brightside"

Present Day

After the meeting, Hayden and I linger at the coffee station. Not because we want to stay, but because Jon's in the middle of a story and he wants everyone to listen.

"...vinyl records flying everywhere like Frisbees. My entire Fleetwood Mac collection—*pfft!*—smashed. Then the whole house started vibrating, as if some giant had picked it up and was shaking it like a Christmas present to see what's inside."

"Same exact thing happened to me," Minh says, her eyes wide. "Only I'm too young for vinyl records. It was CDs in my case."

"Okay, then." A corner of Jon's mouth twists downward. "The next thing I remember, I'm laid out on this glass bench and I'm hearing a power saw rev. I'm the coldest I've ever been in my life. And I'm from Anchorage..."

Hayden clears his throat. He leans close to my ear and whispers, "I need to leave."

"Wait. Please. I have to talk to you first," I whisper back. All through Jon's story, my stomach was doing cartwheels. Not joyous ones, either. I try to hold Hayden's gaze, but he looks at his phone.

"I'm sorry. I just got a message." He points at the phone as a message alert appears, then vanishes. "It's a family thing."

I blink. "Oh, of course. Totally understand. Everyone's all right?"

He gives me a grim, fleeting smile, but that doesn't answer my question. "We'll talk later, okay?"

In a completely unexpected move, he squeezes my hand. It's warm and reassuring, and has the delicious effect of turning my insides to jelly. Before I can recover fully and think maybe I should squeeze back, he slips away and out of the room.

Moira sidles up to me. "I was surprised to see you and your anonymous friend here, Jenny. Although I should have had an inkling when you ran off with my flyer."

"My name's not really Jenny." I offer her an embarrassed smile. "Cassidy. And I was curious."

"About why you have gaps in your memory?" she asks. Her demeanor is a lot softer now and less intimidating. Maybe even sympathetic. Behind her, Alien Man—or Jake Letoa as he introduced himself later in the meeting—lurks. The hideous mask is poking out of a trash can along with the discarded fluorescent light tube.

"I wasn't capital *T* triggered till an hour later." I explain what I overheard in Taco Heaven. "Seems like everyone everywhere is obsessed with UFOs. Or maybe I'm just noticing it more."

"Sightings have occurred since the ancient Egyptians and the Mayans. Probably since the beginning of time," she says. "But news travels so much faster now. Instantly. Widely. People are more open to talking about UFOs."

"I wonder what *T. rex* thought of flying saucers." Despite myself, I grin at the idea of those poor dinosaurs trying to defend themselves against aliens with those short little arms. "So you formed this support group? Is it because you have personal UFO experience?"

"I haven't had a close encounter. First, second, or third," she says. "But I do have a degree of separation from alien abduction."

"What do you mean?"

"My grandfather was one of the gold miners who was abducted in the forties." When she sees the confused tilt of my head, she goes on. "He was part of a group that saw a UFO hovering over the mine entrance one night. It was reported in the newspapers at the time. But the mining company he worked for later 'clarified' that it was just a mass hallucination."

"What did your grandfather think?"

Her gaze is steady, sober. "My grandfather said it went further than just a sighting. He was taken."

"And he remembered the whole thing? What happened to him?"

"My granddad was a chatterbox." Moira shakes her head, a swathe of magnificent dark curls waving down her back. "But there are two experiences he never wanted to talk about. The D-Day landing and the UFO visit. We all know how horrific the first thing was, so I'm sure the second thing was on the same level. Maybe worse. We'll never know. My dad also had a close encounter, but that's another story."

I study the tightness around her mouth. It's not hard to see the subject of her grandfather is a touchy one. Pivoting slightly, I ask, "Do you think *I* was taken last night?"

"There are ways to find out." She hands me her card.

Moira Harris. Registered hypnotherapist. Available all hours to all humans.

"You can hypnotize me?" My heart races as snippets

of the vision I had during the meeting sneak into my mind. Aliens. Needles. But is it a real memory? Or a product of my imagination fed by rumors?

I pull my sleeve up and look at the insect bite on my arm. It's all but gone now. But somehow I can feel the sting like it just happened.

It's not beyond the realm of possibility that it's the mark of a needle and not a mosquito.

I shake my head. Hayden's right. I would have remembered being waylaid by aliens and experimented on. My brain is capable of many things, but scrubbing the memory of a UFO sighting? I'm not so sure.

"Yes, if you're open to it. If your *mind* is open to it." Moira shoulders her bag. "I'd better get home. I hope you'll come to another meeting soon."

Moira sweeps out of the room in the same dramatic way she entered it. Most of the others have drifted away, too, I realize. Waving goodbye to Jon and Minh, I head out to my car, absently scratching at the bite.

Jake is sitting in a sparkling cobalt Tundra right next to my spot. His hands grip the wheel, but the engine's off. He's going nowhere. I give him a wary side-eye as I edge past his front bumper and see his eyes are squeezed shut. He's mouthing something.

Suddenly, his eyelids fly open, startling me.

Jake gets out of his truck. Without the mask, vulnerability is plain on his face. Dark purple circles ring his eyes. "Hey! Can we talk?"

"Um, yeah," I say, transferring my purse onto my left shoulder. He didn't say much more than his real name in the support group. If that actually was his real name. I can't fault him for using an alias. "What about?"

Inching toward my car, I feel into my pocket for my

keys. Just in case I need to make a quick getaway. And Lord knows it's been a helluva long day. I'd kill for a ten-hour nap.

"What about?" He snorts and closes his car door. Out here in the elements, he seems less of a hulking figure than he did inside. Even all rugged in a puffer jacket and beanie. "What do you think?"

"You didn't say boo back there," I say, gesturing at the meeting place with my head.

"Neither did your boyfriend."

I'm about to say he's not actually my boyfriend, but I remember something odd about Hayden's reaction when he saw Jake's face unveiled. Did Hayden lie to me when he said he had a family thing to deal with? Does he know something about Jake? But how? Hayden's new in town. And Jake definitely doesn't go to our school. A guy who looked like that would not go unnoticed.

"He's shy," I end up saying. It's not a lie.

"Okay." Jake shrugs and nods. "I, uh, wanted to talk to you because…once I overheard you say your name is Cassidy and not Jenny, everything got clearer. I recognized you. From pictures. She bombards me with them *all* the time."

My feet are rooted to the spot, even though a warning bell is clanging in my head. It's go time, for sure. "Uh, who is *she* and why is she sending you photos of *me?*"

"Oh." He exhales. "Sorry, I'm in my head so much these days that I can't tell what I've said out loud sometimes."

"I hear you," I say. He looks up. "Figuratively. And literally. Okay, I've confused myself and I need to stop talking. Please go ahead."

"Angie Tanner. My girlfriend."

I choke. "*You're* Jacob?! Angie's Jacob?!"

"Jake. But you know Angie. She'll call you whatever she wants to call you."

"True," I say with a snort. Then I remember something vital. "Wait, hold up, she's mad at you."

He scratches the back of his neck. His lips quirk. "Yeah, because I stood her up. And it's not the first time."

Folding my arms, I say, "So what do you have to say for yourself about that?"

"I didn't actually stand her up. Not intentionally." Torment jags across his features. "I was abducted by aliens."

TRACK 24

"Break On Through (To the Other Side)"

One Year Ago

On the football field, no one could outrun Jake Letoa. No one else could grip the ball and break through the defensive line, shrugging them off like flies. No one scored as many touchdowns throughout his high school career. No one was as focused on the game. Football was going to be his meal ticket to college.

Until an elbow from an opposing player struck his temple, and everything he thought he knew about his world changed.

Because when he came to, fragmented memories flooded his mind. Memories of a time when he could not outrun *them,* could not get a grip, could not shrug off the virtual flies.

Flat on his back, he stared past the concerned teammates who'd formed a ring around him. For a nanosecond, he thought he was surrounded by *them*—the creatures. Tormenters from the past. He kicked. Someone put a bag of ice to his forehead. Overlapping chatter about calling paramedics sounded increasingly frantic.

But he ignored all of them.

He sat up, brushing off hands that tried to help him.

Pain bloomed from ear to ear as he got to his feet, but not for long. A corner of his mind heard the roar of the crowd. They were happy to see their hero rise once again.

He wasn't sure if the humming he heard was the beginnings of a concussion. It seemed to come from outside of his head. Not from the bleachers, but from beyond the goal posts thirty yards away.

Robotically, he put one foot in front of the other, crossing soggy grass. His gaze fixed on a bank of floodlights.

The crowd hushed.

Jake stared unblinkingly at the lights. Studying those glowing, pulsing filaments. Trying to reassure himself. He knocked on one of the metal poles holding up the grid.

It's not them. *Not them watching over me. Thank fuck for that.* A teammate ran up and thumped his shoulder lightly. "You all right, man? You've got me worried."

"Yeah…uh, Luca. I just needed to check something."

"Um, what? To see how many lightbulbs are out?"

Slowly, Jake turned to him. "To check that the aliens aren't coming back for me."

Luca's concerned expression slipped, a look of panic taking its place. He flicked a glance at the coach jogging toward them. "And…are they?"

Lifting his face to the stars, he whispered, "I hope to God they're not."

TRACK 25

"Big Girls Don't Cry"

Abduction #6 - XU-891B
One Year Ago

Cassidy woke up on a cold plinth, with no pillow, no quilt, nothing remotely homely. And *they* were around somewhere. Maybe not in the room, but they were watching.

Jake was sleeping. Every now and then he made a quick, sharp, choking noise.

Cassidy turned her head toward Alondra, grimacing because of the pain. Earlier, the captors put whirring probes into the abductees' ears. The high-pitched sound still echoed in Cassidy's head.

Mustering up a smile, Cassidy signed, *"How do you feel?"*

Alondra's attempt at a smile failed miserably. A fresh tear traced the path of hundreds of tears she'd shed before. *"Could be better,"* she signed back.

"The worst is over," Cassidy signed, wishing she had the strength to stand and give her a hug. No…even better, to escape.

Alondra slowly rolled her head away and stared up toward the far-off white ceiling. *"It'll never be over."*

TRACK 26

"I Melt With You"

Present Day

The next day at school, I practiced all forms of avoidance behavior just so I didn't have to lie to anybody about where I was or why I left. I scraped into classes at the last minute and then bolted out as soon as the next bell rang. Ate lunch in my car and pored over newspaper clippings. Wiped mayo off said newspaper clippings. Claimed I had a low battery when a barrage of texts popped up from my friends.

I didn't have to lie to or avoid Hayden at all, because even if he hadn't been with me yesterday, he wasn't in school today. Part of me wondered if he'd lie to *me* if he was here, about any number of things. I itched to ask him how his family was doing, ask him about his reaction to Jake/Jacob, ask him why the hell he won't talk to me about those missing hours of our lives.

Jake begged me not to tell Angie that A) we've met, B) we've made a "date" to meet up again, and C) that he communed with aliens.

"Just don't mention we know each other at all," he said before he drove off, his face a picture of torment.

Dad, to my relief, left for the office before I came down for breakfast. I did note, however, that he'd printed my list of potential new treatment centers for Mom. All of them had red lines drawn through them. I made an effort to steel myself then. I was just going to have to continue solving the Jane Flanagan case. That should take enough of the mental strain off my mother that she'll be well enough to come home.

Simple.

Which brought me here to Half-Mile Lake right after school, where the only other inhabitants are the bugs and the ducks. However, I'm sure the latter will fly south any minute, because it's forty-two degrees.

In my bag is Mom's dead MacBook. I might as well be carrying a dead body around, but at this point it's a sort of talisman. Something tangible to keep me focused on her. Not on aliens or Hayden or Jake.

On a wide wooden bench, I rest the laptop on my knees and set my phone on top of it. The view of the lake is pretty, but I hardly notice it.

At 3:43, Hayden texts me: Can we talk?

Me: Of course. But now's not good for me.

Hayden: When?

Me: 7:00 at the lake?

Hayden: [Thumbs-up emoji.]

I drop a pin on my location in my navigation app and send it to him.

Hayden: [Thank-you emoji.]

He sends another emoji of a green, gold, and blue flag right after. I wrinkle my nose as I try to figure out which country the emblem signifies and why he sent it. But I soon get engrossed in research.

Eventually, fatigue makes my limbs feel heavy. A pumpkin-colored sun hangs just above the tree line, the blues of the sky darkening to a rich violet hue. The days are getting shorter, but it seems to me like they're getting longer and full of way too much stuff to do.

And all I have the energy for is a nap. Part of me wonders if I really am up to the task of solving the Jane Flanagan case. If it was too much for Mom, I must be delusional to think *I* can do it.

But I'm committed now. I have to do it, no matter what.

Finally, the low rumble of an engine breaks into the symphony of insects. The moon is up. My watch tells me it's almost seven o'clock. I shiver as the weak headlights of Hayden's truck come around the final bend. If he hadn't turned up, I probably would've slept here all night.

Hayden parks in the lot and gets out. Under a lamppost, he shrugs into a maroon puffer jacket. He sends me a tight smile and a wave. There's something almost ethereal in the way he moves toward me, even over the rocks and pebbles lining the lakeshore. Like he's defying gravity. It's more apparent out here in the open than at school.

Hayden flaps out a familiar-looking colorful blanket. "Hey."

"Hey! So *that's* what your flag emoji was meant to symbolize?" I laugh and set aside Mom's laptop and other gadgets.

He grins. "The emoji looked like a blanket to me."

"Are you planning on camping out here?"

"Better than going home." His dark eyes shutter over almost imperceptibly.

I know that look. I've seen it in the mirror every morning for months. "What happened?"

"I just had a disagreement with the parental unit. I won't bore you with mundane stuff." After draping the blanket around my shoulders, he points to my bag and tech gear. "Did you need a quiet place to do your homework?"

"Can't get more peaceful than Half-Mile Lake."

"I'm sure." A gentle breeze tousles his hair as he takes in the towering Douglas firs guarding the lake.

"I'm, uh, working on a secret project, if you must know. I even conducted my very first interview for it." I bounce on my toes with pride.

"I *must* know," he says, crossing arms in faux indignation. "You can't drop something like that on me and not give me juicy details."

After a moment's hesitation, I say, "It's the Jane Flanagan case."

Hayden looks at me, his face blank. "Who's Jane Flanagan?"

"Are you kidding right now? It was only the most high-profile missing person case since Jimmy Hoffa. She was kidnapped right under the noses of the Secret Service." I give him a brief history of the case.

"Oh, *that* Jane Flanagan," he says when I finish, nodding soberly.

"Yes. My mom was working on a book about the disappearance. She never got to finish it because..." *It drove her to a breakdown.*

"Because of her health issues," Hayden finishes when he realizes I'm choking up. "So...you want to pick up where she left off."

"I'm convinced it's what she needs to get better." I pause. "Please don't tell me I'm being too simplistic."

"I wasn't going to," he says, his dark eyes soft. "I can't think of a better reason than to help your mom recover. Aside from giving the Flanagan family some peace."

"Exactly," I say, feeling a rush of relief now that I know Hayden really gets what I'm trying to achieve. "Mom herself said it was too dangerous. Not in so many words, but I know that's what she meant."

"But you're not convinced?" He shoots me a worried look. "Cassidy, what if she's right? What if the person who did it is still a threat?"

"I've thought about that. Jane was kidnapped in 1985. Chances are they're not in a position to do any more harm. You know, because they're presumably ancient. Or dead."

Hayden's lips wiggle. He doesn't look convinced. "I wish I could help."

"You've got your own life stuff to deal with. Not to mention your new job. The boss can be *really* demanding."

"I know. So can the boss's daughter," he says with a wink. He grows serious again, gazing at the laptop with so much concentration I have to wonder if he's trying to view the contents with X-ray vision. "I'll do whatever you want. Make calls. Do letterbox drops. Kick down doors. You name it."

"You're serious?"

"About kicking down doors? Deadly."

Before we started hanging out together, I never would have guessed he had such a fun side to him.

"That's so sweet," I say, picturing those long limbs thrusting out and breaking into dingy lairs. We could both kick down doors and save the day. And Jane. "I thought I'd be able to use Mom's research, but her laptop is fried. I had a tech genius try to fix it, but he said it was beyond saving."

He nods at the laptop lying closed on the bench. "Is that it? I can check it out."

"You're a computer geek?" Of course he is, he's a sci-fi fanatic. I should have guessed.

"Yep, I'm all kinds of geek," Hayden confirms. He picks the laptop up and puts his palm on the lid. He nods. "I can give it a shot. Leave it with me."

"Thank you." My heart flops with gratitude. There's nothing like a geek in shining armor.

He sets the laptop down gently as if it's made of delicate glass, then gazes around the lake. In the distance is a rotting wooden dock. At the end of it, the bow of a partially submerged rowboat peeks above the rippling water. He points. "What's that over there?"

"Just an old boat dock." I'm about to ask him if he can rub two sticks together to build a fire, but he starts walking. "Oh, you want to continue your tour of Dawson? Sure."

I leave my belongings on the bench and draw the blanket tighter around my body. By the time we reach the dock, the stars are all putting on a show. Most of the structure's planks were lost to the lake years ago. Those that remain are slippery with moss. Somehow, the thick pylons are still standing.

Putting on my best tour guide voice, I say, "Okay, so you may think this is *just* an old dock, but to the people of Dawson it is a monument to our proud past. It was built over a hundred years ago by the women who were left here when their brothers, sweethearts, husbands, and sons went to war."

"Wow." Hayden crouches and touches a plank as if he's trying to extract the blood, sweat, and tears of the women who worked on the dock. Eventually, he stands, a frown scored on his brow. "If it's so important to the town, why does it look like it's about to collapse?"

"No one can decide whether to pull it down completely, thus destroying the monument, or try to shore it up," I say, leading him onto the jetty. "What about you, newcomer? What would you do about it?"

He stops and studies the roughened handrail. "Hmm, I would source some reclaimed timber and..."

"Okay, good start," I say when it's clear he's lost his train of thought. "And what?"

"And…" Hayden takes his hand off the handrail as if it has suddenly become as hot as lava. "I shouldn't interfere more than I have already. I can't."

A twinge of sympathy hits my gut. He's obviously not quite at home in his new town. Even hypothetical questions make him uneasy. "It's not interfering. You live here now. You get a say in how things work. Or should work, anyway."

"We'll see." He glances skyward. Maybe for divine guidance, I don't know.

Carefully, we continue navigating over broken and missing boards. Our hands clash together, sending tiny bursts of energy jolting through me. My breath skitters, but I try to stay cool. Because looking at Hayden, it seems he's totally not feeling any kind of internal fireworks.

In a light tone, I say, "If we survive this tour of the dock, then I'd be more than happy to keep being your guide around town. And soon enough, *you'll* be the one giving tours to unsuspecting new citizens."

That earns a decent chuckle out of him at last. The sound of his laugh makes my insides warm up.

When I slip, Hayden grabs my elbow and this time the jolt is more like a lightning bolt. And since we're already in a precarious position, I quickly slide out of his grip and watch where I'm walking. The quarter-moon, hidden by thin clouds, isn't up to the task of illumination.

"It's kind of an obstacle course, right?" I laugh to hide the nervousness that has attacked me out of the blue.

"Nothing you can't handle," he says. His tone is so full of certainty that I take my eyes off the slippery, mossy planks and check to see if he's kidding. I mean, he's known me all of five minutes. He can't possibly know what I can and can't handle. But I like his vote of confidence in me.

We finally make it to the end of the dock without putting a foot through the boards. Gingerly, we sit down, letting our legs dangle over the edge. It may be shallow here, but out in the middle of the lake, dive as far as you can, and you can't see the bottom, let alone touch it.

It grows so quiet that the sound of water lapping against the dock and Hayden's breathing have a hypnotic effect on me. My worries about Mom seem to fade. She's still in the front of my mind, but I'm somehow a lot calmer.

Hayden kicks his sneaker against the boat. It rocks and lurches. "What happened here? Did this thing hit an iceberg?"

I laugh and peer down at the bow. All that remains of its livery is flaked paint that might've been an arctic white in days gone by. "Nobody knows for sure. It's been here for as long as anyone can remember. The lake owns it now. It won't let go."

"What do you mean?

"There's something anchoring the *anchor*," I tell him. "Scuba divers have tried everything to get it out over the decades. They say it's buried into rock. Like Excalibur. There's a rumor that the anchor is solid gold. You know, because this used to be a mining town."

He squints into the water. "So if I used my otherworldly strength and wrenched it out, would that mean I'd be allowed to join the round table at Goldie's Diner?"

"Absolutely, Sir Hayden. That'd be some kind of magic." Parting clouds reveal more of the moon. The lake shimmers with silver-gray light. Talk about magical. "You wanna give it a shot? Right now?"

"Let me bulk up a little more and I'll give it a try. Next summer," he says. I wonder if the hearts of Dawson High could take it if he piled on more muscles. Mine would probably burst. "Why doesn't anybody just cut the anchor chain?"

"Believe me, people have tried everything. No dice. It's a mystery." I look at him out of the corner of my eye and inhale. "Speaking of mysteries… We've skirted around the topic long enough."

Hayden cocks his head sideways like I suddenly slipped into speaking an obscure Indonesian dialect.

The weathered planks beneath me creak as I shift. Watching his face carefully, I say, "UFOs? The meeting? It makes sense, right? We were abducted by aliens the night before last. Together."

He stares into my eyes like he's searching for the meaning of life. "To be honest, I really don't have a clue what's going on," he says finally, sounding genuinely confused.

"It is a lot to take in. *I* can't even believe it myself." I shake my head ruefully.

"But you kind of do. Almost." He gives me a sidelong glance. "Why?"

I pull the blanket closer and chew my lip. "It's a combination of things. Those people in the support group and their stories… When they spoke, I felt something on a cellular level, I guess. It's hard to explain."

Hayden changes position again. I'm not totally sure, but I think he moved farther away. "It's one thing to read those reports that Carole found, but to hear them in person, it's very hard-hitting."

"There's something else that made me think…maybe," I begin, swallowing a lump of emotion, "when I blanked out during the meeting."

"I noticed something was up with you then." His voice

is low and edgy. Hayden's hand finds its way to my knee. Despite the thick denim of my jeans, his touch is searing. I can't move. Don't want to. "What happened?"

A few seconds—more—pass before I can answer. Images flash in my mind, sending chills through every corner of my body. Needles. Burning pain. I pull my sleeve up and check the faded insect bite. "I had a…a vision of being injected."

Hayden's expression freezes, like someone pressed a button on a video. "Oh."

Somehow, that one syllable conveys much more than he probably intended.

Narrowing my gaze, I say, "You had the same vision, didn't you?"

He gulps like he's trying to swallow a whole watermelon in one hit. "Not exactly."

I close my eyes, urging the images to come forward in my mind once again. They come to me in pieces, like bits of a dream. "I think the vision wasn't actually a vision. It was a memory. Of what happened to us on Saddleback Ridge."

His jaw takes on a stubborn hardness. "Nothing happened that night. We were *not* abducted by aliens."

"But you said it yourself. You don't remember." I grab his arm and squeeze hard through a slippery, puffy sleeve. "So how the hell would you know what happened or what didn't?"

"Because if aliens took us, more than anyone, I *would* know," he says harshly, his face inches from mine. His words echo around the lake, bouncing off trees, and stunning the insect choir into silence. Instantly, he's contrite, like the sound of his own voice shocked him. "I'm sorry, I shouldn't have snapped at you."

My pulse races like a runaway stallion, not in the least

because Hayden lost control for two seconds. I don't care that he got upset. I care more about *why* he got upset. "How would you know? Wh-what are you saying? You've had a close encounter? For real?"

Hayden's chest rises and falls rapidly as he tries to pull himself together. More puzzle pieces slot into space. This explains so much about him. His edginess. His reluctance to get too close to people. To me. He's traumatized and he has no one to turn to. No one who'd believe him.

Tentatively, I slide over the splintered planks and drape the blanket so it covers his shoulders, too. I put a hand on his. This time, I don't squeeze so hard. "Why didn't you say anything?"

"I can't. Not to you." He looks away. The pain in his voice puts a tiny fracture in my heart.

"Hayden, we're friends now, right?" I say gently. "You can tell me anything."

Instead of letting a flood of confessions loose, Hayden gives me one of those long, searching looks again. We stare at each other and time seems suspended. He strokes my cheek, just like he did when I had the micro-blank at the support group. Heat radiates from his touch, but before I can melt into it, he pulls away.

But even in the space he created, there's a palpable energy between us. A connection I can't deny. Then again, has my mind been playing tricks on me? Not just about aliens, but about Hayden? Sleep disorders can wreck a person's perspective on reality.

Following his lead, I put a little more distance between us. "You don't have to convince me that aliens exist. I won't think any less of you."

Hayden smiles weakly. "You needed a lot of convincing when you read those tabloid articles."

"Keyword—tabloid. It's not news. It's entertainment," I say, rolling my eyes. "But when you get new information, new *facts*, you're allowed to change your mind. So let's look at the facts. One, both of us agree that there are almost three hours of our lives we can't account for."

"Yes."

"We don't remember anyone flagging us down on the road."

"Nope."

"We didn't see any spaceships or aliens."

"That's right." He folds his arms. "It's not looking good for the alien abduction theory this time, is it?"

"On the face of things, no." My mouth wobbles. "Should we call the cops? The FBI?"

"What? No way. We can't give them any useful information. No description of a vehicle. No lasting injuries. No evidence. No witnesses. Nothing."

I clasp and unclasp my hands. He's right. Whether a UFO really did suck us up into its bowels or...who knows what else it might have been, the police aren't going to take us seriously without concrete evidence.

So I'll just have to figure out how to get it.

TRACK 27

"Creep"

Present Day

As Hayden watched Cassidy drive away from the lake, his gut churned. He knew his kind was made of steely stuff, but every time he lied to Cassidy, he felt parts of his soul corrode.

"It's not lying," Sam tried to explain to him more than once when Hayden brought up the topic. *"It's survival."*

"What the hell are we doing here if we're merely surviving?" Hayden asked.

"That's a question all humanoids must answer for themselves, wherever they are." Sam gave him a wry smile. *"But our task is clear. Gather intelligence. Don't interfere. Don't draw too much attention to yourself. That's all."*

So while he was "allowed" to join the track team—because habitual refusal to participate in activities can also attract too much attention—he had to hold back. Not break any Earth records. Aim for mediocrity. *Whoo.*

Hayden stared moodily at the water lapping around the tethered boat.

He never asked to be in this stifling position. However, that's how things worked on Agua. Life was mission-based. Everyone had a role assigned to them from birth, depending on which family unit you were born into. His unit just happened to be Observers, the most passive on Agua.

The longer Hayden walked on Earth, the harder it was to maintain the delicate balance of being a bystander as opposed to being a regular teen guy.

Right now, the scales were leaning toward the latter.

He wanted to get involved.

Be involved.

With Cassidy.

It was at first difficult to *not* see Kalexy when he looked at her. But the more he observed Cassidy, the more he realized she and Kalexy were like night and day. Kalexy was fun but reckless. She could never be described as deep. Cassidy's dark eyes were often full of shadows and vulnerability. But whenever she squared her shoulders, he sensed grit. A never-give-up spirit.

Every time she got within inches of him, he felt electricity jangle every nerve. Which wasn't as painful as it sounded. Rather, exhilarating. He felt like he could talk to her about anything. Loosen up. Show her who he was.

Whether she would accept the real him was another thing.

As far as he could see, he had only two choices—be his authentic Aguan self with Cassidy. Or remain tied to the family unit and its finite mission.

And if he chose unwisely, someone was going to get hurt.

His gaze zeroed in on the boat. He was reminded yet again that he could never be a regular teen or a bystander. He wanted to make things happen, be not just an Observer but a Protector.

Providing protection was way outside his job description. As Cassidy said, though, when you get new facts, you're allowed to change your mind. Surely that could be extended to changing your mission. Once he had more facts about who had kidnapped him, then he'd think about consulting the family unit on their next moves.

Water rumbled and roiled beneath his dangling feet. He closed his eyes and focused his mental energy on the rusty chain below, on the anchor. Pictured it wiggling loose from its moorings.

Somewhere nearby, a bird shrieked. Concentration shattered, he opened his eyes. The boat was no longer trapped. It was free.

Hayden looked at it with envy, and right then, he made up his mind.

He chose freedom.

He chose Cassidy.

TRACK 28

"The Ubiquitous Mr. Lovegrove"

MEMORANDUM FOR PARALLAX STAFF
CLASSIFICATION: TOP SECRET
SUBJECT: RETIREMENT

September 22, 1977

It is with regret that I announce my retirement, effective December 24, 1977. I thank you all for your service and loyalty. I am proud of what we have achieved in twenty years of Parallax. It has truly become a family.

Please join me in congratulating my successor, Senator Lewis Blake III. The Senator will no doubt steer Parallax into a new era with his characteristic aplomb.

A Christmas/farewell gathering on my final day has been planned by Mrs. Tate, to be held in Level 3 at 1545 hours.

Godspeed to you all.

Dr. Harold P. Elsworth

TRACK 29

"Upside Down"

Present Day

My dad opens the front door when I park the Fiat in front of our garage. His face looks tense. Lately I've noticed his cheeks getting a bit thinner, his eyes a little more crinkly around the edges. He's still wearing his lawyer "uniform" of black wool suit pants and sky-blue business shirt. The shirt's got a lot more creases in it now from lounging around.

"Were you waiting for me?" I ask warily, getting out of the car. It's an hour before curfew, so I know I'm not in trouble. Unless he found out I skipped classes to get Mom's laptop in Bartlett. I'm positive I hadn't lost time between leaving Hayden at the lake and arriving home. The fifteen-minute drive from the lake took exactly that time. No detours. No lights in the sky. No "wheel alignment" issues.

"I couldn't get you on your cell," Dad says, letting me into the foyer and following me through to the kitchen.

Burying my head in the fridge, I say, "Yeah, Half-Mile Lake is turning into a reception dead spot. It's okay around the parking lot, but if you go past the dock? Nada."

Dad frowns. "What were you doing up there? At night?"

I take my time filling a tall glass with milk. My thoughts go around in a circle, just like the leftovers spinning around in the microwave. Do I tell him I'm ninety percent sure I'm an alien abductee? What would he say to that? Would he drag me out for a psych assessment right now? Maybe he'd have me admitted to Eden Estate. Which would be okay if only to be closer to Mom. Finally, I come out with, "Homework. It's very inspiring."

"Yeah, well, I'd prefer if it you didn't go up there by yourself next time, okay? Especially at night."

I open my mouth to say I wasn't alone. But since Hayden is his newest employee and in need of all the money he can get, I close my mouth firmly.

Besides, it's not like anything happened between Hayden and me tonight.

But you'd like something to happen, wouldn't you, Cassidy?

The thought pops into my head along with an image of his soft lips and those brown eyes that are as deep as the Pacific. And the memory of his warm finger trailing down my cheek—

The microwave *dings*, zapping the image of Hayden from my mind.

"Hungry?" Dad says. "Aunt Carole made enough beef *rendang* and rice for a whole football team."

My stomach grumbles, saying yes on my mouth's behalf. "Thanks."

"I don't know what I'll do for lunches and dinners when Carole retires." Using Mom's strawberry-print oven mitts, he spoons the rice and Indonesian-style curry into big serving bowls.

"She'll always be your aunty. Plus, she'll never retire."

"That's what we said about Charlie." Flashing a weary grin, he hands me a fork. We lean on either side of the marble island and dig into the food, not bothering to serve out individual plates.

I glance over at the formal dining room and see echoes of the old days, when Mom and Dad used to cook up a storm and we'd all eat together at the table. As an intact family. I blow on a forkful of meat dripping with a malty, rich sauce. There's nothing like Aunt Carole's comfort food. It can take my mind off almost anything.

Almost.

Dad grabs a light beer from the fridge. With the concentration of a surgeon, he uncaps it and pulls up a barstool. "I called Dr. Davis late this afternoon."

I drop my fork on the floor and don't bother picking it up. "Is Mom okay? What did the doctor say? Does she want to see us?"

"Mom's as good as can be expected," he drawls out in contrast to my rapid-fire questions. He comes around the bench to pick up my fork and gives me a clean one from a drawer. "But she has regressed in a big way. According to the doctor."

An odd feeling blooms in my chest. That feeling I get when I've done something wrong, and I don't know how to make things right again. Is it possible my visit set her off? "Any…any idea why?"

Dad hesitates for a few seconds, confirming my fears. "Don't take this the wrong way— "

But I do. Immediately. "It's my fault. She wasn't ready to see me, was she?"

"No. Don't blame yourself— "

Again, I cut him off. "How could I not, Dad? Just say it. I went there against her wishes."

"Your heart was in the right place," he assures me. "For the record, do you know how many times I've wanted to visit her, only to talk myself out of it? Hundreds. I'm happy you worked up the courage to go out there."

I chew my lip. "Dr. Davis gives me that 'mad scientist' vibe."

"You think so?" Dad chews his lip, too. Like daughter, like father. "He and Charlie go way, way back. Charlie often gave him legal advice informally."

"What, advice about patients? Were there ever any lawsuits against Dr. Davis?"

"Not that I'm aware of." Absently, Dad pushes a few stray rice grains end to end like a conga line. "Charlie took care of business affairs. Dr. Davis has managed Eden Estate for decades. In any case, Charlie didn't consult with me on the Eden file. But he did highly recommend the treatment center."

I stare at the food, no longer hungry. "When can we expect Mom to come home? Did you ask?"

"Of course. And the short answer was not anytime soon." He shoves the bowl away, his appetite clearly lost. "All of those clinics you found for me are booked solid. I'll do more research, okay?"

"Okay." I drag the *rendang* back from the middle of the island, picking out the bay leaves.

Dad rounds the bench. "I've been meaning to ask, did you take your mother's laptop?"

Swallowing, I say, "I tried to get it fixed. The tech in Bartlett said it's a goner. But Hayden's going to take a stab at it now."

"Is something wrong with yours?"

I shake my head. I catch a glimpse of my reflection in the oven door and even I can see I look five thousand kinds of guilty.

"They why do you need your mother's laptop?"

"I needed information." I can't look at Dad. Tears start

to sting my eyes, and it has nothing to do with the spicy food. Gulping, I add, "Because I'm taking over her Jane Flanagan research. The way I figure it, if I solve the case, it'll take a load off Mom's mind. She'll start to improve, and come home faster."

I hear the words coming out of my mouth and I cringe. I sound like my eight-year-old self, when I told my parents I would stay up and wait for Santa to arrive because I had a list of things I needed to fact-check with him.

Dad wraps his arms around me and kisses the top of my head. Just like he did when I was eight years old.

"You think it's a bad idea, don't you?" I mumble into his shoulder.

"I'm not doubting you. You've got the brains, you've got the pedigree. Both from your mother." He pulls back and gives me a sad smile. "I'm worried about your workload, with school and all."

Quickly, I snatch a paper towel from the dispenser and dry my eyes. "I've interviewed someone already, and I'm trying to line up more. Plus…helping Mom in this way also helps me deal."

Dad's eyes redden. His lips tighten, and I know he's trying to hold back on spilling his feelings. "Okay, I get it. You have my support. But please, be careful, this case turned your mother's life upside down. I don't want the same thing to happen to you."

"It won't, Dad." But given how convoluted my life has become already, I hope it's a promise I can keep.

TRACK 30

"Rooms On Fire"

Present Day

"Hello, Ms. Kingston. It's Cassidy Roekiem again. I'm just following up on your email. I'd really love to talk to you about your time in the White House during the Flanagan Administration. Like I've said before, it'll be totally off the record. Please call me." Sitting down in the small room Hayden and I had commandeered at the office, I scroll through the list of songs on Mom's playlist. If she really did add "The Whole of the Moon" because of the logo on the van, *maybe* some of the other songs had hidden clues.

Through headphones, I listen to the dreamy, psychedelic vocals on Siouxsie & the Banshees' "Kiss Them for Me."

"Who's *them,* Siouxsie?" I wonder aloud while Googling the song's meaning. I add "Jane Flanagan" to the search terms. Nothing about the president's daughter comes up. But the song is sad enough in its own right. Turns out it's about Jayne Mansfield, a sixties Hollywood bombshell who didn't make it home to kiss her children good night because she was killed in a grisly accident.

Tears prickle my eyes as the song fades out. How utterly tragic. Does that mean Mom believed our Jane was dead, too?

Hayden strides in, and I hit pause on my playlist. He's carrying three archive boxes as if they're feathers. The boxes thud heavily on the desk opposite mine.

"No luck with the intern?" he asks, opening a lid. The box is jam-packed, and he frowns at dog-eared pages sticking out of folders. Seems whoever filed it was careless or in a hurry or not paid highly enough.

I grimace while I reconfigure my ponytail. "That's the third time I've called her."

"Maybe she's spooked?" He stands at the desk and shifts papers aside. I kind of love that he ignored the casual dress code and came to work wearing suit pants and a business shirt—albeit without a tie.

"Last week she told me she'd love to answer my questions. She actually used the L-word." I stare at my notes thoughtfully. "Something changed her mind."

Hayden's gaze flicks to an out-of-date calendar on the desk. "It's coming up to the holidays, right? She's probably busy."

"They're over a month away." A pang hits me. The odds of busting Mom out of Eden before Thanksgiving are slim to none at the rate I'm going.

He pries a folder out, being careful not to disturb dust bunnies living in the box. "Who's next on your list?"

"A retired reporter from *The Washington Post,* a gardener who worked at the park. Oh, and the FBI. You know, small fry." I smirk. Honestly, I don't think my chances of getting someone in a government agency to comment are super high, but I have to try. "Maybe you're on to something. Anna really could be spooked. Which means I need to change my approach. Not tell people I'm investigating, per se. If I come across like a private eye, it might raise people's hackles."

"How about you tell them it's just for a little ol' school project? It's nonthreatening, and if people underestimate you, you could fool them into giving more info." He skim-reads a document before scanning it.

The scanner drones. Its bright light glides back and forth under the lid, sending the document to the cloud. The process takes ninety-five seconds. I've timed it. *This* project is going to take centuries unless Dad forks out for a machine that can scan multiple pages at once. But I'm not sure I'm in a position to beg for one now, not after begging him to hire Hayden…and then begging him to let me continue Mom's research. That has to be my beg quota.

"You're a genius," I tell Hayden. "And for that, I'm going to make us both a toasted panini."

In the kitchen down the hall, I stare absently at the sandwich press while trying to organize my thoughts. Like the archive boxes, my head is stuffed full. It's hard to even pluck out the most mundane bits of data. I vow to draw up lists, charts, spreadsheets, and Pinterest boards. Anything to help me keep track.

Since our night at the lake, Hayden's been reluctant to talk about aliens or anything even remotely sci-fi. He even declined an offer to see *Close Encounters of the Third Kind* with me. And when I suggested going to the next AAA support group meeting, he said he was busy that night. Which was weird because I didn't tell him when exactly the meeting is.

But I guess I can't blame him for wanting to remain tight-lipped about his experiences. Didn't stop my curiosity from blazing, though.

A burning smell pulls me out of my thoughts. Melted cheese oozes out of the press. I open the lid and, for some brainless reason, use my bare hands to scoop the goo off the hot metal plates.

"Ow!"

In seconds, Hayden comes running. He sees me clutching my right hand—my best scanner hand—and blanches. "What happened?"

"I just burned myself. It's all right." I suck on my fingers.

"No, do this. For at least five minutes, okay?" Hayden firmly takes my hand and puts it under a cold running faucet. Which is exactly what I would have done had my brain been functioning at optimal levels.

My fingers throb under the streaming water. Hayden keeps his hand clasped on my wrist so I can't move. Despite the pain, all I can think about is the fact that Hayden's left side is pressed up against me. And I like it.

I steal a glance at him, but he's laser-focused on my hand. Chances are *he's* not thinking about what it feels like to be this up close and personal. Applying basic first aid—that's all he's doing. For five whole minutes that feels like a delicious eternity. After a while, he loosens his grip and turns my palm, studying it like it's carved with ancient hieroglyphics.

Finally he looks up, our gazes locking. He flips off the tap. "Do you feel better now?"

My voice is MIA. I can only nod.

He checks my hand again. A deep purple streak stretches across the back of four fingers. They're numb from the cold water. That is, numb until he hovers one shaking index finger just above the burgeoning scar.

My skin tingles with energy. The air between his finger and mine feels thick, like they're separated by an invisible cushion. Before my eyes, the purple streak mellows into a light pink. Seconds later, it fades into nothing at all.

"Wha... Oh my God." I breathe raggedly. "How did you do that?"

"Do what?" He rips sheets of paper towel and dabs at my wet hands. Then he gets busy cleaning up what's left of the paninis. The acrid smell of burnt cheese lingers.

I watch him closely. "You took away the burn, the scar. Like magic."

His face reddens. He clears his throat but a sexy huskiness clings to his words. "I didn't take it away. The magic is in the healing power of water, that's all."

"No, after the water. Y-you did something to make the scar disappear. What was that you did with your finger?"

He silences my lips with that same finger. Involuntarily, my eyes close as a dizzy feeling swirls over me. My body leans toward his, drawn by some invisible force. His warm lips hone in on mine, mold to mine. Our tongues meet for a split second and fireworks go off inside my brain. Better than anything I ever saw on the Fourth of July.

My hand, free of pain, reaches around his back. His muscles ripple under my touch. The slow, languid way Hayden's rubbing my shoulder is sending me into a state of yogic bliss.

After a while, the crackling explosions turn to the sound of a phone ringing in the distance. Oh God. That's right. We're in an office. My *dad's* office.

Reluctantly, I take a few steps back. Aunt Carole or Dad could come in any minute and catch us.

"Wow, uh..." Yeah, that's about all I can say out loud. I want to add, *"Can we do that again? Now?"*

The pain of the burn is gone, nothing but a memory. Corny as it sounds, but it's like he kissed it all away.

Hayden runs a nervous hand through his hair. "I'm sorry. I didn't plan that at all. Not like that anyway."

"Oh?" I can't help grinning. Something tells me I won't stop grinning for the next three days. At least. "Has this kiss been in the planning stages for a while?"

He shrugs and smiles, making dimples in his cheeks. Very kissable dimples. "I'm not willing to go on the record for that."

A door slams elsewhere in the office, bringing us back to reality.

"We can continue this line of questioning later? If you like?" I say in my least Judge Judy-like voice.

"If it pleases the court," he murmurs.

A thrill races up my spine as he kisses me again. Shorter this time, but somehow sweeter. I murmur, "It does."

But later that night, when I'm getting ready for bed, I check out the burn wound again. Or lack of it. Did Hayden really heal me? And if so…how?

TRACK 31

"Running Up That Hill (A Deal With God)"

1979

Call her naive, but it was Anna Kingston's lifelong dream to change the world. End hunger, distribute wealth to the poor, and provide free education and healthcare for all—those were her primary objectives.

She thought going into politics would help her achieve that dream, where she could effect real change through the rule of law.

Anna was no fool—she knew that politics was not for the faint of heart. That compromises would need to be made. Values and ethics would be challenged. Truth would be bent. However, she had a strong sense of right and wrong. She vowed she would never be pressured to stray from the high road.

But that was before she started interning in the office of Senator Lewis Blake III.

Blake wasn't her first choice. She would have preferred to work for Senator Janice Kilby. Still, Anna was a beggar, so she couldn't be a chooser.

Like most people who worked for Blake, she rarely questioned him. To the outside world, he was a quiet achiever. Never hogging the limelight or courting controversy. Which, granted, was a good thing for someone who headed up a black-ops agency.

Blake did enough to make sure he was visible to his voters. If only his constituents knew he wasn't "just" fighting for a better deal on their behalf.

No, he was up to far more than anyone dreamed.

Initially, she was terrified about working for him. And in fact, the feeling of terror never went away. She'd seen him "dispose of" staffers who displeased him, even for minor infractions. Yet no one ever had a bad word to say about him. Not willingly, anyway.

She sat in the chair opposite his, her mind reeling as she scribbled his latest orders. What he was dictating was way beyond the norm.

The desk between them was practically an island of mahogany. On it sat a framed picture of his devoted wife—the only personal item in the entire office. Behind him on a credenza was a crystal decanter half filled with brandy and a smaller bottle she'd never seen before. Its label was simple. Clinical-looking. Alongside it lay a case containing what looked very much like a syringe. She couldn't take her eyes off it.

"Did you hear what I said?" Blake said in a crisp voice.

Startled, she looked down at her shorthand notes. "Yes. Yes, sir. You want me to corroborate a witness statement."

He slid a file across his desk. It was marked *Washington, DC. UFO Sighting #62b.*

Anna opened the file, read the introductory paragraphs, and felt a twang in her chest. This was a journey that would take her far down the low road. Yes, she knew lying was an art form in the realm of politics. But this was something beyond art.

It was pure evil.

She took a deep breath before speaking. "Sir, I'm just curious about why this needs to be d—"

"It's not your job to be curious," he barked.

Anna jumped. "Of course."

"Have a draft on my desk by four o'clock," he said, giving her a wave of dismissal from his office. "Then we'll drip-feed it to the press pool tomorrow."

As she crossed the room to the door, she mentally drafted her resignation letter.

TRACK 32

"Under the Milky Way"

Present Day

"Thank you for coming, I know it's last-minute," says a floor manager wearing a headset as she ushers me through a set of doors. Security guards check the lanyard around my neck.

"I'm glad I could help," I say. I refrain from telling her I'd never interpreted live on TV before. My confidence was shaky enough. I didn't want to rock hers minutes before showtime, either.

My ASL teacher, Betty, called me only an hour ago, saying I was her last hope. A sign language interpreter was needed for an emergency broadcast.

"The important thing is not to panic," Betty said while I frantically dug up an all-black outfit from my closet. "If you forget or don't know a sign, fingerspell it."

"Got it. Fingerspell. Letter by letter," I replied. But... what if I totally blanked out and didn't even remember how to do that?

Hayden gave me a pep talk as he drove me up the highway to the State Capitol Building. Said I practiced hard and would do an amazing job. It was sweet of him to say, but he wasn't standing in my sneakers. People's lives and properties are on the line. What if my nerves take over and I give the wrong information? The thought of letting down the Deaf community made me dizzy. When I stepped into the Capitol's grand marble lobby, the frenetic activity amplified my anxiety. Hayden had to stay outside because of strict security measures.

Now, following the floor manager, I try to create a psychological bubble around me, blocking out the sound of people shouting instructions at each other. Try to anyway. The cacophony of ringtones and buzzing from multiple phones makes a blood vessel in my temple throb.

Get a grip, Cassidy.

"Don't move from this mark," the floor manager says, pointing to a cross of red tape on the floor a few feet away from Governor Fairbanks. Cables anchored by duct tape snake around a podium. My heart rate spikes even higher with the realization of what I'm about to do. "I'll count you and the governor down when we're set to go live, okay?"

A makeup artist touches up shiny spots on the governor's face. The governor herself simultaneously listens to an adviser while she reads briefing notes.

I slow down my breathing and ignore the bright lights and chatter of several broadcast crews. A meteorologist and the police chief line up behind the lectern. The governor gives her adviser and the floor manager a final grim nod. She glances at me. "Are you ready, miss?"

You can do this, I tell myself, arranging my features into a picture of serenity while feeling sweat trickle down the middle of my back. On the inside, I'm still churning. I draw a breath in and hold for a few seconds before releasing it.

Finally, I sign as well as say out loud, "Ready when you are."

As soon as the cameras start rolling, I get into the zone.

Don't. Mess. Up.

"Good afternoon, all." The governor pauses slightly, and I launch into interpreting. "As has been reported earlier, a bank of storms has been gathering intensity. The storm cell has veered east and is expected to bring damaging hail. Winds of up to sixty miles an hour have been belting residents in the northern parts of Colorado. The bureau has reported 121,000 lightning strikes in the two hours before noon alone. Evacuation centers in Riley and Waterton are now open…"

Later that night, rather than bathe in the success of my television debut and subsequent make-out session with Hayden, I get straight back to work. I lie on the floor of my bedroom, assessing my to-do list in the search for Jane Flanagan. Outside my window, lightning flashes beyond Saddleback Ridge.

I'd spent hours scrutinizing fuzzy copies of newspapers published on the day of Jane's disappearance. Most of the photos accompanying the articles were tight shots of the playground. Of Jane's dimpled cheeks. Of her parents' grief-stricken faces. None of them showed pictures of cars, especially not the van Mrs. Parkes described.

Following Hayden's suggestion, I'd contacted several DC news stations about my "school project" and asked for footage. One station known back in the day as WHMM said they'd get back to me. The others haven't responded. But they will. Once they get tired of me bugging them.

My phone buzzes.

Unknown: Is this Cassidy Roekiem's number?

I sit up, my papers, lists, and iPad sliding off my lap. My

heart thuds faster in anticipation. Finally a break, though why Anna is coming up as an unknown number is beyond me. She's in my phone contacts. It's possible she's calling from another number. I hesitate for a moment, then tap.

Me: Ms. Kingston?

Unknown: I don't know who that is?

I groan. Of *course* it wasn't Anna Kingston. She's virtually fallen off the planet. I've almost given up on her. Almost.

Unknown: My name is Alondra. Do you remember me?

My face screws up. The name rings absolutely no bells.

Me: Um, not exactly.

Gosh, talk about awkward.

Unknown: Can we meet?

Everything I ever learned about stranger danger and pervs trying to groom unsuspecting kids jumps to the front of my overcrowded brain. Excited as I am about making a possible break in the case, I take the cautious route.

Me: How about we talk on the phone?

Unknown: I can't do that.

I grimace.

Me: FaceTime?

Unknown: How about face-to-face? Downtown?

Me: I need more information. What do you want to talk about?

"Alondra" waits several beats before replying. After half an eternity, she finally sends me one word. Or, rather, an abbreviation.

Unknown: UFOs.

TRACK 33

"Somebody That I Used to Know"

Four Hours Ago

Alondra Santiago yawned, too tired to even lift a hand and cover her mouth. Purple-gray oil paint was embedded in her cuticles. No safe amount of turpentine was able to lift it. She didn't have any energy to scrub anymore. She'd worked all night completing her art class assessment—five weeks in advance. But once she started right after school yesterday, she couldn't stop. Had to get the images of her dreams out of her head somehow. Now that she was done, she wanted to burn her artwork.

That would have to wait until she handed it in for grading.

A lumpy couch and an afternoon of mildly suspenseful *House Hunters* reruns with closed captions was about all she could handle. The show was predictable. Her life was not.

She sat up as a "breaking news" broadcast abruptly interrupted a Midwest couple's search for an affordable fixer-upper.

"Governor Fairbanks is speaking about the severe storm front that has been battering the state in the past hours. Let's cross live to her now."

The video cut to the governor at a lectern, addressing reporters. Left of her onstage, a trembling young woman wearing all black interprets in American Sign Language.

"The storm cell has veered east and is expected to bring damaging hail. Winds of up to sixty miles an hour..."

Alondra's younger brother, Miguel, barreled into the center of the Santiagos' spacious living room. He stopped dead as if he'd run out of battery power, blocking Alondra's view of the broadcast. He bellowed in the direction of the kitchen, "Mom, where are my soccer boots?"

Alondra scowled fiercely and stretched a leg out to tap his ankle. She signed, *"Move out of the way! You're not a ghost."*

Her pulse rate tripled as she tried to look around her very solid brother.

Miguel simultaneously spoke and signed, *"You could've just scooted along the couch."*

"I was here first." She didn't care that she came across like a ten-year-old. She and Miguel had bickered like this since they were toddlers, anyway. But today he was particularly grating. Especially since her nerves were stretched thinner than usual. *"And you're blocking my view of the interpreter."*

"They always blow these things way out of proportion. Besides, the storms are twenty miles away."

"The storm could blow down this way." Alondra knew her brother was probably right, though.

And as intense as the weather pattern seemed to be for folks upstate, she wasn't focused on the storms. Rather, she zeroed in on the girl signing. A girl she thought she'd never see again. One who'd barely changed in five years, albeit with an obvious growth spurt.

Cassidy.

TRACK 34

"Connected"

Present Day

Spine straight, I sit at a table facing the door of Goldie's Diner, my hands hugging a pumpkin spice latte to warm them up. Howling winds hurl rain and small debris into the windows. The staff outnumbers the patrons, and they cast nervous looks at one another. Driving downtown was hell. Torrential, horizontal rain battered my little Fiat. I almost hydroplaned across the lot, but I rode it out and parked safely. Thankfully, there were very few cars around to bash into anyway.

But the lack of people on the streets, and in the diner, royally messed with my plan of meeting "Alondra" safely in a crowded place.

I glance at my phone for the millionth time. 8:14. She's more than forty minutes late. Either the weather's holding up her travels or she's chickened out.

Or…

She's been waylaid by a UFO.

Scrolling through my social feeds, I establish that no one has reported any strange lights in the sky—aside from the storm's inordinate number of lightning strikes. Posts and pics are all about the wild weather and local flooding north of Dawson. But Alondra gave me zero information about which direction she was coming from.

A short while later, the doors swing open. A small, thin girl who looks to be around my age stumbles in, propelled by the wind. Leaves swirl at her wet black sneakers. With a grunt of effort, she pushes the door closed. Long spirals of rain-soaked dark hair cling to her high cheekbones. She dumps her broken umbrella into a trash can near the foyer, then looks around the restaurant.

Her fierce dark gaze drills into mine right away. The diner's host attempts to show her to a booth, but the girl gives her a "stop" signal and stalks straight to me. Her olive-green parka comes to the knees of her dark green jeans. The cloth band of her khaki satchel crosses her chest. It occurs to me then that she's dressed in a sort of camouflage outfit.

She slides onto the seat opposite me, her large eyes never leaving my face. She's breathing hard and fast.

"You must be Alondra?" I ask tentatively.

She gives a firm nod and fingerspells my name.

My hand knocks the mug, sending pumpkin spice splashing over onto the table. "You're deaf?"

"Yes," she signs. *"I'm Alondra Santiago. I saw you on TV today. I got your contact details from the sign language association, in case you're wondering."*

Instead of using my voice, I go into sign language mode. *"I hope I did an okay job."*

A tiny smile cracks through Alondra's sombre features. *"Your movements, your facial expressions were flawless. And appreciated."*

"You're welcome." I allow myself to bask in a little glory, then I realize Alondra's lost her smile already. *"So, if that message you sent me is anything to go by, you're not here to*

give feedback on my interpreting."

"No." She snaps up a bunch of napkins from the dispenser and dries her face. *"I am here to talk about UFOs. Our UFO."*

I slide down on the vinyl bench, my gaze darting furtively at the approaching waiter, Andy. He's worked here for years and I'm reasonably sure he's not a sign language aficionado. No threat of him eavesdropping on our conversation.

My hands tremble as I try to sign. *"Our UFO? What do you mean?"*

Alondra shoots me a puzzled look. But before she can reply, Andy's looming over our table. She watches his lips intently when he asks for her order. She points to my mug. This time she sounds out the words as well as translates with her hands. "I'll have what she's having."

"Coming right up," Andy says. Smiling, with a flat right palm, he then taps his fingers toward his lips and down toward her—*thank you* in sign language.

I gape in astonishment. Just when you think you know somebody, even casually, they surprise the hell out of you.

Shrugging, he says, "That's pretty much all I know. Sit tight, ladies."

"Alondra," I sign as soon as Andy leaves us. My pulse hammers in my ears. If only I could *remember* exactly what happened on Saddleback Ridge. If only I had something tangible to confirm it. *"Are you telling me there really was a UFO landing last Monday? Was I really taken by aliens?"*

"Monday? No." She frowns, her face a picture of confusion. I'm sure my expression is identical. *"Wait, so you don't know?"*

"Don't know what?" I forget to sign and say the words

out loud. The frustration in my voice bounces off the walls.

Andy arrives with Alondra's pumpkin spice latte. In silence, we watch him carefully plunk it down.

The second he leaves, I sign at Alondra. *"You need to tell me what you know. Start from the beginning."*

"Okay." Alondra sips the steaming latte and screws up her face in disgust. She pushes the mug away. *"But first, I need you to know I'm not some fanatic. Despite what you might read when you Google me online later."*

"Noted." I, too, push away my now lukewarm drink. I wish I could order something stronger than watered-down pumpkin.

"I mean, I don't care if you Google me, but you have to believe me and not what other people say about me."

"Got it, got it."

Her shoulders hitch up to her ears. She chews her bottom lip so hard they turn a deep maroon. The pain in her face makes something inside me break for her. She signs hesitantly. *"You asked me to start from the start. Okay, newsflash, you and I have met before."*

"We have? Where? When?" Surely I'd remember meeting her. My memory isn't *that* bad. Anyway, why would that bring her so much pain?

"Yes." Alondra toys with her damp sleeve for a moment. A gray-ish substance clings to her cuticles. Paint, maybe? She snaps a loose thread, then looks up. *"I know this is going to be hard for you to process, but you have to trust that I'm telling you the truth."*

I shift uncomfortably on my seat. But no position seems to be comfortable. Not when my whole body is vibrating with anxiety. *"You're starting to scare me."*

"It's not my intention to frighten you. For some reason, I expected you remembered everything we've been through,

but I guess… I guess I'm an anomaly."

I want to say she's "A" for "annoying" right now for keeping me in such suspense. Then it hits me. This conversation is tough for her, too. I soften and give her hand a sympathetic squeeze. Her skin is so, so cold.

"Take off your parka." I slide my dry duffel coat across the table.

She blinks, her eyes large and emotional. *"That's so like you. Caring about other people's welfare instead of your own."*

"That's…a nice thing to say about me. But how could you possibly know?"

"Because I know you. We're alien abductees," she signs. *"We're alien abductees, okay? We were both abducted when we were twelve years old."*

Alondra's hands fall into her lap.

My brain fizzes and shuts down. It's like all the gray matter has been replaced by a black hole. I can't process anything.

Okay? No, not okay!

She slides along the table and covers my hand with hers. The action wakes my brain again. Shivering, I take my hand back and hug myself.

"I know you must have some questions."

"I have questions, all right. What do they want? Why don't I remember any of it?"

"Why don't you remember?" She scoffs. *"Because you're lucky?"*

"Lucky?" I splutter out loud. Then I look in Alondra's eyes, see the deep trauma in them. I live in an enormous house. Luxurious by anyone's standards. My parents love me. I have great friends, good grades. I'm kinda falling for a really cute boy. And through a strange quirk of my brain,

I have no recollection of being abducted and most probably tortured by aliens.

Yes, compared to most, I'm lucky.

Her eyes soften. *"How about if I tell you what happened to me first? It might give you some answers. You can take or leave whatever I say. I actually don't care. I know the truth."*

Leaning forward, I sign, *"Just tell me. Please. I want to know. What happened to you?"*

I place the emphasis on *you*, because ninety-eight percent of me can't reconcile that it also happened to me—according to Alondra. Yes, there are two and a half hours of my life I can't account for. But anything could have happened. To most people, alien abduction would never be on their radar. Until last week, *I* was one of those people.

She nods. *"I was twelve years old. It was my birthday. My parents had given me a Star Wars lightsaber and a Jar Jar Binks doll."*

I can't help myself. I laugh. *"They gave you Jar Jar? Are you sure that didn't make you want to run away?"*

"Don't blame me. Mom didn't know the difference between Obi-Wan Kenobi and Jar Jar. If she had her way, she would have given me a Barbie. I had a green birthday cake in the shape of Yoda." She allows herself a smile, too. But it disappears at warp speed. *"That night, I went to bed high on the sugar in that cake. Mom had a helluva time getting me to settle down. But I guess I did. Until I woke up. Or was woken up."*

"By them?"

"By a light. Brighter than the sun. But diamond white. Everything in my room looked like it was bleached. And I couldn't move a muscle. It felt like I was being held down. No, pressed down by…by an invisible force."

I go very still as I listen to her story. My heart clenches at the thought of a tween Alondra trapped in that terrifying scene. "*What a nightmare.*"

"*I wish it was just that.*" She shudders like she's reliving every second of the experience. "*There was only one of them at first. He…she…it, I don't know what it was, stood at the end of my bed. All I could see was a silhouette. An outline of a big, triangular head. Skinny arms and legs. Puffy torso.*"

I raise a brow, but say nothing. She's describing E.T., the alien creature in that eighties movie, exactly. Does that mean the fictional alien had an uncanny resemblance to nonfiction aliens? Or does that mean Alondra's mind played tricks on her and the alien was a figment of her sugar-fueled imagination?

"*It floated around to the side of my bed. And then as soon as it did that, another alien appeared at the foot of the bed.*" Alondra shudders again. "*I think right then I wet my pants.*"

"*I would have, too,*" I sign. "*Maybe even before the second alien came along.*"

She nods. "*The first alien put its hand on my forehead.*"

Involuntarily, I clench my fists. "*It touched you? What did it feel like?*"

Alondra's gaze drops. "*Cold. Colder than ice, if that's possible. But leathery. Somehow. And then the second alien put something on my foot. It felt like a red-hot poker. I tried to scream again and again. Tried to kick the best I could. But it was useless. Next thing I knew, the second alien yanked me out of bed. Instantly I was in another room. Like nothing I could have imagined. Just this white, square room with nothing in it.*"

She swallows hard.

"I still couldn't move. I was standing in a corner. Just glued to it. The lights started going on and off. Dim at first, then brighter and brighter. All kinds of colors. I couldn't even close my eyes." Alondra's breathing gets faster. *"Then suddenly, the flashing stopped. And I saw something in the opposite corner."*

"What? What did you see?"

She skewers me with a dark, intense look that's becoming all too familiar. *"I saw you."*

TRACK 35

"Intergalactic"

Parallax Human Intervention Unit
Transmission Received

February 19, 1981

0100110101100101011100110111001101100001011001110110010100100000011100100110010101100011011001010110100101110110011001010110010000101110001000000101011101100101001000000110000101110010011001010010000001101100011010010111001101110100011001010110111001101001011011100110011100101110001000000100000101110111011000010110100101110100011010010110111001100111001000000111100101101111011101010111001000100000011100100110010101110011011100000110111101101110011100110110010100101110

Translation: Message received. We are listening. Awaiting your response.

TRACK 36

"Space Oddity"

Parallax Human Intervention Unit
Transmission Sent

February 19, 1981

0101011101100101001000000110000101110010011001010010000
0110100001101111011011100110111101110101011100100110010101
1001000010000001100010011110010010000000111100101101111011
1010101110010001000000011100100110010101110011011100000011
011110110111001110011011001010010111000100000010011010110
0001011110010010000000100100100100000001110011011101010110
0111011001110110010101110011011101000010000000111011101100
1010010000000110010101111000011000110110100001100000101101
1100110011101100101001000000110100101100100011001010101100
001011100110010110000100000001110100011001010110001101101
0000110111001101111011011000110111101100111011111001001000
000110000101101110011001000010000000110110101100101011001
000110100101100011011000010110110000100000001100001011001
0001110110011000010110111001100011011001010111001100111111

Translation: We are honored by your response. May I suggest we exchange ideas, technology, and medical advances?

TRACK 37

"Careless Memories"

Present Day

"What happened? How did I get in that room with you?" I stare at Alondra. Though I haven't used my voice while signing with her, my throat is bone-dry as if I'd been screaming for days. A thousand other questions race through my mind at the speed of light. The most disturbing one is: If what she's saying is true, why can't I remember any of these events?

"I don't know," she signs. *"One minute, the corner was empty. The next minute, there you were. Staring back at me and looking freaked out."*

I shake my head. It does nothing to help bring back any memories of the abduction. *"What was I wearing?"*

She closes her eyes. *"A long-sleeved Donald Duck shirt over long blue pants. Your feet were bare. Your hair was a lot lighter then. And almost to your waist."*

A faint clanging sound starts sounding in my head, getting louder and louder the more she describes my twelve-year-old self. Accurately. My hair darkened over the years, my features evolving to become more like Dad's side of the family rather than Mom's. But how would she know what I looked like then? How would she know about the

Donald Duck pajamas I got at Disneyland that year? I wore those PJs until they disintegrated, but Alondra couldn't have known.

We. Are. Total. Strangers.

If what she's saying is true—and it's harder to believe it *isn't* true now—then I'm missing a whole other part of myself. It doesn't feel real. *"I really want to understand, Alondra. Help me. What else happened? How long were we there?"*

"I can't say for sure. It felt like forever." She pauses for a moment and gathers a breath into her lungs. *"The room lit up. So bright I couldn't see the corners of the room anymore. It was like we were floating in a big, glowing box, but I could still feel the floor under my feet. I kept looking around for an escape. I still couldn't move. Neither could you. But when those creatures came in… God, I wanted to run."*

"Creatures. The aliens?" The low rumble of thunder outside underlines my words.

She nods. *"Three of them. Floating right through the walls like they were ghosts. Their skin was a grayish-purple. They didn't have any clothes, but I couldn't tell what gender they were."*

The details in her story are mind-boggling. But could it be that this is all just a product of an imagination fertilized by a healthy diet of Steven Spielberg movies? I can relate to that. If I hadn't read Aunt Carole's UFO articles, I wouldn't have leaped to the conclusion of alien abduction when I lost track of time.

But there was one glaring thread that's making it all too real for me—the pajamas. The only way she would know about those is if she saw them. And according to Alondra, she saw them during an abduction.

"Did they say anything?"

"Not verbally," she signs. *"Their mouths reminded me of coin slots. Slightly open, but not moving. Yet somehow… somehow they talked to us with their minds."*

"Mental telepathy?"

"Exactly. And I could understand them. It didn't matter that I was deaf."

"Wait. Back up. Are you saying you could hear their voices…in your head?" I squint. *"You have to explain that to me."*

"I wish I could explain it. But I can tell you I wasn't born deaf," she signs, and averts her gaze. *"I had a virus when I was six. It destroyed the structures that affected my ability to hear."*

"I'm sorry." I start to reach across the table, but she waves me off.

Bristling, she signs, *"Don't be. I'm proud of being Deaf. That's with a capital D. It's my culture. It's who I am."* She smiles ruefully. *"But it floored me that the first sounds I 'heard' in six years were alien voices. I would have preferred to hear my annoying brother's voice."*

I stifle a laugh.

"Anyway, somehow, some way, I could understand what they were telling me. After I stopped crying, that is."

"What did they sound like?" I sign.

Alondra thinks on it for a moment. *"Just like you and me. Like humans. English-speaking people."*

I'm so far removed from everything she's telling me. Like it happened to someone else. I believe her, but I want to know more, to feel what she felt. *"Tell me about the abduction. What did you see? What happened to us?"*

Lips pursed, she closes her eyes. *"Beds appeared out of nowhere. No mattresses or sheets. They might have risen from the floor, I don't know. The aliens told us we had to lie down on the beds."*

"So we could move at this point?"

"Not exactly," she signs. *"I remember seeing you, stiff as a board, kind of drift to one bed, levitate above it, then lie down. And I did the same thing. But I had no control over my body. It just…happened like magic. They put us in silver gowns. Like a hospital gown kind of thing."*

If we couldn't move our limbs…then how did we change our clothes? Did the aliens undress us? Oh my God, what if—

"I was powerless," she tells me. *"I couldn't turn my head to look at you. Both of us were on our backs. The only thing I could see was just a white ceiling that looked five miles high...and those big, triangular faces looking down on me."*

I squeeze my eyes shut. Every horror movie I've ever seen jumps into my mind. *"Then what?"*

Alondra pushes her latte mug even farther away, like the smell of it is making her nauseous. *"They started examining us. Prodding us with those cold, leathery hands. Then they got their instruments out."*

"For tests?" Wild images spring to my mind. Butcher knives. Foot-long needles. Surgical saws.

"They hooked us up to computers, took blood, hair samples, skin samples, nail samples. I can't imagine what else." She pauses. *"Actually, I can imagine."*

"And all extracted from us in the most brutal, painful ways possible?" I think of the alien support group and some of the experiences they shared.

Her brow furrows. *"You know what? No. It was… painless. Like they were taking the utmost care with us."*

"But that can't be right. Practically everyone who says they were abducted by aliens talks of torture and being probed."

"What can I tell you? These ones were… I don't want to say nice. Humane is a better word," she signs. *"Maybe because we were kids? After a while, they left us alone in that room."*

"To recover?"

"I think so." She squeezes my hand. Tears roll down her cheeks. *"It was so, so cold in there, on that spaceship. You somehow got up. Shivering. Came to me. Hugged me. I read your lips when you said we'd be okay, that we'd be home soon."*

"I did that?"

"You did. And you calmed me down. I can't thank you enough for that."

A knot forms in my chest. Alondra grabs more napkins from the dispenser, emptying it. She hands one to me and we both dab our eyes with the scratchy tissue.

I inhale and exhale slowly, taking in Alondra's story. She seems believable. Sincere.

And why would she make it up? Go to all the trouble of tracking me down and regaling me with an out-of-this-world story?

Because, again, we are total strangers.

Or are we?

In my head, I add up what she has said so far about how I looked at age twelve, right down to my Disney PJs. I *know* there aren't any pics of me online wearing those pajamas. Unless Angie posted one of our slumber parties from middle school, but I'm sure she would have tagged me.

"Like I told you, it doesn't matter one bit if you don't believe, because I know what I saw, what I felt. But the minute I saw you on TV today, I had to find you." Alondra gives me a long, assessing look as if trying to think of more ways to convince me. *"It's…interesting that you know sign*

language. What made you want to learn?"

"I want to work for the UN as an interpreter when I finish school. I suck up languages like a vacuum." I laugh.

"But sign language, Cassidy? Really? Most people pick, I don't know, French or Spanish." She leans forward, gaze narrow. *"How old were you when you took it up?"*

I can't move, but my heart rate spikes higher and higher. She is right. Even my teacher was taken aback—but pleased—when I insisted on lessons back then. *"I was around twelve."*

Her right brow arches slowly. *"And one day, out of the blue, you said, 'Mom, Dad, I want to learn American Sign Language.'"*

"It wasn't out of…" I trail off and stare into space, trying to think back to that one moment when the idea of learning how to communicate with the Deaf community came to me.

"Was it, say, around June of that year? June fifteen?"

"It was summer," I sign, mind whirling like a Kansas tornado as I take myself back to the past. In those virtual clouds, pieces of information fly out. Pieces of dreams. Of conversations. Faces I'd never seen before. *"I woke up one day and I…and I dreamed about someone trying to talk to me, but I couldn't hear them and they couldn't hear me."*

"It wasn't a dream, Cassidy." Alondra grins with satisfaction. *"It was real. And that someone was me. It can't be a coincidence. On some level, you knew it was important to learn how to communicate with me. You knew this day would come, when we'd meet up at some diner in the middle of a day-long storm."*

"Yeah." It's hard to find any more words to speak or sign. Something deep down stirs—it's that kernel of truth again. Roiling and popping deep inside me.

"Do you believe me now? Believe everything I just told

you?" The look in her eyes tells me she so desperately needs me to say yes.

We stare at each other for what seems like a century and a half. I just can't see why she'd make up a story like this. What's in it for her? But I also can't use her story to convince the police, or anyone else who might be able to help.

Slowly, I sign, *"The way my brain works is…I need proof. I mean, what you're telling me is over-the-top, unbelievable—"*

She heaves a sigh. *"I knew you'd say that."*

"I'm not finished," I sign. *"I may not remember these abductions, but I do believe you."*

"Thanks. That means a lot." She stares at my hand and squeezes it before letting go. *"Do you…want to remember? Maybe it's better if you don't know every little detail."*

"No, I want to know." I glance at the blank white ceiling. That empty space reminds me of the gaps in my memory. It's unsettling. *"I feel like my life is a jigsaw puzzle, but with missing pieces."*

Again I have to wonder if this goes back to that void Angie talked about. The one I've been trying to fill by doing a hundred projects at once. Is it a coping mechanism for my brain so I'll keep memories of the abduction buried?

Alondra gives a knowing nod. *"Then we have to try hypnosis."*

"Funny you should mention that." I dig out Moira's business card and show it to her.

She reads the card and hands it back. *"You should try it. If you want to remember."*

The clanking of dishes reminds me of where we are. We're the only ones left in the diner. I sit up and look out the window. *"The storm seems to be dying down. Finally."*

She checks her watch and frowns. *"And it's getting super late."*

"Where do you live?"

"Alexandria. It's about thirty minutes east of here."

"Do you want to stay at my place tonight? My dad won't mind."

Alondra looks hesitant. *"I…I should go home. But thanks anyway."*

I watch her book an Uber on her phone. When she finishes, I sign, *"Why us? Why do these aliens keep stalking us? Are we really that fascinating?"*

A riot of emotions charges across her features. Confusion. Fear. *"What do you mean by 'keep'?"*

Rubbing my chilled arms, I sign, *"Until tonight, I didn't know for sure. But now? Now I'm convinced. They're after us. Aliens are after us again."*

Me: *Are you up?*

Hayden: *Yeah. The storm was wild, right?*

Me: *Not as wild as what just happened.*

My thumbs hover over the keypad, wondering where to start.

Hayden: Don't stop there.

Me: A girl named Alondra tracked me down after the broadcast. She said she knew me. Said we were abducted by aliens together.

A minute goes by. Two. These days I like to keep a close eye on the time. No doubt Alondra would, too, now that I told her about the night I lost nearly three hours of my life.

Hayden: When?

Me: Seventh grade.

Hayden: And you believe her?

Me: I think so…? She described what I was wearing—

Donald Duck PJs. Hayden, I wore those religiously when I was a kid. And get this—she is deaf. And I think she's the reason why I took up signing. My parents thought it was random at the time. Now I know it wasn't.

Hayden: Interesting…

Me: Interesting?! I thought you of all people would be excited. You're the one who had to convince me we're not alone in the universe, Jedi guy.

Hayden: Excited, you are?

Me: Very funny.

I put the phone down, wishing I could just laugh it off. But he's been super serious about this alien stuff and now suddenly he's making jokes… I don't know what to think anymore. If Hayden won't take me seriously, who will?

TRACK 38

"Imitation of Life"

November 14, 1977

James:

Good to catch up with you at the alumni luncheon last summer.

I've been ensconced at Parallax for several months now. And I have to say, while my predecessor's studies on hypnosis were groundbreaking initially, it's clear to me that the institution has stagnated from the mid-fifties onward. As a result, some staff members appear resistant to change.

Professor Taylor is particularly loyal to Elsworth. This may become problematic, but given his vast psychiatric experience, it is my hope he will become reinvigorated by the new programs I will be initiating in the coming months.

The CIA director has indicated I will have free rein to inject new life into Parallax. To that end, I'd like to extend an invitation to you to join me here as an engineer. I'm most interested in your use of microchips. Certainly, your focus is on veterinary applications, but I'm confident your technology can be of use on the Subjects still remaining in the Parallax program.

We have in the works a unit involving virtual reality that may interest you also. I look forward to discussing this offer further with you. I believe some truly exciting and innovative times are ahead of us at Parallax.

Regards,

Lewis Blake III

TRACK 39

"It Ain't What You Do It's the Way That You Do It"

Present Day

The next day Hayden turns up on my doorstep, wearing a half grin that makes my heart perform Cirque du Soleil-style somersaults.

"The bad news is I haven't fixed your laptop yet," he says, then pulls me in for a kiss. "Hi."

"Okay. And hi." I wasn't expecting him to have any more luck with it than Javier the PC guy, so that isn't exactly devastating. And his lingering, tingling *hello* kiss went a long way to make me feel better. Much like his healing kiss on the day of the great burning panini incident. "Does that mean good news is on its way?"

"It is if you like flying in small planes." He turns on a full-scale, ten-thousand-watt smile. "I got hold of a Cessna Skyhawk for hire. Not exactly a Concorde like I promised. But are you up for a joyride, anyway?"

My jaw drops to the doormat. "Are you for real?"

"Totally." He flashes a card like it's an FBI badge. "I'm licensed to thrill."

"But what's the occasion?" *Is this a date?*

His gaze darts around the quiet neighborhood, then into the house.

"It's okay. Dad's at the office, prepping for his Copenhagen speech."

He pauses before saying in a low voice, "I thought we could have a break from all the UFO stuff."

"You think it's getting to me, don't you?" My gaze narrows.

"It's all you talk about. I want to take you above it all. Literally." He takes a step toward me, drawing me forward. Nuzzling my neck, he says, "We can consider this part of the never-ending tour of Dawson. Also, I wanted to celebrate your television debut yesterday. You were incredible!"

"I couldn't have gotten up there in front of those cameras without your pep talk. Thank you."

I'm amazed to see Hayden shedding his shyness. Did our make-out session *after* the broadcast have something to do with that? Who knows what several more kissing marathons would do to him? I'm willing to find out.

"Don't thank me now," he says. "Thank me when I get you safely back on the ground."

"I know what you're thinking," Hayden says as he finishes his preflight checklist in the tight cockpit. "'If he can barely drive a stick-shift truck, what the hell is he doing flying a plane?'"

"I wasn't thinking that at all, but I am now!" I adjust the headset he gave me. I'd watched him carefully inspect the aircraft inside and out. The focus and concentration on his face, the steadiness of his hands as he flicked various switches and twisted some knobs on the dials—all of that filled me with respect for him.

Last night's storms brought down branches and even

trees in Dawson, but the runway at the municipal airport is clear of debris. There's barely even a stray leaf to be seen. High clouds punctuate the blue sky.

"Trust me, though, I've been a pilot longer than I've been a driver."

I give him a playful wink. "Okay, I'm better at driving cars than you, obviously. But I could never fly a plane."

"Never say never, said James Bond." Hayden grins, putting on a pair of aviator-style Ray-Bans.

Through his headset, he has short, jargon-filled exchanges with the control tower. My confidence in him soars as he taxis toward the single runway. One hand is relaxed on the yoke, the other smoothly controls the power. Boot-clad feet operate the rudder pedals to steer the plane.

Light winds buffet the plane slightly as it rolls. Hayden keeps the aircraft going in a straight line and gives me a reassuring smile.

"Have you, uh, flown this plane before?" I try to keep notes of anxiety out of my voice.

"Not this exact airship," he says, looking out at a windsock.

Wrinkling my nose, I say, "Airship?"

He shakes his head as if berating himself. "Sorry. Pilot-speak. Ship. Plane. Aircraft. I've flown similar ones back home."

I want to remind him that *home* is here now, but I think better about laboring the point now. Especially when he's about to take us into the clouds.

When we trundle to the start of the runway, he waits for the tower to clear him for takeoff. Finally, he turns to me, grinning from earmuff to earmuff. "No turning back now. Ready? Set?"

"Go!" I laugh.

Even with a headset on, the single-propeller engine roars loudly in my ears. My whole body tightens as we hurtle forward, the markings on the asphalt runway turning from sharp white lines to blurred streaks the faster we go. Gradually, the plane lifts and the earth seems to fall away. Hayden continues talking to the control tower, his gaze shifting from the instrument panel to the windows and back again continuously.

I keep my hands jammed under my thighs. No way in hell do I want to accidentally bump a switch and somehow send us into a tailspin. Hayden banks right, giving me an actual bird's-eye view of Dawson. The plane edges higher at a steady rate. Already, at this altitude, the fields resemble a patchwork quilt in fifty shades of autumn. The lanes of the I-15 are a dark gray crack in the landscape.

As he levels the plane again, I catch a glimpse of pure joy beneath those green sunglasses.

"You belong in the skies, don't you?"

"It's what I was born to do. Contrary to what my parents say." Hayden throws me a bittersweet smile.

Shifting, I say, "What do they want you to do instead?"

"Go into the family business. Real estate."

"Right…" I drawl. "No disrespect to your folks, but flying is a better career choice for you."

There's no doubt about it. Hayden's parents struck me as kind of odd. It was almost like they were playing roles, not being themselves. But I have to remember, the McGraws are living on the edge in Sinkhole City. Or so the rumor goes. They must be stressed to their limits.

"I know. They haven't exactly set the property world on fire." The brightness of his smile dims, and I feel crappy for taking him out of the moment of bliss. "Can we not talk about my parents right now?"

"Forget I said anything." I pitch myself higher in my seat, as far as my harness will allow. "Ooh! Check out Half-Mile Lake down there!"

From up here, the water sparkles a deep navy blue. The treetops are green, orange, and red blobs surrounding the lake. Hayden makes a turn, and more of the lake comes into view.

"Oh my God," I say, leaning closer to the glass. "The boat! It's in the middle of the lake!"

"Really?" Hayden says. He couldn't sound less enthused. But I give him a pass because he's studying the horizon.

"It must have broken free during the storm," I muse, casting another look down at *Excalibur* floating around for the first time in more than fifty years.

"That storm was pretty strong," he says. He peers out the window at a virtually cloudless sky.

I study the instrument panel. With its wall-to-wall analog dials and switches, it doesn't look like something that was built this century. Still, it's in pristine condition. "Does this airship have autopilot?"

Hayden shakes his head. "It's an optional extra."

"So this is all you?" I sweep my hands as far as I can.

"Yep. But who needs autopilot? I can operate this thing with my mind." He waggles his eyebrows and takes his hand off the control yoke.

"Oh my God, Hayden!" I squeak, throwing a panicked look out the windows. To my relief, the little aircraft does not nosedive into the Colorado landscape. The engine drones steadily.

"Don't worry, I'm not *that* reckless. This is meant to be a joy flight, not an oh-boy-we're-gonna-die flight." His hands return to the controls and my pulse slows.

I laugh. "Good."

Distant mountain peaks are dusted with early snow. Way above them, a commercial jet glistens in the sunshine. At least, I *think* it's a commercial jet. It has a red, white, and blue tail, so I'm pretty confident.

"Do you ever wonder about UFOs when you're flying?"

Hayden shoots me a stern *We aren't supposed to be talking about aliens* glance. "You mean, have I ever seen one? While flying?"

"Yeah. Like, the other night, you talked about a close encounter you had a long time ago. I was thinking maybe that's what happened."

"Not exactly." He doesn't elaborate. Instead, he adjusts a knob on a dial.

"Sorry, I didn't mean to distract you. And I forgot that I was supposed to forget about aliens."

"You weren't distracting me. It's just…" He trails off. "It's just something I can't explain. To anyone."

"Even to the support group?"

"Especially them," he says emphatically. He arches an eyebrow. "Are you going to another session?"

"Thinking of it." I toy with the shoulder harness. I have to wonder about his reaction to the group. I would have thought he'd appreciate being around people who understood what he went through. What *we* went through. I shake my head. It would be easier to think of it as my own experience if I could actually remember it. "Well, I want to see Moira anyway. She's a hypnotherapist."

"You want to get hypnotized?" he asks in a voice as tight as piano wire. He keeps his eyes glued on the horizon.

"Apparently it helps with memory recall." I twist as far as I can in my seat. "Do you want to try hypnosis, too? So we can find out what happened to us on Saddleback Ridge?"

Though Alondra had insisted the aliens were kind to

us, I'm a little nauseated by the idea of becoming fully cognizant of the poking and the prodding and God knows what else the aliens did to us. But at the same time, I *need* to know. Need to fit together those random jigsaw pieces hovering in my mind.

After a seemingly interminable time, Hayden nods. "Almost a hundred percent. But let me think it over some more."

"I understand. Personal choice and all that."

"Mm-hmm." He adjusts the power, and that reminds me again not to distract him or talk about aliens.

As much as I want to reach out and touch the line of his jaw, the slope of his shoulder, I have to restrain myself. Though, if I'm being honest, he's flying as confidently as someone with decades more experience. Every move he makes is deft, deliberate.

It's sexy as hell.

"Hey, isn't that Eden?" he says, pointing east.

It could be the altitude wreaking havoc on me, but my chest hurts as I gaze down on the sprawling white building. It's planted in the middle of nowhere, surrounded by evergreen forest. From the ground, it's hidden. From up here, it sticks out like a beacon. Again, there are no cars in the lot. No construction vans, no visitors.

The shadow of a passing cloud darkens the estate. Perfect metaphor.

No, that pain in my chest isn't altitude sickness. It's a giant pang of guilt. I'm no closer to getting my mother out of that place.

I place a palm on the window and manage to squeeze out a few words. "Yeah, that's it."

"How's it going with your research?" Hayden asks.

"Slowly. Two reporters got back to me this morning.

But neither of them had any new info that they hadn't said before. Publicly anyway."

"Do you think they have something to hide?"

"It's hard to tell from emails, but I didn't get a gut feeling, no. The person I'm really interested in talking to is still ghosting me. She's a real insider. Which makes me think…"

"*She* has something to hide. Maybe she's the kidnapper!" he says dramatically. I know he's joking, but still if it's true, I really need to be on guard.

The plane continues a little way past Eden, past an old development.

"See those rusty sheds on the ridge line just past Eden?" I say to Hayden. "Those are the old gold mines. They say the tunnels go for miles, but most of them have collapsed. Total no-go area."

"Have they been shut down long?"

"Yeah, at least sixty, seventy years."

"Wonder why there's a radio telescope array there."

Only when the plane banks to the left do I see what he's talking about. An array of three dishes in a clearing, all tilted up toward us. They're not huge, but definitely noticeable from up here.

"You're right," I say, chewing my lip thoughtfully. "Bringing satellite TV to Eden?"

"They seem big for that," he says in a doubtful tone. "They might not even be connected to the estate. There's a separate fence around them. See?"

"It could be a government or university installation or something."

While Hayden talks to the control tower about landing, I keep my eye on Eden until it's finally out of sight.

I'll be back for you, Mom. Don't worry.

"This plane is one of the easiest to land," Hayden says,

maybe misinterpreting my silence as apprehension about getting on the ground.

"You're being way too modest." I smile to let him know I have every confidence in him. "You have skillz."

He beams at me, then gets to work "configuring the plane for landing," as he technically puts it. My stomach drops along with the plane as it makes its descent. But not in an anxious way. I'm more excited to see him do his thing and land this baby.

As he lines the plane up with the runway, my stomach goes a little haywire with fear. Minutes later, there's one bump, then a second one as the back wheels and then the nose gently kiss the asphalt.

The moment he parks the plane in its bay, I shower him with applause. Taking off my headset, I lean in to kiss his cheek. "Great job, Captain Hayden. *Now* can I thank you?"

"Yes, you can!" Grinning, he whips off his headset. He brackets my face with both hands. They're a little sweaty, but I don't care. The heat radiating from them makes every cell in my body hum. I'm in serious danger of melting under his touch. "Cassidy, no matter what happens, on the ground or off, I want you to know I'll always keep you safe."

"Oh, really?" Feeling awkward, I laugh. What I've learned about Hayden McGraw in the past few days is, apart from being a stellar kisser, he can be so old-fashioned. But he wears that description in an adorable way, not a chauvinistic caveman way. "Same," I tell him. "No matter what, I'll do whatever it takes to keep *you* safe."

His gaze sears into mine, then he kisses me. Despite my vows not to, I lose all track of time.

TRACK 40

"Don't Bring Me Down"

MEMORANDUM FROM THE DIRECTOR OF THE CENTRAL INTELLIGENCE AGENCY

CLASSIFICATION: TOP SECRET

SUBJECT: PARALLAX DISBANDMENT

November 15, 1984

ATTN: Senator Lewis Blake

As you are no doubt aware, President-Elect Thomas Flanagan has announced spending cuts to nonessential programs. To this end, my office has been instructed to identify programs that no longer fulfill a purpose within the CIA's overall operations. Under your stewardship, the program's budget has blown out by forty-five percent and, frankly, we have seen very little in terms of cost benefit. No new studies or developments have come forward from Parallax in the past two years. Therefore, we regret to inform you the project must be disbanded.

We expect decommissioning of the Colorado facilities to begin January 2, 1985, with a view to completion by no later than June 30, 1985. It is understood your existing budget will cover the removal and disposal of equipment, staff redundancies, and deprogramming of remaining Subjects.

Parallax can be proud of its history in developing advanced hypnosis techniques and furthering microchip technology. The President-Elect and the CIA thank you for your loyal service. If you wish to discuss joining another project, I would be happy to schedule a meeting.

Sincerely,

Edward P. Philips
CIA Director

TRACK 41

"Saturn's Rings"

Present Day

"Thanks again for seeing me on short notice, Moira."

"I knew you'd take me up on my offer," she says, sliding a steel door open and waving me in. Dressed in a flowing gold gown with pleated batwing sleeves, she looks more like a magician than a licensed hypnotherapist. Her black hair is javelin-straight today. On each of her elegant fingers, she wears two gold rings.

When I called, Moira suggested I come to her home office. I didn't expect *this*. The industrial loft conversion is totally open-plan, including the bathroom. Massive abstract artworks hang on red-brick walls. Thick layers of oil paint look like they were lashed onto the canvas by someone in a fit of temper. I was excited on the drive to Bartlett, but now my body's all locked up with tension.

I *so* hope I don't need to use that bathroom while I'm here.

"I'm not saying you're transparent or predictable, but you clearly have a certain level of curiosity," she says in a knowing tone. "I had a feeling your anonymous friend *wouldn't* come knocking on my door. He's a very closed-off person, isn't he? Very guarded."

"Only with people he doesn't know. He's been burned in the past." I shift from foot to foot, suddenly consumed with the thought that I hadn't done a background check on Moira. How could I be so careless as to just trust that she is qualified? Anybody could print up a business card and say they are a hypnotist.

Moira gestures for me to sit on an electric-blue velvet sofa that incidentally matches her eye makeup. A camera is set up on a tripod.

"You record the sessions?"

"Yes, but it's totally up to you. It doesn't have to be recorded." She sinks gracefully into a purple paisley armchair opposite me and rearranges her sleeves.

I stare at the camera. "How do I know the footage isn't going to end up on YouTube or something?"

"I promise it won't, but if it makes you feel better, I will not press the record button while you're under. Sound good?" When I nod, she continues. "I write notes for my own clinical files. Even my memory can be fallible."

"Can't you hypnotize yourself if you forget?"

"Sure. There are ways." She smiles. "But let's bring this back to you. What exactly do you want out of this session?"

"I just want to know if I really have been abducted by aliens." I fold and unfold my hands. I'm still not totally relaxed, but I am feeling less suspicious about her qualifications. "Since the support group meeting, I've been *told* I was abducted when I was twelve."

Moira's mouth falls open. She quickly recovers and sits straighter. "So you've had multiple abductions."

I cringe. "Maybe. Possibly? And if that's the case, I want to figure out what the hell to do about it."

One thing I won't be doing is selling my story to Aunt Carole's favorite tabloids.

What would my dad say? If I tell him, he'll probably find some way to have aliens arrested and put on trial.

"Okay, so here's where I explain a couple things before we start," Moira says. She crosses her legs and grabs an iPad from the coffee table between us. "Sometimes when we use hypnosis to bring up memories, it's not always an accurate, objective picture of what happened in the past. Memories may be colored by your own perceptions, by your distortions."

"You mean, what I remember might not actually be what happened?" I frown. "Then what's the point of doing this?"

"It can still give you clarity. Peace of mind, even."

"Peace of mind that I'm not *losing* my mind?"

"Some people like to think of it that way. I call it enlightenment." She chuckles, putting me at ease. In her natural environment, despite the costume, she seems less theatrical and more like a regular human being.

"I'm ready to be enlightened. On film."

Moira smiles and presses a button on the camera. She grabs the tablet and brings up a GIF of black-and-white stripes moving in an endless spiral. "Keep your eyes on the white swirls. Watch them go around…and…around…and around. Take a deep breath in. Five, four, three, two, one. Breathe out. Five, four, three, two, one."

My thoughts soon slow down as I focus on the sound of Moira's soft speech and the perpetual spiral.

"Breathe in…breathe out. That's it. Your legs are feeling heavy. You're sinking into the sofa. Breathe in. Breathe out. Now your torso's getting heavy. In…out. Your shoulders are heavy. Eyelids are drooping. Your head's like a bowling ball. Sinking. Breathing in. Breathing out. Entire body completely relaxed. Listening only to me."

I want to keep my eyes open to keep watching Moira

and the ribbon of white in the spiral. But it's hard. All I want to do is sleep.

"Don't fight it, Cassidy. Let your mind go still. Breathe in. Breathe out..."

I become aware of wind rushing through my nostrils, filling my lungs. Feel the muscles contract to force air back out. Behind my closed eyelids, I sense the room becoming dimmer and dimmer, till there's no light at all. Just pitch-black darkness. I've sunk so deep into the couch that I no longer feel the softness of the cushions. Still falling.

Moira's voice sounds far away, eventually fading into nothing.

I'm still falling into oblivion.

When will I hit rock bottom? Is there a rock bottom? Does the universe have a bottom?

As soon as those thoughts whirl through my brain, my fall is broken.

I land on a hard bench. The force of the fall startles me awake. Looking up, I see a blank white ceiling. At least I think it's the ceiling. It seems to be several stories high.

The walls are white now. Everything's white. It's like I'm in the middle of a blizzard but without the snow driving into my eyeballs. I'm cold. So, so cold.

Beside me is a figure silhouetted by a bright white light shining from a source that I can't figure out.

I sense strong shoulders. A determined posture. So familiar. So...Hayden.

"Hayden, is that you?" I murmur.

The figure leans over me. A face sharpens. A gray-purple alien face with eyes that look like gaping black holes.

My body jerks in response. The figure's slit-like mouth opens ever so slightly.

"It's me," says the alien in Hayden's voice. "I'll keep you safe."

I scream. "No! Get away from me! Don't come near me! Oh God, why can't you let us go? Haven't you done enough?"

The alien screeches. Two more aliens rush to the bed and stare at me, also screeching. Then more surround me. Their cries are loud enough to shatter glass.

Suddenly, a voice cuts through the noise like a thunderclap. "One, two, three. Wake up, Cassidy."

Groggy, I struggle to sit up, then fall back on the cushions. "Am I awake?"

"You're awake. You're in my loft," Moira says in her soothing, melodic voice. "You don't have to get up right away. Ease into it."

My vision sharpens. Those violent-looking paintings glare down from the walls. Sunlight bounces off spherical glass paperweights. This is no spaceship.

"How do you feel?" Moira asks. In no way does she seem alarmed or even the slightest bit concerned.

"Did you get it all on video?" My heartbeat thunders through my body. The coldness I felt in the presence of aliens is still with me.

Moira's brow furrows. "Yes, it was running, but to be honest, there wasn't a lot to capture."

"Capture. Not the best word choice," I mutter, catching my breath. I zero in on the worn knees of my jeans. In the vision, I wasn't wearing much. Just some paper-thin gown that reached halfway down my thighs.

"Of course. I'm sorry." Moira takes the camera off its tripod. "I mean you didn't respond to my suggestions out loud. But that's okay. People respond to hypnosis in different ways."

"Let me see that clip." Sure enough, there I am lying

serenely on the couch as Moira's soothing voice pulls me under.

In the ten-minute recording, I moan once or twice. My eyelids flutter here and there. A twitch of my foot. But most of it is me just…sleeping like a lamb.

There was no sign of me freaking out. No clue that I saw my new boyfriend morphing into an alien.

Moira peers at me curiously. "What did you see when you were under?"

Grimacing, I say, "It…it's too embarrassing. It had to be a nightmare, not a memory. My subconscious is making stuff up."

"Are you sure?" She tilts her head in confusion.

I picture Hayden's firm jaw, espresso-brown eyes, and rosy lips I'd kiss all day and all night given the chance. Conjure the sexy slope of his shoulders, lean torso, and long legs. Think about the strong hands that have gently cupped my face and turned me into a puddle. Yep, physically he's a fine example of a male human. He's not a bobble-headed alien.

"I'm sure. Can we try something else?" I ask Moira. "Like, I've read that you can use hypnosis to stop bad habits."

"Yes, I've helped people stop smoking, stop procrastinating, you name it."

"Is it possible, then, to plant a suggestion in my head? Something that'll help me remember my next alien abduction?"

Moira leans forward, her eyes intense. "You think you'll be abducted again?"

I steel my spine. "The last thing I want is for aliens from planet Zimbot to make a habit out of kidnapping me. But if they do it again, I have to be able to remember."

And then stop them once and for all.

TRACK 42

"The Fear"

November 30, 1985

Charles Hobart, Esq.
Attorney at Law
15653 First Avenue
Dawson, CO 80009

CONFIDENTIAL

Charlie:

Enclosed is my signed letter of engagement with your firm. I look forward to many years of working together.

Allow me to take this opportunity to reiterate the need for utmost confidentiality with regard to the sensitive work of the Parallax Human Intervention Unit. As per our agreement, neither you nor your office is permitted to communicate with my staff in any manner, including by telephone, by mail, in person, or by electronic means, et cetera. All contact must be through my personal telephone number, which I have previously provided to you. And, of course, the work of Parallax must not be discussed with anyone—period.

On another note, I invite you to enjoy a little down time at Eden Estate. The spa facilities are coming along nicely. Perhaps you'd like to become one of my first guinea pigs, so to speak.

Senator Lewis Blake III

TRACK 43

"Rapture"

Present Day

"No shortcuts this time, okay?" I strap myself into Hayden's truck on homecoming night. It's filled with the sweet aroma of a spilled soda mixed with the earthy cologne Hayden uses. I lift my delicate shoes to make sure I haven't put my foot into a puddle of Coke.

Almost a week has passed since Moira hypnotized me and buried the suggestion in my mind about remembering UFO visits. I've not encountered an alien in that time. Which means either I truly have not been paid a visit or I have been abducted but the "spell" Moira cast failed.

I spent a lot of time drilling down on Mom's playlist choices, listening for clues. "The Man Who Stole a Leopard" by Duran Duran has really grown on me. The song tells the story of a man who took an animal from the wild and kept her confined for his own selfish enjoyment. He told himself he loved the big cat. But keeping something trapped in a place where they don't belong isn't love. It's torture.

After interpreting every element of that track, I researched convicted animal hoarders and cyber visited some very dark places. If Jane is still alive, I hope to God she's safe.

Hayden turns on the engine and grins. "I can take the long way, if you want. Drive down every street in town until we get to school."

When he told me he's never been to a homecoming dance before, I very cordially asked him to be my date. Since that day, nothing has wiped the smile off Hayden's face. It made a nice change from the shy, guarded Hayden who arrived here weeks ago. I noticed he's become a lot more social lately, not hiding away.

Dress-wise, I went for the KISS principle—a navy-blue jersey boat-neck dress with three-quarter sleeves that I'd pulled from Mom's old closet. It's tighter and shorter on me than it ever was on her, but still kind of warm enough to keep the fall chill at bay. I'm regretting the silver pointy-toed heels I also took from my mother's abandoned stash. It feels like I'm walking on needles. Maybe, after a while, my feet will go numb and I won't notice the pain anymore. And also temporarily forget that my work on the case is going as slow as molasses.

Hayden's sartorial choice is a black slim-cut suit. The top of his crisp pale-blue shirt is unbuttoned. No tie. The ensemble fits him so well, though. We look like a pair of yuppies from the eighties.

As we drive out of my cul-de-sac, the hulking form of Saddleback Ridge comes into view. A small shudder rolls through me. I cast a wary, thoughtful look out the windshield. "You know what we need? Dash cams."

"So if *it* happens again, we'll have it on camera?" He raises his brows, impressed. "Genius idea."

My mouth puckers. "Of course, I would rather not be kidnapped by aliens again."

"But just in case." He reaches across the bench seat and finds my hand, then he very deliberately runs his thumb along my skin. The warmth of his body heats up mine.

Do we have to go to the dance?

I just want to be alone with him.

Behind us several cars honk us into reality. Hayden jumps, his hand flying back to the steering wheel. In his haste, he messes up with the clutch again and stalls the truck.

Red-faced, he gives a courtesy wave to the driver behind us before they get another chance to honk.

I can't help but laugh. "Where did you learn to drive anyway?"

"YouTube. It's the repository of all wisdom." He flashes a grin. "Kidding. I got through driver's ed. Barely. But practice makes perfect, right?"

"Yeah. A *lot* of practice," I tease.

The truck glides down Second Avenue and turns into MacKenzie. Looks like he's taking the shortcut after all. Hayden turns up the radio. A fiddle twangs as a singer moans about being oh-so-sad and lonely because his "woman" cheated on him. He turns it back down again.

At a traffic light two blocks from school, Hayden angles his head toward me. "I have to make a confession—I can't dance. I'm like an octopus on roller skates, just so you know."

I hide a grin at the image of tentacles flailing and doing awkward splits under a mirror ball. "And this is a big deal because…?"

"Isn't that why people go to dances? You know, to dance?"

"No, people go to show off and make out." I laugh. But instead of laughing with me, Hayden looks even more nervous. He wipes his hands on his freshly ironed trousers. "You'll be fine. I'm no Maddie Ziegler on the dance floor, either."

When we finally reach the school parking lot, it's

heaving with cars and kids. A pink stretch Hummer blocks the main building's entrance. All around us I see bright, happy, excited faces. In direct contrast, Hayden looks terror-stricken. Eyes like a startled meerkat. He's so rigid I'm afraid I'll have to use a crowbar to get him out. My heart melts for him. He's obviously lived a very sheltered life up until now.

Softly, I tell him, "We don't have to go in if you're too freaked. It's not like we get extra credit for attendance."

Cutting the engine, Hayden turns to me. His dark eyes pierce into mine. I want to look away, but I can't. I take in a view of a jaw slightly roughened by stubble. Dark pink lips drawn in a firm line. A strong chest that's rising and falling rapidly. His fingers curl around the steering wheel, and for a few seconds I imagine those hands wandering all over on my body.

"Okay, let's make a deal," I say, forcing hot and steamy thoughts from my mind. "We have one drink. Spiked, preferably. One conversation with friends. One dance. And if you're still not having fun, we can leave. Together."

"We have to do each of those things?"

"At least once. And it can't be one out of three, or two out of three. We have to drink, talk, *and* dance like octopuses on roller skates." I hold out my hand for him to shake.

"All right." He slides his hand into mine, and his warmth makes my head swim. "But if that drink isn't spiked, we are outta here."

"Just as long as by 'we,' you mean 'you and me.'" I grin and grab the door handle.

"Wait, don't move."

Hayden jumps out, goes around the front of the truck and opens my door. He takes both my hands and pulls me up. My feet get tangled in his, and I lurch into the door. He puts his arms around my waist, steadying me.

I stop breathing.

An electric pulse seems to throb between us, drawing us closer. Inch by inch. His warm, minty breath brushes tantalizingly on my lips. The voices around us fade out like a song. I swear the only sound I'm conscious of is a thunderous heartbeat. His or mine, I'm not sure. Probably his, because I'm out of breath. But the thudding is fast and furious. Overwhelming. Hayden's hands rest on my hips like they belong there.

Just as fast, the spell breaks with the noisy arrival of a carload of kids beside us. We blink at each other.

Voices become louder and more intrusive. Someone calls out to me and says something. I don't know who. Don't know what. I just send a distracted wave and smile in their general direction. The group of kids moves away.

I take a slow, unsteady step back.

"I know what you're thinking," I say, my voice husky. Oxygen starts to return to my brain. "And you're wrong."

"Oh? What am I wrong about?" he croaks. Hayden takes my hands and twirls me once before releasing me. All. Too. Soon.

"What just happened there does not count as dancing. So our scoreboard is still zero out of three."

"This punch isn't spiked," I note with disappointment, swirling ice around the plastic cup. I also note the glares shooting from some of the girls around me. One trio of freshmen in particular alternates between looking at me with envy and looking at Hayden with lust. Hayden seems oblivious to all types of stares.

Shifting from foot to foot, I try to keep my weight off these toe-squishing shoes. I wonder where Angie and Jake are.

I'm half hoping he says he can't make it on account of a spontaneous coma. I'm not sure I can pretend I don't know him. Of course, Angie would be heartbroken if he stands her up for a third time.

"Let's just pretend we're drunk. No one will care." He puts down his half-empty cup. "Aren't those your friends over there?"

I follow his gaze to the gym's south entrance. Lisa and Billie are sauntering through the door hand in hand. The two of them giggle like elementary schoolgirls and make a beeline for us.

"Cassidy! You look amazing," Lisa says, squeezing me in a bear hug. Her red hair is coated in glitter. She turns to Hayden. "Doesn't she look incredible? You did tell her, right?"

"Three times." Hayden throws an arm around my shoulders. I could get used to the buzz of electricity I get every time he touches me. "Using different adjectives, too."

Lisa and Billie laugh uproariously. It's not hard to see they've had something a little more risqué than Budweiser.

Billie looks over the dancers to the DJ booth onstage. The end of a bouncy pop song mixes seamlessly with a bouncy hip-hop song. "I love this one! Let's get out there, you guys!"

She drags Lisa behind her, and they shimmy into the middle of the crowded dance floor. Every now and then, they jump head and shoulders above everyone else.

Beneath my feet, the polished timber vibrates. More kids are drawn to the dance floor.

I pry the cup out of his hand and tug on his arm. "We'd

better do what Billie says. No telling what she'll do if we don't get out there. Report us to the dance police, is my guess."

Hayden stares at the dancing crowd. There's a range of styles going on out there. Body-locking by stiff-legged jocks. Vigorous arm-waving and high kicks by the cheerleaders. Vague swaying movements from the less coordinated. Tangy salsa in the shadows by a couple out of the chaperones' eye line.

A few kids are scattered around the bleachers lining one wall of the gym. Misery's stamped over their faces, making me wonder if they really are here only to get extra credit.

"If you want, we can check out a few dance tutorials on TikTok. Wanna learn how to pop and lock?" I bust into a poor imitation of hip-hop moves.

"Confession time. I may or may not have watched *Dirty Dancing* right before I picked you up." He snares my hand. "Let's see if anything sunk in."

He spins me twice, then leads me toward the center of the floor. We get bounced around like we're inside a pinball machine. But no one seems to care about getting pinged. Smiles glow broadly under the black light. Everyone's in their own groove. The beat's frenetic. My pulse accelerates in time with the music. In this cauldron, it's hard to move. I shuffle my feet from side to side in an approximation of dancing while others take to simply jumping up and down on the spot. The crowd pushes Hayden and me closer.

He grabs me by the wrists, then starts reeling me in and out before spinning me around three times. A colorful blur races before my eyes as he spins me again. On another part of the dance floor, Lisa and Billie are flailing their arms, oblivious to everyone and everything.

Hayden leads with a fast pace. I keep waiting for one

of those teen movie moments, when the music changes to something slow and sexy. When the teen movie couple is left standing with their arms folded, looking around awkwardly, watching everyone else draw together as if pulled by a magnetic force.

None of that happens.

A strobe light flashes, burning right into my retinas at millisecond intervals. White light captures people in funny mid-dance poses as if they're in a stop-motion cartoon. But in the dark phases, when I should see nothing, faces are odd. Not-so-funny. Large, elongated heads. And black eyes. Big, wide, staring black eyes.

I stop dead.

But still under the spell of the strobe, Hayden doesn't notice. He goes on dancing the mambo with his eyes closed.

Turning my head, I see dozens of figures swaying and moving. Thin, insect-like arms fling in all directions. The kaleidoscope of colors blend into a putrid khaki green.

My skin starts to boil. Thousands of tiny hot needles seem to poke up and down my body like in a stadium wave formation. At the same time, those eerie black eyes all stare intently at me. I blink hard, but that does nothing to clear away the image of those damn eyes.

"Hayden…" I try to shout his name, but it comes out like a whisper from a mouse. With my arms extended out wide, I try to grab onto him. But, inexplicably, I can't connect with him. My arms go straight through him.

This isn't real, I insist to myself. *It's got to be a dream. It's got to be. That'd make sense. Why else would you be out on a date with someone mega-hot like Hayden McGraw?*

The strobe light pulses impossibly fast.

Now I can't move, even if I wanted to. I try to lift my arms. They're sticks of lead dangling at my sides. My legs are stuck to the floor, too. Heaviness sets in my chest, making it hard to breathe.

All the while, Hayden dances on and on.

I try to shout again. "Hayden!"

This time he hears me. His eyelids snap open, and he sees me paralyzed in front of him. He squeezes my shoulders with both hands. I feel the heat and pressure of his touch.

I guess I'm not dreaming after all.

"Cassidy?" Hayden shakes me gently.

The moment he speaks, color returns to the dance floor. Those spooky faces and eyes vanish.

Were they even there in the first place?

TRACK 44

"Science Fiction"

Present Day

My head hurts. The music suddenly sounds sharp and sinister. But as I look around me, everyone else seems to be enjoying it.

"Cassidy?" Hayden says, squeezing my shoulders again.

I duck away. The look of concern he's giving me makes me feel guilty for ruining his night. "Can we go? I'm not good with crowds. I…I just have to get out of here."

He frowns deeply. Taking me by the hand, he pulls me toward the refreshments table. "You're really hot."

Now that I'm out of the sweaty, pulsing dancers, I can manage a weak smile. "Thanks. So are you."

Hayden doesn't laugh or even smile. "No, I mean you're burning up."

"Yeah, maybe I'm coming down with something. A fever," I mumble.

I cast a wary look at the dance floor. There's just a bunch of ordinary-looking high school kids. All shapes. All sizes. All kinds of fashion sense—Jim Edwards in his shiny silver pants, case in point. Some may be strange. But I don't think any of them look like they're from out of this world.

"Drink this." Hayden hands me an icy-cold cup.

Thirsty as I feel, I push the cup away. "That stuff's spiked after all. I'll get something from the vending machine outside."

I push past Hayden and run straight into Angie.

"Hey, guys!" Angie squeals. The sweet odor of weed wafts from her as she hugs me. Her gold dress slides under my hands. "I saw you guys dancing. Aren't you so cute together? Where are you going? You can't leave now! Jacob hasn't arrived yet."

"I…I'm so sorry. I'm not feeling well." I pull away from Angie. Every instinct screams at me to get out of here before the vision of insect-like creatures comes back.

Hayden steps closer and puts an arm around me. "We made a deal before we came here. One drink, one convo, one dance."

"Three out of three," I say. "So…we've got to go now. We've seen and done it all."

Angie's lips curve mischievously. "Okay, then. Run along. I won't wait up for you."

The sound of her giggles chases after me as I run out to the corridor, following the white cinderblock wall closely. A few kids linger outside the restrooms. I head in the opposite direction for the glowing red vending machine. Hayden catches up to me.

He takes me by both arms and searches my face. A shadow darkens his eyes. His jaw clicks. "Something happened."

I lean back against the wall and grip my head. A tremor rockets through me. Those green angular faces seemed so real. "I shouldn't have watched *Close Encounters of the Third Kind* last night."

"What's that got to do with anything?"

I wince and look back toward the gym. Hayden would

have seen aliens if they were really there. Hell, the whole school would've seen them and stampeded. "I just thought I saw something weird on the dance floor. I'm sure it was all those flashing lights messing with my vision."

A gym door bursts open, and the sound of music and laughter crashes into my ears. I watch a freshman dry-heaving as he sprints up the hall to the restroom.

"Come on, let's get out of here," I say. "Before these kids turn into zombies."

"Where do you want to go?" Hayden asks, running after me.

"Somewhere peaceful." I glance at the mayhem around us, my heartbeat still thudding hard. I look back at Hayden, who's standing there looking at me like I'm the most important thing on the planet, and my pulse gets out of control. "But I'm so not ready to go home."

Hayden chews his lip thoughtfully, then smiles. "I know a place. Let *me* show you around for once."

At Watkins Lookout, somewhere over Saddleback Ridge, we lean against the warm hood of Hayden's truck. The place is deserted. Up here, without the ambient glow of city lights, the constellations are brighter than I've ever seen them. Stars pulse blue, green, even pink. I've always been fascinated by the night sky, but now I'm frightened by what's in the dark spaces between the stars and planets. What's up there? *Who's* up there?

With the lightest of touches, Hayden puts a finger under my chin. "Is this the peacefulness you were looking for?"

"Uh-huh." It's beyond corny, but staring into his eyes right now, I get lost. Even if I had a compass, I wouldn't want to find my way back to Earth. Right now, nothing else matters but the two of us here.

His hand finds its way to the back of my neck. He holds it there for a few moments. The warmth of his palm seems to melt into my muscles, leaving me relaxed, yet almost giddy.

Little by little, he leans close. His breath wisps over my cheek and hair. Heat radiates from his body to mine, and I feel like every cell in my body is a whirling dervish. All either of us has to do is shift forward by a fraction and our lips will meet.

Hayden strokes my cheek, setting a fire there that quickly spreads. He breathes my name before slowly lowering his head, bringing his lips to mine in a light-as-a-feather touch. Before I know it, my hand inches into his hair. His kiss grows firmer, deeper, and that fire becomes a full-on inferno.

Time is lost. Again. But this time, I don't care. This kiss can stretch on for eternity as far as I'm concerned.

Sooner rather than later, though, we have to come up for fresh air.

"Phew," I say, panting. "I guess I'm forgiven for cutting your first homecoming dance short?"

He brushes my lips with his for a sweet, lingering moment. "You are now."

I laugh and snuggle under his arm. "How is it possible that you never went to a homecoming dance before?"

"Correction, *any* dance." After a thoughtful sigh, he says, "I just tried not to get involved with social stuff at my other schools."

"Because you had to move cities so much?"

"Yeah."

I watch a plane move across the sky, high above the

horizon, its lights blinking intermittently. Along with the chirping of insects, all I can hear is the sound of Hayden's breathing. It's quiet, but fast. And I'm not so sure it's because he's still trying to refill his lungs after kissing me senseless.

"Tell me about her," I whisper at last.

He gulps audibly. "Who?"

"The girl you left behind." I arch back a little so I can see his face, but he turns away. "Did you break your no-socializing rule because I remind you of her?"

Hayden takes a step back. Which gives me just enough room to kick myself for ruining the moment. He looks down at the dirt. "Her name was Kalexy. She, uh…she passed away."

My hand leaps to my mouth. "Oh my God, I'm so sorry—"

"It's okay, really." He gives me a sad smile. "It's just that I didn't get to say a real goodbye to her. We had…we had already moved."

"To Dawson?"

"Uh, n-no," he stammers. "We'd moved to Maine. She was far…far away. And then I got word she was gone. It happened last year."

I watch myriad emotions swirl in his eyes. Torment, even. My heart aches for him. It's hard for me to feel envious of a girl whose life was cut short. "I can see she meant a lot to you."

"She was my best friend. We were young but had been told we were destined to be together. We learned to fly at the same academy." He angles his head to the sky as if picturing her soaring above.

And maybe she is. Maybe that satellite that's passing overhead is actually her spirit. If you believe in that sort of thing.

"That's really special," I murmur.

"You have a lot in common with her. She would never let anything get in the way of what she wanted." Hayden stares at me, his arms encircling my waist. "But I know you're not Kalexy. And I wouldn't want you to be, anyway. I like who you are, not who you're not."

"Maybe we're long-lost relatives, if we kind of look similar," I say. "There aren't a lot of Dutch-Indonesians in this corner of the world. Wouldn't it be great to find out? Do you have a picture? What's her last name?"

"No, she wasn't Dutch-Indonesian, that I can tell you." He shakes his head. The sorrow in his eyes makes me think twice about pumping him for more information. It looks like it physically hurts him to talk about Kalexy.

I think back to when I met his family. "Is…is that why your family was a little weird the night I met them? They thought they saw a ghost?"

His eyes grow huge. "You thought my family was weird?"

"Well," I laugh awkwardly, "if you remember, I said your parents seemed kinda tense. Meaning…weird. And in my defense, you *did* mention your little sis was a monster."

"It's true." He laughs along with me. "But they couldn't see the resemblance."

I can't help noticing he doesn't shed any light on why his mom and dad seemed uptight that night. Which is totally fine. Still, I'm curious.

"I'd love to hear more about Kalexy someday," I say, squeezing his hands. "But you don't have to say anything if it's too painful."

"Yeah, someday." Hayden squeezes my hands even harder. "But you know what? Finding you here, I think it's a sign. I want to make the best of things right where I am. I'm meant to be here. Be with you."

In reply, I hook my arms around his neck and kiss him

deeply. We're interrupted sometime later by the arrival of a couple of cars. Their headlights shine into our eyes as they each veer left and right a short distance from Hayden's truck.

"Oh, damn. The dance must be over," I say, my arms still wrapped tightly around Hayden.

He heaves a sigh as two more cars crest the hill behind us. "Should we head home?"

"Do we have to?" I say in a suggestive tone, running a finger down his face.

Hayden checks his pockets and frowns. "Maybe not. Since I think I've lost my keys."

"Ohhhh," I say. "I didn't hear them fall out."

"Neither did I." He drops to the ground and uses his phone's flashlight to look under the car. He kicks at small rocks and shrubs.

"I'll check inside the truck." I clamber in, searching the most obvious place first—the ignition. But the key slot is empty. The weak light from the overhead bulb is useless. I pat around the floor and in between the seats.

Hayden pokes his head into the cab. "Anything?"

"Nada." I sit back on the vinyl bench seat.

He scratches his head. "I don't understand how I could've lost them."

"We were kinda preoccupied," I say. My blood heats as he shoots me a seductive look. "Are you in the auto club?"

"Not yet. I was planning on joining." A corner of his mouth twitches as he drums his fingers on the dash. He looks deep in thought. "I could, uh…do something. I'm not sure what you'll think of me and how I learned how to do it."

"What, are you going to push this beast down Saddleback Ridge?" I say, arching a brow.

"Not exactly. Shuffle back. I'm coming in." Hayden

swings into the driver's seat. He fumbles under the dash, pulling down a bunch of colored electrical cables.

"Ooh, you're going to hot-wire this baby?" I fan myself. "Don't tell me—you learned this on YouTube."

"Where else?" He grins. "Okay, don't watch me. I get self-conscious when I boost cars. I wanna get this right the first time. And not electrocute myself."

"Fine." I scoot across so my back is against the passenger door. Though I cover my eyes with my hands, I detect a small flash of light. Then comes a *click* and a faint sparking sound. Within seconds, the starter motor whines, then the engine rumbles to life.

"Huh? Huh?" he says triumphantly and beats his chest. I slide across the bench seat, and he pulls me closer. Deliciously close. "Who needs keys?"

"Just don't do anything to lose the keys to my heart." *Wow, Cassidy. Who ordered the cheese?*

"Never." He kisses me, and a tingle shimmies from my lips to my toes.

I shut out the world around us and melt into Hayden. The only thing that could tear us apart now is an alien invasion. And seriously, what are the chances of that happening?

TRACK 45

"Boom Clap"

Present Day

Call it a Jedi mind trick, but Hayden could sense right away that Cassidy was disturbed by whatever it was she'd seen on the dance floor. Taking her to Watkins Lookout to debrief seemed like a great idea to rebalance the Force.

Until she questioned him about the girl he'd said resembled her.

He couldn't lie to himself. Losing Kalexy had cut him like a laser beam. They *were* best friends. All their short lives, they were told they would be partnered once they reached adulthood. Once they were ready to form a family unit. As he grew older on Earth, he realized he wasn't in love with Kalexy. Still, he mourned her when he got word she'd passed away.

And, yes, Cassidy bore a resemblance to Kalexy. And, yes, it stopped him in his tracks when he first saw her in the crowded halls of Dawson High. It made his job as an Observer even harder.

Kissing her, though, was easy. He was attracted to her drive to save her mother, to her open smiles, to her authenticity, to the way she was determined to help him fit in. The latter, of course, was something he didn't know he craved until he met her.

He just wished he could show her *his* true, authentic self. Time and time again, Sam and Lindsay warned him not to use his Aguan abilities on Earth. He wanted to obey. He really did.

But after losing his keys—such an Earthling thing to do—he had no choice but to use telekinesis. Cassidy was none the wiser as he "hot-wired" the truck not with his hands but his mind.

Also very human? To be so caught up in the moment of kissing Cassidy that he did not see they were about to be ambushed.

TRACK 46

"Wicked Game"

Four Years Ago

"Retired Senator in Curbside Scuffle"
The Capitol Hill Courier
Staff Writer

In extraordinary scenes outside the Capitol Building today, Secret Service agents were forced to shield Senator Lewis Blake III (R - CO) from a lone activist, who claimed he'd been "brainwashed" by the senator.

Witnesses say the activist, a man described as being in his fifties, approached retired Senator Blake.

"The guy was polite at first," said an onlooker. "But then he snapped and pulled out a bunch of papers and started shouting about aliens and UFOs and black-ops cover-ups."

The man allegedly pushed a Secret Service agent into the senator before absconding down Maryland Avenue on foot. The senator ordered the agents not to give chase. However, the onlooker observed a car from the senator's convoy quietly leaving in the direction of the activist.

Senator Blake appeared to dismiss the man's actions, declaring loudly that he was "harmless" and "exercising his democratic rights." The senator was swiftly escorted into a waiting limousine.

Senator Blake is known for running a tightly controlled office and for his hardline stance against immigration intake. In 2002, he introduced a controversial bill designed to curtail freedom of information laws, which was voted down after weeks of heated debate.

Calls to Senator Blake's office were not answered. It's understood the senator is traveling to his home state of Colorado for long-planned meetings with constituents.

TRACK 47

"I Will Follow You"

Present Day

"Trust Angie to call a snap post-dance debrief and show up late!" Lisa laughs as our waitress brings her an espresso.

"Where's Billie?" I ask, scratching my arm. That insect bite site has flared up again. Maybe I'm allergic to something.

"Sleeping in. She was smart enough to know Angie wouldn't turn up on time anyway."

Lisa and I both arrived this morning on time, five minutes ago. But in between getting our orders taken and fielding apologetic texts from Angie, we haven't had a chance to talk yet.

"I could have done with an extra couple of hours in bed. If there isn't a law about compulsory sleeping in on weekends, there should be." I yawn and slosh an extra helping of half-and-half into my coffee mug. By the time Hayden got me home, it was almost one a.m.

"That reminds me," Lisa says, digging into her purse and producing a fist-sized amber bottle. "I bought these for you at the drugstore."

Screwing up my face, I say, "Vitamins?"

"To stop you from falling asleep in class."

"Ah, you mean 'vitamins,'" I say, using air quotes.

"Legit vitamins, minerals, and herbs," she insists, dropping the bottle into my bag. "Take two and call me in the morning."

"Thanks, Dr. Cannon." I grin, touched by her thoughtfulness.

Through the window, I watch Angie rush out of her convertible. She points the remote lock over her shoulder as she runs across the diner's crowded parking lot. Once she's inside, a few people wave at her as she makes her way to us in the corner.

Angie looks a bit less put-together than usual. Her brown hair is tangled. Eyeliner uneven. Russet-colored dress rumpled. But her huge grin is big enough to make anyone overlook those things. This is not the face of someone who'd been stood up at homecoming.

"Hi and hi!" She slides into the booth, bumping me. Coffee splashes out of my cup. "Oops, sorry."

"Hey, you!" I mop up the coffee spill with a paper napkin. "Good to see you all chipper this very early morning. I'm guessing Jake, uh, Jacob turned up after I left?"

Angie nods happily. "But since we all went our separate ways so quickly last night, I want to know everything that happened." She points a chipped-polish fingernail across the table at me. "Starting with you."

"Give her a chance to wake up," Lisa says.

I throw her a grateful look. "There isn't a lot to say. Hayden and I are a thing. I'm sorry I didn't tell you about him. I wanted to find out for myself first whether my feelings for him were real. And they were real. *Are* real."

"I'm really happy for you, Cassidy. Nothing to apologize for," Lisa says. "We get it, don't we, Angie?"

"Totally." Angie nods. After the waitress takes her order, she continues. "Maybe we could all go out on a triple date, huh? It's a shame you didn't meet Jacob last night, Cassidy. He's gorgeous, isn't he, Lisa?"

Angie shows us a series of photos from last night. I can't help but notice Jake's gaze looks blank in every single one. Hands in pockets. Broad shoulders hunched. It's in sharp contrast to Angie—arms either spread wide or wrapped tight around Jake's waist. Judging by the size of her smiles, you'd think she'd won a Powerball jackpot.

Lisa shrugs a shoulder. "He's not my type. But I'm not blind. He's definitely movie-star material."

As Angie continues extolling Jake's/Jacob's physical attributes, my mind stays stuck on how traumatized he looked at the support group. Even to me, a virtual stranger, he seemed to be walking a virtual tightrope across the Grand Canyon. No harness, no net. And he was seconds from falling.

Furtively, I check my messages. Nothing from Jake, though I'd texted him a few times. Why was he being so elusive?

Movement outside catches my eye. A tall, muscular figure stumbles through the parking lot. His dark hair sticks up at odd angles. A streak of blood runs from one nostril. He leans against my car, gasping for breath.

"Holy shit," I say, startling the others. "Is that Jake?"

"What…?" Angie leans over me to peer out of the window. "Oh my God! Jacob!" she shrieks before running out of the diner. Lisa slips out of the booth after her.

"Wait for me!" I grab a handful of napkins from the dispenser and chase my friends.

Angie skids to a stop at Jake's side. "Baby! What happened to you? Have you been in a fight?"

Jake looks up, dazed and confused. He clutches at his right arm. "I don't know. How did I get here?"

"Maybe he's got a concussion," Lisa says.

"But from what?" Angie clutches at Jake's cheeks. They're drained of color, like a vampire had sucked ten pints of blood out of him. "Baby, talk to me. Did you fall? How many fingers am I holding up?"

Jake blinks at Angie's index finger. "Four?"

Calmly, Lisa says, "Yep. It's a concussion."

Angie wrings her hands. "We should get him to a hospital."

"No doctors! No hospitals!" Jake shouts. "I'm not letting any more quacks near me."

"But, Jacob, you're a mess! You're covered in blood. What the hell happened?" Angie looks hurt as Jake flinches away from her touch.

I step forward and press a wad of napkins to his nose. "Tip your head back, Ja…cob. That's it."

A flash of recognition lights Jake's eyes. I pinch his nose tight at the bridge while supporting his muscular neck. A silent agreement passes between us—pretend we're total strangers. I'm loath to ask him what happened in front of all these people, even in a whisper. What if he says he was abducted by aliens?

Angie wedges between us and takes tissue-holding duties. Jake waves her away and clamps his nose. More blood soaks through the tissue. A dried river of blood runs down to the neck of his long-sleeved shirt.

Lisa backs away. "I'll get more napkins."

"Babe, how long have you been wandering around like this? Where's your car?" Angie asks, fighting back tears.

Jake simply shrugs. "I need some water. Can you get some for me?"

She kisses his cheek. "Anything for you, baby. I'll be right back."

As soon as she's out of earshot, Jake takes my wrist

with an iron-like grip. "Cassidy, tell me I'm having some insane dream right now."

"I'm afraid you're wide awake, but you're safe," I say, trembling inside, but trying not to show it on the outside. Passersby look at us curiously. I move to shield Jake from view.

"Last night…after the dance… I saw you."

I frown. "Where? At the lookout?"

He drops his already deep, low voice. "You, me, your friend from the group, and a deaf girl. We were together. On a spaceship."

My body turns to stone. I guess I was dead wrong about the chances of another abduction. Moira's hypnotic suggestion was supposed to help me remember my next abduction. What if her suggestion went the other way and helped me mentally bury it instead?

"Are you sure? What was I wearing?"

Jake groans. "You don't believe me."

"I do. I believe something awful happened to you."

His bloodshot, fear-riddled eyes look up at me. "You were wearing a dark blue dress and silver high heels. And… Anonymous—"

"Hayden."

"He was in a suit but no tie."

I choke back a golf ball-sized lump in my throat. We *were* taken last night. But how? When?

Running footsteps approach us. I turn around to see Angie with two bottles of water and Lisa carrying an entire napkin dispenser. My pulse keeps going up and up.

Lips hardly moving, I say, "We'll talk about this later. Follow my lead for now."

"But—"

I shove the bloodied napkins against his face to keep

him quiet. I have to get him out of here, maybe meet up with Hayden and Alondra so we can figure out this mess together.

Angie rushes up to us. With two fingers, she tosses the napkins to the asphalt. She clumsily opens a water bottle, spilling almost a quarter of it. "Drink this, baby. It's ice-cold, just the way you like it."

Jake grimaces. "Thanks."

"Ohhh, you're still bleeding," she moans and gingerly touches his face. "Lisa, give me those napkins."

Jake guzzles the entire bottle of water. He takes the napkins out of Lisa's hands. I can't see any other marks on him. No bruises or cuts. If we take Jake to a hospital and they find some sort of alien device implanted inside him, what'll happen to him?

"Babe…" Angie says. "You've gotta let me help you."

I cut in. "You know, Aunt Carole will know what to do. Jake, I can take you to her house if you don't want to go to a clinic or hospital."

"Yes." Jake pushes himself off the bumper of my car. He looks much more alert now. "Let's go to your aunt."

Angie puts up her hands in protest. "Jacob, tell me where your car is so I can grab it and follow you. Lisa, you'll come with me, right?"

"Sure," Lisa says, kicking the blood-soaked napkins into a pile. "I'll get rid of all this stuff."

"No!" Jake's forceful tone makes us all take one step backward. Seeing that, he softens his tone. "No, Angie…uh, baby, I don't want you to see me being, uh, examined."

My throat constricts even more on that last word. Examined. Studied. Probed. A flash of white blinds me for a split second. Nausea sets in as a silhouette seems to loom over me. Woozily, I lean against Lisa.

"Hey, you're sick, too? Is there something in the water?" Lisa pushes me upright. Her touch brings me back to reality. The nausea washes away almost instantly.

"I'm fine, I'm fine. Must've been the sight of blood that got to me," I tell her. I spin around. "Jacob, I'm gonna run in and get my purse. I'll be right back to take you to my aunt."

I have no intention of taking him to Aunt Carole's. She'll only ask questions and it'll get back to Dad. But I've got to get Jake somewhere safe. Now.

On my way back to the diner, I quickly fire off a text to Hayden: Where are you? Jake's with me. He's in trouble.

I wait a few seconds. No response. After a second's hesitation, I text Alondra.

Angie catches up to me inside the restaurant. "Cassidy, something's not right here."

It's hard to meet her gaze. "Yeah, it's so weird the way guys hate looking weak in front of their girlfriends, huh?"

"Yeah," she says faintly, looking over her shoulder at Jake and Lisa. "I don't know. This whole thing is bizarre. He turns up here all disoriented and bleeding. Bleeding! And he doesn't seem to know who I am!"

Of course Angie's confused. But what can I possibly say to her? That her boyfriend was abducted by aliens, who scrambled his brain and did God knows what to him? Inside the diner, my vision blurs as it sweeps over plates of untouched strawberry pancakes, hash browns, and sunny-side-up eggs. Digging into my purse, I find enough money to cover the check for all three of us and dump it in the middle of the table.

Angie grabs my arm. "Do you think he'll be okay? I don't understand the big deal about the hospital."

"Don't worry. I'll try to convince him to go." Ignoring the stares of other diners, I run out to the parking lot. I can't answer the stream of questions Angie's firing at me as we go.

Jake's standing now, head back, still holding a wad of tissues against his face.

"Can we go now?" he mumbles.

"Yep." I remote-unlock the Fiat. "Get in."

He obeys as I start the engine. Angie leans down and I open the window so she can kiss him one more time. When she's done, she peers over at me. "Drive carefully, okay?"

Hands gripping the steering wheel, I reply, "You know I will."

"And call me. One of you call me. No, both of you call me," she begs.

"Will do, Ange." I back out of the parking space and try not to look at Angie and Lisa.

Once I get out onto the main street, Jake turns to me. In a nasal voice, he says, "Thanks for getting me out of there."

"No problem. Keep your head tilted back and your eyes closed. Rest for now."

Privately, I hope he doesn't pass out. The flow of blood has not stopped. Seems he's lost five pints. What if bypassing the hospital is a big mistake?

TRACK 48

"Kiss Them For Me"

Earlier This Year

Nina paused outside Charlie Hobart's office door. Through the glass, she watched the elderly man peck away at his keyboard.

The weight of the archive box Nina was carrying deadened her arms. She cringed, thinking of the mini-tantrum she threw when Ethan first asked her to help Carole digitize decades' worth of documents for the firm. Sure, she'd hit a dead end in her Jane Flanagan book. She'd traveled to DC and back so many times she was on first-name terms with the crew of the Colorado Springs-to-Dulles route *and* their spouses. There were no more leads to follow, no more interviewees willing to talk to her, and she'd burned a few bridges. That didn't mean she had time to do a job an intern could easily do.

But she resigned herself to the task. Out of boredom, she started reading those dusty government documents.

Dusty *explosive* government documents.

She peered through the office door. Sweet old Charlie. Was it really possible? Ethan's own partner, a man they'd both known since college, had a link to Jane Flanagan's disappearance? She had to find out for sure before acting on the information.

Nina cleared her throat. "Hi. Do you have a minute?"

Charlie looked up sharply as if startled. But he smiled as soon as he saw Nina's face. "Of course, come in. How are things?"

Stepping inside and closing the door with her foot, Nina glanced down at the box. She dumped it on the floor. Decades of dust puffed out of the pages. It kind of represented how she felt until a few days ago. Exhausted. Old. Tired. Now, the fire within was back.

"What do you know about the Parallax Human Intervention Unit?"

Charlie stood, his face becoming even more wrinkled thanks to his deep frown. "Parallax? It no longer exists—"

"They had a file on Jane Flanagan," she interrupted. She had no time to lose.

He blinked in confusion. "As far as I understand, there were many government agencies involved in the search for her."

"According to this, Jane *was* found. At this unit." Nina carefully pulled out a folder from the box, then leaned on the desk. He looked at the folder like he'd never seen it before. "Charlie, you knew all this time! Is it true? Is she still alive?"

"Nina, I didn't know!" With a shaky hand, Charlie opened the file. His knees buckled, making him land hard in his chair. "Where did you get this?"

"It was with all the other boxes in your storage rooms." Nina wanted to believe him. After all, Charlie was known for his commitment to the truth, to honesty, to justice. She stood over him, watching his jaw slacken as he read.

"I've never seen these files before." Finally, he looked up at her with watery eyes. "Just let me make a phone call."

Her voice sharp, she asked, “To Jane’s parents? The president? Because that would be the right thing to do.”

He hesitated, then picked up his desk phone. “No. To an old friend.”

TRACK 49

"Come Together"

Present Day

Alondra's pacing outside her house when I pull up. She'd texted me her address and insisted I come straight over. Jake's nosebleed had slowed somewhat, thanks to the spare tampon I'd stuck up his nostril. I once saw a triage nurse do that while waiting in an ER, so I figured it'd work for him as first aid. Judging by his look of abject horror, it seems he would have preferred another abduction.

I pop a couple of Lisa's vitamins in my mouth and swallow them without water.

"Are you all right?" is the first thing I sign to Alondra when I tumble out of the car.

She nods, then does a double take when she sees Jake staggering toward her. *"Is he all right?"*

"He will be. I hope." I wave Jake around to my side. "Jake, this is Alondra."

"I saw you on the ship," he says, loud enough for the sleepy neighborhood to hear him.

I sign what he says for Alondra. Never did I dream my interpreting skills would be needed in this way.

Well, obviously a part of me knew they would. I'm glad I took notice of the voice inside me that insisted I learn how to sign.

Alondra's eyes grow huge. She beckons us down a path alongside her house. *"Come this way to my studio. We won't be bothered by anyone down there."*

I interpret what she says for Jake and try to lead him by the arm.

Jake shrugs me off. "I can walk—"

"And bleed at the same time?" I finish.

He dabs his nose gingerly. "I think it's stopping. Can I take this thing out yet?"

"Soon."

Alondra leads us into a walk-out basement that smells of oil paint and turpentine. She bundles us in and closes the curtains. Lights buzz on, then dim.

Jake and I stand side by side, our mouths falling open. The walls are covered in canvases of varying sizes. Abstract figures and landscapes are all painted in the same gray-purple color palette.

We're surrounded by aliens.

Depictions of them, anyway.

These are disturbing. Slashing lines. Dangerous curves. Oppressive colors. Just looking at them makes me break into a sweat.

I'm drawn to a half-finished painting. It's an extreme close-up of large bulbous eyes. They're deep onyx at first glance. Then in the center, the tone fades to a dark gray, where I can just pick out a human silhouette.

Looking sheepish, Alondra moves close to an easel. A charcoal sketch shows the outlines of four figures. Whether they're human or not, I can't tell. *"I may be a little obsessed."*

"A little," I sign after interpreting for Jake, who seems to have forgotten all about the tampon in his nose.

She touches the easel, her face contorting. *"This isn't*

art. It's a documentary."

"What are you going to do with them?" I spy dozens more canvases stretched on pine frames stacked in corners and on metal shelves. She's sure as hell prolific.

"I'm torn," she signs. *"Some days I feel like I can sell the paintings. Other days I want to pile them up and start a bonfire."*

"Happy to help." Jake puts his hand up. "But first, can I take this thing out of my nose? I think the bleeding's stopped."

Alondra gives him a grim smile. She points at a door. *"There's a trash can in the bathroom."*

"Thanks," he mumbles, ducking his head to avoid a painting hanging from a shelf.

"Who is this guy?" Alondra asks me when he's gone.

"Jake was at the support group meeting," I sign. *"It turns out he's my best friend's new boyfriend. But he's been standing her up a lot because he says he's been abducted by aliens."*

"He is a mess," she signs.

I chew my bottom lip. *"He claims we were abducted last night, too."*

"We?"

"You, me, Hayden, him. The reason why I brought him here is because he saw me communicating with 'a girl' through sign language on the ship. That could only have been you. How many deaf abductees could there be?"

"I get that it's uncommon. No one in my Deaf community has ever admitted to being abducted." Alondra's brow wrinkles in concentration. *"But I don't remember anything."*

"Neither do I."

I check my phone again. Nothing from Hayden. Not even an irrelevant emoji.

Jake finally gets out of the bathroom. He scrubs at his right arm, making the skin raw with nail marks. At least his nose is all cleaned up.

"Guys, I think I found a needle mark," he says.

Bile races up from my stomach. I whisper, "What?"

Stepping forward, he rolls his sleeve up higher. Slowly, I do the same with my right sleeve. So does Alondra.

There, right in the crook of our right arms, is a raised red bump. We stare open-mouthed at each other, frozen to the paint-stained tile floor.

"I thought…I thought it was another insect bite," I sign, then something inside me stills. Yeah. Another insect bite in the same spot as before. What a coincidence. But why would I have thought it was another kind of injury? We live in semi-rural Colorado. Even now, in early October, mosquitoes are more common than needle-wielding aliens.

"So did I," Alondra signs. She inspects the wound again and winces. Alondra motions for us to sit on a group of mismatched furniture. They're splashed with dried paint.

But I can't sit. I start pacing. *"Okay, obviously we're connected somehow. We should compare stories. Alondra, you remember the two of us getting abducted five years ago."*

Jack jerks backward in surprise. "You didn't mention it at the support group."

"That's because I have no memory of it," I tell him and sign for Alondra. *"Maybe it's my brain's way of protecting me."*

Alondra signs, *"After I saw you at the diner, I did a little research into memories of alien abductions. It seems some people, lucky people, get to walk away from abductions blissfully unaware they even happened in the first place."*

My gaze drops as guilt overwhelms me. What made me so special? Why do other people suffer so much through every waking hour? Or could it be that it's manifesting in other ways with me? Like disturbed sleep patterns?

"Do you think aliens have the power to wipe people's memories?" I sign.

"Yes, but obviously their methods are hit and miss," signs Alondra.

"Pretty sure my brain got erased after an abduction," Jake claims. He sets himself down in the middle of an overstuffed couch. "Didn't realize what happened until about a year ago."

"What happened then?" signs Alondra.

The jiggling of Jake's left leg gives away his nerves. "I got knocked out during a game. When I came to, all these visions started coming back. It freaked the hell out of me."

"Visions of an abduction?" I sign and speak. He nods.

"I'm going to take a wild guess," Alondra signs. *"Were you abducted at around twelve years of age?"*

He nods again. Much more slowly this time. I let out a tiny gasp in response.

"I've been seeing a shrink on and off since I got that concussion on the field," Jake says, and I continue interpreting for Alondra. "Thought I was starting to deal with the visions okay. But these past few weeks, I've felt… tormented, I guess is the right word. That's another reason I've been bailing on Angie so much, 'cause I've been seeing the doc more often. Trying to get my head screwed on straight."

Alondra grabs cans of sodas from a bar fridge, hands them to us, and sits on the padded arm of a chair. *"Seeing a psychiatrist is nothing to be ashamed about."*

"I know," he mutters. We watch Jake intently. His right hand shakes as he tries to sip his drink. "Stop looking at me like that. I've been studied enough for one day."

Both of us look away from him. I feign deep interest in the graphics on my soda can, then notice his left nostril start trickling blood again. I hand him some clean tissues from my purse. He'd taken my last tampon.

"Jesus, why won't the bleeding stop?" he says.

"They must have really done a number on you," Alondra signs, her eyes full of concern.

"It's not like the first time this happened to me." Jake sits up straight again, which is a real feat considering how soft and fluffy those cushions seem. "Something's different."

"In what way?" Alondra signs.

"Last night's guys were mean sons of bitches. It was out-and-out torture. I mean, look at me, no wonder my nose is bleeding." Jake's eyes water. As I sign for Alondra, a rush of sympathy wells in my chest. We look bleakly at each other.

"What if these are a different breed of aliens than the… nicer ones who've taken us before?" Alondra signs. *"Maybe there's something we have in common that makes us attractive to aliens from all kinds of planets."*

From a physical standpoint, none of us have anything in common. Alondra's small-boned, Hispanic, and deaf. Jake's built like a towering Polynesian warrior, all muscle and brawn. Me, I'm Eurasian with a penchant for fried brains. But could there be something in our collective DNA that the aliens want? It's an unnerving thought that I'm not ready to share.

Jake sighs heavily. "Yeah, I can imagine an interstellar network where they're saying, 'Hey, guys, we've struck gold. Found a tri-county area full of chumps here. Guarantee you they won't fight back.'"

"There must be a way to fight back, if that's the case," I sign, drawing my spine upward.

"Cassidy. I'm a hundred-and-ninety-pound football

player and I didn't stand a chance against them last night." Jake grimaces. "Why are they even messing with us? What's the point?"

"Science? Curiosity? Exploration?" I sign. *"Maybe it's the same reason we go out into space. One small step for alien, one giant leap for alien kind."*

"You sound like you're on their side," Jake says, his blood-encrusted nostrils flaring.

"I'm not!" Shuddering, I sink onto the couch beside Jake. *"Look, I seem to be lucky enough to have amnesia when it comes to these abductions. I wish it were the same for you guys. Moira tried to hypnotize me, but my memories aren't reliable."*

"Hold on. You remember what happened now?" signs Alondra.

I wave my hand. *"Not really. When she put me under, I had a vision of aliens but it wasn't real."*

"How do you know?" she signs.

"Because one of them was Hayden. Or had his voice, anyway." I gesture at one of her many art pieces. *"And he looked like a classic alien in the vision. Clearly, that was just my mind compiling every sci-fi movie and conspiracy story I've ever seen into one nightmare."*

"I wish I had abduction amnesia," Jake says, his tone bitter.

I shift on the chair. A spring pokes into me. *"I asked Moira to plant a hypnotic suggestion so I would remember from now on."*

"Then why didn't you know about this latest abduction?" Alondra signs.

"Maybe she's not a legit hypnotherapist? Or it simply didn't work?" I turn to Jake. *"Tell us what happened to you last night."*

"Uh... Okay, last night..." Jake swigs from the soda can. He runs a hand through his hair. "I dropped Angie off at her house. Maybe twelve thirty. So this morning, really."

Hayden left my house just after one. It seems like our goodbye kisses under the streetlights outside my house happened a millennium ago. But does it seem that way because we were again intercepted by aliens at some point?

"Then what?" I sign.

"I drove a few miles. Switching stations on the radio 'cause I couldn't get decent reception. And the Bluetooth wasn't working between my phone and the car stereo."

"Electronic interference," signs Alondra. *"That's a classic sign of an approaching UFO. Sorry. Go on."*

"I started driving across that ridge between Dawson and Bartlett," Jake continues. "You know how dark it is there, right, Cassidy? No streetlights, no houses. Cliffs on either side of the road."

"Why did you go that way instead of the freeway?" I ask him as I sign.

Jake's cheeks redden. "I was trying to avoid the highway patrol 'cause I had a swig or two of whiskey early in the night at your homecoming. A mouthful. I swear to you I wasn't drunk. Stone-cold sober. Angie wouldn't have gotten in the car with me if I wasn't."

It's true. Angie might drink like a fish, but she doesn't get in cars with people who are any more or less drunk than she is.

I hesitate for a few seconds, then sign, *"Did you smoke anything?"*

"You mean like weed?" Jake's lip curls. "No, not last night. And no marijuana gummy bears or brownies, either. I swear to you."

"Just wanted to cover all bases."

Alondra signs, *"Then what happened, Jake? When you were driving."*

"Oh yeah," he says, shaking his curly head. "Driving along. Doing the speed limit 'cause, you know, those turns are tricky up there. All of a sudden, the engine starts sputtering. Now, I work on that truck myself. I know it's running sweet. And I know there was three-quarters of a tank of gas left. The battery's a few months old.

"But the engine just cuts out. Completely dead. The lights flick on and off and then die. I roll the truck onto the shoulder. I get out. My phone won't work, so I can't even use that as a flashlight, let alone call the auto club. Total darkness. No one around. No crickets chirping. It was like I was in a bubble. And the air felt different, you know? Thicker. Like I was underwater, but not wet. I can't explain it."

"I know that feeling," Alondra signs. *"There's, like, resistance against your body."*

"Exactly. That's exactly it." Jake nods. "I popped the hood. Couldn't see a damn thing, of course. Until…suddenly, this bright beam of light just shone down. I swear to you it was like somebody flicked a light switch right above my head. I tried to look up, but it was so fucking bright. It felt like my skin was on fire."

"It was a UFO? Could you hear anything? What did it sound like?" I sign. What he's saying is so vivid. And the fear on his face is real. How could I not believe him? Or Alondra?

"It didn't sound like anything. Seriously, no sound. It's impossible, I know. But you're gonna have to believe me." Jake straightens.

I think of my dad's electric car and the way it glides

almost silently along highways and byways, but I let Jake's words go unchallenged. For now.

"Did you get a good look at it?" I sign. *"How big was it? How low was it flying?"*

Jake holds up his palms. "I'm getting to that. It was kind of hard to see because its lights were literally blinding me. But then my eyes adjusted to it. The thing was maybe a hundred feet above me. Not directly above. Just north of where I was standing. And it was gigantic. Like, I don't know, half a football field. And triangular shaped. As well as the white light on its underside, it had colored lights running really fast around the edges. Green and purple lights. They were kind of hypnotizing. I was paralyzed. Or frozen. Couldn't move a hair."

"We should check social media, see if anybody else reported it last night." I doubt if a ship that big and bright would go unnoticed, even in a sprawling area like Dawson. Jake nods vigorously. *"How did you get inside the ship? Did they beam you up, too?"*

He scratches his head. "Can't remember that part. What I do know is that one minute I was standing next to my truck and the next I was horizontal next to you guys. God, everything was so white, I thought I was in heaven."

"Then the aliens came in and you knew they were no angels," Alondra signs.

Jake's mouth moves wordlessly at first. "Man, those horrible operations. No anesthesia. Digging and poking and scratching with those weird instruments. It seemed to go on forever. And Alondra…your screams. I can still hear them in my head."

"I'm glad I don't remember that." Alondra's hands shake.

I shudder at the mention of instruments and torture. I close my eyes. A blurry vision of something silver glinting under a spotlight flashes. It's gone before I can make out exactly what it is. A scalpel? A probe?

"What about the inside of the ship?" I sign. *"What did it look like?"*

He squeezes his eyes shut. His breathing is sharp and quick. "I was in a white room. That's where they did their worst."

"I know the one you mean," signs Alondra. *"It's like you're in a snowstorm. You can't see where the walls and ceilings are, but you know you're trapped in there."*

I clear my throat. *"How did you get out?"*

Jake's leg jiggles faster. "You guys all went home before me. I was the last one standing. Or lying down."

"What do you mean, we all went home? How? Did they carry us out? Wheel us on gurneys?" I sign.

He faces us, jaw clicking. "You just vanished. Like, *pop*, *pop*, *pop*. You, Alondra, then Hayden. Gone like bursting balloons. When it was my turn, I woke up behind a McDonald's dumpster. How's that for shitty valet service?"

"We just vanished?" Only weeks ago, I would have dismissed a story like Jake's as an intense hallucination or even just a nightmare. This is straight out of *Star Trek.* But there are a bunch of things I can't deny. Alondra described my twelve-year-old-self perfectly during our abduction or whatever we're calling it. Jake saw me communicating in sign language with Alondra. And now we all have suspicious needle-marks on our bodies. It can't be coincidental.

Jake blows out a big sigh. "If you don't believe me, I don't care."

"We believe you, Jake," Alondra signs. *"Right, Cassidy?"*

"Yes," I tell them. *"There's something bizarre happening to us as a group."*

"So…what do we do next?" Alondra signs, then wrings

her slender, paint-encrusted fingers. *"Can we do anything?"*

"Like what? Call the cops?" Jake says. "They can't protect us from these alien assholes. Even if we did ask them, I'm sure they'd give us some serious side-eye and tell us to get lost." Jake digs his phone out of a pocket. He sighs heavily. "Angie's left me a dozen messages. We need to get going before she gets even more upset."

"Hayden's a part of this, too. If we're getting abducted as a group, then we should try to figure out how to deal with the abductions as a group," I sign. Though, inwardly, I'm not so sure he'll be open to forming a sort of *Scooby-Doo* mystery-solving crew. Hayden clams up whenever I try to press him on his experiences. I check my phone for the millionth time.

Still nothing.

As I fire off another message, I'm suddenly overcome by a dizzying thought. "Oh my God," I whisper.

Alondra studies my face and her expression darkens. *"Cassidy? Did Hayden reply? What did he say?"*

"Nothing from Hayden." A shudder rattles every bone in my body. Jake said he saw Hayden vanish, but that doesn't mean he was sent home. *"What if they still have Hayden?"*

TRACK 50

"Superman"

Present Day

"How many times has this happened?" Lindsay asked in a clipped tone. She folded her arms tightly across her chest.

Hayden gulped. Contrary to his sister's prediction, he felt no relief about finally revealing his abductions. "Twice. The first time was the same night Cassidy collapsed here."

Sam rested his chin on steepled hands. "Why didn't you tell us?"

"I wanted to gather more data before I involved you, find out who they were," Hayden said, straightening his spine. "Technically, I followed our rules—I didn't interfere. I pretended to be just another Earthling."

"You didn't interfere, I'll grant you that, but you let yourself get captured and stupefied. That's careless, Hayden," snapped Lindsay. "No matter what, we must always protect ourselves. Who knows what was done to you while you were unconscious?"

"If there's good news from this, it's that their methods are imperfect. My system metabolizes their medications very quickly."

"Did it occur to you that they may be refining their 'methods' as we speak? The next time they drug you, *if* they catch you again, it may be with a stronger formula." Lindsay raised a brow. "You are not to leave this house until we consult with our diplomats."

"I think it would draw less suspicion if he carried on as normal," Sam said.

Eyes wild, Lindsay said, "But in the meantime, he could be taken again!"

"Not if I use my abilities. You know, to protect myself," Hayden drawled pointedly.

"That's out of the question," replied Lindsay, ignoring her son's growl of frustration. "You are well aware of the consequences if you were to expose your abilities here."

"Yes, yes, banishment to the deep, dark, undersea bases," said Hayden. Truthfully, he thought those caverns were an Aguan myth. His people weren't that brutal.

Weren't they?

"You won't see the sky again, much less fly through it," Lindsay bit out.

The prospect of never being at the controls of an airship again put a lump in Hayden's throat. His mother knew how to push his buttons. He looked away.

"Does this mean we have to find another place to live?" Trudy spoke up in a tiny, plaintive voice, sounding all of her five Earth years. She hugged Yoda till he squirmed.

Lindsay drew a deep breath and crouched before her daughter. "It might mean an extraction to Agua. But we will do our best to stop that from happening. Right, Hayden?"

Hayden nodded. Damn straight, he'd stop it.

Trudy kept her gaze on the carpet. Hayden knew what she was thinking. Guilt hit him like a baseball bat to the stomach. She didn't want to leave. Moving here from Maine, across the country, was hard enough for her. How would she cope with moving to another galaxy?

TRACK 51

"Love Is a Stranger"

Present Day

A shirtless Hayden blinks at me from his front door. "Cassidy! How are you?"

How am I? My mouth is dry as a desert rock. I'm going to need a body of fresh water to drink from. And my brain? Devoid of all sensible thoughts. Exactly what made me race here as fast as my tiny Fiat engine could go?

He closes the space between us and we kiss. Heat from his bare chest radiates through me. When he ends the kiss, I'm left wobbly-kneed on the doormat.

"Y-you're still in your pajamas. Or half of them."

He looks down at his long cotton pants. Thin blue, white, and green stripes run down the legs. I can't take my eyes off a set of well-sculpted abs that Michelangelo's *David* would envy. I tell myself to focus on other good things, like the fact he's alive and well and in his sinkhole-prone home.

Rubbing his eyes, he says, "The doorbell woke me up. But it's okay. Come on in."

From the hat stand in the foyer, he plucks a gray hoodie and zips it on. The house is warm, but empty. Clearly they've not invested in any furniture since I was here last.

"I've been trying to reach you for ages." My voice

bounces off the plate glass windows overlooking the valley. "Is anyone else home?"

Hayden plucks a note off the fridge and frowns. "According to this, they've gone to the market. Back soon."

"Good."

"Agreed." He snares me by the waist and pulls me close. A delicious giddy wave washes over me as his lips tease my neck.

Reluctantly, I wiggle away and get a good look at him. In particular, his nose. "I need to talk to you. Alone."

"Why are you staring at my nostrils like that?" he says, fidgeting.

I stand on my tiptoes and give his face a closer inspection. "I'm checking for bleeding or signs of trauma."

Hayden covers his nose, which I found to be, well, perfect. "Why?"

"One sec." Next, I push up his sleeves. If I hadn't been blinded by his abs on the doorstep, I might have spotted a needle mark on his inner arm then. There's a tiny, tiny mark on his right arm, but even from half an inch way, it's barely visible. It's certainly not raised and red like the injection site on my own arm. I brush my fingertips over the spot. Goose bumps pop up in response. "Does this hurt? Sting? Burn?"

He steps away and slides the sleeves down again. His face reddening, he says, "Um, no. What's this all about?"

I grip both of his wrists. Despite knowing his family is out, I look around nervously. "Hayden, we were abducted by aliens again after homecoming. And not just us—Jake and Alondra, too."

Hayden turns and moves toward a set of sliders leading to the barren terrace. But he stops right there at the glass. In the reflection, I see his face is taut. Unreadable. Slowly, he nods.

My voice soft, I ask, "Do you remember something?"

He faces me, his dark eyes stormy and tortured. "Yeah. I just remember lights coming toward us. I thought…I thought they were cars."

"Lights?" I close my eyes as I struggle to think back. "The last thing I remember is you hot-wiring the truck." When I open my eyes again, Hayden is staring at his hands like they'd just been sewn on by Dr. Frankenstein. "What about you?"

"Let me think." A bead of sweat starts to form on his hairline. I narrow my gaze. It's not *that* hot in here.

"Hayden, please. Let this sink in—we have been abducted by aliens. Twice." I grab him by the shoulders, my fingers clenching his rigid muscles. There's real fear in his eyes. Even talking about his past alien experiences seems to be bad enough for him. Is it possible he's suffered more than any of us in the skeletal hands of the aliens? Even more than Jake? In a softer tone, I say, "I know this is really hard for you. We need to work together if we're going to stop it from happening again. You're not Han Solo."

"I know, you're right." He speaks so softly I can barely hear him. But his face relaxes somewhat, like he's unburdened himself. "We have to get organized against whatever's happening and tackle it together."

"I'm glad you feel that way, too." I breathe out a sigh. "I'll get in touch with Alondra and Jake. We'll figure out when we can all get together."

Hayden nods without looking at me. "I have to object to one thing, though. I'm more of a Lone Ranger than a Han Solo."

"I know." I quirk a smile at him. It's a famous one-liner from one of the original *Star Wars* movies. The sound of his laugh makes me feel just that little bit lighter. I get on my tiptoes and kiss him.

"Oh, hey, change of topic..." he says in between landing short kisses on my lips and face. "I've fixed your mom's laptop."

I gasp. "What? How? Javier said it was ready for burial."

"I have special powers." He gives a modest shrug and takes my hand. "It's upstairs."

I raise a single brow, Angie-style, trying to look cool. But on the inside, my heart's taking off at lightning speed. "That is the best pick-up line I've heard all day."

"No, really, it's...um, that's where I've been working on it." His deep red blush is super adorable, but he doesn't let go while he leads me through the house. "But hurry, my family unit will probably be home soon."

"It's so cute that you call them that," I say as we walk upstairs.

He laughs weakly. "Some habits are hard to break."

Funny, though, how there's no family pictures visible anywhere. In my house, there are picture frames on mantels, on side tables, on walls. When Mom left, I was concerned Dad would take them all down. But he even left their wedding picture up in his room. So much for moving on.

Near the landing, I peek inside Trudy's room. I can't help it. The door's wide open. Her desk is right by the door. I expect to see her coloring book and crayons scattered on it. Instead, there's...a calculus textbook?

"Hayden, is your little sister doing your homework? I'm not sure that's allowed." I wink and point at the book.

"Trudy's classified as a genius here." He pulls a face and moves on. "And she likes everyone to know it."

"Your parents don't encourage it?" I follow him to a door diagonally opposite Trudy's.

"At home...uh, inside our home they do. We're all proud

of her enormous brain," he says in a measured voice. "But we learned a few states ago that some kids get singled out for all the wrong reasons."

"You mean she was bullied? For being smart?" I can't imagine what it would be like to move from place to place, forever trying to fit in.

"Mm-hmm. People are strange. Trudy rose above it, though." Clearing his throat, he opens the door. "Anyway, welcome to my domain."

Hayden's room is pretty much like the rest of the house. Cream walls. Polished hardwood floor. Sparse, but lived-in. The top half of his PJs is neatly folded over a chair, like he made a deliberate choice to sleep *sans* shirt. A pair of striped socks lies near the bed, perhaps discarded during the night. There are no sports trophies, no posters of heroes, no instruments. But there are books—lots of them—jammed into shelves that span an entire wall.

I run my fingers over the spines, most of them creased and worn. Fiction-wise, there's a thoughtful assortment. Everything from Allende to Zusak. And on the nonfiction shelves he's got worn copies of all the *-ologies*—anthropology, sociology, psychology, et cetera.

Hayden McGraw really is the perfect, well-rounded-in-all-the-right-places human being.

"Wow, your collection is amazing." I take out a book about Mars exploration.

"It's pure escapism. Like this one." He tilts his head at a *Star Wars* novel.

I move to another section of the bookcase and find a self-help book. "This looks like a fun read. *How to Behave Yourself.* You haven't read it, obviously."

With an embarrassed smile, he quickly puts himself between me and the shelves. "Okay, that's enough browsing."

"Right," I say, spying Mom's laptop on his uncluttered desk. Shaking my head, I open the lid to wake it up. The familiar desktop image pops up. It's a selfie with Mom, Dad, and me in our backyard. I remember the day it was taken—just before I started my sophomore year. Our smiles are wide, faces relaxed and happy, despite spending the day painting the tiny guest house in the blazing August heat. Who knew the three of us would be blown apart just over a year later?

"I can't believe you got this working. It's like magic. How did you do it?"

Hayden shrugs. "Magicians never reveal their secrets."

"I'm going to search your library for your magic handbook." I grin and hit a key on the laptop. It prompts me for a password. I try a combo of family names and birthdates, but none open the virtual door. "Do you have the password in your bag of tricks?"

"I'm afraid not," he says, rocking back and forth on his bare feet.

"It's okay. You've raised the laptop from the dead. That's more than enough. How can I ever repay you?" My arms encircle his waist.

"I can think of one way." He angles his lips against mine and the rest of me turns into mush. His hands tangle through my hair, unbinding the ponytail.

I tilt my head and he runs a trail of kisses along my jaw, right to the delicate little spot below my earlobe. Knees buckling, I lean into the bookcase for support. And he follows. Closes the space between us.

The heat from his body sears into me. I feel the *ba-bomp, ba-bomp* of his heart. For a few excruciating seconds, he arrests me with an intense stare that almost makes me forget my own name. My brain has been erased. In a good way this time.

I only want to think about Hayden and how every touch from him sends thrills racing all through me. A hot shuddery breath escapes from him, then our lips find each other again, moving slow, then fast like there's no tomorrow. When his palm finds its way under my shirt, I swear I see stars. "S-so," I stammer a little while later, straightening my clothes. I'd repaid him thoroughly and passionately. "Now that I've got Mom's laptop back, I'm going to get to work on unlocking it. Are you good to meet up with Jake and Alondra this weekend?"

The sound of a vehicle makes Hayden dash across the room in two bounds. He looks out the window and scans the driveway below.

"Is it the family unit?" I ask.

"No, it's just a passing car." His jaw clenches and unclenches, then he turns to me with a sheepish grin. "It's just weird hearing any kind of traffic in this ghost town."

"Do you think you'll get neighbors anytime soon?"

"My parents kinda like having the place to themselves while they're settling into town." He takes my hand. "We'd better get downstairs in case they come home. They're touchy about me having girls in my room."

"Girls? Plural?" I tease, and he rolls his eyes. I hold the laptop close to my chest.

Downstairs, my attention gets pulled to the butler's pantry beside the kitchen. I fainted last time I was here. Fainted while doing the simple task of grabbing cutlery. Silver cutlery.

Without a word, I drift over to it.

"Can I get you something?" Hayden asks, following me.

"Sorry, I'm not being nosy. I just wanted to check something." I run a hand over the bench tops on either side of the narrow room. An iPad and other gadgets sit charging on a corner of the stone counter.

Now, which drawer was it?

Bumping Hayden aside, I pull open one drawer and dig around.

"Uh, you need help? I know where everything's kept," he says.

My fingers close over the silver instrument. It has a long handle with short prongs on one end. This time I don't feel faint. Exhilarated is more like it. Holding it up, I say, "Jake mentioned aliens using instruments on us."

He takes the instrument out of my hand and frowns. "Like lemon zesters?"

"What?"

"Lemon zesters. You don't watch the Food Network? They're used to scrape the top layer off of lemons." Hayden demonstrates on the back of his hand. "I'm not taking any skin off, don't worry."

I watch him and I should be reassured. But I'm not. "Are you sure?"

"Cassidy, trust me." He laughs. "It's a normal everyday lemon zester found at a Crate & Barrel near you." He rips the charging cable off the iPad and does an image search. "Check it out for yourself."

I scan the results. Image after image shows lemon zesters closely resembling the one in my hand. There's nothing that suggests these things are from out of this world.

"Okay, it does seem like it's an ordinary household gadget," I murmur.

"It is." Hayden nods emphatically. "Sure, maybe in another world, some alien came up with an instrument that looks just like this. And maybe they use it on lemons, too. If lemons exist in other galaxies. But this lemon zester is my dad's lemon zester. Nothing more."

"So. I freaked out over a lemon zester," I say flatly.

"Don't be embarrassed." Hayden rubs my neck in slow, lazy circles. "Something about this gadget triggered your memory. Of lemons. Look, if it makes you feel better, I'll throw it away right now. Dad will just have to deal."

True to his word, he tosses the so-called lemon zester in a trash can on his way out. I stare down at it like it's a zombie that could jump up and attack me. I can't escape the feeling that there's something about this seemingly innocent gadget that isn't so innocent after all.

My heart pounds so hard it could crack a rib or two. After a few seconds' hesitation, I reach into the trash and pocket the lemon zester. I don't care that I might go to the devil for stealing from the McGraws because, if Alondra and Jake are right, I've already been to hell and back.

TRACK 52

"Ring of Fire"

Six Weeks Ago

TO: LBlake@phiu-gov.com
FROM:JDavisMD@edenestate.com
SUBJECT: Re: Classified — Simulation Trials

Sir,

We've had encouraging successes with the latest simulation trials. Support group leaders in four sectors have reported vivid alien encounters among attendees. However, while I appreciate the financial benefits, I hold grave concerns about plans to insert nanochips into Subjects in addition to the unstable Suppression formula. Both methods are in their infancy and adverse side effects may be profound. I believe it's unwise to push these trials, particularly with the influx of inexperienced staff.

This brings me to a related matter regarding the direction of Parallax as a whole. I have several concerns. Could we arrange a time to discuss as a matter of urgency?

Kind regards,

Dr. James Davis
Eden Estate

TRACK 53

"The View From the Woods"

Present Day

"I'll be back a week from today," Dad reminds me on Sunday morning. He inhales coffee and leaves the empty *World's Best Dad* mug on the counter.

"Yes, I remember. It's in my calendar." Plus, he's already told me twice this morning.

"Aunt Carole's going to check in with you every day. The Robinsons next door will, too. And the Wangs across the road. And I'll call you as often as I can, okay?" he says. I track him through the house, carrying his wool overcoat on my arm. "And don't open the door to strangers. I mean it."

I swallow thickly. "I won't, Dad."

He has no clue the strangest of strangers have no problem getting me in and out of the house without him, the Robinsons, or the Wangs noticing.

But we're going to put a stop to that. As soon as we figure out how…

"No wild parties, either. I *really* mean that, too," Dad says.

"How about a wild study party? I have a lot of research to do." And thanks to Lisa's magical vitamins, I've been feeling a lot more alert lately. Alert enough to stay up past midnight working on my project.

Standing on the porch, he smirks. "You can have the study party minus the wild part. Don't forget, everybody's watching you."

He's joking, but I squirm. So close to the truth. He kisses me on the forehead.

"Break a leg, Dad. Love you."

"I love you, too. Be good. Now go inside and lock the door." He grins and heads for his Tesla.

I smile and wave, then do as he says. I lean my back flat against the door. No lock or alarm system is going to stop the aliens. One slash of a proton beam and they'll storm through and snatch me.

Sighing, I look around. It's silent and still and lonely already. I have the whole three-thousand-square-foot house to myself, and yet there's somewhere else I'd rather be.

I grab Mom's resurrected MacBook and head out to her tiny house in the back garden. I described it as an upscale IKEA dollhouse at the time it was built. All clean lines, light-colored wood. Clever storage. No amount of hidden drawers and cupboards would have been enough to contain Mom's vast wardrobe and shoe collection, though. The bulk of her clothes and shoes are in the main house's spare room.

The work desk is a tiny-space marvel. When not in use, it folds down into a shallow niche in the wall. I release a latch, and the cantilevered timber desktop pops up. Dragging a chair over, I sit before the laptop, contemplating possible passwords. I found a bunch of tutorials on how to recover a forgotten password, but none of it seemed simple.

Mom hasn't answered any of my calls for help or my texts. By now, that shouldn't surprise me. Intellectually, I accept she's in treatment. She's doing what she needs to do. Still feels like a stab in the guts when she doesn't reply.

I drum my fingers on the desk and stare out the window at the overcast sky. When she wasn't on the road, Mom would have spent countless hours looking at the same mountain view. A row of six towering pine trees acts as a kind of border between the yard and a ravine. Dad built even tinier houses in each tree for the squirrels.

As I watch two feisty squirrels fight among pine needles on the ground, an idea crystallizes. On paper, I scratch out a list of various combinations of six, pines, and squirrels. The combo that finally does the trick? *666Squirrels.*

For a few seconds, as I watch the status bar, guilt jabs sharply at me. This is Mom's personal laptop. What if there's something on it that she didn't want me to see? What if there's something *I* don't want to see, like rejected selfies or her journal?

Then I think of her locked away in Eden Estate, a place that sounds idyllic but in reality wouldn't even rate a star on Expedia. I purse my lips and remind myself why I'm breaking into her files. Ultimately, it's going to save her.

Yep, just keep telling yourself that, Cassidy.

Her computer desktop is a cluttered mess of folders with cryptic filenames. Some contain documents with titles and headers but no contents. Either they'd been wiped or she hadn't done any work on them at all.

"Mom, what the hell were you doing all that time?" I murmur. This is not like her at all. What I'm looking at is the digital equivalent of a thousand filing cabinet drawers that had been emptied onto the floor, papers scattered to the moon and back.

It occurs to me that the state of her computer mirrors her state of mind. Or at least, how frenzied she became the longer her investigation went.

I click on the Notes app, hoping to find a roadmap of

sorts to her filing system at the very least. My hopes are dashed, but there are dozens of unfinished sentences that start with *"What if..."* One of the most recent ones had *"Daisy chain"* written on it.

There's no question. Mom was stuck. Confused. Lost.

Opening her calendar, I note that she'd already met with the same DC reporters that I'd contacted. That's a good sign that at least my approach was similar to hers, albeit more organized. I skim through dates from the first half of this year. Mom went into treatment in June. My eyes zero in on an entry early in that month: *Elsworth v. Eden + Parallax archives.*

Heart hammering impossibly hard, I stare at the words on the screen. *Elsworth v. Eden?* Someone tried to sue Eden?

"It doesn't mean *that* Eden," I mutter to myself, trying to be rational, trying to stop hyperventilating. But my gut is screaming that it sure as hell is *that* decaying, decrepit, and downright scary Eden.

As for Parallax, is it connected to Eden or are they two random, unfinished thoughts? The word "archives" makes me think of the never-ending digitizing job at Dad's office. Mom helped out there occasionally. What if she means she stored physical research files there? Because she couldn't have squeezed them into this tiny home.

I close the laptop and grab my keys. I have to find out.

"Alondra!" I'm so stunned to see her sitting on my front porch that I forget to sign. I drop my satchel and car keys. *"How long have you been sitting out here? You should have texted me."*

In the cul-de-sac, little kids shout and play tag. A drone flies erratically, obviously someone's new toy. I've been seeing more of them around lately. All shapes and sizes. I swear some are the size of a dining chair. This one's motor makes an annoying, mosquito-like buzz.

"I wanted to get myself together before actually knocking on your door." Her eyes are swollen and bloodshot. Her curly hair is bunched into a messy topknot. The laces on her boots are untied. She so does not look like she has it together. At her feet lies a bulging army surplus tote.

Alarm bells clang inside my head. *"What happened? Did they…? Have you been abducted by those alien assholes again? Tell me!"*

"It's nothing like that." Sniffling hard, she signs, *"I had a fight with my family. Can I stay with you? Just for a night. Until everything settles down. I had nowhere else to turn."*

I squeeze her tightly. *"Of course, stay longer. My dad's away, so it'll be good to have some company."*

"Thank you." She points her toes at my satchel. *"Are you on your way out?"*

"Yeah, I have to go to my dad's office and check something out. Come with me."

By the time we reach the office, Alondra's sniffles are gone. She used the cup of the frozen Coke we bought as a sort of icepack on her eyes.

I show her the kitchen and also the couch in my dad's office where she can lie down. She'd refused to tell me what the fight with her parents was about, only to say things will get better once everyone cools their hot heads.

An hour later, I'm sitting on the floor beside Aunt Carole's desk, surrounded by a forest of papers.

Alondra pads across the carpet in bare feet and yawns. *"Are you looking for something?"*

"A needle in a haystack," I sign and grimace. I give her a shorthand version of what I've been working on to get my mother out of Eden.

When I finish, she signs, *"So what does this Eden Estate have to do with Jane Flanagan?"*

"Well, it doesn't." I push down another guilt pang. *"But maybe if I find some dirt about the place, then it might finally convince her to check herself out."*

She gazes down at the stacks of folders I'd semi-sorted. *"I want to help. What can I do?"*

Standing up, I give my stiff legs a shake. At Aunt Carole's computer, I click on a database and a desktop folder. *"We've digitized a fraction of a trillion documents. Only got another trillion to scan. How about if you search terms like Eden Estate and maybe therapy? And Dr. Davis."*

Alondra nods as I write the terms on a sticky note. *"Easy."*

"Great! And while you were napping, Jake texted. I asked him and Hayden to come by the office. I figure we can safely talk about the aliens here."

She glances up at me. Her pink-stained mouth tightens. *"What is it?"*

"That's what the fight with my parents was about. Aliens." Her face contorts, but she reins herself in. *"They're ashamed of me because they believe I've been telling people heinous lies. Science fiction."*

"But this is science fact, am I right?" I sign. She high-fives me. My phone buzzes. *"The guys are here. I'll have to go downstairs to let them in. Be right back."*

The elevator ride from the eighth floor down to the lobby seems to take forever. I lean against the cool, waist-high steel railing running along the mirrored walls. Green numerals tick down the floors.

The elevator doors finally slide open. But before I can take a step forward, a light explodes before me, turning everything brilliant white. Reeling backward into the wall, I try to shield my eyes from the painful glare. The phone slips out of my grasp.

Cold, leathery hands grip my arms. I know that touch. It's not a comforting one. Then at the speed of light, those hands rip me out of the elevator so fast I barely have time to scream.

All the while, my aching brain registers one thing and one thing only—aliens.

TRACK 54

"Planet Earth"

Present Day

Three, two, one. Wake up, Cassidy.

My eyelids feel so heavy I can barely open them. Wincing, I turn my head from side to side. I'm lying on something cool and solid.

"Wake up, Cassidy," says a familiar voice. "Open your eyes."

Startled, I sit up and look straight into my mother's blue eyes. There are more lines around those eyes, more dark circles than I'd ever noticed before. "Mom!"

Mom hugs me. She's so gaunt I feel like I might accidentally break her bones if I squeeze too hard. "Oh, baby," she murmurs into my hair. "I'm so glad you're okay."

I pull back slightly from her and grip her angular shoulders. So, so thin. "What about you?"

Giving me a wobbly, tearful smile, she says, "My day's getting better by the second."

A warm hand settles on my back.

I jump and turn. "Hayden!"

"People keep telling you to stay awake, Cassidy. And what do you do? Snooze." I can see he's trying to smile, but he can't quite make it happen. He draws me up into a hug that melts me with its comfort.

"What's going on? Where are we?" Frowning, I look around the room. It's not the arctic-white space Jake and Alondra described. The walls are clearly visible. Dull gray cinderblock walls. The ceiling tiles are made of a pitted material, very much like those found at school. A dark gray door with a porthole stands in one corner. It's hardly the space-age, high-tech room you'd expect to see on a UFO. I pat my back pocket. My phone's gone. Of course it is.

"Welcome to the Twilight Zone," Jake says, giving me a limp salute. He's sitting in a corner, his back to the wall.

I stand up and peer through the porthole, but there's nothing to see except the reflection of my own face. Turning around, I look from one weary face to the other. "We've been abducted by aliens again? How did we get here? Where's Alondra?"

"We don't know," Hayden says. "Maybe she'll arrive soon."

"Maybe she won't, if she's lucky," I say darkly. "This doesn't look like the regular ship."

"Ship?" My mother sags against the steel gurney I woke up on. It's the only one in the room. The room is bare, with run-of-the-mill gray linoleum on the floor.

"This is Earth," Jake says. "We think."

"And the aliens brought us here?" I ask. "Is this like a base camp? Home away from alien home?"

Mom speaks drowsily, "Cassidy, where did you meet these boys? Will someone explain to me all this talk of ships and aliens?"

Oh God, she's medicated to the hilt. Would she even comprehend it if I told her we've been kidnapped by extraterrestrials?

Hayden pulls me into a corner. In a subdued voice, he

says, "I didn't see who kidnapped us. Just a bright white light. Then they must have knocked us out and brought us in here. Your mom was in here when I came to. I recognized her from the photo on the laptop."

An unsettling sensation burrows in the pit of my stomach. On one hand, I'm relieved Mom's here with me. And on the other, I'm terrified we're here in this room. Just what are *they* going to do with us?

I blast out a breath. "Okay, I *think* we're still on Earth. That's...that's good, right? Alondra's at the office. Maybe she'll send for help."

"Or maybe she'll assume aliens got to us again. And she'll know the cops aren't gonna help them search for E.T." Jake starts pacing. "We could die here."

I'm struck by the strange expression on Mom's face. It's almost like relief. Like dying is a viable way out of this mess. Well, I'm not content to give up. I don't want any of us to die in this concrete box. Dad would never get over it. I don't want him to forever wonder what the hell happened to his family.

"If they can't help us, we're gonna have to get ourselves out of here." I stare at the door again, wishing I could fire laser beams from my eyes and burn it down. There's nothing fancy about it. Nothing to suggest it's made of some space-age material. It's like any other door found on Earth. Pop rivets. Flat gray paint.

So if we're still on Earth, there must be a way out to safety. If I manage to escape, I surely wouldn't find myself on some hostile planet in another galaxy. But I'd have to get past our kidnappers.

"It's no use," Mom says. "The boys tried their best to break down the door and smash that window. There's no way out."

Hayden's hands clench and unclench as if he'd like to try it one more time. He puts his palms to the metal, his expression equal parts fear and defiance. I'm kind of feeling the same way. Scared out of my wits, but at the same time, I just want to fight against these aliens. Stop them once and for all.

"So what do we do? Just wait?" I pace the room. Twenty feet by twenty. The walls are rock-solid and cold. A vent above the door is, I guess, our air supply.

"That's all we can do," Mom says, rubbing her temples.

Tentatively, I sit beside her on the gurney. "Mom, I visited you a couple of weeks ago. At Eden. Do you remember?"

She looks at me in surprise, then looks thoughtfully at a blank wall. "I…I thought I was dreaming."

"No, I was there. In the flesh." I hug her, just so I can validate again that she's really with me. "Do you know where we are now? This doesn't look like Eden."

Mom looks around the room as if for the first time. Her forehead furrows deeply. She seems to be working through a mental fog. "It's…possible. I've never seen this room before, but come to think of it, that ceiling looks awfully familiar. God knows I've memorized every inch of my cell."

Hayden's still pressing on the door, glaring at it as if he's trying to open it with the power of his mind.

"You mean your suite, don't you? You're not a prisoner," I say, anger rising in my chest as Mom looks away. If I ever get a hold of Charlie, he'll be sorry he recommended that hellhole for my mother.

She stares at her bony hands, peeks at me, then looks away again. "Sometimes, I feel that way."

"Why, Mom?"

"Because…" Her voice is no louder than that of a mouse.

"I can't leave Eden, even if I wanted to."

Her words hit me with the force of an asteroid impacting the ground. I gasp. "I knew it..."

"There's something really off about Eden," she says, brow wrinkling in concentration.

"Mom, I have been saying that all along." But my gut instinct about the place is nothing to celebrate. I should have fought harder to bust her out. "I found a note on your laptop. Something about a lawsuit against Eden. Do you remember?"

"No..." She tilts her head, deep in thought.

"Mom?" I prod.

"I'm sorry." She gives a mirthless laugh. "I get these moments of clarity sometimes, where I make up my mind to check out. And I tell the doctor, I do. Demand to be released. I want to get back to my family and my work. Then...I don't know. He'll start talking to me and the next thing I know, I'm unpacking my bags."

"What does the doctor say to you?" Jake asks. "He must be pretty convincing."

I glance at Hayden. He's mouthing to himself now, forehead pressed against the door.

Mom shakes her head ruefully. "I can't pull the words from my brain. But I feel like this scenario happens every few weeks. Days, maybe. I can't keep track of time."

The sound of a lock turning makes us all jump. We stare at the closed door, then at each other with wide, startled eyes. Trembling, Mom puts her arms out protectively and tries to herd Jake and me toward the back wall.

"Hayden," I whisper. Cold air rushes against my face. "Get back here."

He looks from the door to me. A smile tugs at the corner of his mouth, then extends fully across his face. He pumps a fist in triumph. "It's unlocked."

Jake suddenly breaks from the huddle. "Well, what are we waiting for? Let's get out of here."

"We can't go charging out like a herd of bulls," I say, grabbing his muscly forearm. "Who knows what's on the other side?"

Hayden looks at the ceiling, nose twitching. His smile falters. "Shit."

"What is it?" Mom asks. "Do you smell something?"

"I *feel* something." He shakes his head vigorously and reaches me in one big stride. "Stand still. Can you feel it, too?"

Holding my breath, I become a statue. Hayden pulls me close. An infinitesimal vibration pulses under my feet. A low-pitched droning gradually fades up into my ears. It seems to beat on my eardrums, sending shockwaves to every cell. I whisper, "I feel sick."

"What's going on, man?" Jake says, clutching his head. "Is it an earthquake?"

Against Hayden's wall of muscle, I mumble, "The door's unlocked. Let's just run."

The entire room seems to vibrate as the droning gets louder and louder. The walls, the floor, the ceiling. Us.

"It's not an earthquake. They're using sound frequencies to render us unconscious," Hayden says, his voice grim and distorted.

Jake staggers away from the door. Face red and sweaty, he asks, "And you know this how?"

Hayden coughs. "I read an article about some... experiments. In a science journal."

Mom moans and sags against my side. I tear myself away from Hayden. "Mom!"

But she's already unconscious. I try to check her pulse.

It's hard to distinguish the beats of her heart from the increasingly unbearable droning. A vein in her neck throbs under my fingers. She's alive, but unconscious.

My thoughts swirl dizzily as first aid training from a summer camp kicks into gear. It takes all the strength I have—which is not much—to roll Mom onto her side in the recovery position. Feels like pushing a boulder uphill. Nausea overwhelms me. I wobble all the way down to the floor. Hayden's hands scoop my head to stop it from cracking on the hard linoleum.

"I can't feel my body," Jake pants beside us. Moving his hand as if it's filled with concrete, he pats down his thigh. "I can't…"

When he doesn't finish his sentence, I try to reach out to him. But my arm feels like an anchor. I can barely move it. "Jake?"

"Jake's okay. He's breathing." Hayden's face hovers above mine. It's hard to focus on him. He's becoming a blurry shape.

"What about you? Are you breathing?" I mumble. Hayden's face rubs against mine. I'm grateful for the rough stubble of his face. Makes me feel like I'm still alive. His arms wrap around me. I try to hug him back, but my brain has no jurisdiction over my muscles.

"Yes," he says softly, rocking me. "I'm still here. And I'm so, so sorry."

"For what?" My breathing slows. The room starts to darken. Or is that consciousness fading away?

"It was me." It's in that gloom, right before everything goes pitch-black, that I hear Hayden's anguished whisper. "I'm the one who unlocked the door. Now we're being punished."

TRACK 55

"Message to My Girl"

Present Day

I wake to the sensation of cold hands coming at me from all sides. With superhuman strength, they pin down each arm, each leg. A cloth is strapped over my mouth to stop me from screaming. A blindfold covers my eyes.

Cool breath glides over my sweaty forehead. "Shhh, shhhh."

Then hot pain jabs into my left arm. Instinctively, I try to kick at my captors, but it's no use. And soon, there's no need for them to hold me down. My muscles weaken. Fog starts to roll through my brain. I hear the sound of feet slowly shuffling away.

"What did you do to me?" I try to yell, but my words come out all jammed together and incoherent because of the gag.

"Shhhh." Cool breath. Soothing tone.

"Who are you?" I mumble.

A light turns on somewhere. A very dim one that makes everything monochrome. It does nothing to reveal where I am or the source of that voice.

"Shhh. Easy does it. You're okay." It's a female voice, I realize. Her hand presses against my open palm. But her touch is leathery.

No, not leather. Latex. She's wearing a glove like the kind found in any hospital or kitchen. Slowly she removes the blindfold and loosens the gag.

"Are we still on Earth?" I mumble, desperate to stay conscious, to get my bearings. "Are you human?"

She leans over me. So close I see only her eyes. Two human eyes. And in a very human voice, she whispers, "Shhh. Stay still."

Another set of footsteps echoes through the room.

"Is she under?" asks a gruff, male, human voice. He sounds like an older guy. Older than my father. Grandfatherly, even.

"Hey! What's going on here? Let me go!" I yell. At least, that's what I try to yell. To the others in the room, my words probably sound like a series of high-pitched grunts. The woman's grip on my hand gets tighter.

"She's had ten cc's, Director," says the female. My eyes adjust to the light. She has blond hair. Hazel brown eyes you could almost describe as lifeless.

The man's voice is low and ominous. "All right. When she's fully under, give her five cc's of the Suppression formula. I want to see how far we can push her."

"Yes, sir," replies the woman robotically. Her hand closes around my right wrist. Heavy footsteps recede, and a door closes somewhere. A soft breath whispers across my cheek as she leans down and loosens the gag over my mouth even more. Her demeanor changes completely. Her dull eyes seem to light up from a fire inside. "I have to talk fast before he gets back to the God Room."

Jesus. God Room?

Lips barely moving, she says, "Do you know who I am?"

"Are you an alien in human form?" I whisper. I'm surprised by the look of sorrow and regret in her gaze.

"I am Daisy."

"Daisy? Do you work for the aliens?" My brain might still be navigating the fog, but it finally registers the phrase from Mom's notes. *Daisy chain*. Eyes bulging, I squeak, "What—"

"Shh. I've disabled the listening devices. It should take the Director a while to figure out the problem. But there are cameras on us. Just stay still and nod if you understand."

Head heavy from the injection, I nod. The gag slides.

"Help me, and I'll help you," she says. She adjusts the cloth so it covers my lips again, but loose enough so I can speak through it. "For both our sakes, be quiet and listen. I have limited time in which to explain everything. I know I don't deserve your trust, but right now, I'm your best friend."

Daisy flicks a surreptitious glance at a row of mirrors embedded high in the wall. One-way glass.

"Who's up there? The guy who just left the room?"

"The Director. Someone I used to trust." The woman swallows hard. "But someone I do trust completely is your mother. Nina."

"Mom?" I start to wriggle. "I have to get back to her."

"Please. Hold still." She shushes me again. "You will see her again in good time." Again, her gaze drifts to the observation window. When she speaks next, she sounds in control. Not because she's trying to remain emotionless for her alien bosses, but because she's trying to keep her emotions from taking over.

"What is she doing in this place?"

Her upright posture falters for a split second before recovering. "Nina was looking for me."

"Looking for..." A burst of adrenaline surges through me, defying whatever substance they'd given to me earlier. *Suppression formula*. I shudder, imagining what that drug could do to me. And that surge shifts some more puzzle pieces together.

Daisy.

Daisy chain.

Daisy…Jane.

"Holy shit," I rasp. "You're…you're Jane Flanagan."

Her nod is almost imperceptible. Under her lashes, she throws another cautious glance at the observation windows. "Daisy was my code name."

My hands curl into tight balls. "You've been here almost forty years! Why haven't you tried to escape?"

"I have a tracker implanted inside me. It's crude technology, but it works. *They* will find me, just as they've found other workers who've tried to run." Jane gives a mirthless laugh and scratches the base of her skull.

"Do *I* have a tracker?" I whisper. "What about the other abductees? Hayden?"

She shakes her head. "I'm told abductees are easy to track through data now. Unless you are off the grid, your digital footprint is everywhere. And we…*they* have some fail-safes in place."

"Stalking?"

"Drone surveillance. Stakeouts," Jane adds, her lips angling downward.

"I don't understand. How can you be a part of all this? It's criminal!" I want to feel sorry for her, but at the same time, I'm filled with disgust.

"I realize that. Now. But I had no choice. This place is all I've known since I was a child." Her eyes fill with tears. She blinks them away, but the anguish in her face remains even as she tries to hide it. Her pain is palpable. The disgust I felt melts away. "For a long time, I didn't even know what my real name was. Didn't know I had a life before I was brought here. And then your mother came along. She helped me remember my past."

"Jane—if you really are Jane—"

"I am." She glances down. A fat tear drops to the floor.

"Who brought you here? Who kidnapped you?"

Her hands shake as she whispers. "I don't remember."

"Something doesn't add up," I say, staring hard at her. "Mom would've called the cops the minute she found you."

"She knew about the tracker inside me. Plus, she was… persuaded to stay quiet." Her eyes dart to the tray of needles and medications beside me.

"Drugged?"

"And hypnotized," Jane replies soberly. "Then she was brought here."

A tremor violent enough to measure on the Richter scale rocks me. My mother didn't check herself in here. She was trapped. Abducted.

Hypnosis—at least the kind practiced here—is hazardous.

"Where are we? Are we all gonna get out of here?"

"Cassidy, I would love to answer your questions. Really. But I have a job to do, and fast. As do you." She writes something on a slip of paper. Then she picks up a needle and draws clear fluid from a small vial. I recoil as the silver needle glints ominously under the lights.

"What are these 'jobs'?"

"*Your* job is to get out of here and find my parents while I look after your mother. I know you can do it. But discreetly. It's important you tell them my code name. Only they and the Secret Service know it."

I stare at the menacing needle. "Are you sure that needle's not gonna kill me?"

"This vial contains a new formula that's meant to

suppress memories," she says. "Don't be afraid. I'll only inject a minute amount this time. I'm so sorry I have to do this at all, but *he'll* know if I don't. Please know that I never wanted to hurt you. I wanted to fight them as much as you did. But I couldn't. Someday, you will understand."

I keep my lips taut while Jane pushes my right sleeve up. The needle tip presses lightly against my skin. Cold, viscous liquid oozes uselessly down my arm, making me tremble. By not injecting the full dose, she wanted to show she's trustworthy.

And it's a very good show.

"All right, now breathe deeply, like you're trying to get to sleep. I know you want to sleep anyway. The sedative is quite powerful." Her voice is calm as a lake in summer. Hypnotic. Warm. "But I will give you a way to remember something extremely important. It'll be part of your soul."

Wait. She's trying to hypnotize me. This woman who claims she's a former president's long-lost daughter. But almost forty years have gone by since Jane Flanagan disappeared. Who knows what she would look like today? How do I know she's telling the truth? She was five years old at the time of her disappearance; surely she wouldn't remember much about her past?

Stay awake, Cassidy! Don't fall for it!

I swallow a ball of fear as she discreetly mops up the now useless drug. Fog invades my brain. Slurring, I say, "There are no aliens, are there? It's all a lie."

Jane eyes me. She carefully pats down my arms and legs. Slips off my sneakers and inspects them, then slides them back on again.

"We have all been deluded by our fellow human beings. For what purpose, I don't yet know. The Director only tells us what we need to know. The big picture isn't one of those things." She checks equipment beside my bed. "Forgive me, but the sedative I gave you a few minutes ago should start to take full effect now. You won't wake up again until after you're transported. There will be side effects, but they won't last long."

"What's going to happen to me?" I whisper, my tongue thick with fatigue.

"You'll be okay. I'll protect you as long as I can, I promise."

Behind her, the door thuds open. The room plunges into blackness.

The Director's voice carries across the room in deep, ominous notes. "Now, now, Jane. Don't make promises you can't keep."

TRACK 56

"They Don't Know"

Present Day

A loud buzz, followed by a bone-jarring jolt, wakes me from a deep sleep.

"Whoa!" Beside me, Hayden grabs my hand. Judging by the startled expression, he just got a rude awakening, too.

My head feels thick and heavy. I look around and see my reflection everywhere. And Hayden's and Jake's. Green numbers on the wall count up. I'm in a familiar place.

"What the hell happened?" Jake's slumped against another wall. His eyes move around dizzily. "Are we in a spaceship?"

"It's just an elevator in Dad's building. We're okay. I think." I grip onto the cool steel bar running along three sides of the car. My legs are wobbly, but they have just enough strength to support me. Hayden slowly rises along with me.

"But we *were* in a spaceship, right?" Jake asks. He's not even attempting to stand. His body looks limp and weak.

"Give me a few minutes to unscramble my brain," I mumble. The elevator's inching along at a sloth's pace. Seems like it's taking forever to crawl from the ground floor. Seven more floors to go. "I saw you guys in a concrete room.

And my mom…my mom was there. At least, I think she was…"

"Yes, she was there," Hayden says, then gives a troubled frown. "But everything else is foggy."

Closing my eyes, I try to put myself back in the moment. Images and sounds come at me. They disappear quickly like water down a drain. I force my brain to drag those memories back, but it's a struggle. "The room we were held in, it seemed so ordinary. Like something you'd find on Earth."

"Yes!" Jake snaps his fingers. "It had cinderblock walls. They reminded me of my school gym."

"Maybe we were put in some transition or holding room before being taken to their ship," I say.

Jake forces a laugh. "What, are the aliens renting a warehouse here? Why would they bother doing that? Can't they just suck us up into their spaceship with their tractor beams?"

Hayden paces the tiny elevator like a caged leopard. Suddenly, he stops and checks his arm. We all do. We've each got a tiny puncture in the crooks of our arms. I'm too out of it to feel a sting.

Anger bristles off of Hayden as he grates out, "We were drugged."

"Yes." I stand straighter and squint as if trying to squeeze a memory out. And it works. A stronger vision flashes and fades quickly. A human face. "There was a woman working on me. She had orders to give me a second dose of some formula, but…"

"A woman? You mean an alien?" Jake asks.

"No, definitely a woman. Blond. Close to my mother's age, or a little younger." My voice strengthens with conviction. "She's an abductee, too. Said I had to help her."

"Another abductee?" Jake asks, using the bar to hoist himself up at last. "What did she want you to do?"

"I don't remember." I growl in frustration with myself. I'm so confused. Is it possible that we were taken by aliens that *look* like humans? Are humans in cahoots with aliens? Can I trust the blond woman? What the fuck is going on? I turn to Hayden. "Did you get out of the room, too?"

"If I could give you a blow-by-blow, I would." His voice is splintered, raw. He pounds a fist into his palm so hard I could swear I hear a bone crack.

The elevator bell *dings*. We all stand frozen in place as the doors glide back. A long hallway fitted with blue patterned carpet stretches before us. Deserted except for a few potted plants dotted near the suites' doors. A fluorescent light at the far end flickers. I put a foot out and carefully test the floor. It's firm and stable.

Unlike me. I steady myself against Hayden. "My feet are numb."

"Mine, too." He slings an arm around me.

I snarl. "They have no right to mess with us like this."

"No argument from me," Hayden replies.

"Oh yeah?" says Jake. "And how are we gonna put an end to it? Think about what just happened to us. They took us away in broad daylight, and we were completely powerless."

Hayden and I exchange glances. Jake's right, of course. The aliens have proved time and time again that they're in charge.

"I'm not giving up. They've got my mom."

Up ahead, the glass doors of my dad's office suite open. Alondra tumbles out, relief carved into her features.

"Where the hell have you been? The power and phones went out, and I've been stuck in here forever. These fancy

electronic doors don't work in a blackout. That's so dangerous!" she signs as I push past her into the office. She's mad. Fire-breathing-dragon mad. Her gaze falls on Hayden and Jake. They're disheveled and tired-looking. *"Are you all okay? What happened?"*

I translate what she says for the guys, then tell her, *"We were abducted."*

Alondra gapes, stunned into silence. Her hands stay by her sides.

Muscles burning, I tap my back pocket. They gave my phone back. How considerate. *"How long have we been away?"*

"More than three hours," Alondra signs. *"My phone went dead and I couldn't charge it."*

"And you were definitely here the whole time? You weren't snatched?" Jake asks.

Alondra frowns. She checks her arm for a needle mark. *"No, I was here. I'm sure."*

The numbness in my feet fades, and pain sets in. My whole body aches. It's like every cell of my body has been expanded and shrunk and expanded again. I force myself to focus. *"I'm sorry about you getting locked in here. That's not supposed to happen, believe me."*

The glass entrance door *whooshes* open. "What are you all doing here?"

We whirl around as one.

"Aunt Carole!"

"I got an alert about a blackout." She strides in. Her beehive hair isn't as high as it usually is. The fingernails on one hand are painted a bright yellow. The other hand is naked. "I was in the middle of a mani."

"I'm so sorry," I say in a wobbly voice. "Everything's under control."

With narrowed eyes, she looks at Jake and Alondra. Both are trembling. "Is it?"

"Okay, no." I glance at the others. *"Should I tell her?"*

They nod with varying degrees of apprehension. Hayden holds his temples, his skin growing red and sweaty.

Taking a deep, deep breath, I sit Aunt Carole down and tell her everything. About the aliens, about the abductions, about seeing Mom locked in a room with us. Hayden is largely silent, either rocking on the balls of his feet or pacing from one corner of the room to the other.

When I finally stop talking and signing, Aunt Carole stares at each of us, her expression a mix of shock, awe, and terror.

"Are you okay?" I wave a hand in front of her eyes. She doesn't blink. For the first time in history, Carole Roekiem is speechless. With good reason. I hold my breath and wait for her to react.

"UFOs…are real?" mumbles Carole at last. "Aliens… are real?"

"Yes!" we exclaim in unison.

A wide grin spreads across Carole's features. "Aliens are real. I *knew* it. Didn't I tell you guys? Didn't I show you those videos?"

"Yep, you did!" I say, relieved. I counted on her being a believer in tabloid stories and dodgy UFO footage to start with. Carole doesn't seem to need much more proof. What evidence could we give her, really?

Her grin is short-lived. "Wait a minute, kids. Aliens. Are. Real. And they're coming after all of you?"

"Yes, that is the downside," Jake says flatly.

"Understatement of the millennium," I sign, without a drop of humor.

Carole frowns, confused. "And you want *me* to stop

them? It's one thing to believe, but…I'm an old lady. I can't even fire a slingshot, let alone a laser gun."

"We're not asking you to go into battle against aliens." Gently, I touch her arm. *"We don't know how to stop them. Yet."*

Carole eyeballs the entrance. "What about Nina? She didn't come back with you. Do you think she's okay?"

"No, I don't know where she is now." I don't want to say out loud that I have no idea if she's okay. My stomach tightens at the thought of her all by herself. Then light bulbs ping inside my head. *"Wait a second. If Mom was there with us three, that must mean she's also an abductee!"*

Pressing her yellow-painted fingers to her chest, Aunt Carole looks faint. Her eyelids flutter rapidly. "That's not possible. In all the years I've known her and talked about UFOs, she's never said she even *believed* in aliens."

"But Cassidy didn't know about her abductions," Alondra signs. *"It's possible her mother had no idea, either."*

"Goodness, how can you even forget something so big?" Aunt Carole says.

"There are ways," Hayden says. His mouth flattens as he jabs his phone's keyboard. "The human mind is adept at suppressing painful subjects."

There's something about hearing the word *suppressing* that forms a knot in my stomach.

"Who are you texting, Hayden? The cops?" I sign.

"I'm thinking that's a good idea. Maybe they can check CCTV footage," Alondra signs. *"There are cameras everywhere, right?"*

"Right." Hayden looks up sharply, then taps on his phone so fast that I'm sure he's breaking the world record for texting.

"First we have to convince them we've been kidnapped

at all, let alone by aliens," Jake says. He scrolls through his phone and frowns. "I can't find any posts about any UFO landing today. You'd think there'd be thousands already."

"I'm not contacting the police. This has to be handled another way." Hayden reads an incoming message, and his features turn to granite. He pockets his phone and continues pacing.

The knot in my stomach tightens. *"Hayden, you're going to wear a groove in the carpet. Talk to me. Is there something going on with your family unit?"*

"You could say that." Hayden turns. His eyes are full of conflict. He grimaces as his phone buzzes again, but he doesn't answer it. "I've just received orders. We have to move."

"You can't. You just moved in," I protest. Hayden puts a palm to his head. *"Oh. Wait. Is there a sinkhole in your neighborhood now?"*

"No. It's more like a black hole," Hayden mutters. He pulls out the phone and reads the message again as if to make sure he'd read it right the first time.

Jake's eyes are wide and wild. "We're dealing with sinkholes now? As well as aliens? What the fuck?"

I give him a rundown about the rumors, all the while keeping my eye on Hayden. He looks like his whole world is crashing down on him. *"But you're sure the orders are because of sinkholes, right, Hayden?"*

Grasping my hand, he says, "I need to talk to you. Alone."

TRACK 57

"I'll Feel a Whole Lot Better"

Winter 1994

I'm doing the right thing. I know I am. This is my insurance, James Davis chanted to himself as he schlepped another box of files from his trunk and headed into an elevator.

It was after ten p.m. He stared at his gray-haired reflection in the elevator mirror. Working for a black-ops department was a boyhood dream. Hell, Parallax was so secret that nobody in the government apart from Blake knew about it.

But lately his conscience was starting to prickle him. He hardly recognized himself anymore. Could he really continue conducting experiments? Sometimes it felt like torture, both to him and the Subjects. He hoped that one day he'd have the guts to end it. Right now, though, it was the money that motivated him. He had debts. Big ones.

The elevator *dinged*. James got out on the eighth floor and headed to Charlie's darkened office.

Charlie was expecting him. Silently, he showed James down a hallway and unlocked a door. The lawyer knew not to ask too many questions. As far as Charlie knew, James was simply following orders from Blake and delivering files for safekeeping. Sure, James could've hired a storage locker in which to put the stolen documents. But the nearest facility had suffered first a break-in and then an arson attack.

No, this was the safest place. For now.

He hefted the box onto a shelf along with two others, then turned to a poker-faced Charlie. “There’ll be more.”

TRACK 58

"I Got You"

Present Day

The downtown building that houses Dad's office is only ten stories high, but it's considered a skyscraper in Dawson. I have to sprint to keep up with Hayden as he climbs the last set of fire escape stairs that leads to the roof. Hayden, on the other hand, is barely puffing. Then again, he's the newest member of the track team and fitter than I'll ever be.

At the landing, he waits for me to catch up. His dark eyebrows are drawing toward each other. Jaw clenched so hard it twitches. He rests a hand on the door's iron-bar handle and looks back at me.

I'm not sure if it's because all the oxygen has gone to my legs, but my vision begins to blur. I grip the cold steel handrail and squint. Two overlapping, translucent Haydens swim in front of me.

"Cassidy?"

"I'm sorry…"

Swaying, I squeeze my eyelids shut as Hayden's voice echoes in my memories.

"…unlocked the door… I'm the one who unlocked the door…"

Panting, I say, "Hayden, what did you mean by that?"

His gaze darts. "By what?"

"By what you said when we were in that room with Mom and Jake," I say, pulling myself up to the landing at last. Fleeting images of a gray cinderblock wall tease me. I glance at the thick steel fire exit door beside us and a *clank* plays in my head. The clank of a lock. "You said you unlocked the door, but you couldn't have. It's not like you had a key."

Hayden bites hard on his lip, turning that soft skin from pink to a brutal shade of red. Finally he releases his lip and nods. "You're right. That's what I said. I unlocked it."

"How?"

"You can do anything," he says with the briefest of smiles, "if you put your mind to it."

"Your *mind*?" I scoff. He really has taken his collection of self-help books to heart.

"It's hard for people to believe, I know." He takes a step toward the fire door, then turns to me. The fierceness in his expression relents bit by bit. "Before you regained consciousness in that holding cell, I realized my abilities were weakened."

"Your *abilities*? What are you talking about?"

He swallows audibly. "Can I show you?"

I splutter and step back from the door. "Please. I'd love to see your mind do some heavy lifting."

Hayden's eyes shutter over, like he's uneasy but he realizes there's no going back now. He gives me a sober nod. Putting his hands behind his back, he faces the door. "This should only take a second."

As Hayden's gaze drills into the door, the air around us thickens. Electricity pulses. But there are no sparks. No fireworks. No strings. No smoke. No mirrors. The iron bar clunks downward and the door opens.

Just like that.

All by itself.

And it really did only take a second.

But what the hell was *it*? What enables a person to use their mind to move inanimate objects?

Fresh air rushes in from outside. My chest heaves. I keel dangerously toward the concrete stairs. Hayden hooks my waist and brings us toe to toe. My bones have turned to jelly. I wish I had recorded him on my phone, because I keep replaying what just happened in my mind and I can't understand it.

I'm not sure how long it takes to regain my voice, but when it comes, it's hoarse. "What do you call that? Witchcraft? Are you like Harry Potter?"

"Nothing like that." Hayden puts his foot out to stop the door from swinging shut. I tremble in his grip. "Whatever they drugged us with when we were taken turned out to be my kryptonite. At one point, I had to resort to trying to physically break us out."

"If you couldn't use your…your mind and you couldn't use brute force, how did you unlock the door then?"

"Is now a good time to tell you I'm also blessed with a fast metabolism?"

"You're saying the 'kryptonite' wore off, Superman?"

"Yes."

"And *then* you put your mind to unlocking the door?"

"Yes," he repeats. His brow wrinkles. "I hope I'm not scaring you."

"I don't know how I feel," I say honestly. He has opened a door—two doors now—using the power of his brain. Normal people don't do that. Normal people *can't* do that. And yet here's Hayden McGraw, showing me he is a thousand levels above normal people. Something tells me this is beyond simple magic, like something you'd see at a flashy show in Vegas. He might even be supernatural, despite what he said about not being a wizard.

"You're in shock. I can understand that. You don't see this kind of thing every day." He slides his hand into mine. I look down at our entwined fingers, still not fully understanding what I just witnessed. "Come on, let's go outside. There's a lot to explain."

The building casts a long shadow over the mall and quaint specialty shops. In summertime, it's party central on the rooftop, where people hang out under a pergola strung with fairy lights. Heavy chairs and tables anchor a big square of artificial turf. On an October afternoon, you're likely to freeze your ass off. Which is why there's nobody else here, with only the occasional bird around to spy on us from above.

My feet stumble over themselves as I make my way to the chairs and sit on the very edge. Vertical timber slats of a pony wall act as a windbreak, but cold air turns my breath into vapor. Hayden pulls a chair as close as he can. Using his hands this time. He takes off his coat and drapes it over my shoulders. He's still the slightly old-fashioned but sweet Hayden I've gotten close to. But I don't move an inch.

"So," I say, trying to keep my voice steady, like I can handle whatever he's got to tell me. Because, for better or worse, we're dating. Shouldn't I be accepting of him no matter what? Is being able to move inanimate objects a deal-breaker in the grand scheme of things? "What was that back there?"

"It wasn't sorcery." He hesitates a second, then says in a matter-of-fact way, "It was telekinesis. The ability to focus on an object and make it move without touching it."

"Telekinesis," I repeat, then suck in my cheeks. "Is this

something you learned? Like magic tricks?"

"Uh, no. I was born this way. I'm proud of my abilities. I hate hiding them from you. But I have to. For survival." He dips his head and his shoulders droop. "It gets me into trouble sometimes. Notably today. If I hadn't lost control of myself and unlocked the door, they wouldn't have retaliated."

"You don't know that. It could have been a coincidence," I rationalize in spite of this wholly irrational conversation. "Those aliens were probably testing us somehow. Seeing what we'd do if the door were unlocked. They wouldn't come all this way to Earth without a plan."

He looks up sharply. "They weren't aliens. I'm one hundred percent sure."

"How do you know?"

"Because *I* am an alien."

A smile spreads across my face, but it falters when I see the seriousness in Hayden's gaze. "Come on," I say. "Stop messing around."

"It's true. I'm…I'm from a planet very much like this one called Agua. It's fourteen thousand light-years away from Earth." He looks at me without blinking, and right then I feel like I'm having an out-of-body experience.

Shaking, I shrink back in my chair and take in his handsome *human* features. Two eyes that look like pools of melted dark chocolate. Soft lips that can be tender one minute and scorching-hot the next. I almost want to run my fingers through his glossy hair, just to see if it would move and reveal something terrifying.

Like the faces in Alondra's alien paintings.

My heart hammers against my ribs like it wants to break out. Faintly, I say, "Stop. You're *not* an alien. Aliens don't drive badly the way you do. Aliens don't go to stupid school dances. And…and they sure don't kiss the way you do!"

"How do you know?" he asks wryly.

"They just don't!" Another memory of Hayden blazing a trail of kisses down my neck surfaces. It was quickly followed by another—the first time his tongue slicked against mine, making me see stars.

He inches toward me and I shift back even farther. My skin feels hot and clammy, like I'm coming down with a fever.

My boyfriend can't be an alien. It's not humanly possible.

He's not human, a nagging voice inside me says.

Until five minutes ago, I felt safe around Hayden. Swoony, even. Breathless every time he so much as brushed his fingertips across my skin. Now? I'm freaking out. Because he's telling me he's an intergalactic being. Next thing he's going to say is there's nothing to be afraid of.

But I've watched *V*, the old TV show where beautiful, humanoid aliens come to Earth, hang out, fall in love with humans. Everything's hunky dory until someone realizes the aliens are actually guinea pig-eating, bloodthirsty reptiles with world domination on their agenda.

I swallow hard. "If you really are an alien, what are you doing in a random place like Dawson?"

"You'll let me explain? You won't run?" he says, sounding relieved.

I shoot a quick glance at the fire escape. I could make it there in a few big strides if I really had to. After that, I'm not sure what would happen. Maybe he'd catch me. Maybe he'd release me. Slowly, I nod.

Exhaling, he says, "We were just…existing. Minding our own business. Going to school and work like normal… people. But, uh, that night I followed you home, when we lost time? What happened that night scared the hell out of me." He scrapes his hair back with his interlocked hands. "It was days before I worked up the courage to tell my family unit. They were furious, of course, that I was so irresponsible as to get captured and not remember any details. Trudy even tried to hypnotize me, but it turns out I'm resistant to hypnosis. My mother contacted our diplomats and confirmed that there were no scheduled missions in the quadrant..."

Listening to him, my brain spins like a hurricane. I can't get enough air into my lungs. When Moira hypnotized me, I had a vision of Hayden as an alien. Albeit as a bobble-headed, creepy-faced one. But maybe deep, deep down, I knew he wasn't from Earth.

As if reading my mind, he plucks at his stubbled cheek. "I'm not wearing a mask to look like this."

"How did you know what I was thinking? Are you a mind reader?" If I sink any farther into the chair, I'm going to be embedded in it. Why I don't run instead, I'm not sure. Maybe because I have to know more. If he wanted to hurt me, he would have done it by now.

Or is he using *alien* telekinesis to hold me? Or somehow controlling my mind and body?

I'll always keep you safe.

That's what he said after the joy flight. I hold onto that thought for as long as I can. Because a big part of me wants that to be true, now more than ever.

"I can communicate telepathically with fellow Aguans," he says, "but I mostly choose not to."

"Oh, *mostly.* Okay, then." I can't help being sarcastic. It's like a coping mechanism.

"It's true," he says, looking at me with an earnest gaze. "We're not about being intrusive, not mentally. Your private thoughts are just that. Private. But I have exceptional intuition."

I shake my head as if that'll rattle my brain into gear. "I don't understand. You're from another planet. Why do you look like…" *The hottest human ever to walk the halls of Dawson High.* "…like that?"

"Do you think all aliens look like Yoda? Not my dog Yoda," he clarifies. "The little green guy."

"No, not exactly. You heard Mrs. Walters. She said aliens exist only in the form of bacteria."

"Yeah, I really wanted to school her that day." His grin dies a quick death. "But she mentioned panspermia. You know, the idea that a species can be distributed across habitable universes—by hitching a ride on an asteroid, for instance."

"I wasn't exactly paying attention at that point." I was thinking of my mother and the Jane Flanagan case. In the space of two weeks, life has become one big complication after another. Now *this*?

"Okay, well, she was right. Long story short, through panspermia, civilizations of humans have been seeded across multiverses over time. Earth is a planet that holds one of those civilizations. Agua is another. My planet." He stops for a moment and watches my reaction carefully. I'm pretty sure I resemble a stunned trout at this point. I gesture for him to continue and he nods. "Like Earth, Agua hosts a number of different species, including humanoids like me and 'Gray' aliens. Those are the beings you typically see demonized in horror movies here."

"I'd say they're demonized for a reason." Images of Alondra's artwork make me shiver. "They abduct people. You heard the people at that support group."

His lips twist. "There are civilizations of Grays who deserve the bad reputation. But on Agua we live in harmony with them. They are kind. Knowledgeable. They have a role to play, and so do we."

As he speaks, his language becomes more formal. Less twenty-first-century boy. Is *this* the real Hayden?

"Cassidy, when you were abducted the first time—the *only* time—by real aliens, by the Aguan Grays, when you were twelve, they would have painlessly taken data and marked your DNA."

"With a lemon zester-like instrument?" I say archly, though what he's saying does match part of Alondra's story. She said it was painless that first time.

"Um, I don't know what to tell you. Our Grays don't use anything that resembles a lemon zester." He peers at me. "My dad wants his back, by the way."

"Fine." A red-hot blush climbs up to my cheeks. I change the subject away from my pilfering, which is not the most terrible thing in the world, really. "Why did they mark my DNA?"

"To identify you as an abductee, and one who cannot be taken again. The Grays use a retinal scan, using certain light spectrums, to determine who must be left alone."

Gasping, I grip the arms of the chair. "That's what you were doing in class that day? Trying to ID me? And Trudy, too, with her so-called light experiments?"

"What I said about you reminding me of Kalexy was true. The first time I saw you, it threw me because I was still processing her death." He slays me with an intense stare. "But then that's when I realized you were also…marked."

I gulp uncomfortably. Alondra was right. I was abducted by kindly Gray aliens. "What's *your* role in this game?"

"It's not a game, trust me." He looks up at the sky, where dark clouds are coming together. "Think of us as anthropologists. Teams of us have been tasked with finding humanoid civilizations. Earthlings are doing the same thing. Just not on the same scale."

I close my eyes. "Oh yes, I feel so much better now that I'm picturing you as Sir David Attenborough."

"My family unit is here to observe. That's it." He shrugs both shoulders. "We're not to interfere. We can interact, of course. Buy real estate to support ourselves and drive clunky old trucks."

"A family unit? That's really what you call yourselves?" I ask. He nods, but I can't help feeling like the name has military connotations despite his "we come in peace" spiel.

"Yes, we are a real family," he says. "We arrived here when I was seven. Trudy was born in Upstate New York, but she's an Aguan through and through. She's aware she's not like Earth girls. Lindsay is homeschooling Trudy until it's deemed safe for her to mix with others."

"You should tell her not to leave her calculus textbooks lying around on play dates, then." I allow a small grin. He returns a relieved smile, sensing that what he's saying is sinking in. And it is. A little. But most of it is still out-of-this-world unbelievable. "What does it mean to be Aguan? Like, how are you different from us, aside from telekinesis?"

He inhales deeply. "By what we can determine, the Earth civilization is younger, much less evolved than our own, with fewer genetic mutations."

"So you're saying we're primitive?" I blink. "Why would you hang around us? I mean, we have to move things around manually. We can't just use our brains."

Again, he shrugs. "I'm telling it as it is. We Aguans are evolved humans. We have advanced hearing, vision, and language skills, use mental telepathy, telekinesis—as you now know—and are fifty percent physically and mentally faster than Earthlings."

My mind boggles as he reels off his people's abilities. "So *that's* why you're a big track star. Isn't that an unfair advantage over your competitors?"

"Which is one reason why I dial it back a little when I'm competing here. I deliberately run fifty percent slower than usual." He laughs. "It was Trudy who fixed your mom's laptop. But I checked her work on the chip."

"Well. Can't deny it's impressive. And it sucks to be an Earth human in comparison." I look down at my hand, and instantly I'm reminded of the panini incident in the kitchen. There's no evidence of a burn. Even the paper-cut scars have vanished. My jaw drops as realization hits. "You really did heal me."

"Yes." He flashes a modest smile.

"Hayden, you get that's a superpower, don't you?" I grab his wrist. "You could change the world! *This* world."

"We can't. That's part of the bargain we made to live here."

"So…you do everything in your power to *not* use your powers?" I frown. "Who did you bargain with? The devil?"

He pauses and looks anywhere but at me. "Your government."

His words crash into me like a speeding truck. Air knocks out of my lungs. "The *government* is in on this?"

"An agreement was made many decades ago. We would share some of our technology in exchange for safe arrival, documents, seed money, the chance to study your planet. To learn from Earth's mistakes." His solemn gaze rakes over mine. "I think you can see why this needs to remain confidential. The panic it would cause across the world?"

My thoughts swirling, I nod. "There are already thousands of conspiracy theories."

"Some of them draw attention *away* from our presence

here, so that's a good thing. From what I gather, a deal between universes is so far-fetched that few people believe it." Sadness creeps across Hayden's face. "In any case, about changing the world, there are limits to being able to heal others. Contrary to what you said, we don't have superpowers. If we could bring people back to life, we would. But no one gets to live forever. No one."

"Kalexy," I whisper. His fists clench as he gives a short nod.

"She passed away in a flying accident." Gaze solemn, Hayden leans forward, his hand on my knee. Heat radiates from his palm. His story isn't the only bamboozling thing. "I've overwhelmed you."

"A little." A big lie.

His gaze is hypnotic. Spellbinding. "Cassidy, I need you to know I would never hurt you. That goes against everything we Aguans stand for. Our mission is only to observe and not harm."

I rub my arms and shift on the hard seat. Quietly, I say, "You know, it is possible to harm someone emotionally. Lead them on. Pretend you like kissing them, when really you're just observing them?"

He straightens. "Believe me, I tried to stay *away* from you. But I couldn't. I didn't want to. You're an extra-special terrestrial. What I feel for you is real. You bring out the best Aguan in me."

I stare at his hand—his alien yet very human hand—as it winds its way to mine. I can't move. I don't want to. The memory of his hands exploring my body brings a little ache in my heart.

"For years, I've been told to hide who I am," he says, never keeping his intense brown gaze off my face. "The one time I did show someone what I could do, things didn't go the way I intended. It could have meant the end of this world for my family unit. But we were given a second chance."

"In Dawson. Sinkhole City. You were set up to fail."

He snorts. "There are no sinkholes. It really is a rumor to discourage people from living near us."

"So you can continue your nefarious activities in *private*?" I say pointedly. Then a thought ricochets through my skull. I gasp. "There are more of you coming. You're all going to live on that estate like some kind of cult."

His jaw clicks. He releases my hand. "I'll ignore what you said about it being like a nefarious cult, but that was the basic plan. Until now."

"What's changed?"

"We've been exposed." He looks away. "The abductions we've experienced recently? I'm telling you, it's not aliens who are intercepting us. It's humans. And they're using elaborate means to do so."

Blood drains from my face. I shiver inside and out. In a whisper, I say, "Why?"

"I've been trying to find out," he says in a grit-filled voice. "But my parental unit thinks I'm the real target. We believe they've discovered I'm not from this world." Despair makes him tremble. "Lindsay has called for an extraction before they do something worse."

It feels like a boa constrictor is winding around my heart and squeezing it dry. "That sounds very painful."

"Yes. In more ways than one." His shaking hand reaches for my cheek. He strokes it in that special way of his, creating little fires wherever his fingertips roam. "But, Cassidy, I can't go back to Agua. You have to help me. I'm begging you."

TRACK 59

"A Soul Kind of Feeling"

Present Day

"What do we tell Jake and Alondra? And Carole?" I ask Hayden as we head back down the stairwell.

Hayden sucks in a huge breath. I can practically see his brain working overtime to assess the pros and cons. Finally, he gives a firm, decisive nod. He speaks as well as uses sign language. *"Everything. But I'll do it. In my own way."*

My eyes pop. "You know how to freakin' sign?"

"I told you," he says with a shrug. "We're good with languages. Even nonverbal ones."

"Just don't scare them. They've been through enough." I stop to adjust my shoe. Something sharp is sticking into my foot. When I stand up again, Hayden's staring at me and fidgeting. "What's wrong?"

"You're not scared of me?" There's a hopeful plea in his voice.

A millennium seems to pass as we look into each other's eyes. I see beyond the obvious hotness that would make a modeling scout double back and offer him a *Vogue* cover job on the spot. In the past few weeks, Hayden's been nothing but the best kind of human—gentle, sweet, funny, smart. Not to mention brave. Some people say moving from one city to another is a pain in the butt. Hayden and his family unit moved from their galaxy to ours.

"No, not one bit," I say, my throat thickening with emotion. With a slight tremor in my hand, I cup his jaw and bring his lips to mine.

But I'm scared *for* him.

Scared because he's counting on me to stop the abductions.

A little while later, I'm handing out cups of cold water to Jake, Alondra, and Aunt Carole. But they're all frozen in shock on the couch in the reception area.

And it's all Hayden's fault.

They barely said a word as he methodically explained his story. Though, at one point, Jake asked for unequivocal proof. Hayden made the couch levitate by an entire two feet off the carpet.

Finally, Aunt Carole moves to her desk, arms and legs stiff. Without a word, she draws out her gin stash and drinks straight from the bottle. She gasps and delicately wipes her lipsticked mouth. "Okay, now I've heard *everything.*" She pauses. "That *is* everything? What else are you going to say? There's an invasion coming?"

"That's it. We're not invading. We're...leaving. Soon." Hayden signs as he speaks. As I listen to him, my chest seems to crush in on itself like a black hole.

Alondra's studying Hayden like he's an artist's model. She looks intrigued and intimidated all at once. I can tell she appreciated him using her own language.

No one is running in panic to the door or making any threatening moves toward Hayden. Much to my relief.

I clear my throat. *"I think we can agree that there's a common enemy here, right? And it's someone terrestrial. They're kidnapping humans—including my mother—and aliens."*

Nodding soberly, Alondra signs, *"Didn't I tell you the aliens were nice to us, Cassidy?"*

"You did. Aliens are the good guys." Glancing at Hayden, my heart flops over. I blink rapidly to hold back the tears. The question now is who the hell is doing this to us? And if they can overpower someone who has supernatural abilities, what chance do we have against them?

"Should we really call you an alien, Hayden?" Aunt Carole puts away the gin and straightens. "You just don't *look* any different to us."

He gives her a lopsided grin. *"I'm fine with my Earth name. I like it. I'm used to it now."*

"Do you have an Aguan name?" I sign. Hayden McGraw, to me, is such a movie star kind of name. Something that a talent agent would pluck out of a phone directory and say "There's a name that belongs on a theater marquee."

He signs one letter at a time. *"Zhor."*

"No last name? Just Zhor?" I sign, and he nods. *"Nice."*

"Yeah, nothing weird or alien about Zhor," Jake says. "Do you also have a hammer and cape? A brother named Loki?"

"No," Hayden replies, *"but I do have a five-year-old sister who could probably create a thunderstorm if you just give her an afternoon to work out the kinks."*

I slide my hand into his and give it a tender squeeze. I don't care what his name is. As long as it's not Darth Vader.

"How am I gonna tell Angie?" Jake says, sweeping his curly hair off his forehead with both hands.

"You can't," I sign. *"It's been killing me to keep secrets*

from her, too. Not to mention my dad. But for everyone's safety, we have to keep this between us."

Jake's nose starts to twitch. He pales and gets up fast. He trips over an archive box. Pages scatter. "Fuck. Nosebleed."

"Nosebleeds are a classic sign of alien abduction. In movies, anyway," Carole says in a subdued voice as Jake runs down the hall.

Alondra frowns at the files spread across the reception area floor. She crouches and starts stuffing them back into the box. I move to help her, but something sharp literally stops me in my tracks. I sit on the couch and ease off my shoe.

"Hey, something just fell out of your sneaker." Aunt Carole seizes on a piece of paper lying under my dangling foot and passes it to me.

I read the looped handwriting. My heartbeat judders. I let the page fall to the carpet. "Oh my…"

Another memory from the abduction surfaces. Earnest brown eyes. Golden blond hair. A whispered voice.

"Your job is to get out of here and find my parents."

"You'll feel it in your soul…"

Hayden picks up the note. Blood drains from his face. *"Daisy/Jane Flanagan is alive. PHIU."*

With a shriek that could shatter glass, Aunt Carole jumps up and down. "She's alive!"

Legs shaking, I get to my feet. Another fuzzy-edged memory swirls to the fore. *"Jane wrote this. She meant I'd feel it in my sole, not soul. My shoe sole."*

Hayden gives Alondra the note, then runs to a back office.

Blood roars through my ears. *"Jane is the woman who injected me with the drug! She wrote the note!"*

Aunt Carole turns sober in an instant. "Little Jane

Flanagan is behind your abductions?"

"No, she was trying to help me," I sign. Putting a hand to my temple, I beg my brain to hurry up and sort through the jumble of images and sounds and memories. Pieces of a conversation echo in my head.

"Perhaps she has Stockholm syndrome," Aunt Carole says thoughtfully. "That's when kidnap victims sympathize with their captors."

Jake returns with tissues stuffed up his right nostril. He looks over Alondra's shoulder. "Holy fuck. What the hell is PHIU?"

Hayden comes back with a box. He drops it on the floor with a thud and extracts a file. *"I came across this last week. A land acquisition from D.W. Prospecting to the U.S. government in 1947."*

I frown. *"Governments buy back land all the time. Even contaminated property. What's that got to do with anything?"*

"Your federal government sold it in 1985 to a new corporation called the Parallax Human Intervention Unit. PHIU."

"Human Intervention Unit? Sounds totally dehumanized." Jake's lip curls. "Like a human resources department."

"There was a note in Mom's computer about Parallax," I whisper. She *was* close to finding Jane. *"Let me look at the note that was in my shoe again."*

This time, it's not just the handwritten text that grabs me. It's the faint gray logo letterhead in the top right-hand corner that depicts five moon phases. Crescent, half, full, half, crescent.

Strains of "The Whole of the Moon" thunder through my head and get louder by the second. The brass section, the drums, the piano, the vocals—they all come together in a heart-thumping crescendo.

Gasping, I poke the note. *"I interviewed a woman named*

Mabel Parkes. She and her kids were in the playground in DC on the day Jane Flanagan went missing. She gave me a description of a van that had this logo on it!"

"What does this all mean?" Jake says.

Cracking my knuckles, I pace the room. *"Before my mom had her breakdown, I'm pretty sure she found out who kidnapped Jane."*

"Why didn't Nina tell anyone?" Aunt Carole asks. I detect a slight hint of hurt lacing her words.

"She needed to verify it first, prove it wasn't a hoax," I sign.

"Do you believe this woman?" signs Hayden. *"What if she isn't who she says she is?"*

"I don't know for sure, but even if it isn't Jane Flanagan, this woman is crying out for help. I can't ignore that," I sign. Our "mission" seems to be expanding by the second. Rescue Mom. Rescue Jane. Stop the abductions. *"How hard would it be to get in contact with an ex-president? DM them on Twitter or something?"*

"There's probably a hundred protocols to follow if you want them to take you seriously," signs Alondra.

Hayden shrugs. *"Well, we'll just have to go through every one of those protocols. Or find a way to bypass them all."*

"Don't they have a charity or foundation?" Aunt Carole asks. "Maybe we can reach them through that."

I snap my fingers. *"Anna Kingston! She was a White House intern. I've been trying to get in touch with her for weeks, but we keep missing each other. She must know someone who can help."*

Alondra dumps a box of files on Carole's desk while I call Kingston. There's no answer. Of course. I'm forced to leave a message. I make room for Alondra and turn to my phone's internet browser. My finger slips on the screen, taking the browser page back to Lewis Blake's Wikipedia page that Billie tapped on days and days ago. His late wife's name jumps out at me.

Eden Marie Blake.

The page has a single, decades-old picture of a dark-haired Blake. Impressive, hawklike nose. Eyes clear and sharp, even behind a pair of wire-rimmed glasses. He seems familiar somehow. But if he's a senator, it's possible I might have seen him interviewed in the media.

"You need to see this." Alondra shoves a file that bears the U.S. government seal under my nose, but I can't focus.

Instead, I read the Wiki page. *"When Eden Marie Blake was diagnosed with terminal brain cancer in 1985, Senator Blake retreated from public life to care for her…"*

Eden.

What are the chances that Blake has something to do with Eden Estate? He's a Colorado native. A mining heir. But he could also be involved in the health care industry somehow.

He named a mental institution after his wife?

Alondra snaps her fingers under my nose. *"Memory experiments. Sleep studies. Mind control. Nanochip implantations… Are you getting this? These are files about a CIA black-ops program that was canned in the eighties."*

"What about it?" Hayden steps closer, brow furrowed. His phone bleeps incessantly, but he ignores it.

"There was a debriefing center for the program." Alondra throws the file onto the desk and looks from Hayden to me steadily. *"Guess where it was."*

"Eden Estate," I sign, simultaneously spitting out the words with venom. Flashes of the rundown, rotting building hit me like lightning. That's no "wellness" center. My mother's not a patient. She's a captive. I've got to get the man who stole her from me. Steel pours into my spine. I

stand straighter. *"Do you know what this means? The same people who've got Mom and Jane are the same people who are kidnapping us. We have to break them out of there."*

"Hell, yes! Right now!" Aunt Carole exclaims at the same time Jake yells, "Fuck, yeah!"

Alondra nods vigorously. *"I'm ready to kick butt."*

"Wait, tonight?" Jake asks. Excitement fades from his face. "I'm supposed to take Angie to that new James Bond movie."

"Oh…" My chest twinges. I try to find the right words. *"You can't stand her up again. It'd shatter her."* Selfishly, I need Jake and his considerable brawn if we're going to storm the castle. At the same time, the thought of Angie getting hurt again kills me. If only she could understand why Jake had to bail on her.

"Thanks for adding the 'again.' Way to rub it in." He smirks and I cringe. Guess I found the *wrong* words.

Alondra signs, *"You could take her with us. Wouldn't that be more thrilling for her than sitting through a crappy movie that's full of CGI stunts?"*

"No, I won't put her in danger," Jake says. He paces, his jaw firming as he mulls over his options. "I can't keep lying to her, man. Can you guys at least give me a chance to explain everything? She deserves to know. Then, depending on whether or not she breaks my balls, we can meet up later to jailbreak your mom. Without Angie."

"Yes. She deserves to know. And you both deserve each other. You're good for her." Eyes blurring with tears, I hug Jake. *"Hayden, are you okay with us telling Angie? I swear to you she will keep it quiet. Hayden?"*

But Hayden's not paying attention. He's staring at his phone like he wants to hurl it into the nearest dumpster.

"The Aguan Grays are coming," he bites out without

looking at me, but he signs it, too, so I know he meant for me—and everyone—to understand him.

My breath hitches. *"What does that mean?"*

Finally he looks at me, dark eyes blazing like twin wildfires. *"They're extracting my family unit within the hour."*

TRACK 60

"The Last Day on Earth"

Present Day

From my car, I peer out at the McGraw house. There isn't a single light on, not even over the fake-timber portico.

"Doesn't look like anyone's home," I say, killing the engine. Even in the vacuum-sealed cabin of the Fiat, the silence of the neighborhood around us is palpable.

"Oh, they're in there," Hayden says. His lips are set in a hard, grim line. "Probably watching us."

Twisting to face him, I ask, "Are you *sure* you have to go right now? Ask for a stay of extraction. What if we can keep you safe somewhere until we find Mom and nail the kidnapper?"

"What, like a bomb shelter? A submarine?" He lets out a joyless chuckle. "Maybe there's time for me to commit a minor crime and get myself thrown in the county jail for a night."

I bite my lip and think it over. "There are some merits to all of those options. I know a good lawyer who can get you out of jail when the coast is clear."

He shakes his head. Dark bangs fall into his eyes. I want to reach out and brush them away, just to give me an excuse to touch him some more before he gets on that spaceship. "If I were still on Earth, I'd want to be there when you get your mom out. Kicking down doors and fighting with you, if that's what it comes down to."

"Then stall for more time," I say, hating the whine in my voice. Leaving Earth is hard enough for Hayden; I cringe with the realization that I'm making it even harder. But I have to try. How am I going to do this without him? I mean, he can move things with his mind. An awesome skill like that would come in handy.

"I have my orders. I'd be letting my family down if I don't follow them." He gives me a desolate look before opening the passenger door.

My legs wobble under me as I get out and wait for him on the curb. I'm numb, and it's got nothing to do with the icy air blowing around us.

He punches a fist into his palm. "It's all my fault. If I'd kept my mouth shut and left the abductions out of my reports, then we wouldn't be on the first ship back to Agua. Every choice I make seems to be the wrong one."

"That's not true. You've made some excellent decisions. You took me to a homecoming dance. Brought a dead laptop back to life when everyone else gave up on it." Leaning against the car, I grab his hand and squeeze as hard as I can. "Most importantly, Hayden, you risked your life to show me who you really are. That took guts."

Hayden kicks at the artificial turf. "Not really. I slipped a few times when my ego got in the way."

"Oh yeah? When?"

Wiggling his long fingers, he says, "There were a few minutes during the flight when I wasn't actually using my hands to control the plane. The landing was on alien autopilot."

"Hayden!" I gasp and bump my hip against his. "I mean,

obviously we survived, but…"

"But we were totally safe. I used my head." He smiles coyly. "Also…I know you were super impressed with me hot-wiring my truck after homecoming, but it was—"

"Don't tell me!" I butt in, laughing. "It was your beautiful mind!"

"If you ever go back to the lookout and find my keys, the truck's yours." He grows serious and slides his arm around me. "I hated hiding my true self from you. I get what Jake said about Angie. I didn't want to lie to you anymore."

I snuggle into him, wishing I could somehow weld us to the spot. At least until winter sets in. Softly, I ask, "What would happen if you disobeyed your parental unit? Stayed with me instead? I could ask my dad to give you a raise so you can support yourself."

"That's impossible. You've seen *Star Trek*, right? Where they teleport people from one place to another?"

"That's actually a thing?" I say, amazed. Part of me wonders if that's something I would miss if I were a sophisticated Aguan stuck on primitive Earth.

Hell yes, I would.

Am I being selfish for not letting him go, not letting him reach the safety of his planet?

Hell yes, I am.

But that's not going to stop me from doing my best to convince him that heaven is a place on Earth. There *has* to be a way to keep his whole family protected.

He shrugs like teleportation is no big deal. "We are transported as a family unit. All for one, one for all."

I wring my hands, twisting each finger till they burn. In no way does it take away the pain of saying goodbye to Hayden. Things between us have only just begun. I breathe faster as a brilliant idea pops into my head. "Okay… Okay, what about Trudy? And Yoda?"

He tilts his head. "Of course they'll come with us. We have dogs there, you know. They're not as smart as Earth dogs, but Yoda will feel at home."

I spin and face him. "But they were born on Earth! They can't go to a planet they've never seen before. That would be too cruel."

My brilliant idea only seems to crush him more.

Burying his face in both palms, he says, "What have I done?"

I pull him as close as I can and hold him tight. His muscles coil and flex in my arms. "You just have to tell your parental unit you need more time. Tell them you're about to find out who's been stalking you. That you're going to take them down so it never happens to another Aguan again."

"Or another human," he growls.

"Right."

"You could…come with us?" Hayden holds his breath. My mouth moves soundlessly. Then he shifts, putting centimeters between us. "No, that was a stupid thing to say out loud. You have a life here. You're going to save your mom and a president's missing daughter. You'll be world-famous."

"I'm not chasing fame. I'm chasing Mom." The more I look at our situations, the more I realize we both have to do what's right for our families.

"You'll find her, I know it." Hayden's hand snares mine. He squeezes so tightly I can feel our pulses throb.

"Oh? Are you psychic, too?" I sniffle quietly.

"No. I just have faith in you." He lifts my hand to his mouth. My eyelids flutter shut as he kisses my jaw line, then my lips.

Slinking my hands around his neck, I kiss him deeply. Every bump and valley of his body fits perfectly to mine. My thoughts float away like stardust as his kisses get more intense. I just want to bottle this moment forever.

Hayden draws away, his fingers trailing down my arm till he reaches my hands. He holds me there, our gazes locked. Every inch between our bodies becomes a mile.

"Hayden." Trudy's girlish voice calls from the porch. Yoda's on a leash at her side, wagging his little yellow tail, clueless about the journey ahead of him.

"This isn't goodbye," he says, bracketing my face in his hands. Tears glimmer, and I bet he's willing them not to fall. Meanwhile, I can't stop thick tears falling hard and fast.

Lindsay walks out. She gives me a taut smile and puts a hand on her son's arm. "It's time, sweetie. They're nearly here. We have to get to the rendezvous point."

Straightening his shoulders, Hayden draws himself up to full height. "You should go now."

"But I want to stay. Wipe my memory of it later. You can do that, right?"

"No, that's one of the Grays' special talents."

"Okay, order them to erase my memories."

"They don't take directives from family units when it comes to mind-altering tactics." He can't look at me. Tension and chaos radiate from every muscle fiber. "Please…just go. It's better this way. For both of us."

Lights begin to flash on and off. Not just the streetlights, but every house on the street. My Fiat jumps up and down on its suspension, every light going like a fit-inducing strobe.

My gaze darts to the sky, searching for a UFO, but all I see is a blanket of bulbous storm clouds.

Then just as suddenly as the light show began, it stops.

My car door opens. Without me putting a hand on it. This is an invitation I would like to decline.

I gaze at each of the aliens and their oh-so-human faces. Trudy's sobs are quiet. Yoda licks her tears away.

Lindsay orders her family into the house but waits by my car door. She faces me, authority dripping from her square shoulders and determined jaw. Gone is the absentminded mom who worried about ruining dinner. With a single index finger, she beckons me forward. She doesn't say a word, but I can feel disapproval in her gaze. My muscles tighten in response, but somehow I put one foot in front of the other.

Once inside the car, I swivel and say, "I-I'm sorry, Mrs. Mc—"

The door shuts in my face with a brutal *thump*.

We stare at each other through the tinted window. Hayden said Aguans can read minds. Well, if she won't let me speak out loud, I'll broadcast my thoughts to her.

I tell her everything that's in my heart, everything I told Hayden just now.

Please let him stay, Mrs. McGraw! I'm so close to finding out who's behind the kidnappings. I'll nail 'em, and you'll never have to worry about being exposed again. You can just live your lives in peace. Observe us all you want! Let those Grays erase my memory of Hayden when I'm done, but please just let him continue his mission on Earth.

Whether she hears my silent pleas or not, there isn't even a hint of emotion on her face. She turns ever so slowly and stalks toward the house.

The ignition turns without human intervention, making me jump. The Fiat's engine roars. Immediately, I put my hands on the wheel and jam my feet on the brake and clutch to thwart further alien intervention.

The engine revs again.

"Okay, I can take a hint," I growl.

I peek over my shoulder just in time to see Hayden looking out from the shadows of the portico. Despair pulses between us. He backs away and disappears into the darkness.

And right then, my heart shatters into a trillion little pieces. There'll be no putting it back together again. Not in quite the same way it was during my happiest times with Hayden.

My phone buzzes.

Alondra: Sending you and Hayden all the hugs. Jake drove me to your house. If you still want to go ahead with the plan, we're in. We'll wait for your go.

I thump my head backward and sigh deeply.

The plan.

Yes, I have to pull myself together and get Operation Mom back on track. I failed to convince Hayden to stay, but there's simply no time to wallow.

Hands trembling, I do a U-turn and travel uphill, past darkened, uninhabited homes that seem to be calling out for people to come and live in them. Going well under the speed limit, I take the same route over Saddleback Ridge that I'd taken after my first fateful visit to the McGraws'.

When I lost hours of my life.

My hands squeeze the steering wheel. I push aside that last image of Hayden and check the time. Eight o'clock. If I'm not home by 8:20, I'll know I've been abducted.

I slam my palm against the wheel. Why didn't I find time to buy a dash cam?

"Wait," I mutter to myself. "I can use my phone. Duh."

At the border between Sinkhole City and Saddleback

Ridge, I stop in the middle of the road. As I reposition the phone holder on my dash, the storm clouds light up intermittently. They're closer now. More voluminous.

By the time I roll video, the lightning is much more intense. I wind down the window, waiting for the first crack of thunder.

But there's no thunder. Not even a chirp of a cricket or a hoot from an all-seeing owl.

The air feels thick. Getting out of the car is a laborious task, like I'm wearing shoes of lead. I cling to the door and look around, unable to take another step. The woods lining the road light up with every streak of lightning. The hackles of my neck have hackles. They stand at attention.

A mammoth triangular shape moves just above the tree line, casting a shadow over the woods and blocking out the storm clouds above. It stalks silently. Slowly. Ominously.

"A U-fucking-O," I gasp. But there's nothing unidentified about it. To me, anyway. It's an *Aguan* flying object.

Scrutinizing the coal-black undercarriage, I make out three gray bubbles on each corner. Windows? I squint harder. No. They're lights, I realize. Throbbing, it seems, to the beat of my racing heart. The tops of the trees ruffle as the ship breezes overhead. Burnt pine needles rain down on me, their pungent scent stinging my nostrils.

My hand trembles violently as I raise a palm to the sky, hoping in some way, Hayden can sense me down here.

This isn't goodbye, I vow. *We'll find each other again.*

The circular lights swirl in shades of purple, blue, and red. Churning faster and faster, brighter and brighter. Then, without warning, the ship shoots straight up at warp speed, burying itself in a flashing nimbus cloud.

In an instant, the woods become alive again. Insects scream. Bats swoop from trees, their wings flapping wildly.

The storm clouds thin, leaving a full spectrum of sparkling constellations. Feet scrambling, I climb onto the roof of my car and search desperately for those purple lights.

But it's no use. Hayden is already far, far away and out of my reach. Forever.

TRACK 61

"This Tornado Loves You"

Present Day

"*This is it. We'll walk from here,*" I tell Jake and Alondra on the service road leading to Eden Estate. And I tell myself to keep my focus on the task ahead.

Easier said than done.

Alondra filled me in on a few of the documents they'd found while I was getting my heart torn out at Hayden's house. But I could barely concentrate on what they were telling me. Government experiments. Cover-ups. Charlie *must* have known. Those files were stored at his and Dad's firm. Is he in on all this? My father, too?

I cast another bereft look at the clear night sky. The storm has well and truly passed.

When I met Jake and Alondra at my house, they were both pale. They'd worked out a way to communicate through text messaging each other. They, too, had witnessed the ship as it passed like a black cloud over Saddleback Ridge, carrying the McGraws to an unknown universe. Incredibly, not a single post on our social media feeds reported on it.

It's still hard to comprehend that I'll never see Hayden again. Never feel the warmth of his kisses or his intense dark eyes. I can't even send him a random text and expect a reply—not all the way from Agua. No Instagram account to stalk. No glimpse of him in the hallways at school. It'll almost be like he's…dead.

I shake my head to vanquish that thought.

Hayden is *not* dead. He will always be alive in my heart and in my hopes. Some way, somehow, we'll see each other again. I have to believe that.

Jake parks his truck under shadowy trees on the interstate's shoulder. From a tool chest in the back, he gets out a pair of bolt cutters. Alondra gives my shoulder a sympathetic squeeze, then glances around uneasily. Tall pines tower around us, forming an almost impenetrable wall along the lonely highway. Apart from distant coyotes and nearby crickets, there's not a soul to be seen or heard.

"I don't think we should go in without weapons," Jake says.

"You mean guns?" Alondra signs. *"Do you know how to use one?"*

"No," he admits. "But I'm a quick learner."

"Putting aside the fact we can't just raid a gun shop at ten o'clock at night, we are not using guns." I turn my phone on vibrate-only and slide it into my back pocket. *"Someone could get accidentally hurt or killed."*

"I agree with Cassidy," signs Alondra. *"Besides, I want answers from these guys. Can't get anything out of them if they're dead. But feel free to knock them upside the head with those bolt cutters."*

"Hands, feet, knees, nails, teeth—those are our weapons." I start tramping uphill. A three-quarter moon illuminates our path. I'm grateful it gives just enough light for Alondra and me to communicate meaningfully. It's vital she sees my facial expressions as well as gestures..

"Guys, we should head into the woods instead of sticking

to the road," Jake suggests.

"Good idea." I shine my phone's flashlight onto the overgrown shrubs. Vines tangle with rusty barbed wire. *"Could you do the honors, please?"*

"Sure." Using the bolt cutters, Jake clips away sections of the slack barbed wire. "Through here."

A few steps away, Alondra's standing by herself, frowning toward the interstate. I round back to her and sign, *"What is it?"*

"I just feel like we're being watched." Alondra shifts from foot to foot. *"Or followed."*

I squint at the tarmac stretching into the distance. *"Did you see something? Like a drone or another car?"*

"I saw a black town car at that gas station we passed a few miles back."

"What about it?"

Alondra peers back at the empty highway. *"I'm probably just paranoid, but…it seemed to be following us. Not closely. For a few miles, every time I turned around, there it was."*

"Where did you last see it?"

"At the turn-off. They kept going on the interstate."

"Are you guys coming?" Jake whisper-shouts.

I cast another look down the road and listen. There isn't a soul around. Or a black town car. *"Yeah, we're coming."*

In the thick woods, we dodge spiky bushes and prairie dog holes. Ten, twenty, who knows how many minutes later, we're facing Eden Estate.

"*This* is your mom's hospital? It looks like it needs to be bulldozed," Jake says.

"I think they want it to look uninhabitable so no one would disturb whatever freaky shit they do here," I sign. The guard's booth is empty. Somewhere close by, a creature squawks.

"But why not just hire tons of security people?" he asks.

"Budget cutbacks?" I study the sprawling, rundown building. Boards cover windows. Gutters hang sideways, dragged down by years of dust and cobwebs. Over the front gate, a single feeble light shines. I move to a dark section of chain-link fence and grab the bolt cutters. *"Let's get started."*

I clip a single rusty wire. Each of us stops breathing. Waiting for an alarm to wail or for a fleet of drones to dive-bomb us. When nothing happens, I keep going. Each snip sounds like a shot from a cannon to my ears.

"What are we gonna do once we're inside?" Jake asks me.

"Search room by room until we find my mother. And we'll do it as quietly as possible. So turn your phones on silent. Switch to dark mode, too, so your screens won't stand out."

"You know what we should do? Split up. We'll cover more ground that way," Jake says. I stare at him, incredulous. "I'm kidding. I've always wanted to say that. Classic horror movie stuff."

Alondra signs, *"I think you're right. Someone needs to keep a lookout. I'll hide out here and let you know if someone comes."*

Jake shakes his head. "I can't leave you out here alone."

"Why not? I'm deaf, not helpless. I'll stay behind these bushes."

Jaw clicking, Jake nods. "Point taken."

"Okay, guys." I push through the fence. Sharp wire scrapes my arms and legs, but I ignore the pain. "Text me if you see anyone coming. I'm going in."

The sound of an engine in the distance makes me freeze. I squint in the direction of the interstate. There's no glow of headlights.

"What is it?" Alondra signs.

I signal to both of them to crouch and be still.

Car doors thump quietly, as if the people were trying to close them without drawing attention to themselves.

"Someone's coming," I sign as I whisper, tightening my grip on the heavy bolt cutters. I glance at Jake. He's low to the ground, looking like a coiled spring. *"Don't move a hair."*

Alondra taps on my knee. *"It's those people who were following us. I'm sure of it."*

I shrug helplessly and peer through the bushes. The tops of two heads bobble. Right. Toward. Us. Not a word passes between them. They must have been tracking us. With every cautious footstep that crushes dry, fallen leaves, my heart pounds. Though the night is cold, sweat forms on my brow. As they come ever closer, I bunch myself into a ball, keeping my head down.

"Cassidy?"

I snap my head up, almost giving myself whiplash. I blink once, twice, a hundred times before I can believe what's in front of me. Or rather, who.

"H-Hayden?"

With Olympic-level agility I didn't know I possessed, I leap up onto him and wrap my legs around his waist. Hayden doesn't even stagger at the sudden acrobatics. I slide down to the ground. He buries his face into my neck, the stubble tickling me, telling me I'm not dreaming.

"It's really me." Hayden stares at me with a tide of emotions washing over his features. He cups one side of my face, then kisses me sweetly. When he drags himself away, I'm so dizzy I have to cling to his arms to keep from falling.

"But I saw your ship leave," I say, savoring the taste of him on the tip of my tongue.

"It left without us." He grips my hand like he's never letting go. "I don't know what you said to Lindsay, but it worked. She and Sam are circling on the interstate with

Trudy, ready to back us up."

"I'm so glad your mom saw the light." I didn't say much to her. Not out loud, anyway. She must have heard my silent pleas. I just hope there won't be any consequences for the family unit. Like being sent to an icy planet on the far side of the universe for disobeying an evacuation order. *"Does this mean you're staying?"*

He clears his throat, then signs as he says, *"For as long as we can."*

It's not lost on me that he means there'll be a time in the future when it really will be goodbye for good, when his mission on Earth is officially over. But I can't allow myself to think of that day right now. There's still tonight to get through. Still time to find a way to stop whoever's abducting us.

"Ahem. Did you miss me, too?" Angie taps me on the shoulder and grins. She's entwined with Jake, whose face is a picture of bamboozlement, eyes wide with shock. Instead of her usual top-to-toe fall colors, Angie's wearing all-black clothing. Behind them, Alondra looks bemused, her lips turned downward. "Jake told me everything."

"Angie…" I breathe.

"Don't worry. My lips are sealed shut. If you don't believe me, Hayden—aka Zhor of Agua—will permanently seal them for me."

"I would never do something like that," Hayden signs.

"Right, your type of aliens don't interfere, blah, blah, blah." She tosses her hair and turns to me. "I went to your house to see if you were okay after saying goodbye to Zhor. Imagine my surprise when I saw him trying to laser down your front door."

"I wasn't trying to break in," signs Hayden, darting glances from me to the others then back to Angie. *"And I did not use lasers."*

"I know. You used your brain power," I sign. Then I squeeze him tight as if to prove to myself he's really here and not a hologram or something.

Angie beams at all of us and claps her hands. "Okay, so what's the plan? Are we gonna get these creeps or not?"

A ring of overgrown shrubs surrounds the sprawling building. I gesture for Hayden and Alondra to follow me single file into the shadows. When we're in line with the wide front porch, we wait. I scan around for surveillance cameras or movement inside the dark building. Since the three of us can communicate with sign language, I figured it would be best to let Jake and Angie keep watch from the estate's perimeter.

I shiver. Not just from the cold, but from a burst of anxiety. What if we are being watched and we're heading into a trap? What if I'm putting Mom in even more danger by breaking in?

But the way I see things now, I have no choice. I've got to take this risk.

Hayden nudges me. *"I see a broken window on the side. What do you say we try that first?"*

"Yep. Not as noisy as jimmying open the door," I sign, fingerspelling some of my words because I'm distracted by the thought that Mom could be hurt during this operation. *"And we should keep singing with each other, too, instead of using our voices."*

Hayden smothers a laugh.

"What's wrong with that?" I sign.

Alondra grins. *"I'm presuming you meant signing, not singing."*

"Yes, signing." I give myself a swift mental kick. The movements for the two words are completely different. Even a beginner in ASL wouldn't mix them up. Flustered, I sign, *"Sorry. It won't happen again, I swear. I'm a bundle of nerves right now. I just want to bust my mother out of this horrible place."*

"I get it. But if you're looking to get more interpreter gigs on TV, you'd better practice a hell of a lot more," Alondra says, then she flashes me a sympathetic smile that tells me all's forgiven. *"Come on, let's go."*

We sprint across the shadowy grass. Of course, with his long legs and Aguan speed, he quickly takes the lead. Using his height advantage, Hayden peers into the broken window.

"See anything?" I sign once Alondra and I catch up.

He shakes his head. *"It's empty. Just a big desk and a wall of bookcases."*

Carefully, he chisels off jagged glass from the windowsill with his bare hands. He grabs me by the waist and hoists me up. On the other side, I land on a rug. Dust puffs around my ankles. The others clamber in behind me. The room looks like a study. One nobody has used for half a century or more.

Dr. Davis had mentioned renovations were underway. But I can't smell fresh paint or newly sawn timber.

A big clunky typewriter sits on the enormous desk. Cobwebs cling to the keys. The spider that crafted them is long gone. One corner of the desk houses a black rotary phone. Impulsively, I pick up the handset. To my surprise, there's a dial tone.

Which means the phone service is still connected.

Interesting.

Tilting my head, I listen to the building. Listen for a presence other than us. Try to get a sense of whether or not it's truly abandoned.

I gesture for the others to follow me, and open the door a crack. The creak of the hinges is so loud it might as well be gunfire. Grimacing, I check the hallway. All's quiet. Nothing's stirring, not even a mouse. I tiptoe out of the study and realize we're in the corridor beside the main staircase. Hayden's so close behind me that his breath heats my neck.

Moonlight spills in from the windows, showing dark stains in the tired linoleum. The reception desk is silent.

Something glitters in the corner of my eye. I glance down. In a trash can by the desk is the foil pack of *speculaas*. Unopened. A quake ripples through my body, making me convulse.

"Oh no…" I moan.

Hayden's at my side in a nanosecond. *"What is it?"*

"Those are the Dutch cookies I brought for Mom on my first visit here." I breathe rapidly, trying to calm myself down. *"She wouldn't have thrown them away. I bet that asshole doctor did it. And if a basic thing like trash is being neglected, what does that say about how well they're taking care of her?"*

Hayden gives me a sympathetic squeeze. *"Let's keep looking. We're gonna find her. You can shower her with cookies once we're out of here."*

Steeling my spine, I glare around the foyer. I point to the next level. *"I think Mom's room is up there."*

Hayden pulls my arm as I make a move to go upstairs. *"I thought we were going room by room. There are still a couple down here to look at."*

I swallow hard. Pale rectangles stand out against peeling, grimy walls—ghosts of long-gone paintings. *"I know I said that, but…I've just got to check there first. I'll come right down, I swear."*

Alondra plasters herself to a wall at the bottom of the staircase. *"I'll wait here and keep watch. Don't dawdle."*

"I'll go with you." Hayden takes the stairs three at a time alongside me.

My heart hammers as I stare at the first closed door. Could Mom be in there? Pressing my ear against it, I listen for the sound of a TV or some other signs of life.

"Anything?" Hayden lifts an eyebrow. When I shake my head, he reaches for the doorknob and twists it.

Even before the door opens fully, I know the room's empty. Stagnant air greets us. I turn on my phone's flashlight, revealing a timber floor covered by a small area rug. A bed stands in the middle of the room. Its wafer-thin mattress and dark iron frame scream *prison bunk* to me. Next to it is a nightstand, bare. A wardrobe, bare. Two windows on either side of the bed are nailed down. Behind the thick curtains, I find glass that's almost opaque thanks to a stubborn layer of dirt.

My heart splits in two. There's nothing personal in this room. No books, no artwork, no TV. No stimulation of any kind. Even the walls are a lifeless gray.

His face lit from below, Hayden looks slightly scary. But a lot scared. *"This might be another patient's room."*

"I hope it's no one's room."

He kisses me on the head and flashes a quick smile. *"Don't worry. I think we're close. We'll find your mom."*

He's lying through his teeth. Or rather, through his hands.

But I love him for it anyway.

I watch him head out to the balcony overlooking the main foyer, then cast one last look around the cold, lifeless room as I back out over the threshold.

"Oh, sorry, Hay—"

A strong set of hands grips me so hard I yelp.

My whole body turns to ice as a low voice growls into my ear, "Nice to see you again, Cassidy. You're earlier than scheduled, but I'm sure we can accommodate you."

Panicked, I whip my head around. All I can glimpse is an old man wearing a calm, yet intimidating smile.

"Dr. Davis?"

He grins. Right before he stabs me with something sharp. My skin burns. I try to scream, punch, claw, but somehow it feels like my muscles are dissolving into nothing.

In a soothing voice, he says, "If you think it'll make you feel better, sure, I can be Dr. Davis."

TRACK 62

"Friends of Mine"

PARALLAX MEMORANDUM
SUPPORT GROUP REPORT

Sunday, May 3, 1992

Attention: Director

Our inaugural meeting this evening attracted twenty-seven participants out of a catchment area of thirty-two thousand. Names and contact information have been added to the database.

Of those who attended, none experienced genuine sightings. However, I have identified two impressionable participants who may be suitable Parallax inductees:

James Harris
Carmela Martinez

While our classified newspaper advertisements were clearly successful, may I suggest we begin exploring the use of forums and Listserv on the World Wide Web to further the objectives of Parallax? With time, I am sure this method will help generate more interest and interconnectedness with potential and existing Subjects.

Kind regards,
Kimberly M. Johnstone

TRACK 63

"The Man Who Stole a Leopard"

Present Day

I wake up strapped to a chair that's bolted to the linoleum floor. My fuzzy brain detects a room filled with hard shapes and metal objects. Lights from racks of equipment blink intermittently. A wide console with even more lights and switches runs the length of one wall. Above it is a huge panel of glass, tilted at a downward angle. The whole setup looks like it's from another era.

Twisting my neck, I see the doctor working at a desk. Three flat-screen monitors are lined up side by side in front of him. On the wall above are a bank of screens. A couple display what looks like an air traffic control radar.

Through an open door to my left, I spy a room that houses more monitors. I can't make out any clear images on the flickering screens, but they look like CCTV. More racks of electronic equipment flash with lights of red, green, and yellow.

I flex each finger one at a time. Good. At least my muscles have recovered from whatever Davis injected me with. I glare hard, as if trying to burn holes in the back of his silver head.

In that same second, a blinding floodlight turns on in

the next room. I squeeze my eyes shut.

"I trust you slept well," says the doctor. His chair creaks as he swivels around to face me. That cold, dangerous smile stretches his aged features.

I blink him into focus. The black-and-white image I'd seen on a Wiki earlier surfaces in my mind. With his hawkish nose and piercing gaze, Dr. Davis looks like a way older version of…

If you think it'll make you feel better, sure, I can be Dr. Davis.

Oh. God.

"You're Senator Blake." My jaw goes slack.

"Director Blake," he corrects me. I guess the distinction must be pretty important to him.

"So you're definitely not a doctor?" I point at his lab coat, monogrammed with Davis's name. It's the same one he was wearing when I first visited Mom.

Blake rises from his chair. He takes off the white coat and grabs another from a coat rack. This one has his own name embroidered on it. He chuckles and puts it on with a deft shrug. Like the first time I met him, I'm semi-impressed by the way he moves for someone of his vintage. "So easy to get these things mixed up, you know. They all look the same."

"Where's the real Dr. Davis?" I demand, fully awake now. And alarmed. "Was there ever a real one?"

"Of course there was. Until about six weeks ago. And I decline to say where he is at this present moment. It's none of your concern."

Glaring, I say, "He's my mother's doctor. I'm concerned. No one told us he'd left. You didn't correct me when I called you Dr. Davis the day I met you."

"I didn't feel it was necessary."

"Because you were impersonating him," I growl.

Stooping, Blake busies himself with scrawling on a notepad. "We have other physicians on staff here. You needn't worry."

I peer at the array of monitors again, but I'm not close enough to see what's on them. "What *can* you tell me? This really is a black-ops program, isn't it?"

Raising a bushy silver brow, he jots another note. "Been researching, I see."

"I know what you've been up to all these years," I spit out.

"Is that right?" he says in a way that indicates I'm wrong. "Tell me, then."

"You study alien abductees, try to find out what they know about alien technology so you can replicate it and make a fortune." I peer at him closely. "But the more you try, the more you fail."

He bristles at my last word. "That's all?"

"And you're also holding Jane Flanagan hostage. My mother tracked her down, and now you've got both of them under a spell."

"I'm not holding anyone hostage. And spell? Goodness, this isn't Hogwarts, my dear."

I purse my lips, noting he isn't confirming or denying specifics. "Where are we? Eden Estate?"

"I thought you'd researched us." He frowns with faux confusion. "Yes, we're at Eden Estate. Or rather under it. Five stories under, in fact. The branches of Eden run wide and its roots are deep. Down here, you're in the Parallax Human Intervention Unit."

"Eden Estate is a front for this place?"

"The two organizations work synergistically. Eden Estate is the public face, if you will. I named it in honor of my wife."

"Oh, I'm sure she was flattered by that."

"Eden was very supportive of everything I did. We were quite a duo," Blake says, his face taking on a wistful look for a split second. It *almost* makes me feel sorry for him.

"Everything? Including kidnapping people?"

"She understood what I was trying to achieve." Blake unbuckles my wrist and ankle restraints. When he's done, he backs away. He turns around to the console. My gaze locks on the old-fashioned fire extinguisher sitting nearby. It looks nice and heavy. Lethal in the right hands.

I clench my sweaty fists. "What do you do at Parallax? What are you trying to *achieve*?"

He smiles over his hunched shoulder. "Tremendous leaps in science."

While some of the equipment looks new, paint peels from dented metal bulkheads and the floor is scored with furniture marks. I smirk. "Yeah, that's obvious."

"I'm talking about the brain and what it's capable of," he says, pushing his glasses onto the bridge of his nose. "It's been quite a day for you. Would you like to see something even more exciting?"

My jaw clicks with tension. "I'd like to see you in hell."

"Soon, perhaps."

"What does that mean?"

He gives a thin smile and tweaks a knob on the console. The light shining through the window dims to a less retina-burning brightness. "Come step up next to me. I won't hurt you."

"Oh? Why stop now?"

"My dear Cassidy—" he begins in a condescending tone.

"I'm not your dear."

He continues without missing a beat, nodding at the

window. "Take a look."

Stubbornly, I stay in the chair, checking for an escape path. There are two other doors in this control room, and I don't know where either of them leads.

The God Room.

Yes. That's what Jane said during my last abduction. This has to be it.

Curiosity gets the better of me. But still, I stand three feet away from Blake, close to the fire extinguisher.

At first, all I see is an expansive white room. So white it's hard to tell where the walls, floor, and ceiling meet. Then I look down, way down at the bottom.

Bodies lie motionless. Three bodies. Stretched out on gurneys with their arms crossed over their chests.

As if they're dead.

Waves of nausea hit me, sweep me away in a riptide. I grab onto the console to stop myself from falling.

"They're quite all right," Blake says, but I'm in no way comforted.

I stare mutely at the bodies as I take in their faces. They look so small and vulnerable. My mother, Hayden, and Alondra. Stainless steel carts and surgical instruments gleam beside each of them.

Far below in the room, a pair of doors opens. Wearing a lab coat, Jane trudges in, pushing another gurney.

"Is that Charlie?" I exclaim.

"He's a good man, Charlie. Very much enjoying his retirement," Blake says with a proud smile. "He spends most of his days virtual-fishing here at Parallax. He's very skilled. Must say better than he was in real life."

Again, my jaw drops. "Why is he here?"

"He was a man who knew too much. He was getting… difficult for us. Together with your mother, he was threatening to expose Parallax to the public."

Silently, I cheer for Charlie and Mom.

Blake goes on, "Our team here has worked hard to keep Charlie's knowledge of the abductions and of Parallax buried in his unconscious brain."

"In other words, you brainwashed him?"

"I prefer the term 'hypnosis,' Cassidy. If Moira Harris were here, she would agree." His watery eyes stare steadily at me.

I choke. "Moira works for you?"

"Don't tell her that." He winks, and goose bumps sprout on my arms within half a nanosecond.

"I don't understand. What is she up to really?"

"*Most* of the people in the support group she runs are Parallax subjects. Notably, subjects who've been conditioned to think they're alien abductees or UFO witnesses."

"Why would you want people to think that?"

"Deflection," he says. "In order to draw attention from Parallax's activities, we perpetuate the idea that UFO witnesses are mentally ill. We do whatever it takes to discredit genuine encounters. Parallax is about sowing confusion and doubt. Operatives encourage conspiracy theories on top of conspiracies."

"What a load of shit…" I murmur.

"I admit that we did lose our way when the government pulled the funding rug from under us. We had to scramble for new objectives. Without their blessing. However, our prospects have improved of late." His smug chuckle makes me shiver. "But as I say, Moira isn't aware that she's collecting data or procuring new subjects on our behalf."

I shudder, wondering what else Moira unwittingly passed on to Blake about me. Thank God Hayden didn't go to her for hypnosis.

Then again, he still got caught up in Blake's net. My mind whirls as I try to figure out my next moves.

"Why *are* you telling me any of this? Is it because you're so sure you can brainwash me into forgetting?" I straighten and look him in the eye, challenging him with an outward confidence I don't actually feel. But I can't let him know that. "Or do you plan on killing me?"

"Why would I kill you?" he asks like it never crossed his mind. "You're quite useful to the project. And I've genuinely enjoyed tracking your progress, seeing how you handle certain situations in life. When you took up sign language so you could communicate with Alondra, well, I knew you were special. You both are."

"You have no right to do this to me or anyone." Anger simmers inside me. I *really* want to knock him out with the fire extinguisher. Maybe do worse. But it's better I wrench some information out of him first.

"I like to think of you more as family," he goes on. "My wife and I came to think of Jane as ours. But I do take exception to your accusations. What Parallax has done is no worse than what aliens have been doing for generations." Blake's arctic smile freezes all the water in my body.

"There's no such thing as aliens," I say with as much conviction as I can.

"Oh, Cassidy, admirable try. I'm aware of countless UFO visits. It's a government treaty with aliens that allows them to exist here on Earth, after all."

Damn. Of course he would know.

"What *exactly* is the government's role in all this? If you really need me to help you," I add, hoping he buys it, "then at least tell me about what I'm helping you with."

"It started with a good old-fashioned cover-up," he says, settling back. "Perhaps you know the story of the local gold miners who saw a UFO in the 1940s? My uncle owned the mine. Fifteen of his workers witnessed it. The government established Parallax to find out what happened to the men, to study them. But what the public didn't know was that the men were abducted again and again. The survivors returned with fantastical tales of alien creatures, stories extracted right here through hypnosis."

"Why did you say survivors? Are you saying some *died*?" Dear God, how close did I come to dying when I was abducted? Jake's massive nosebleeds are bad enough.

"Regrettably. A few suicides. I recall one man died due to complications from alien surgery. Parallax did what it could for the injured ones. And as the years progressed, we discovered some of the miners' descendants were also being abducted. Not quite the inheritance those descendants expected, I'm sure."

I drag in a quivering breath, thinking of Opa Henk, who I never got to meet. His mind and body were ravaged by his job in the mines. Mom said he was a quiet man who never explained, never complained. But I guess it's clear now why I'm one of the "chosen ones." Henk must have been part of that first group of abductees.

"You said your uncle owned the mine. Was he abducted, too? Were you? Are you an abductee, too?"

"Uncle Derek? Perhaps. Me? To my deep regret, no."

"Maybe you should try it someday. Couldn't happen to a nicer guy."

Blake seems to find that funny.

"What about Jane?" I ask.

He gives me a sharp look. "She was never an alien abductee."

"No. *You* kidnapped her. The president's daughter."

"That's a very serious accusation, Cassidy." Blake stares

down into the room below.

"It's true, though, isn't it?" I watch Jane line the gurneys up in a straight line before she slips out of the room. "That *is* Jane Flanagan down there."

"She's a very useful presence at Parallax," he says slowly, pressing a button on the console.

Useful. That word again. Like we're machines, or tools. Not people.

"Why did you push that button? What does it do?" I search for signs of gases in the room. Panic's really starting to set in. It takes everything in me to hide it, because God knows he'll exploit that.

He brushes off my questions like lint on a sleeve. "Jane's father was in a position of power. I won't say he was the most powerful man in the United States. Most people don't realize how impotent presidents really are. Or shortsighted. He couldn't see the potential in Parallax. Said it was too expensive. Immoral. What's immoral about inexhaustible studies into the human mind? It's a tremendous cause. One I was prepared to pour my own money into after Flanagan cut the program."

I stare at him in shock. "Isn't it immoral to keep Jane here for revenge when she still has a family who misses her? Wonders about what happened to her?"

"I can hardly let her go, can I? She belongs here. This is her life now. Besides, she has built up quite a rapport with your mother. And she hasn't been starved of stimulation. There's always much to do here. We didn't expect young Hayden to move to Dawson. It was quite a marvelous surprise when he was captured for examination. He's one reason why things are looking brighter for Parallax." He pauses. "You *do* know your beloved is an alien, do you not? Yes, we had to resort to using a dart gun to administer our formula to him tonight. We're nothing if not resourceful here."

"Leave him alone," I say in a low, gravelly voice.

"No, I don't believe I will." He claps his hands, breaking the stillness of the God Room and scaring the bejesus out of me. "We're engaging in a new kind of mining. Data mining. We can literally dig into the minds of genuine abductees like yourself and download information about other worlds. Seems appropriate considering my mining heritage, don't you think? But the gold we're looking for comes in the form of technology. Some aliens' cerebral cortexes are *quite* the puzzle. Hard to extract data. Hard to keep sedated, too. I suspect this has something to do with the way they metabolize our drugs."

"The aliens know you're after them. They're furious that you've broken the agreement. You're supposed to let them live here in peace."

The triumphant little grin Blake gives makes me nauseous. "Well, once my team gets the formula right—and they will—your alien friends won't know what's being done to them here in the noble name of science."

"Th-they're sending reinforcements," I say, hating the tremble in my words.

"Oh my! How exciting for Parallax." He rubs his hands. "Tell me, since you appear to be their envoy now, would they care to leave a ship at Parallax for us to study? It's all very useful to be able to delve into the brains of an extraterrestrial. But to have a fully functioning ship? Tremendous."

The door behind me *whooshes* open, interrupting Blake's horrific "musings." Head down, Jane ghosts to the center of the room. Her hands are clasped so tightly together her knuckles are white. She doesn't dare look at me.

"Ah, Jane. Are the Subjects prepped for surgery?"

I whip around to face him. "Haven't you dug up enough data for a while? Jake's been getting serious nosebleeds. He's been through too much already. We all have. Just let us go for one day."

"Yes, those nosebleeds are concerning. A side effect of certain surgical interventions, I'm afraid. Our interventions aren't normally this frequent. But we had to seize on opportunities when they presented themselves." He gives me a look that I suppose is meant to be that of a kindly grandfather. Instead, it makes me feel like I'm facing off with a serial killer. Maybe I am. "Still, trust me, it's safe to conduct tests."

"You want me to trust you? That's not gonna happen."

He smiles. "I could make it happen."

I'm reluctant to say *Over my dead body* aloud. "Who's the surgeon? You?"

"I'm a man of many talents, but I leave all surgeries to Jane, since the, uh, departure of Dr. Davis."

Wide-eyed, I look at Jane. She remains mute, gaze fixed on the floor. "When did she gain her medical degree? How?"

Blake says without batting an eyelid, "Don't worry. Your friends and family are in good hands. Like I told you, Jane trained under Davis. She knows exactly what's required of her. Isn't that right, Jane?"

"Yes, Director," Jane replies immediately, robotically.

Heart pounding, I peer down at the others in the white room. I need to stop this. I don't know how, but I have to try.

"Why don't you take Cassidy downstairs and get her prepped," he suggests.

I throw a panicked look at Jane. She stares at the floor and says, "Yes, Director."

He smiles and moves to his bank of monitors. "Thanks

for stopping by, Cassidy. I trust you won't remember our meeting."

Jane steps away and opens the door. Trying to look as meek as possible, I start to follow, then quietly snatch the fire extinguisher. Jane's jaw drops. With my eyes, I beg her to stay quiet.

Easing the pin from the extinguisher, I call out, "Senator Blake?"

"Director." He looks up.

Without another word, I aim the hose *directly* at his face. I soak the floor and a bunch of consoles and equipment for good measure. He slips in the mass of white foam, cracking his head on a desk on the way down. I force myself to wait a few seconds to see if he gets up.

He doesn't.

Throwing the extinguisher down, I run out, taking Jane with me.

TRACK 64

"The Emperor's New Clothes"

Present Day

"You shouldn't have done that! I was going to get you out of here!" Jane exclaims. She locks the God Room door.

"Sorry to screw up your plan. But can you blame me? You were doing a really convincing job of playing the role of compliant employee. I had to do something." I glance around the corridor. The place looks like a nuclear fallout shelter from the fifties. All gray metal and cheerless cinderblock walls. "How do we get down to that white room? Show me. Before he wakes up."

If he wakes up.

Jane nods and grabs my arm.

We rush down a hallway to a single set of steel elevator doors. Jane punches the call button several times. Apologetically, she says, "It's very old and slow. Resources are getting to be in short supply here."

It seems incongruous to me that a rundown place like this is capable of researching and testing alien technology.

And Blake thinks he can mess around with people's minds and bodies. That makes him even more dangerous.

I cast a look down the hallway. "Fire escape?"

She nods to the other end of the hallway. "Yes, this way."

Jane rushes down flight after flight of industrial metal stairs. Even in sneakers, my feet make thunderous noises as I follow her.

After a couple more flights, Jane opens a thick door. We enter a long, wide corridor. The atmosphere down here is cool and the walls are painted stark white. No windows, and barely any features other than ducts and utilitarian lighting. Even though I'm with Jane, I feel isolated from humanity.

"I'll try 911." I reach for my back pocket. "Wait. Where's my phone?"

"In my coat." Handing the phone to me, she says, "But it won't work here. We're deep underground."

Might as well be in a bunker on Pluto.

As we race down the corridor toward a pair of white doors, Jane speaks breathlessly. "I was ordered to tranquilize the others. I gave them very small doses. But they won't be able to move by themselves. We can wheel them on their gurneys to the elevator here and unload them into the car when it comes."

"What about Jake and Angie?"

She throws me a puzzled frown.

Furtively, I check the area for cameras and find none. Voice low, I say, "They were keeping a lookout by the fence line."

Jane shakes her head. "They weren't captured."

Relieved, I sigh. "Good."

"Not to my knowledge, anyway," she adds.

My pulse rate shoots for the stars. *Please, God, let them be okay!*

When we reach the white doors, Jane punches a green button and steps back.

Nothing happens.

Jane punches it again. And again. She tries one of her

keys. The door stays obstinately shut. "He must have used the override lock."

I look around for something I can ram the door with. But there's not so much as even a janitor's mop lying around. Pushing her aside, I say, "Then I'll kick it down."

With all my strength, I smash my right foot beside the doorknob. Jane joins in. Together we break the door open with a couple more swift kicks. A vast white room lit by blinding lights greets us. Cold air blasts my face.

In the middle of the room, Hayden groggily tries to sit up on his gurney. But wrist and ankle restraints keep him down. Trays of surgical instruments and syringes lie on carts at the head of each gurney.

Hayden squints. "Cassidy? Is this another abduction?"

"Technically, yes. We're underneath Eden Estate." Rushing to his side, I kiss him all over his face, then get to work on unbuckling his restraints. No doubt the drugs he was given have diluted his telekinetic powers. I just hope he wasn't bragging about his metabolism and that he recovers fast. "Everything's going to be fine. I'll explain later. First, we've got to get everyone out of here. Can you stand up? Walk?"

"I think so." Gingerly, he gets up. He wobbles a little on his knees and clutches the gurney. His gaze lands on Jane. "Who are you?"

"This is Jane Flanagan," I say. Hayden gapes. "She's going to help us. Now, come on." I hurry first to Mom, then the others, checking their pulses, looking for signs of consciousness.

Kicking a lever on the wheel of Mom's gurney, Jane says, "We'll have to wheel everyone out."

Loud clanging and sliding noises make us all freeze on the spot.

"What was that?" I whisper. "The elevator?"

Jane puts a finger to her lips. She gestures for Hayden to lie down again, then forces me to sit on the floor at the head of Mom's gurney.

I glance at a cart of instruments. Hesitating for only a second, I jump up and grab the sharpest, most lethal-looking thing I can find.

A big, long needle.

Jane stares at me. Realization crosses her features. She nods and grabs a glass vial of clear fluid from the tray. Silently, she crouches, fills my syringe, then hands it back to me. I sit back down and hide the needle under my thigh. Jane fills another syringe with fluid and puts it in her coat pocket.

"Pretend I've immobilized you," she whispers. "I'll give you a signal when it's time to act."

"Got it," I say, and lean back. The polar-cold steel of the gurney's leg prods my spine.

Slow, steady footsteps make their way down the corridor. Straight for us. Finally the footsteps stop.

"Jane." A voice ricochets off the hard concrete walls. Blake.

Her back to the door, Jane freezes. Slowly she turns. Somehow she makes her voice flat, zombie-like. "Yes, Director?"

"I see you've brought Cassidy under control after that moment of unruliness," he says. "Good job."

"Yes, sir. Dr. Davis's tranquilizer works very well, very fast. It's what we used on the Subjects earlier today with great success," Jane replies. "I trust you were not hurt?"

"Not at all, not at all." His voice sounds kind of strained. A long pause follows. Through my lashes, I watch Blake's polished black loafers walk away from me. Foam clings to the hems of his beige trousers. He stops two gurneys away, where Hayden's playing dead. "Jane?"

"Yes, Director?"

A buckle rattles. "This Subject is not restrained."

"Of course, Director. He is fully tranquilized," she explains after a heartbeat passes.

Another pause. "I see."

Blake's toes point toward Hayden's gurney. I peer at Jane. She pats her pocket and looks down at me.

"*Wait,*" she mouths. Affecting that stiff, zombie-like walk again, she steps to Hayden's gurney. "But if it pleases you, I will fit the restraints again, Director."

"I would prefer that, thank you. Davis's work on this new tranquilizer formula was rather sloppy, in my opinion."

"Yes, Director."

The buckles jingle. When is Jane going to signal me, dammit? Slightly more importantly, *how* is she going to signal me?

Inch by inch, I rise to my knees and peer over my mother's body. Her breathing is slow and even. Good. Blake's leaning forward over Hayden. Even from six feet away, I can see Jane's hands shaking as she fumbles with the buckles on Hayden's ankle restraints.

"And you, Jane, you disappoint me, too," Blake says.

Jane pauses. "Excuse me?"

"I know it's not your fault. Not entirely. But I'm still very disappointed."

"D-Director, I don't understand," she stammers, losing the zombie act fast.

Blake takes one step in Jane's direction. She takes one step away from him. "I know Dr. Davis was trying to deprogram you. He didn't give you a choice about that, did he? And he was most certainly going against my orders."

On the gurney, Hayden's head moves a fraction. I cringe. But Blake's not looking at him. He's looking at Jane, who's quivering like a newborn foal.

"He…he wanted to help me."

"Help you escape, Jane? Escape your home?"

She whispers, "I have a family. Out there."

Keeping low, I move around the gurney, being careful not to brush the instrument cart. My sweaty fingers grip the syringe. I beg my rubber-soled sneakers to remain silent.

"There's nothing and no one out there for you, Jane," Blake shakes his head. "They're long dead."

I turn to stone.

What an asshole.

Jane lets out an almighty wail that could shatter crystal. Syringe poised, she charges at Blake. He grabs her by the wrist so hard the veins in his hand pop up under his thin skin. The syringe drips to the floor, where Blake stomps on it.

I lunge forward and stab his butt with the needle. His glasses fly off as he jerks in pain. Meanwhile, Hayden thrashes on his gurney and wraps an arm around Blake's throat. But he loses his balance—and his grip on Blake. Hayden topples backward. His head makes a sickening *thud* on the floor.

"Hayden!" I shout.

"I'm…okay…" he says, despite a trickle of red sliding down the side of his face.

"You are *not* okay." I start to move toward him as he tries to use the gurney to pull himself up.

Hayden's eyes widen. "Cassidy, look out!"

The old man staggers. Ignoring broken glass piercing my skin, I try to grab hold of his legs.

I catch sight of Jane racing across the room. Mouth flat

with determination, she picks up a scalpel from a cabinet and runs back.

"Get out of the way!" she yells at me, her voice reverberating around the theater.

I scramble, crashing into a cart. Instruments tumble to the floor around me, the harsh sound of falling steel hurting my eardrums. I look up just in time to see Jane standing over Blake. Her body practically vibrates with rage. She raises the scalpel and jams it into Blake's neck.

"Liar!" she screams, throwing down the scalpel. Blood pulses in time with Blake's heartbeat. "They're coming for me. And even better, they're gonna let you rot!"

Blake's face contorts and turns a volcanic red. He starts to go limp. Hayden finally gets to his feet and staggers to my side.

The three of us stare down at Blake, panting. I glance at Hayden, unsure of what to do next. I hated Blake for everything he did to my mother, to Jane, and all of Parallax's victims. I wanted to see him live long enough to be tried, convicted, and thrown in solitary confinement.

"Don't touch him," Jane says in a bleak voice, as if sensing the conflict spiraling inside my head. "He's not gonna make it. Trust me."

Blake's breath comes in rasps and wheezes and gurgles. Slowly, those noises subside.

Until there's total silence.

Jane crouches. She puts a finger to his bloody neck and stays there for a long, long time. Finally, she rises.

"He's gone. And I'm free. I'm *free*," she croaks. A sudden flood of tears runs down her cheeks. At her feet, Blake lies sprawled. Motionless. Eyes open. Wrinkled face drooping. Blood seeping. "We're all free."

"Not yet. Not till we're out of this place," Hayden says,

looking around. During the commotion—and the demise of Blake—no one so much as twitched. "When will everyone else wake up?"

"I can give them an antidote. The vials are in a supply room. I'll go get them." She stares at Blake's body. Her mouth twists. I almost think she's going to spit on his dead, crusty face. But she turns abruptly and enters a side room I hadn't noticed before.

Hayden steers me away from Blake and the widening pool of blood ebbing from his body. He lifts my chin. "Are you okay?"

"I'm fine…ish," I reply. "What about you?"

He focuses on an unbroken syringe resting on a cart. It wiggles almost imperceptibly. "Getting there. Once I fully metabolize the drugs they gave me, I should be back to my normal self."

"Your normal, out-of-this-world self."

"I'm part of this world, too," he says, drawing me to his chest. With a shaky sigh, I look over at my mom, Alondra, and Charlie. All of them peaceful, oblivious.

Gingerly, I step over a pile of polished instruments strewn on the floor. One of them stands out to me like a beacon. Something that resembles a lemon zester, only it's sharper, longer. Was this an instrument of torture used on us by Blake?

I glance around at the brutal starkness of the theater and shudder. No doubt in my mind.

"I'm…I'm fine. I *will* be fine," I finally answer. I pick up the instrument and hurl it into the God Room's windows. Never has the sound of glass breaking sounded so satisfying.

The elevator grinds and groans in the corridor nearby.

I freeze. "Someone's coming."

"Guards?"

"Maybe," I whisper.

Hayden stands in front of me protectively. "We might have to get more of those tranquilizers to fend them off. My telekinetic powers are still sluggish."

Two men dressed in black suits and ties, like they're going to a dinner party, soon fill the broken doorway. Only instead of holding cocktail glasses, they're holding guns. Small but dangerous-looking guns. With any wrong move, their suits' seams could rip apart thanks to their broad shoulders and pecs.

"Cassidy Roekiem?" one of them barks.

My legs wobble. "Um…"

"Yes, that's her!" A black-clad blur crashes between the two men and streaks toward me. In seconds, the blur engulfs me in a bone-crunching hug.

"Angie!" I gasp.

Over her shoulder, I spot Jake grinning alongside the stoic men. They holster their guns. "It's okay. They work for the Flanagans."

"Secret Service, Miss Roekiem." One man steps into the room, his eyes darting left, right, up, down. I realize he's kind of old. Like, over sixty. He holds his ID out long enough for me to read it. Agent Jeremy Hicks. He pockets his ID. His face twitches, then becomes as stony as Mount Rushmore.

"Who sent you?" I ask, incredulous. His partner checks Blake's body and gives a grim nod.

"President Flanagan got a message from an old friend of his, a Ms. Anna Kingston."

"Oh, thank God." Relief surges through me. "Trying to contact her has been like trying to contact aliens…" The words die in my throat. Hayden looks away.

"Ms. Kingston received credible threats after agreeing

to speak with you and had to bunker down."

"Oh… *I* put her in danger." I swallow, looking at the floor. At the body of the person who mostly likely wanted to harm her.

"We have reason to believe she was in the perpetrator's sights for a long time," Hicks says.

Rubbing my temples, I ask, "How did you get here so quickly?"

"We've been stationed in this sector for several months now, ever since we got a tip-off about Daisy from a source in the area."

I glance at my still unconscious mother. The tip-off had to come from Mom before she got locked up. Who else would have known?

"Jerry?"

We all turn as Jane barrels back into the room. I glance at Hicks. His craggy face softens. Without a word, she runs to him. And as Jane squeezes him hard, the big guy starts sobbing. The rest of us look at each other tearfully. Even Agent No-Name.

"I'm so sorry, Daisy Jane," Hicks chokes out. His macho image fades with every tear that slides down his cheeks. "It was my fault you were kidnapped. I should have taken better care of you."

"No, you were the *best*, Jerry," Jane whimpers. "When I started to remember my old life, it was you I saw in my head. I never really forgot you."

Jerry tries hard to compose himself. Angie tries to give him a tissue, but he waves her away. "I never forgave myself for losing you."

"I was taken. You didn't lose me," Jane says soothingly. She casts a dull look at Blake. His blood oozes across the floor. Who knows how many others he tormented in this very room? "It's going to be okay."

Grimly, Agent No-Name takes a sheet from a nearby cart and covers Blake's body. And the deep crimson puddle around it.

I edge toward my mother while the others fuss over Jane. Her chest rises and falls steadily. My hands shake as I undo her restraints. Hayden's standing beside Blake's body. Silent. Face taut. "Hayden, can you check on Alondra?"

"Sure." Without moving from his spot, he turns his head toward Alondra. Her chrome buckles clink and fall open.

Gaping, I stare at him. I can't believe he did that with everyone milling around. Fortunately, no one seems to notice "magic" just happened. He puts a finger to his lips. "I've still got it."

"Show-off," I say with a good-natured grin, then focus on my mother. When I sweep tendrils of blond hair off her forehead, her eyelids flutter. I squeeze her hand, but her fingers stay limp. "Mom, can you hear me? It's Cassidy."

Jane steps beside me, syringe in hand. Softly, she says, "Let me help."

I stand back as she administers the antidote to Mom, then to Alondra. Minutes go by like hours as we wait for them to wake up. I can't take my eyes off Mom. I grip her hand tighter and tighter, till my knuckles turn white.

Meanwhile, Hayden, Jake, and Angie stay with Alondra. She comes to first. Hayden signs, *"We're here for you. You're going to be all right."*

All she can do is nod. Her smile is faint, but relieved.

I'm not sure if it's my death grip or the antidote that did it, but finally Mom opens her eyes.

"Cassidy?" she croaks, her lips dry. "I'm so happy you're here."

"I am, too." I hug her as tight as I can. She yelps in

response, then laughs as I ease off. A little.

"I've been wanting to tell you for so long…." Fatigue makes her eyes fall shut again. But her smile remains.

"Tell me what, Mom?"

"I did it. I found Jane…Flanagan," she whispers.

"Yes, you did. Know what that means? You can go home now." I beam at Jane. Her face is a blend of sadness and joy and uncertainty, like she can't believe her life is about to completely change. For the better. "We all can."

TRACK 65

"Never Tear Us Apart"

Two Weeks Later

I don't want the dream to end.

Warm beach sand feels silky between my toes. Hypnotic, exotic music plays somewhere in the background. Waves send a salty mist over me. And the smell of barbecued shrimp makes my mouth water and stomach growl. All I need is for Hayden to show up and complete the fantasy. Maybe wearing a T-shirt that molds to his rippling chest and six-pack. It doesn't matter what he's wearing or not wearing, really. As long as I get to kiss him again in my lifetime.

Something cold and wet brushes against my bare ankle, taking me out of the dream a little. The music stops, replaced with a low whirring noise. Eyes shut tight, I turn fitfully. My back rests on a hard, creaky surface. Quivering, I order my brain to take me back to the warm beach, and the dream goes on.

The wet sensation on my ankle is replaced with growing pressure. It squeezes and squeezes till I can't ignore it anymore. I glance down, straight into an ashen face dominated by enormous black eyes.

"Welcome to Agua," it says through a toothless, coin-slot mouth.

I jolt awake to full consciousness and gasp. A muscular figure crouches beside me on the lake's dock. It takes a millisecond for me to register the intense eyes grazing over my face. "Hayden!"

"I've missed you," he says. Unlike the Gray alien's voice, his is deep and textured with huskiness. Still, I shiver. He hugs me to his chest.

I scoot even closer and angle my lips to his. "I've missed you, too. Two Earth weeks is a very long time."

He pulls me to my feet. It's only then that I notice Yoda's with him, dancing excitedly at the end of a leash. The puppy noses my ankles, leaving a trail of cold slobber.

"Oh, so that was *you*!" I laugh at him as he yips excitedly. Seems the dream was just a dream. Reality is much sweeter. Again and again I kiss Hayden. Delicious heat radiates from his lips and reaches all the way down to my toes.

"You weren't scared waiting here in the middle of the night, in the middle of nowhere?" His deep voice rumbles into my ear.

"No, because I was anticipating this super-romantic reunion," I say, grinning. We face each other, holding hands. His lips are a breath away from mine. "And it's not the middle of nowhere. We're still in good old Dawson."

"Ah yes, the rural home of nefarious government conspiracies." Hayden brushes hair across my forehead. "How was it for you? At the hospital? No one would tell me much."

"It was hell. But it could have been worse. Like at Eden/ the Parallax Fucking With Humans Unit." My lips curl. The whole time we were sequestered, I had no phone contact, not even a text, with anyone except family. For "operational reasons," we were told.

Former President Flanagan had me, Alondra, and Jake

whisked to specialist hospitals—bona fide ones personally checked out by Dad—for full check-ups and debriefings, as the therapists liked to call it. The whole time I was there, not once did anyone mention extraterrestrials. And I didn't want to be the first to say the words. I hope Alondra and Jake did the same.

Yesterday, in a feat of stealth only the Secret Service could perform, Jane Flanagan was quietly flown to Europe for treatment with her relieved parents. None of us knows how Jane's disappearance and reappearance is going to be explained to the world. But President Flanagan assures my family he'll do whatever it takes to protect us from publicity.

My blood boiled when I learned Blake got a funeral with full honors thanks to "his contribution to governance as a federal senator." My guess is no one but a select and unfortunate few will ever know how twisted he really was. The conspiracy rolls on.

Until I write my college thesis about him anyway.

He turned Parallax into a private "research" company. He told his workers the government still had oversight. Running it without government money literally cost him his fortune. That's why the place was so rundown. He'd decorated Eden with furnishings from the home the bank had taken away from him.

We learned Mom most definitely hadn't checked herself into Eden. She'd been working part-time at Dad's office and dug up boxes of old secret files about Parallax. When Blake found out she was planning to expose him, he pretty much kidnapped and brainwashed her. Charlie was collateral damage.

Mom and I were placed in the same recovery facility. She's still there. It's going to take a while before she's truly herself again. A long time before the mess Blake made of her neurons can be completely untangled. Makes me wonder what kind of debriefing Parallax employees like Moira might get. Dad says there'll be years of litigation to come.

"I can't get over the stunts they pulled to make people believe they were alien abductees. It's unbelievable how easily the brain can be tricked. I feel so stupid!" My grip on him slackens.

"You're not stupid," he says, nudging me. "To be fair, Blake's mind games didn't work so well on you. It wasn't until he started changing up his formula that you started remembering Parallax abductions."

"What about *you*?" I ask, feeling marginally less stupid. "What was Aguan lockdown like?"

"Lonely. We didn't leave Sinkhole City." Hayden's sigh is so heavy it could generate waves across the lake. "But we felt a lot safer knowing both Blake and his program are dead."

My time in isolation gave me plenty of time to think. Angie was right. I did race around in circles, trying to plug up every gap in my schedule. Not that taking on Mom's investigation wasn't worth it. Obviously it was the best form of distraction I could have ever taken.

But deep down, I didn't have the guts to confront an uncomfortable truth—that I had been forever altered when I was abducted by Grays. I wanted to push it down, have things go back to the way they were. I know now that's impossible. You have to deal with the cracks that occur in life, patch them up, and move forward.

It's funny, though. Five years on from that abduction, and my life has again been altered by an alien.

In a good way.

I gesture for Hayden to follow me to the edge of the

rickety dock. He sits beside me, swinging his legs over the lake. Yoda nudges his way between us like a canine chaperone. Squawking animals and singing insects provide a soundtrack. In the distance, the newly free rowboat bobs on gentle waves.

"Is the treaty dead, too?" I close my eyes, not sure if I want to know the answer.

When Hayden doesn't answer, I open my eyes again. He purses his lips tightly, fighting for control. But his desolate gaze tells me everything I need to know.

"You're going back," I croak through a painfully dry throat. I fix my gaze on the constellations above. Billions of secrets lie up in the stars and in the blackness between them. Humans are kidding themselves if they think they can uncover them all.

He nods like his skull is made of cement. "Once our rotation ends."

"Which is?" I clench my hands, nails biting into the flesh of my palms. *Please don't say five minutes from now. Don't even say five days from now.* Selfishly, I want him to stay forever. He'd crossed galaxies and somehow found me in this tiny dot of a town. That had to mean something.

Hayden clasps my hands and kisses them. "We have six months. Till the end of senior year. And in that time, we have to keep our heads down."

I let out a deep, energizing breath and start pacing the rickety dock. Yoda follows my every move. "Six months. I can work with that."

He squints. "What do you mean? What are you going to do?"

"Plenty!" I exclaim. "We can cut a new deal. President Flanagan will help. Hell, he said he owes us and wants to help in any way he can. This is just one way."

His face is a kaleidoscope of emotions. He leaps up, making the dock creak. "You'd do that for us?"

"I'll do it on one condition," I say, laughing. "You teach me to fly."

He licks his lips as he considers my offer. "Hands-free?"

I take his hands and place them on me in strategic places. "Hmm, I was thinking more hands-on."

Hayden's grin lights a fire inside me. He kisses each cheek before nibbling my earlobes and finally connecting his scorching lips to mine. Our hands restlessly explore each other. I gasp as his touch glides under my shirt and wanders over my bare skin.

Yoda's restless whines bring me back to Earth. A sudden stiff breeze whips around us.

"We should get back home before we all turn into icicles," I say, rubbing spray from the lake off my cheeks.

"I don't know. I'm feeling pretty hot here." Hayden grins. Yoda prances and yips loudly, his leash tugging around my legs. "Okay, buddy. We'll get you home soon."

But Yoda isn't listening. His barks become more insistent. Suddenly, he's gone from innocent puppy to rabid dog. I follow Yoda's laser-like gaze. He's watching the middle of the lake. Water churns like crazy. Lit up by… What? It couldn't be moonlight. The light source is coming from *below*.

"Hayden…the water…"

"I see it," he says, grimacing as he tries to keep Yoda from diving in.

The lake rumbles faster and faster, like a pot of water coming to boil.

Then, quick as lightning, a silver disk as big as a basketball court shoots out of the water. Blinding blue-white light trails after it. The disk itself spins, does a round of the lake, then launches high above us.

My neck strains as I try to keep sight of it. In seconds, a shock wave ripples the night sky.

And the disk, the…unidentified…flying…object, is gone. Out of this world.

It takes minutes, maybe hours, for words to come out of either of us.

“Okay, h-here’s where you get to tell me not to worry. It was one of your s-ships,” I stammer. “Right, Hayden? Zhor?”

He doesn’t answer. Oh God—

“Do you think they’ll be back?”

Hayden turns to me. I squeeze his hands. They’re drenched in sweat. His face is devoid of color and full of fear at the same time. He swallows. “Count on it.”

ACKNOWLEDGMENTS

Everyone says writing is a solitary pursuit, and for the most part it is. But I could not have finished this book were it not for a constellation of supportive people around me.

Lydia Sharp, Stacy Abrams, and Liz Pelletier—my incredible editorial team. I'm so grateful to you for your expert guidance and for making a dream come true. Riki Cleveland, what a gem you are! To my cover artist, Elizabeth Turner Stokes, thank you for bringing my characters to life in such an adorable way. Heather Riccio, Meredith Johnson, Curtis Svehlak, Bree Archer, Jessica Turner, Katie Clapsadl, and everyone at Entangled Publishing, I so appreciate all you've done to launch this ship.

To Beth Miller, my literary agent at Writers House, thank you for always being there for me, no matter what, no matter when.

Pintip Dunn, thank you for unwavering friendship, sage advice, and critiquing prowess. Anna Campbell and Annie West, I admire you so much. I wouldn't be the writer I am today without you two. Much gratitude to Tina Ferraro, A.K. Wilder, Darcy Woods, Sally Rigby, Amanda Ashby, Amy DeLuca, and Marlene Perez—fabulous, talented women. Shelly Chalmers and the Dreamweavers, you are all incredible writers and generous friends.

Ellen Lindseth, my lovely writer friend and pilot, thanks so much for your technical advice on the fine art of flying a light aircraft.

Heartfelt thanks to Bel Licciardello, Cathy Smith, Darynda Jones, Karen Rose, Kiah Morante, and Sarah McCarthy for providing invaluable expertise on sign language and interpreting.

Javier Arriaga, my eternal gratitude for your generosity, understanding, and encouragement. You and Omar Abunaser, the king of cakes, have an uncanny ability to deliver dessert at just the right moments. Javi, seriously, this novel would not have made it to the printers without you.

To my brilliant workmates—including Linda Baker, Cecilia, Ella, Peter, Ming, Monika, Paul—thank you. Special thanks goes to my brains trust and "frens"—Murray, Lindsay, and Philip. You've helped me through more difficult patches than I can count.

Thank you to Alison Myers and Helen Velkov for your steadfast support and abundant supply of M&M's.

Many thanks to Brinsley Marlay and Wade Goring for so confidently saying I could get through it all. (You were right.) Jason, ready for another round of pizza? Mitch and Les, what a brilliant duo. Cheers to Blake at Mr. Burrows Hair, who despite what he says, is not at all evil—unlike his namesake.

Thank you to the artists whose music moved me and my characters throughout the entire writing process. Among them, The Model School/Brendan Wixted, Megadon Betamax, and Duran Duran.

Special thanks to Hanee Kim and everyone at Discovery Asia for inspiring me with literally hundreds of program hours over the years.

Humongous thanks to the nurses, doctors, and staff at the Royal Prince Alfred Hospital, the Chris O'Brien Lifehouse, and the Leukaemia Foundation.

Much love to my father, Marcel, who encouraged me to not only look to the stars but to reach for them. To Nancy and Debbie, to Anne and Sasha, and all my family members scattered around the planet, thank you for your never-ending support.

Last but never least, more eternal gratitude and love to Frank. Thank you for the music. You're the brightest star in my galaxy.

Sink your teeth into the instant New York Times *bestselling series that has turned into a global sensation.*

crave

NEW YORK TIMES BESTSELLING AUTHOR

TRACY WOLFF

My whole world changed when I stepped inside the academy. Nothing is right about this place or the other students in it. Here I am, a mere mortal among gods...or monsters. I still can't decide which of these warring factions I belong to, if I belong at all. I only know the one thing that unites them is their hatred of me.

Then there's Jaxon Vega. A vampire with deadly secrets who hasn't felt anything for a hundred years. But there's something about him that calls to me, something broken in him that somehow fits with what's broken in me.

Which could spell death for us all.

Because Jaxon walled himself off for a reason. And now someone wants to wake a sleeping monster, and I'm wondering if I was brought here intentionally—as the bait.

The exciting release from author Molly E. Lee is a pulse-pounding paranormal fantasy with epic worldbuilding, swoony romance, and heart-pounding action!

EMBER OF NIGHT

I am a weed.

Unloved by my abusive, alcoholic dad. Unwanted by my classmates. Unnoticed by everyone else.

But I'd suffer anything to give my kid sister a better life—the minute I turn eighteen, I'm getting us the hell out of here. And some hot stranger telling me I am the key to stopping a war between Heaven and Hell isn't going to change that.

Let the world crumble and burn, for all I care.

Draven is relentless, though. And very much a liar. Every time his sexy lips are moving, I can see it—in the dip of his head, the grit of his jaw—even if my heart begs me to ignore the signs.

So what *does* he want?

I need to figure it out fast, because now everyone is gunning for me. And damn if I don't want to show them what happens when you let weeds thrive in the cracks of the pavement...

We can grow powerful enough to shatter the whole foundation.

From Lindsey Duga, author of Kiss of the Royal *comes another fast-paced, unique, romantic read for fans of Holly Black and Meg Kassel.*

Briony never planned to go back to the place she lost everything.

Firefly Valley, nestled deep within the Smoky Mountains, is better kept in her past. It's been six years since an unexplained fire gave Briony amnesia, her mother disappeared, and her dad moved them away.

But now her grandmother needs a caretaker, and Briony's dad insists she be the one to help. The moment she returns, she feels a magical connection to the valley, as if it's a part of her somehow.

And when she meets a hot guy named Alder who claims he was her childhood friend but now mysteriously keeps his distance, Briony starts piecing together her missing past...and discovers her mother didn't leave to start a new life somewhere. She's trapped in the hidden world within the valley.

Now, Briony will do whatever it takes to rescue her, even if it means standing up against dangerously powerful gods. But when saving her mother comes with the ultimate sacrifice–Alder's death–how can she choose?

Discover the New York Times *bestselling series from Jennifer L. Armentrout.*

Obsidian

Starting over sucks.

When we moved to West Virginia right before my senior year, I'd pretty much resigned myself to thick accents, dodgy internet access, and a whole lot of boring…until I spotted my hot neighbor, with his looming height and eerie green eyes. Things were looking up.

And then he opened his mouth.

Daemon is infuriating. Arrogant. Stab-worthy. We do not get along. At all. But when a stranger attacks me and Daemon literally freezes time with a wave of his hand, well, something… unexpected happens.

The hot alien living next door marks me.

You heard me. Alien. Turns out Daemon and his sister have a galaxy of enemies wanting to steal their abilities, and Daemon's touch has me lit up like the Vegas Strip. The only way I'm getting out of this alive is by sticking close to Daemon until my alien mojo fades.

If I don't kill him first, that is.

Let's be friends!

@EntangledTeen

@EntangledTeen

@EntangledTeen

bit.ly/TeenNewsletter

entangled teen
an imprint of Entangled Publishing LLC